Afterwards, Annys was asham̲ ̲ ̲ ̲ ̲ ̲not think why she had told the lie, except that if she ̲ ̲ ̲ ̲ ̲ ̲ ̲ ̲ ̲ng Kit O'Brien, the charming young Irishman, her ̲ ̲ ̲ ̲ ̲ ̲ ̲ ̲ ̲uld have scolded, and forbidden her to go to marke̲ ̲ ̲ ̲ ̲ ̲ ̲, at fifteen, is old enough to want her freedom; and M̲ ̲ ̲ ̲ ̲ ̲ ̲ugh she is with the sister she has mothered since infancy, ha̲ ̲ ̲ much else on her mind to notice Annys's evasions.

For Mhairi can no longer conceal from herself how much she loves Fergus Adam, owner of the rich Silvercairns granite quarry, and bitter rival of their own quarry at Rainbow Hill. Despite the years of sworn enmity between their families, Fergus has acknowledged publicly the esteem in which he holds Mhairi: he has invited her to his sister's wedding. Holding the expensive white card, Mhairi is torn between elation and despair. How can she accept, when her brother Tom is so violently against it?

The sins and jealousies of the past, acts of violence and treachery long ago, dominate the loves and longings of the families in *Willowbrae* – third in Agnes Short's much-loved 'Silvercairns' trilogy. And, as the hatred between Tom Diack and Fergus Adam leads to tragedy in the great granite bowl of the Silvercairns quarry, it is young Annys, holding fast to her own love, who inspires Mhairi to fight for truth and honour, and for the man she has wanted so long.

Also by Agnes Short

The heritors (1977)
Clatter Vengeance (1979)
The Crescent and the Cross (1980)
Miss Jenny (1981)
Gabrielle (1983)
The first fair wind (1984)
The running tide (1986)
The dragon seas (1988)
Silvercairns (1990)
Rainbow Hill (1991)

under the name of 'Rose Shipley'

Wychwood (1989)
Echoes of Wychwood (1991)

under the name of 'Agnes Russell'

A red rose for Annabel (1973)
A flame in the heather (1974)
Hill of the wildcat (1975)
Target Capricorn (1976)
Larksong at dawn (1977)

Agnes Short

Willowbrae

Constable . London

L823 SHO KW
922707
ZOO 6367

First published in Great Britain 1992
by Constable and Company Limited
3 The Lanchesters, 162 Fulham Palace Road
London W6 9ER
Copyright © 1992 Agnes Short
The right of Agnes Short to be
identified as the author of this work
has been asserted by her in accordance
with the Copyright, Designs and Patents Act 1988
ISBN 0 09 471230 1
Set in Linotron Ehrhardt 11pt
and printed in Great Britain
by Redwood Press Limited
Melksham, Wiltshire

A CIP catalogue record for this book
is available from the British Library

F
1351442

Part 1

Annys picked her way carefully over the trodden snow, packed hard by the daily feet of the quarry workers and ice-crusted after a night's hard frost, turned a bend in the track and saw, to her left, the red glow of the forge where Mr Bain's apprentice was already feeding the fire for the day's trade. The glow cast a pink sheen over the snow-spread field, sparked diamonds from the rutted track and strung the bare hedgerow with tangled stars. The quarry horses were shooed at the Bain forge, with the horses from all the neighbouring farms and any passing traffic on the Aberdeen road a mere hundred yards away. The Bain girls had been her friends when they attended the local school together, but both had jobs now, one in a neighbouring farm kitchen, one in a big house in town. Annys envied them. But today Annys herself had a job: to go alone to the town market and sell the family produce. Ina Bain might even be among the marketers, sent by her mistress to buy eggs or cheese.

The thought was cheering, as was the bright square of the black-smith's open doorway in the chill winter landscape, and when Annys reached the end of the track and turned south onto the road which led to Woodside, Kittybrewster and eventually Aberdeen she felt her spirits lighten even more, in spite of the bitter wind that sliced across the open landscape straight from the arctic sea. The trees beside the river in the dip to her left traced black lace over the ice-cold water and there were deep lids of snow on the rocks. The light was strengthening – or her eyes were growing accustomed to it – for she found she could see bird-prints in the snow beside the road and once the paw-marks of a fox. Already there was at least one set of wheel-ruts on the trodden surface, possibly two, and several sets of fresh foot- and hoof-prints. She pulled her plaid tighter about her to keep out the wind and, to speed her journey, began to count them, trying to separate small from larger: a man and a boy, a farm-horse, another man, a pony . . .

'Good day, ma'am. 'Tis a fine morning.'

The voice too close behind her and the touch on her arm made Annys flinch with terror. For a horrifying moment she was back on the canal path, in a nightmare of contorted face and thrusting fists and then, like a smothering blanket, the canal water which doused her eyes and filled her lungs with death. The next instant she was on the Woodside road again, in the half-light of an empty winter morning, alone with the stranger and no one in sight to protect her.

Where had he come from? She had heard no footstep. Unless the snow on the road had muffled the sound? But it was crisp snow with a skin of ice, and though when the sun strengthened the white might turn to brown sludge underfoot, she realized her own feet made a light crackle with every step. Perhaps he had not come up behind her at all, but had been hiding behind the leafless hedgerow, to jump out, snatch her basket and ... and ... oh dear God protect me. Eyes desperately on the road ahead, as if not to see him were to obliterate him, she clutched her market basket tight against her pounding chest. Though she dare not send even the smallest glance in his direction, she willed him with all her strength to see she did not want to speak to him, whoever he was: willed him to stride on and leave her in peace.

'I am sorry, I did not mean to startle you, lass.'

It was a light voice, unnervingly close, but musical and warm. In other circumstances she might have listened to it with pleasure, but she could think only of his threatening proximity and of her own weakness. Oh God, why had she begged her sister Mhairi to let her go alone? Needled and persisted and withdrawn into hurt silence until, against her better judgment, Mhairi had given in? And now all Mhairi had feared was coming true. Her brother Lorn had more strength in his little finger than Annys had in both arms together, and her brother Willy the same. All men, even the most puny, were stronger than women and when driven by lust ... she quickened her steps till she was almost running.

He fell into step beside her, matching his longer stride easily to hers, and said, 'You see, I mistook you for a woman.'

For a moment the words penetrated fear and released a small spurt of anger. It was bad enough that Mhairi still treated her as a child, watched over her, fussed and fretted and guarded her as if she were no older than six-year-old Catriona, as if Mhairi were her mother instead of her older sister, though Annys stood a good two

[8]

inches taller than Mhairi, and three in her Sunday shoes. But for a stranger to deny her maturity too ... Today, with fresh snow fallen in the night and a keen wind blowing, Annys wore her serviceable, everyday boots under thick flannel petticoats and heavy blue serge skirt, a plaid over head and shoulders and wrapped tight across her chest, but in spite of that missing Sunday inch the woman in her was insulted.

And at the same time afraid. To be a child was safe and protected: with womanhood came vulnerability and a new fear. Mhairi had warned her of drunken Irish navvies from the railway workings, of wandering strangers and deserters from the army, of all sorts of riff-raff waiting to molest the unsuspecting, especially young women alone. And there was something odd in the man's voice, a lilt and cadence that was not of these parts. She bit her lip hard while her eyes darted over the road ahead, over the surrounding fields and hedgerows, praying for a house, a ploughman, Mr Dickie's market cart, anyone familiar to help her. *Please God, keep me safe.*

'There now, I have offended you,' he said. 'You have taken umbrage. I can see it in the turn of your pretty head, and who could blame you? Wasn't my own mother always telling me to curb my tongue and now I've let it run away with me again, unthinking idiot that I am. But I meant no offence, lass. From behind, bundled as you are against the weather, I took you for a grown woman, a mature woman with the years upon her, a woman well used to the open road. And now I see you are nothing of the sort, but a walking angel straight from heaven. Surely the plaid must be the most deceitful of garments in all God's creation, or my name's not Christopher O'Brien.'

O'Brien. An Irish name. Last week an Irishman from the railway workings near Inverurie had been drunk from Saturday till the following Wednesday, Willy said, and had fought his way in and out of every tavern in a ten-mile radius, leaving a trail of screaming women and bleeding men, till at last the police had caught up with him. And though this O'Brien spoke with honeyed words that had begun to soothe her fears in spite of herself, that meant nothing. Didn't all Irishmen kiss the Blarney stone and by so doing receive the gift of the gab which made them the smoothest liars in all Christendom? She dare not look at him lest she see the gleaming, lascivious eyes, the unkempt hair. It was only later that she remembered the 'walking angel'.

[9]

'There is no need to quicken your steps on my account, lass. The path is difficult enough as it is, with the snow playing tricks with the potholes and iced smooth over rocks and rut alike. Why, if a man did not keep his wits about him any one of those rocks which are lurking everywhere out of sight might leap up and send him flying. There, what did I tell you?' and he skidded, half fell and righted himself again in a comical display of jerking limbs. Though she wanted to smile, she kept her eyes on the road ahead and refused to look at him.

'Sure and I did not intend to scare the daylights out of you, Miss Traveller, nor to bring the fear to your heart. And me wanting only a civil direction to my doom and company on the way. But I will gladly go back down the path again and walk respectfully twenty paces behind you, if it will bring back the bloom to your cheeks, and the light to your pretty eyes. I give you my word, and Christopher O'Brien's word is his solemn bond.'

Suddenly he laughed, a soft, rippling laugh that twitched the corners of her mouth in spite of her fear.

'Will ye listen to the arrogance of the man? Christopher O'Brien is it now? And me plain Kit to my friends. If my traitorous tongue has not driven them all away and left me friendless before I'm a year older.'

Then at last she half-turned her head, slid a swift sideways glance at the stranger, and looked away again, but in that instant the thumping of her heart slowed. Her fear had misled her: he was no older than her brother Lorn, though shorter and stockier in build. She risked another glance and saw that he was little taller than she was, with a fresh-complexioned face, wind-ruffled hair and a jaunty swagger to his walk in spite of his undoubtedly shabby clothes. Slung over one shoulder was a well-worn canvas bag such as she had seen sailors carry at the docks, when a ship was embarking for foreign parts, or unloading after a long sea voyage. The bag was half empty and she wondered, with a stir of concern, if it contained all he owned.

'Well, you have inspected me, Miss Traveller, and do not deny it for I caught that timid glance, like a roe deer cornered and looking for escape. Sure and you must have seen I am no brigand, but only an Irish lad with an inclination to seek his fortune. Are you going to say you forgive me, Pretty Dancer, and favour me with the pleasure of your conversation, or must I walk all the way to Aberdeen in silence?'

Irish. She hesitated, remembering Mhairi's warnings, blushed and could think of nothing to say.

[10]

They walked a dozen yards or so, not speaking, before he sighed aloud and said, with woeful solemnity, 'Then silence it shall be. Unless, of course, I talk to myself. Kit my lad, I shall say, you have trudged all this blessed night, with the snow at your feet and the wind at your back, but with all the stars of heaven to light your way and did not the Pretty Dancers themselves throw their rainbow beams across the skies to bless your passing? If the morning sprite you took to be an angel has taken a vow of silence, or if the Prettiest Dancer of them all, come down from heaven to bless the earth, turns out to be a Trappist nun on a sacred pilgrimage, then who are you to complain, Kit my boy? No matter that you are marching to your doom, that you had hoped for a cheerful word to sustain your spirits, that you have left brothers, sisters, parents, all behind you across the water and have no kind face to speed you on your way. No matter, Kit my lad, that danger, bitter cold and the risk of a violent death await you. Your country needs you and you must do your duty.'

He began to whistle, softly, a lilting tune she recognized but could not place. He talked as if he was going to join the army, like Willy Macrae. Since the outbreak of the war in the Crimea, many of the young men of the area had done so and even Lorn had talked of going, till Mhairi had taken him aside, reminded him he had barely served out his apprenticeship, told him to leave soldiering to the soldiers and pointed out where his true duty lay. It was different for Willy Macrae who was a fourth son and the farm not big enough to support all of them, though his mother had been set against it and white-faced with dread. Annys had read letters in the paper from soldiers in the Crimea. It sounded a terrible place.

But the stranger had mentioned seeking his fortune. Surely you could not do that in the army? Again she risked a look at him and this time he caught her eye and winked. There was a look of her brothers' cheerful honesty about him and she was searching her mind for something suitable to say when she remembered Mhairi's voice only that morning. 'Do not speak to strangers, Annys. Keep your eyes on the path ahead of you and come straight home. There are too many wanderers in the streets these days. Speak to no one.' But surely this time Mhairi was wrong. What harm could there be? She bit her lip in indecision, shifting the weight of her basket from one arm to the other.

'Here, let me carry that for you.' He stopped, held out his hand and grinned. 'I may have walked all night but I've still the strength of

[11]

my arm, God be praised, and a good thing too or I'd be no use to anyone, let alone Messrs Peto and Betts. And you don't have to speak if you haven't the inclination. Just nod, and smile as you are doing now, and give me the basket.'

The basket was heavy, but no more than she was used to. If anything it was lighter than usual, for the winter months meant the hens did not lay as freely, the cow gave less milk for butter and cheese, and vegetables were scarce. But today her mittened hands were cold where they gripped the wicker handle and she welcomed the chance to warm them inside her plaid. Besides, it was a kindly offer. Not all lads would risk being seen with a woman's market basket. She pushed Mhairi's warnings to the back of her mind as the last of her fear slipped away.

'Thank you. It is a little heavy. Usually by now a farm cart has ...' She stopped, embarrassed by the way he was looking at her. With triumph and teasing, as if he had set a trap to catch her.

'So my Pretty Dancer can speak after all, and with a voice like a mountain stream.' He took the basket and said gravely, looking at her with green-flecked eyes, 'Please continue now you have begun, or I shall think I imagined it.'

Annys was instantly tongue-tied, looked wildly about her as much to avoid his eyes as for any other reason, and with relief saw help approaching.

'Oh! Here is Mr Dickie now.'

She waved, stepped back onto the verge, forgetting the snow and the hidden ditch, and cried out in alarm as her sturdy boots broke through the ice crust and plunged downwards. She floundered in a spray of snow and waving arms and would have fallen had he not swiftly caught her hand and pulled her up again. Even so her blue skirt was patched thick with clinging snow. Safe on the road again, she stamped her feet, shook the heavy folds and brushed at the snow with trembling hands, saying 'I'm all right, truly I am,' and at the same time blushing with embarrassment.

'It is a good job I had the basket and not you, my lass, or there would be frozen omelettes for all the carters in Aberdeenshire by now,' he said, grinning. 'But take my advice, lassie. Next time you want to beg a lift, don't hide in the ditch like a timid rabbit, but do as I do.' He stepped into the middle of the road, spread his arms wide, the basket hanging incongruously from one of them, and called cheerfully to the approaching vehicle.

[12]

'Ahoy there, ship of the highway! Is it the big city you are bound for?'

The farmer drew his horse to an abrupt stop, one hand on the reins, the other on his whip. Behind him, the cart was half-filled with bundles of straw, piled up like a rampart behind the driver's perch. He glared at O'Brien and the whip in his hand stirred. 'If you are wanting a lift, Annys lass,' he said, his eyes still holding O'Brien's, 'Jump in.'

'Thank you, Mr Dickie.' She moved to the rear of the cart and drew back the bolts which held the flap in place.

'Just a minute,' warned the farmer as O'Brien moved to follow her. 'You stay where you are. Was this fellow bothering you, Annys lass? I saw a scuffle, and there's him with your basket ...' He looked threateningly at O'Brien who still had that object in his hands, its red-checked gingham cover bright against the work-worn moleskin of his trousers.

'No,' she heard herself answer. To her surprise, she added, 'I slipped, that is all, and ... and he helped me regain my footing. As to the basket, he kindly offered to carry it for me.' She blushed in sudden confusion and looked away.

Mr Dickie, a dour-faced tenant farmer from Sclattie who supported wife and eight children on a farm little bigger than a croft, but a good neighbour and responsible family man, looked searchingly at Annys. He knew the Diack family for honest, hard-working folk, knew the widow Mhairi and the care she took of her sister, knew Annys herself to be a timid, God-fearing sort of a quine 'who wouldn't say "boo" to a gosling, let alone a goose' as his wife unkindly said. But there was no guile or mischief in the lass, not like most of the young baggages hereabouts, his own daughters not excepted. After another hard look at both stranger and girl, he decided to believe her story, inept though it was, but he frowned a warning at O'Brien. It said as clearly as words, 'She may be a gullible girl with a trusting nature, but she is under my protection and I don't trust you one inch, for all your so-called help and kindness. So watch your step or you'll have me to deal with.'

'Mr O'Brien has walked all night, Mr Dickie,' dared Annys. 'In the snow.' She put her foot on the tailboard and scrambled up into the cart, then held out her hands for the basket. With a wink, Kit handed it to her.

'Though to be sure,' he murmured, one eye on Mr Dickie, 'I

[13]

would gladly have carried it to the ends of the earth for you, my Pretty Dancer.'

He put a hand on the side of the cart as if to vault into it, and Mr Dickie's whip sliced the crisp air within an inch of his face.

'Who offered you a lift? I'm nay a public omnibus.'

There was a moment's silence in which the stranger stood immobile, his brown hand still resting on the side of the cart. The scent of the straw hung strong in the frosty air and the wood under his fingers was worn smooth as glass, the once-bright paint flaked away years ago.

'But Mr Dickie,' began Annys bravely. 'It is . . .'

The whip cut across her words with whistling malice and this time sent the horse leaping forward in the shafts. As the vehicle gathered speed, wooden wheels rattling over pothole and rutted snow, straw bundles swaying, every board creaking with the strain and tail-board flapping, Annys clutched the side for support with one hand and hung onto her basket with the other, while the bare hedgerow bowled past her not three feet away and spray arched up from the wheels in a shower of splintered ice. When at last the speed slowed to a steady walk she dared a glance back, along the way they had come. But the road was empty.

Then she heard a soft sound behind her, whirled round in alarm and would have cried out had he not put a finger to his lips and rolled his eyes in comical appeal. Separating passenger from driver, and forming a concealing barrier between, were the stacked bundles of straw that were all the Dickie farm could spare for the morning's market and his back against one of them, feet outstretched and ankles crossed, was Kit O'Brien, his bag on the dusty boards beside him. There was straw in his hair and more on the shoulders of his work-worn jacket. She was still looking at him in horror when Mr Dickie turned his head and called over his shoulder.

'You all right back there lass?'

Above the bristling palisade she could see the farmer's hawk-nosed profile under his dour black hat and, beneath the whiskers, one white corner of his collar. The straw cut off the rest of him from view, but above its pale gold prickles the swaying tip of his horse-whip was clearly visible.

Annys licked dry lips, but when the stranger put his hands together in mock prayer and, by some Irish trick, no doubt an aspect of the Blarney stone, made his eyes look twice the size and emerald

[14]

green, she called out, 'Yes thank you, Mr Dickie,' and Kit O'Brien grinned. His teeth, she noticed, were startlingly white.

He settled back with a sigh of content against his chosen bale, reached a hand up behind his head, selected a straw and with a wink at Annys commenced to chew it. He looked relaxed, untroubled and completely at ease.

Annys, on the other hand, passed the journey in a torment of confusion and anxiety. If she looked at him, he winked or grinned or pulled a comical face and if she did not look at him, but deliberately studied the hedgerow or the lightening sky or the road strung out behind them, she felt his eyes like green fire burning into her back. The force of his personality was a powerful magnet which it took all her strength to resist. Until, inevitably, she gave in and the process began all over again. It was a sort of conversation, intimate as a tête-à-tête, and afterwards Annys had difficulty remembering that no words had been spoken. But she could not answer his silent laughter with even the smallest smile because of her fear, which was no longer for herself, but for him. Suppose Mr Dickie looked round, saw those outstretched feet? In imagination Annys saw the farmer rise in his seat, heard the whip scream, saw Kit O'Brien flinch, arm raised in futile defence, then the vivid red stripe across his face and the oozing pinpoints of blood. *Oh God*, she prayed over and over. *Please keep Mr Dickie's eyes on the road ahead. Please don't let him turn round.*

Only when the stranger, warning finger to lips, dropped soundlessly and undetected from the tail-board on the outskirts of the town did her anxiety ease. He raised a hand in silent farewell and, with a glance behind her to make sure she was concealed from Mr Dickie, Annys timidly returned his wave. She saw him adjust the bag over his shoulder, hitch the waistband of his trousers, kick a pebble into the air and, before it could fall, kick it again in a joyous arch straight towards the back of the cart. With a final lurch of terror she reached up to catch it before it could smack onto the boards or, worse, into the respectable dome of Mr Dickie's hat which, she suspected afterwards, was probably its goal. The pebble stung her mittened hand, but her fingers closed safely over it and the last sight she had of the stranger before the road turned and lost him from view was of his raising his hands aloft in mimed applause.

Then at last, the fear of discovery past, she allowed herself to relax. With a long, quivering sigh, she opened her fingers and for no reason other than relief, idly studied the object which she had snatched from the edge of disaster. It was an ordinary enough stone, about the size of a large walnut, grey for the most part, but speckled here and there with pink and green. The green reminded her of the stranger's eyes. On an impulse, instead of tossing it aside as she had meant to do, Annys slipped the unremarkable pebble deep into her pocket. Then, smiling to herself, she began to check the contents of her market basket, lest any of the eggs had been cracked.

It was bitterly cold on the Green. The biting wind from the north had strengthened until it swirled and snatched at every unprotected cranny, teased the straw from under the produce in her basket and tossed it aloft like whirling yellow snowflakes; caught at her skirts and set the corner of her plaid snapping like a ship's pennant in a storm. There were fewer fisher lassies than usual in the market, the weather being too rough for their menfolk to put to sea, and those there were had pitifully few fish to sell: a handful of yellow smokies here, a half dozen haddies there. Annys took up her usual stand beside old Kirsty and though today there was less competition among the sellers, there were also fewer customers and trading was slow.

'I reckon the only folk abroad today are in Waterloo Road,' grumbled Kirsty, her lined old face tinged blue with cold except for her nose which was purple and adorned with a trembling diamond drop. Impatiently she shook it off and another instantly formed. 'And good luck to them, poor sots.'

'Who?' called Annys into the wind and caught the precious gingham covering of her basket just in time as a gust snatched it.

'They navvies and such. Them as wants to go to Balaclava to dig a railway for the soldiers. Since before dawn they've been gathering, seemingly, and now there's hundreds of them, pushing and shoving to be chosen, as if it was a privilege to have your fingers and toes froze off in yon Crimea when you can find the same, nay bother, at home. They say they Russians is savages, too. Dinna bury their dead like Christian folk, but leave them lying where they drop, for the wolves and suchlike to . . .'

Annys closed her ears. She was remembering Kit O'Brien and his cheerful whistle.

At first she had been afraid of him: but instead of harming her, he

[16]

had called her a walking angel and carried her basket. The thought warmed her heart, but not her frozen fingers and she stamped her feet and clapped her arms across her chest to keep the circulation moving. Off to seek his fortune, he had said. Then he had talked of doing his duty because his country needed him. She had thought he meant the army, but perhaps he was one of those hundreds Kirsty talked of, wanting to build a railway in Russia and fighting to be chosen? Either way, she did not wish to hear Kirsty's horror tales of death and mutilation.

'Dinna care for their wounded, neither,' the old woman was saying. 'There was one man lying six days with his leg shot off and no...'

'Eggs! Fresh eggs!' called Annys in desperation, to drown whatever dreadful words were coming next. 'Only ninepence the dozen.' But though she tried her best to shut out the sound of the old woman's voice and concentrate on the simple trading of the Green, Annys spent the rest of the day wondering about the stranger, where he had come from, where he was going, and, with new anxiety, what fate would befall him.

Annys was home later than usual, Mhairi's fatherless children Hamish and Catriona already long back from school and settled at the table with their copy books.

Alex Grant, Mhairi's husband, had been killed in a blasting accident at the quarry when Hamish was still a baby and Catriona not yet born, but the house was not without menfolk. Alex's brother Donal and two of Mhairi's own brothers, Lorn and Willy, still lived with the family in Rainbow Cottage, still worked at the quarry on Rainbow Hill, or at the granite-polishing yard in town. Both quarry and yard were owned by their friend and business partner, old George 'Headstane' Wyness, and with his support, as well as that of her family, Mhairi Diack Grant had survived.

But her widowhood had made her anxious, especially if any member of her precious family was away from home for longer than expected, and for the last half hour Mhairi had been drawing back the curtain from the window every five minutes to peer into the gusty gloom of the lane for a glimpse of the young sister she had 'mothered' since their own mother died in child-bed when Annys was four. So, when Annys's slim, bundled figure eventually appeared

[17]

out of the gathering darkness, Mhairi drew her swiftly inside and fussed over her to remove her damp outer clothing at once. She must change her stockings, wrap a warm shawl around her shoulders, come close to the fire and drink hot soup. When she was younger, Annys had fallen into the canal and as a result had almost died of a fever. Ever since, Mhairi had seen pneumonia in the smallest raindrop, and death in the damp hem of a skirt. Mostly this solicitude touched Annys and filled her with affection for the woman who had been sister and mother to her for as long as she could remember, but this evening she had to fight to keep irritation at bay. She was no longer a child: why could not Mhairi see that and treat her as a young woman? As Kit O'Brien had done?

But the thought of the stranger on the road brought a shiver of remembered danger and excitement. Unfortunately Mhairi saw and misunderstood. She pressed a hot whisky toddy into her sister's hands and, impervious to her protests, stood over her till Annys swallowed every last scalding drop. Only then did Mhairi relax enough to ask about the day, while at the same time she busied herself with the broth pot, moved the children aside and laid places at the table. Lorn and Willy would be home at any minute, with her brother-in-law Donal. Donal was deaf and dumb, but through determination and his own intelligence had become a skilled and talented draughtsman: his designs for the pattern-book at the Wyness polishing yard were unsurpassed and renowned throughout the trade.

Lorn, like Donal, made the three-mile journey to the yard and back again every working day of the week, often more than once, and while Willy worked mostly at Rainbow quarry, over the hill beyond the cottage, he too went often into town, for the work of quarry and yard was inseparable. In consequence, the men were invariably weary, footsore and hungry at the end of the long working day. Now, having checked the huge black kettle for hot water, Mhairi took two freshly-baked loaves from the open bread-oven and set them on a wooden platter.

'Let me do that,' said Annys, half rising from her stool, but Mhairi motioned her back again.

'You stay where you are, lass. We don't want you taking to your bed with a chill. Catriona will fetch the cheese, won't you my pet, then when the others come home, everything will be ready. Tell me, Annys, how much was butter fetching today?'

[18]

Finally, when Annys had answered Mhairi's questions about market prices, and Mhairi had counted over the money and checked the few household purchases, she held the new length of ribbon against the old and studied it, frowning. Years ago, before her marriage, when her mother was dead, her father unemployed, and with only her eldest brother Tom's wages as a quarryman to support the family, Mhairi had taken up dressmaking to earn what little extra she could. Over the years her skill had increased and since her husband's death she had found both purpose and much-needed money in developing her talent further until she had built up a regular circle of distinguished clients, in both city and surrounding area. But Mhairi's standards, like those of her clients, were high.

'Is it all right?' asked Annys anxiously. 'I took it into the daylight, like you said.'

'Perfect,' pronounced Mhairi. The frown fell away and she smiled. 'Thank you, Annys dear. I could not have done better myself.' She stowed the ribbon away in her work-box and turned to more frivolous things.

'Did you meet anyone on the road this morning?'

Fractionally, Annys hesitated, avoided Mhairi's eye, then heard herself say, 'No. No one.'

Afterwards she was ashamed. She could not think why she had told the lie, except that if she had mentioned Kit O'Brien, Mhairi would have been cross with her, said 'I warned you,' and gone pale with horror at the thought of what might have been. Mhairi would have forbidden her to go to market alone again, fussed and fretted and set her face even more firmly against the idea of Annys taking any sort of job. But that was not the whole reason. Part of it was the wish to keep her small adventure to herself, to go over every detail in secret, to relive fear and excitement and remember the strange things he had said. He had called her a walking angel, and had winked at her with green-flecked eyes.

'No one?' repeated Mhairi in surprise. The road from Inverurie was usually busy on a market day, and grew busier as it approached the town, collecting travellers at every hamlet. 'Are you sure?'

Annys turned away, pretending to warm her hands at the flames, but before Mhairi could question her further the door burst open on a gust of cold air and Lorn and Willy spilled in together, rubbing their hands and shivering, and made straight for the fire. 'Brrr, but it's a raw evening.'

Donal followed, stooping his head to negotiate the lintel, then shut the door behind him and, for good measure, drew the heavy curtain across to keep out the cold night air. Catriona began to babble excitedly to her two young uncles about the doings of her schoolday, but her brother Hamish leapt up from his stool and flung himself across the room to greet the third arrival. Since infancy, Hamish had learned to communicate with his deaf uncle and now Donal seized the boy under the armpits and swung him high into the air in their usual ritual, to hold him for a moment, their faces on a level, as they exchanged their private greetings. Then, Donal set the boy down again, but when Hamish tugged impatiently at Donal's hand to make him look at a drawing he had made, Donal for once resisted. With a shake of the head and a gesture of the hand which said, 'Not yet,' he felt deep into his pocket and produced an envelope which he handed solemnly to Mhairi. It was a large envelope, white and square, and of expensive quality.

Mhairi looked from envelope to Donal while her face echoed the pallor of the missive in her hands. She had no need to open it to know what was inside. Already she had been given excited orders by several of her richer clients for special outfits suitable for a society wedding. Word of mouth had preceded written invitation, hope had leapt ahead of certainty, and no one who was anyone in 'best society' expected to be left out.

But Mhairi Diack's family was not 'society', 'best' or any other kind, and never would be. Her father had been a humble causeway-man in Silvercairns quarry, until he was sacked and died of dust in the lungs and despair. Therefore the reason must be one of cold-blooded business. Unless...

The thought of Fergus Adam was swiftly suppressed, but not before Mhairi's heart had quickened with excitement and a hope she knew to be both dangerous and futile. Whatever would her brother Tom think of her if he could read her mind? But she had been a faithful widow for six years. Why should she not emerge into the living world again, if the chance presented itself? She was young and healthy and widowhood was lonely. It was all very well for Tom to talk of keeping faith with the dead, but Tom did not have to go to bed alone and now that her children were both at school and did not need her so demandingly, Mhairi was increasingly conscious of an emptiness in the core of her life. Now, for the first time, she shaped that emptiness into daring words: *she would like a man to love again*. And if that man could be Fergus Adam...

But her family was watching her, waiting for comment. With her thoughts in such turmoil and all her effort needed to keep her face expressionless, Mhairi dared not attempt to speak. Instead, her raised eyebrows asked a delaying question. It was Lorn who answered.

'A fellow delivered it to the granite yard just as we were leaving, with a similar for Tom and another for Mr Wyness. One of the Adam men, from Silvercairns.'

There followed a silence in which even six-year-old Catriona joined. Silvercairns was the richest quarry in Aberdeenshire, some said in the whole of Scotland, but the Adam family who owned it were their sworn enemies and rivals. Mhairi's father had worked there loyally for twenty years, only to be sacked on a whim. Her eldest brother Tom and husband Alex had both served their apprenticeship there as stonemasons, until a private quarrel between Tom and Mungo's younger son Hugo, the details of which Mhairi preferred to forget, resulted in Alex and Tom being thrown into jail. Mungo Adam was forced to retract the charge and the men were freed, but the memory still stung. Then the old autocrat had fixed his greedy eye on George Wyness's granite yard and been thwarted in his devious attempts to add it to his empire. As a result of that particular contest, George Wyness had found himself the quarry at Rainbow Hill, had 'rescued' Tom and Alex and taken them on as working partners. He had given the family Rainbow Cottage to live in and, with their loyal support, had set up in defiant opposition to the all-powerful Adam family and Silvercairns.

Mungo Adam had been apopleptic with rage. Had vowed, in a purple fury, to destroy them all and had tried his evil best to do so, until he accidentally killed himself instead. Remembering, Mhairi shuddered. The mystery of the explosion which killed her husband Alex had never been satisfactorily explained, and there might well have been other, similar, 'accidents' had Old Man Adam lived.

Everything in the history of the Diack and Adam families only served to set them further apart, in background and in enmity. So an expensive invitation from that quarter – and in such an envelope and on such paper it could only be an invitation – was astounding.

'Open it, Ma,' urged Hamish. 'See what it says.'

Slowly, Mhairi did so, read silently to herself, then looked up with

[21]

a face carefully washed clean of emotion, though Annys was sure she saw elation and something more in the bright, evasive eyes.

'What is it, Mhairi?' she asked, and the others joined in the clamour. When she did not answer, Lorn deftly lifted the card from Mhairi's fingers.

'Well, well,' he said slowly, with a whistle of disbelief. 'Mr Fergus Adam only requests the pleasure of Mhairi's company at his sister's wedding!'

This time the silence throbbed with amazement and awe. They passed the pasteboard card from hand to hand and even Catriona solemnly studied its baffling spider-marks before giving it back to her mother. Then they waited, their eyes on Mhairi's face, but still she did not speak.

'Ma?' Hamish's young voice again broke the silence. 'Will you go?'

Tom Diack paused on the steps of his solid, granite-built house in Elmbank and, as he had done every day since the day he had carried his bride over the threshold, allowed himself a moment's secret pride and awe. When he had chosen Fanny Wyness for a wife, though her father was his boss and rich enough to buy his only child a dozen houses if she wanted them, Tom had vowed not to touch a penny of George Wyness's money. He would support his own wife, unaided, or remain unmarried. But a quarryman's wages, even at Rainbow Hill, were little enough and his share of the quarry profits likewise. He had sought George Wyness's permission to go to Australia for a spell, on quarry business, and to make his fortune. Though Fanny had been desolate, her father had understood and grudgingly approved. Tom's sister Mhairi had not approved, though she had understood, and Rainbow Hill had managed well enough without him. At least . . .

Remembering Alex Grant, Mhairi's husband and his own dearest friend, Tom felt the familiar twinge of guilt and pain. If Tom had not gone to Australia, perhaps Alex would still be alive? It was a futile speculation and, as always, he fought it down. Besides, if he had not gone to Australia, he might never have married Fanny. As it was, Tom had returned three years later, if not with a fortune, with enough money to build Fanny a house, and with a wealth of new experience and skills which he quickly turned to good account on behalf of his father-in-law's quarry and polishing yard. For though

[22]

Tom had gone to Australia a raw quarryman, he had returned a shrewd and competent building contractor with a flair for building houses for the newly affluent. In his absence, his brothers Lorn and Willy, with Donal Grant, had managed the Rainbow Hill quarry and polishing yard perfectly well without him, but the building opportunities, Tom pointed out, had not been fully explored. George Wyness had given his new son-in-law a free hand to explore them and, at a time when increasing prosperity was pushing the boundaries of Aberdeen steadily outward, Tom had seen his chance and taken it.

But though whole streets of the city were, directly or indirectly, his achievement, no house gave Tom Diack more pleasure than his own, built with the fruits of his own hard labour, for his dear wife Fanny. Once more he let his eyes run proudly over the simple, elegant façade, then, smiling to himself, opened the heavy door and stepped inside. He doffed hat and overcoat, tossed them onto a chair and was about to open the door of the parlour, where he knew Fanny would be waiting for him, when he saw the white envelope on the hall table. He picked it up with one hand, opened the door with the other, kissed Fanny, then smiling down at her ran a paper-knife along the fold and drew out the pasteboard card. The smile vanished.

'Out of the question!' exploded Tom Diack. 'Who does the fellow think he is?'

'Who dear?' said his wife calmly, though she had a shrewd idea. She had seen a similar envelope only that afternoon at the house of Amelia Macdonald Burnett and had witnessed its opening, with the torrent of speculation and comment, from the vitriolic to the plain envious, which had followed.

'Adam, of course. The bare-faced nerve of the man. After what his family has done to ours, I wouldn't accept his hospitality if he was the last man on earth.' He tore the card in two and tossed it contemptuously into the coal scuttle.

'That is hardly Christian, Tom,' said Fanny gently. 'Nor even fair. It was his father who wronged you, and his father is dead. You can have nothing against Fergus, surely? He has always treated us with courtesy and respect.' In the days before Mungo Adam and George Wyness became enemies, Fanny had moved in the same social circle as Mungo's elder son Fergus and his sister Lettice, and for the most part on amicable terms.

'Us?' glared Tom. 'Speak for yourself, Fanny. I certainly remem-

[23]

ber no such dealings with the man. But before you talk of forgiveness, I would remind you that it was because of the Adams that
my father died ...'

'Indirectly,' dared his wife, but Tom ignored her.

'... and because of the Adams that Mhairi is a widow and my best
friend dead.'

When Alex Grant died in that quarry accident, there had certainly
been whispers that Mungo Adam had had a hand in it, though
nothing had ever been proved. Fanny, however, thought it prudent
not to remind Tom of this. Instead she diplomatically busied herself
with her needlework while Tom glowered in silence into the fire. In
the short years of her marriage she had learned the wisdom of
silence, for without the fan of argument to stimulate it, the heat of
Tom's anger soon died. Now she bent her head over her stitches,
while the ormolu clock on the mantel ticked away the evening with
careful precision and the fire crackled softly behind its polished
brass fender. The clock had been a wedding present from her
father's workers at the granite yard and bore a small plaque to record
the occasion.

Gradually the warmth of his own fireside melted Tom's anger,
and the hard knot eased. It was a source of continuing wonder to him
that this solid granite house on the sunny side of the canal bank, with
white scrubbed steps leading up to a solid, brass-handled front door,
with a portico to shield waiting visitors from rain and an iron railing
with a gate to the basement steps should be his very own, built by his
own hands and with his own, hard-earned money. To a man who had
been brought up in a family of seven, in two damp-spotted tenement
rooms on a shared stair, it was both palace and paradise. There was
even a garden at the back, with fruit trees and flower beds, a plot of
herbs for Fanny's kitchen and space for their children to play.

There was space for his brothers and sisters too, and it was the
least he could do, as head of the family and having made his small
way up in the world, to remove them from the cramped quarry
cottage and offer them the shelter of his own home. But he had been
grateful when they refused, and secretly glad. Tom had Mhairi to
thank for that: she understood that after a lifetime's overcrowding
and family responsibility, he wanted his wife, and his house, to
himself. But on the days when he called at Rainbow Cottage, clean
and cheerful though Mhairi kept it, he still felt guilty that she had so
little happiness and he so much. Perhaps, as Fanny had hinted more

[24]

than once, she ought to marry again? But the idea of anyone replacing his dear friend Alex brought the usual angry pain and he thrust the thought aside. What man on God's earth could take Alex's place in Mhairi's heart?' And why should she remarry? She had a home and independence, with her children about her and her memories.

Besides, Mhairi's happiness apart and on a purely practical level, a new brother-in-law might cause complications. Tom was not proud of such down-to-earth calculations, but the fact remained that since her husband's death, Mhairi held a thirty percent share in the Rainbow Hill quarry and he did not relish the idea of some stranger getting his hands on that, with the power such a share would give him. Tom himself owned a mere ten percent, and though his wife had brought another thirty percent with her as dowry, pride prevented him including her share with his. Fanny's father owned the remaining shares, and the situation was no doubt safe enough, but all the same he would be happier if his sister remained a widow, at least until young Hamish came of age. And when that time came, if Mhairi grew lonely, there was always a loving home waiting for her with himself and Fanny.

Lamplight and firelight sent gentle shadows over the plain but comfortable furnishings, glinting on the glass of framed sepia photographs (Mr and Mrs Wyness, himself and Fanny with baby George), on the brass bowl of the parlour palm on the *jardinière* (presented to them by Mrs Wyness when she had taken a dislike to it) and touched the brown sheen of Fanny's hair and the dark red folds of her dress. She wore white lace at her neck and there was more lace on the tiny garment she was sewing for their infant daughter, asleep in a crib beside her older brother's cot, in the nursery upstairs.

Little Georgie would be two in April and was already the apple of his grandfather's eye. Old George Wyness had been beside himself with delight when his wee grandson was born and it had been all Tom could do to stop the old man showering riches on the lad at the least excuse. Now, looking at Fanny across the hearth of the house he had built for her with the strength of his own arm, Tom felt the last of his anger drain away. Fanny was plumper than when he had married her, especially now, so soon after their daughter's birth, but motherhood suited her and she looked both youthful and serene. When she looked up and caught him studying her she said, 'What is it, Tom? Is my hair escaping from its pins?'

'No, you little ninny. But if it was it would only make you look more charming.'

She blushed and smiled into her lap, while her fingers continued to fold the tucks of the tiny bodice. Tom sat down on the sofa beside her and slipped his arm around her waist.

After a moment, Fanny said, 'Lettice Adam was my childhood friend.'

'Was,' repeated Tom, with a returning frown, but her warm proximity disarmed irritation. He had had a long and arduous day and had earned the pleasures of his own fireside and his own delightfully appealing wife.

'I am glad she is getting married at last.'

'Is that a roundabout way of saying you want to go to the wedding, because if so . . .'

'Of course not, Tom dear. I meant only that I am happy for her – and for any girl who marries the man she loves.'

'She took long enough to trap him, poor fellow,' began Tom, but Fanny laid a warning finger on his lips.

'No more. We will talk about it another time. Tonight I want to tell you what little Georgie has been doing. You will not believe the mischief he got into when Mamma came calling. You know those amber beads of hers and what store she sets by them? Well the little horror reached up and tugged and . . .'

'Do you remember,' interrupted Tom, tracing the line of her cheek with a teasing forefinger, 'when Mhairi's Hamish did the same to your hat, and sent your hair tumbling? I think I fell in love with you there and then.'

'Well I assure you wee Georgie's efforts produced a quite different effect on my mother,' laughed Fanny and proceeded to tell Tom all the delightful trivia of her domestic day until the Adam invitation was apparently forgotten. Nevertheless, later that evening, when Tom was out of the room, Fanny found the opportunity to retrieve the torn invitation, dust off the grime and put the two halves carefully away in her writing desk. After all, as she had reminded her husband, Lettice Adam was her childhood friend.

In the library of Silvercairns House, the log fire burnt bright and welcomingly warm. On one side of it sat Lettice Adam, a coffee cup in her hand; on the other, her brother Fergus, his attention wholly on

[26]

the day's newspaper. The folding wooden shutters had been closed against the winter night and the lamps turned up, so that the gilt tooling on the ranks of leather-bound books gleamed like a miriad trapped stars and the gold pattern which threaded the Persian rugs throbbed bright amongst deep reds and blues. It was a cheerfully comfortable and reassuring room, though in their father's day, no amount of firelight and warmth could have counteracted the brooding threat of his presence, especially in his last years when he grew increasingly devious and evil. Mrs Adam had died years ago and Lettice ran the household, but there had been a time when even Lettice dare not speak, lest she bring her tyrannical father's anger thundering down upon her, with the threat of some loathesome old man or poisonous younger one for a husband if she did not toe the line. As to Fergus, his father had threatened him with disinheritance on more than one occasion, usually if the quarry output had not reached Mungo's impossible targets, for the old man was deep in debt.

But even the weight of those inherited debts could not mar the sense of freedom which flowed over Silvercairns when Mungo Adam was safely underground. Lettice ran the household with autocratic efficiency and an arrogance worthy of her father, while doing exactly as she chose. She ordered new dresses or mantles whenever she felt like it, drove out in the carriage with her fiancé or to pay morning calls, invited amusing guests to dinner.

Her brother Fergus, for the first time in his life, was free to run his beloved quarry exactly as he saw fit, with no grasping tyrant of a father breathing down his neck and countermanding his orders. In the evening, pleasantly tired after a hard day's honest work and with no one to accuse him of deliberate idleness or skiving, Fergus was equally free to enjoy an untroubled meal with his sister, or with guests if Lettice had chosen to invite any, and to relax, as he was doing now.

Lettice, however, was not relaxed. Of a naturally impatient nature, which beauty and arrogance made more so, she was plainly irritated, her lovely brow creased in a frown. From the depths of the house came faint noises: a child's voice, a woman's remonstrating, an indeterminate murmuring from the kitchen regions. But inside the library there was silence except for the soft crackle of burning wood, the regular ticking of the mantel clock and the occasional rustle of Fergus's newspaper. When Lettice put down her empty cup on the

[27]

small table beside her with a clatter that would have startled anyone else out of the deepest reverie, Fergus merely shifted a little in his chair, crossed one leg over the other and turned another page. Exasperated, Lettice spoke.

'Who do you think *will* come?'

For answer her brother merely shrugged and Lettice abandoned all attempts at sisterly compliance. In the absence of her affianced, who was as yet unaware of the less civilized aspects of her character, she felt free to give these a thorough airing, such as they had not received for months.

'That's right, shrug your shoulders as if it is of no concern. Well it may be of none to you, brother dear, but it certainly is to me. I am not going to be shunned at my own wedding. I told you from the first that you should never have invited anyone from the Wyness camp, but would you listen? Oh no. A time for forgiveness, wasn't it? For burying the hatchet, patching up old quarrels, and similar maudlin and sentimental platitudes? Invite them all, you said, to show we harbour no ill feeling – and all your so-called generous gesture did was to give them the chance to throw the invitation back in our faces. "Previous engagement" indeed! Some tin-pot, hole-in-the-corner foursome at whist, after cold mutton and a shape, no doubt arranged solely to cover the lie. They are fools if they expect us to believe it, when there is nothing on the social calendar of any interest whatsoever except my wedding. But they don't expect us to believe it, do they? They mean us to see the snub and to squirm. But I'll not squirm for anyone and certainly not for that odious, verminous sewer-rat Niall Burnett and his simpering idiot of a wife. If I'd had my way none of them would have been invited in the first place, not Wyness nor Burnett nor Macdonald. That would have kept them in their proper place, under the nearest stone.'

Fergus looked up briefly from the page. 'I hope you will remember not to speak so scathingly of our fellow-men in Dr Marshall's presence, Lettice. It would be a pity to frighten him off after three years of careful luring. It is not too late, even now, for him to change his mind, choose battlefield instead of consulting room, and go to the Crimea after all. His skills are certainly needed there and should win him recognition far more quickly than at home. Look at Miss Nightingale's fame. All those splendid pages of contributions to the Patriotic Fund are due in large part to that young lady's efforts. An

[28]

injudicious fit of temper from you and Dr Marshall may well decide to follow her example and seek his patients in the Bosphorus.'

Lettice blushed, bit her lip in annoyance, but for the moment held her tongue. 'Careful luring' indeed! Fergus knew perfectly well that it was David who had pursued her, not the other way round. Nevertheless, there was too much truth for comfort in her brother's words and she was well aware that behind her back malicious tongues were wagging freely on the subject of how long it had taken her to 'catch' the doctor, and whether or not he might slip the noose even now. Lettice Adam might be rich, well-born and beautiful, but her arrogance and the sharpness of her tongue were legendary. Why else would she be still unmarried at twenty-seven? At the Assembly Meeting only last week, coming into the supper room unexpectedly, Lettice had actually caught the tail-end of a wager on that very matter, with the ominous phrase 'only after her money'. Those words had nibbled away at her confidence ever since, but, she told herself briskly, it would take more than a gaggle of spiteful Aberdeen matrons to defeat Lettice Adam of Silvercairns.

She did not deny that had she been a penniless nobody Dr Marshall might have looked elsewhere for a spouse. If he had been a penniless nobody, she would have done the same. It was only common sense.

Dr Marshall was, admittedly, almost penniless. He had told her himself that he was only 'a Buchan lad made good' with nothing but his uncle's patronage behind him and the patronage of a country doctor, though welcome, was little enough. But Dr Marshall was certainly not a nobody. Handsome, charming and undoubtedly talented beyond the ordinary in his chosen field, Lettice expected him to go far; even, with her help, to the very top of his profession. Already she saw the words 'Physician to Her Majesty the Queen' after his name, and why not? David was the best doctor in Aberdeen as well as the most personable: all that was required for his talents to be recognized in high places was a word in the right ear. Lettice saw his progress as clearly as if it had already happened: first the cream of Aberdeenshire society, then by natural progression, Balmoral. The castle was only fifty miles away and when the Deeside railway was completed the distance would be nothing. Though David himself seemed unaware of such social possibilities, Lettice knew exactly the route to take and had ambition enough for both of them.

For, in spite of her brother's sneers, she intended to ensure that

[29]

her husband achieved success. In the social pool the Burnetts and Macdonalds were nobody, mere small fry who she was free to insult as they deserved. But there were other, larger fish to whom she was more than willing to be polite, for David's sake, and who she was equally prepared to beguile with hospitality of the most elegant and persuasive kind whenever expedient. The Adam town house in the Guestrow (let to tenants ever since her father's death, but reclaimed now for her personal occupation) though not as modern as Silvercairns, was of a solid worth and comfort ideal for the purpose.

Lettice had laid her plans early. She had not exactly relished the idea of a consulting room in her own house, or of the dispensary which must inevitably go with it, but for the sake of David's career she had been prepared to make the sacrifice. Besides, part of the kitchen wing, with the servants' room above, could be adapted for the purpose with little disruption to the normal running of the household, and after all, only the better class of patient would come to the house. The others would attend the public clinic nearby where David would still be obliged to work from time to time. The best patients, it went without saying, would be visited in their own homes, and the alterations to the house could be carried out at far less expense than renting and equipping similar premises elsewhere. She had consulted an architect in private and instructed him to draw up plans.

She had meant to have the work done without David's knowledge. It was to have been her wedding present to him, and a glorious surprise. But when the architect asked what design of shelving she had in mind for the dispensary, and whether she required special provision for poisons, she changed her mind. The question recalled all the unpleasantness of specimens pickled in glass jars, of scalpels and probes and other such instruments of torture ominously simmering over spirit lamps, of rows of jars and bottles containing unguents and potions of a generally malodorous nature, and her shuddering distaste vanquished all idea of secrecy. David must deal with that side of things himself.

But when she told him of her plans for his comfort and advancement, he had not, as she had expected, overwhelmed her with gratitude and undying love. Instead he had frowned and told her quite brusquely that he had no intention of establishing a surgery in the Guestrow house, thank you very much, that he intended to continue working as before, for his uncle, the hospital or the public

[30]

clinic, exactly as he chose, and would take it as a personal favour if she would not interfere in his professional life. When she had urged that he must not be coy about accepting her money, because what was hers was his also, he had told her she had missed the point entirely.

'I will conduct my professional career in my own way and by my own efforts. I will not advance it by taking advantage of my wife's family home. Nor have I any use for an oak-panelled consulting room with Turkey carpets on the floor, old masters on the walls and a succession of neurotic county gentlewomen with nothing better to do than indulge their imaginary aches and pains. You must understand, Lettice dear,' he had continued more gently, 'that the town hospital and the town clinic are where my work is, with real patients and real diseases for which I hope to make it my life's work to find the cure. Already we know enough to see that poverty and dirt breed disease faster than anything else. How could I possibly advance my research into septic poisoning, for instance,' he had finished, teasing, 'with only the pampered rich for patients?'

Then, to soften the sarcasm, he had taken her hands in his, smiled at her, and said gently, 'Thank you, Lettice, but no. Save your money for a more worthwhile purpose. Or send it to the Patriotic Fund.'

Nothing she said could persuade him and in the end she had given up the attempt. But not the idea, which she put carefully away for a later date. It was male pride, of course. Once they were married he would think differently. But at least it proved that he was not merely after her money as malicious tongues were whispering.

Besides, Dr Marshall could easily have chosen elsewhere, had he wished. Lettice felt a moment's warm reassurance. For in all her casual inquiries she had heard no tales of any such tentative attentions to other women. Only that rumour long ago about him and Fanny Wyness, which was patently untrue.

The memory, however, was a sobering one. Fanny would undoubtedly have made the doctor a compliant and eminently suitable wife. Lettice considered herself to be blessed with many talents and virtues, but compliance was certainly not one of them. Thinking of what an up-and-coming society doctor might require in a wife, Lettice had done her best to subdue the more autocratic side of her nature and to keep her tongue in check. For whatever he said about hospitals and clinics, Lettice knew in her bones, as he must know it, that David's destiny was higher than that. Though he roundly denied it, Lettice was sure that to be one of the Queen's physicians must be David's secret ambition, as it was hers, and to achieve it courtesy of the first order would be required. If she so much as hinted to David that, the wedding ring safely on her finger, she would deal out sarcasm and intolerance instead, she might indeed lose him, even at this late stage in the mating dance.

It had been a slow measure, without particular passion on either side, but she and David Marshall got on well together. They understood and respected each other and the fact that Lettice had learnt early that he would not submit to her dominance in spite of her money and social advantage, merely sharpened her interest and added an unaccustomed touch of humility to her usually overbearing character. For, as much as she was capable of loving anyone except herself, Lettice Adam loved Dr Marshall. The fact that she did not know, even now, how he really felt towards her made an uncertainty in the core of her confidence and, impossible though such an eventuality was, the shame and humiliation and heartache if he should leave her before they were safely married was too awful to contemplate.

Though she could not forgive her brother for it, Fergus was right. If Dr Marshall was to scale the heights of professional success, he would require a wife who could control her temper.

Lettice took a long, slow breath, but before capitulation allowed herself one last barb.

'There is still no answer from the lovely widow. That must be disappointing for you.' When Fergus ignored her, she said sweetly 'I would advise you to forget her, Fergus dear. You have made futile sheep's eyes in that direction for far too long and it is time you came out of your adolescent dotage and grew up. You are past thirty now and should take a wife. After all, who is to run your household when I am gone?'

'There are such things as housekeepers ...' began Fergus, but Lettice interrupted him.

'More to the point, who is to take charge of the wee Australian horror?'

'Leo?' This time she had her brother's full attention.

Their brother Hugo, Mungo Adam's younger and favourite son, had fathered a child on one of the Silvercairns scullerymaids (who had promptly purloined a handful of Lettice Adam's jewellery in compensation and fled to Australia) and had been banished to

[32]

Jamaica for his sins. There, Hugo had caught a tropical fever and died. Mungo Adam, consumed by grief for the son he had lost and venom towards the son who remained, had sent to Australia for Hugo's child and his last years had been spent gleefully planning how to cheat Fergus and Lettice of their inheritance so that illegitimate Leo might have it instead. Fortunately for Fergus, for whom Silvercairns quarry was his life, Mungo Adam had planned one explosion too many, toppled the west wing of Silvercairns house and killed himself in the process, before he had reached the stage of altering his will. But the child remained.

'Leo?' repeated Fergus, frowning. 'Naturally, you will continue to oversee his upbringing, as you have done for the last four and a half years.'

'Oh no, brother dear.' Lettice rose elegantly from her chair, shook her silken skirts into place and moved gracefully towards the door. With her hand on the doorknob she paused, turned and said, in a voice of sweet reason, 'I shall be far too busy "overseeing" my own establishment, in the Guestrow. *Naturally*, Leo will stay here at Silvercairns, where he belongs. With *you*. Unless, of course, that dreadful mother of his comes home to claim him. I believe the most ignorant and brutish of people have made fortunes from the Australian gold diggings. Perhaps she has done the same? Perhaps she is on the high seas at this very moment, speeding her way homeward to her long-lost son?'

With that gleeful taunt, she slipped through the door and closed it firmly behind her, cutting off Fergus's alarmed protests in mid-flow. Though he pretended otherwise, she knew how fond her brother was of the 'wee Australian horror' and how appalled he would be should the child's mother indeed return. The idea had come to her on the spur of the moment, but hours of concentrated thought could hardly have thrown up anything more likely to shatter her pious brother's composure. Smiling with triumph, she made her way upstairs, first to the nursery wing to tell young Leo to make less noise and go to sleep at once 'or there will be no pony for you tomorrow, and certainly no trip to the quarry.' Then to her own room to savour her victory and to go over yet again the contents of her clothes press and the plans for her wedding.

After his first futile outburst, Fergus subsided into silence while the full implication of his sister's words sank home. The idea of Lizzie Lennox coming back to claim Leo was ludicrous, of course. A mere moment's thought was enough for him to realize that. Even if she had made money, and it seemed unlikely, she would hardly waste it travelling half way across the world to burden herself with a son she had never bothered to write to and had probably forgotten long ago. The idea was absurd, but the rest of what his sister had said was not so easily dismissed.

Fergus had not considered the effect of Lettice's marriage on his household. Except for the purely practical point that from the day of her wedding someone else would pay his sister's dressmaker's bills, he had assumed that things would jog along much as usual. After all, the servants would remain, presumably knew what was expected of them and would do it. Mrs Gregor would see to that. As for Leo ...

The more he thought, the more he realized that the matter of Leo was more complicated than the paying, or otherwise, of a dressmaker's bill. His dead brother's bastard had been sent for and adopted by their father almost five years ago and, since Old Man Adam's death, Fergus and Lettice between them had been the boy's guardians. Leo was seven now, still 'a proper handful' as Mrs Gregor put it, but less wild than when he arrived. Thinking back to the struggling, kicking, swearing scrap of flea-ridden humanity they had collected on the quay that day, the child's skinny limbs in ragged hand-me-down's and over-large boots, his pathetic defiance and frightened eyes, Fergus sighed with remembered pity and exasperation. His father had had no business to 'buy' the child unseen, to have him wrenched from mother and home and posted like a parcel half way round the world. No wonder Leo swore and kicked with all his puny strength, and had no more sense of civilized behaviour than a new-born savage.

Old Man Adam's gleeful indulgence had not improved matters, until the old man's death sobered Leo as nothing else had succeeded in doing. After that, the child was more manageable, though far from perfect. He followed Fergus around with exasperating tenacity, demanding to be shown how to blast granite from the quarry, how to lay a fuse, drive a bore-hole, or shape a sett to regulation size, 'so I know how to run my quarry when I'm big, like Grandpa said I could'. If Fergus refused, Leo pestered Lettice to play with him, take him riding or in the carriage to Aberdeen, got in the way of the servants and made himself a general nuisance. He was shamelessly persistent

[34]

and impervious to rebuff, even if that rebuff was accompanied by a clip on the ear or a well-aimed smack on the backside.

When he was five, Lettice had endeavoured to teach him the rudiments of reading, to which he brought little interest and no application at all. The minister's wife had tried with no more success than Lettice. In exasperation Fergus had packed him off to the local school where he went cheerfully enough, to return each evening with scraped knees, a bloody nose or similar signs of fisticuffs, several choice additions to his vocabulary, but little in the way of learning. At last, Fergus took him aside and told him sternly that he would not be allowed to set foot inside the quarry yard again until he could read and write: 'For how will you read the instructions on the blasting powder tin or work out the proportions otherwise? If you do not apply yourself,' he had finished, frowning in a passable imitation of his own intimidating father, 'I shall assume you have no interest in the quarry and that you would prefer to be a scullery boy and scrub potatoes. Or sweep out the stable yard for the rest of your life.'

After that, the boy had at least tried, though it soon became obvious that he would never be a scholar. But he could read a little now and write after a fashion, and his daily homework sessions with Lettice, though tempestuous at times, had brought a slight improvement. On Leo's pleading, Fergus had relaxed the quarry ban, though with the threat of its immediate re-introduction should the boy's schoolwork suffer, and since then they had jogged along together well enough. But how would the boy react when Lettice left? Children needed a woman's care, and Leo could hardly go with her.

Perhaps Lettice was right and it was time he married?

Into his mind came the usual picture, of a dark-haired woman with clear blue eyes and an air of quiet sorrow which tore at his heart. He had kissed her once, aons ago ... But her family and his had long been in separate camps, divided by too many treacheries to forget or forgive.

For the first time he admitted that Mhairi Diack, more correctly Mhairi Grant, had been the reason for his wholesale dispensation of forgiveness and bonhomie. If he invited to his sister's wedding every quarry owner in the neighbourhood, including old enemies, then no one would notice his invitation to the one person above all others he hoped would accept. And when she came, he would take her aside, ask her forgiveness, and they would talk together, as they talked in his dreams, easily, intimately, until ... Abruptly he summoned

[35]

common sense. Her invitation had been sent by hand a week ago and he had had no answer. Far better to banish daydreams and concentrate on reality.

Mentally he ran through the names of those who had accepted, and stopped at those of Philip and Henrietta Drummond, St John's Wood, London. Brother and sister. Second cousins of some kind on the bridegroom's side and invited, less from courtesy and to redress the balance, for the Marshall guest list was a quarter the length of the Adam one, than from deliberate calculation. Dr Marshall had said only that Mr Drummond had shared rooms with him once, in London, but Fergus had read in the paper, quite by chance, that Mr Drummond had a connection with railways, his father being a major shareholder in several, and had recently expressed interest in those north of the border, particularly if there was a possibility of royal patronage. No doubt Dr Marshall hoped friend Drummond would divert some of the royal patronage in his direction, thought Fergus sourly, but that was not where Fergus's interest lay.

Fergus's father had squandered too much of the Adam fortune on railway shares which instead of doubling their value had halved it, and brought no dividends to speak of. In the debt-ridden days that followed Old Man Adam's death, Fergus had sold most of the wretched things, but he had held onto the Deeside railway shares out of sentiment. The line was to pass close to Silvercairns on its westward route along the Dee valley towards Balmoral, where young Queen Victoria was building herself a new castle. He had not admitted to sentiment of course: merely to business speculation. Quite apart from the benefits to his quarry of accessible railway transport, if the Queen favoured the route, profits should be good. And if a London wedding guest with influence enjoyed the Adam hospitality, might not a lucrative railway contract or two come the quarry's way?

'You are growing as devious as your own father,' Fergus told himself, frowning. But those debts had been massive and he had not shaken clear of them yet. The Deeside line was laid only half way, as far as Banchory, and these would be plenty more bridges, stations and related railway cottages to build before it reached its full length and was complete. Larger houses would inevitably follow, as the town grew more congested and the railway made the country more accessible, and granite would be much in demand. Fergus intended to fight for every contract going, and if an unknown wedding guest might help him win them, then it was worth every magnum of champagne he had to open in the process. At least he was not lining up his children to make cold-blooded marriages of convenience, as Old Man Adam had been in the habit of doing.

But the thought of marriage reminded him again of Lettice's words. If Mhairi Diack refused the olive branch, it would mean the feud was as bitter as ever, his dream impossible. Or was that dream no more than 'adolescent dotage' as Lettice had said? A mere excuse to maintain his bachelor status? He stared morosely into the fire trying to make sense of his own feelings, but all he knew with any certainty was that no one had ever appealed to his heart as Mhairi Diack had done. And he had hardly spoken a dozen words to the woman. Impatiently he thrust such fanciful thoughts aside and turned to that other, greater certainty: his beloved quarry.

Over the years since his father's death Fergus had worked like a man possessed to claw Silvercairns back from the edge of bankruptcy: to win contracts, meet deadlines, produce maximum output with minimum damage to quarry and house. For Silvercairns House stood too close to the quarry workings. Since the disaster which had killed his father, all blasting on the north face of the quarry had been forbidden, but no matter how careful the planning, whenever a new section was blasted, a tremor inevitably passed through the flesh of the hillside to Silvercairns itself. It would be manifest in no more than a patter of falling dust from worm-eaten panelling, a sudden quiver of petals among hot-house camellias on a side-table, or the stirring of a crystal chandelier. Nothing alarming: except that every quiver and breath was a solemn warning in a house which had suffered as Silvercairns had suffered. One day, Fergus promised himself, he would make good the damage, rebuild the west wing, strengthen the foundations, make everything safe and solid as rock. But the quarry must come first.

As he had done every day since his father's death, Fergus went over in his mind, the amount of the outstanding debt, the wages of the workforce, the contracts fulfilled and pending, the money owed to him and by him, the sum of interest to be paid. It was growing steadily less. Soon, in a year or two perhaps, he hoped to pay off that Shylock of a moneylender his father had become embroiled with and rid himself of that particular burden for ever. He should have sold the Guestrow house long ago and settled it that way, but sentiment had intervened and at least the rent had helped. When Lettice moved in, there would be no more rent, of course. But there would be no more dress bills either. Perhaps one could be set against the other?

The fire simmered gently, the house settled into silence and even the tick of the clock seemed pleasantly somnolent. Fergus gave up trying to recall particular figures in those interminable accounts and thought instead of his quarry. It was 180 feet deep now and wide as a breakfast cup. The granite harvest was as clean and pure as ever, with that particular mix of white mica and black mica, felspar and horneblende which was distinctive to Silvercairns and which gave it its fame. But how much longer could he continue to harvest its precious granite before he strained that cup to cracking point and let in who knew what turmoil and destruction? They said that granite was made many centuries ago when molten matter, trapped under-ground, solidified slowly into igneous rock. Suppose, under the floor of his quarry, streams of trapped lava still bubbled, white-hot and unsolidified, waiting only for the smallest fissure in the roof of their prison to burst through and engulf them in liquid fire? Or in a thick, grey sludge of semi-molten, smothering death, which would bubble up and up to the very rim of the cup, spill over and . . .

As always when he let his imagination stray along that forbidden path he shuddered with a primeval fear and hauled his mind firmly back to reality. There was no need to quarry deeper. It increased the haulage costs for one thing, and for another, there was land to the west of the quarry, on Willowbrae. Scrub land which the farmer used for rough grazing and little else. Suppose he were to lease that land, work the quarry westward, even start anew? He remembered hearing that someone had tried to start a quarry there years ago, but had done no more than scratch the surface before giving up in disgust. Fergus knew that it took more than surface scratching to prove a quarry's worth: Aberdeenshire might be full of granite, but it was often masked from the surface by sandstone or layers of inferior 'barr' which had to be scraped away before the real treasure was revealed. Even Silvercairns had started life as a discouraging scratch on the earth's surface, and look at it now. But at the same time such initial scratching could be costly, especially if it came to nothing, and he was reluctant to risk a further debt. He would need to investigate the terrain, get hold of a geological survey. One of the railway engineers on the Deeside line might be persuaded to help, if he was lucky. Or

[38]

perhaps he should start in his own quarry and plot the probable lie of the rock from there ?

He was trying to remember the exact direction in which the banks of stone lay when he became aware of a faint sound at the door. Startled, he turned his head and saw, framed in the open doorway, a forlorn, bare-footed child in a cotton nightshirt, his red hair ruffled and on his freckled face an expression of mingled defiance and fear.

'What on earth are you doing out of bed, Leo? And with nothing on your feet. What would Mrs Gregor say if she knew?'

'I had a dream, Uncle Fergus. A horrid dream.'

'Did you indeed. Then why did you not call Mrs Gregor?'

He bit his lip and looked at the floor, bare right foot rubbing the back of bare left leg. 'She said she'd tan my hide if I woke her again.'

'Really?' Fergus struggled to hide a smile. 'Then you should have called Aunt Lettice. I expect she is still awake.'

Leo looked up. 'She is. I saw a light under her door. But she said if I did not go to sleep I couldn't go riding tomorrow.'

'Then I suggest you turn right round and go back upstairs to your room this instant, before she finds out you have left it. The best place to sleep is in your own bed.'

'Not if you have a horrid dream.'

'All right,' sighed Fergus. 'Come in and shut the door. Sit on the hearthrug there – not too close or you'll set your nightshirt alight, you little idiot. Now, what was this dream about?'

'The house fell down,' said Leo in a small voice. 'Mrs Gregor was squashed flat, like a playing card, and Aunt Lettice and you ...' His voice trailed away and he looked pathetically at Fergus for reassurance. All trace of the fist-fighting, knee-grazing, cheerfully foul-mouthed and confident schoolboy had gone, leaving only a small, frightened and motherless child who had had a nightmare.

Irritation disappeared under compassion. After a moment's thought, Fergus said lightly, 'And were you squashed too?'

'No. I could see the sky and the trees and everything, just as they always are, but I was frightened. I was all by myself...'

'Well you are not by yourself now, are you?' said Fergus. 'Is the house still standing?' Leo nodded. 'Am I squashed flat?' Leo shook his head. 'Do you want us to go upstairs to Aunt Lettice's room and see if she is squashed flat?' Leo shook his head. 'Then shall we go to the servants' wing, and see if Mrs Gregor is squashed flat? Though I think if she was she would make a very large playing card, don't you?'

[39]

Reluctantly Leo smiled. 'That's better. Now, to show that you are far too sensible to be frightened by a dream, and brave enough to be my right-hand-man in the quarry one day, how about a sip of my best brandy before you go back to bed?' Fergus held out his own glass to the boy who took it gingerly in two hands, sipped, shuddered, grinned and handed it back.

'Will you come upstairs with me, Uncle Fergus?' he said in the doorway and added, before the usual reminder, 'Please?'

'I suppose so.' Fergus made great show of heaving himself reluctantly out of his chair, took the lad's hand and led him on tiptoe upstairs. He saw the boy into bed, lit a night-light for reassurance, told him to think of something exciting he would like to do tomorrow, though not too exciting or it might keep him awake, and softly closed the door.

But as he made his way downstairs again, his face was troubled. Was it any wonder the boy had nightmares? Mrs Gregor was kind enough, but she was only the cook–housekeeper. What the boy needed was a mother. Perhaps Lettice was right and Fergus ought to marry? If only for Leo's sake?

For some reason he remembered Philip Drummond and his sister. If the Diack answer to his invitation was a refusal, as seemed increasingly likely, perhaps he should cut himself free from the past, start again and look at Miss Henrietta Drummond with speculative eyes? A second cousin of one's sister's husband was certainly not on the prohibited list and a second cousin-in-law with railway connections had a positive advantage. He tried to visualize the unknown Miss Drummond, giving her blonde ringlets and a Saxon complexion, a small, neat figure and dimpled smile, but however hard he tried, the shadow of Mhairi Diack somehow intervened.

'Damn the woman,' he said aloud. 'Will she never leave me in peace?'

The Adam invitation caused heated discussion in more than one house in Aberdeen, both among those who had received one and those who had not. It was soon known throughout the town that Niall Burnett and his wife Amelia had refused: and who could blame them after Old Man Adam's disgraceful behaviour on the occasion of their engagement. Old Man Adam might be dead and gone beyond reach

[40]

of reprisals, but his daughter was not. Let her swallow their snub and make the best of it. Or choke in the process.

Others were more hypocritical. Invitations to grand society weddings were not exactly thick on the ground and no one wanted to pass up the opportunity, whoever the inviting family might be. It was a gesture of friendship, they told each other virtuously, which it would be churlish and unchristian to refuse. An olive branch to be accepted in the spirit in which it was offered. What that spirit was, no one ventured to specify, but all agreed that any quarrel they might have had with the Adams (and they were numerous) should be laid at the father's door, not the son's. By mutual agreement, no one mentioned Miss Adam herself in these justifications: her dissection was reserved for those intimate tea-parties and morning calls that had always been present in the social calendar, but which now proliferated as thick as mushrooms on a particularly succulent dung heap.

'I think we should go,' announced Mrs Wyness firmly over breakfast, when her husband had eaten sufficient of the excellent buttered kippers to be in a benign and generous mood. 'After all, Lettice and Fanny used to play together, if not exactly in their cradles, then certainly in their childhood years. They went to the same dancing classes, too. I know you and Mungo Adam did not see eye to eye, especially after that dreadful canal affair, but the man is dead now. It seems hardly fair to visit the sins of the father upon the children. Besides,' she finished, 'I like a good wedding and so do you.'

George Wyness glowered into his breakfast cup, but it was only a token glower, designed to cover thought. He knew how young Tom Diack felt about the Adams and though he did not entirely agree with the lad, he could sympathize and see his point. If you had seen your father die, your best friend killed and your sister widowed, you could be forgiven for harbouring resentment against those who had caused it all. The fact that Fergus Adam had had little to do with it was irrelevant where Tom was concerned: the Adam family was the enemy and that was that. Tom was a senior partner in the Wyness enterprise, married to Wyness's only daughter and an excellent quarryman as well as a shrewd building contractor and businessman. Wyness was more than pleased with his son-in-law. Which made it all the more difficult to know what to do in the matter of the Adam wedding. Fanny was a loyal wife and naturally would do as Tom wished; his sister Mhairi likewise. Which left only himself and his wife ... Suddenly he saw his way clear.

[41]

'Like it or not, lass, I reckon it's our duty to go. A grand wedding like that and all the quarrymen for miles around invited. There'll be builders and architects too, likely, and I heard talk of a Marshall cousin from London coming, someone with clout in the railway world. We don't want to find that all the best contracts have changed hands over the wedding cake and champagne and we've been left out in the cold, all on account of a bit of grudge-bearing and pique. We'll likely bag a couple of useful contracts ourselves. Then yon London cousin might be needing a railway station or two. Aye lass, you can send our answer this morning. We'll go.'

Mrs Wyness beamed her satisfaction. 'Good. I think you are very wise, dear. I wonder, shall I wear my mazarine, or my Venetian red?' Then a thought banished the smile. 'Oh dear. What do you think Tom will say?'

'I've no need to ask my son-in-law's permission before I accept an invitation.'

'No dear, of course not.' She refilled his breakfast teacup before adding, 'But he is your partner.'

'Aye, and this affair is strictly business. Someone from the firm has to go, and I reckon he'd rather it was me than him.'

'I'd rather no one went at all,' glared Tom, when Wyness told him of his decision, later that morning. Tom had come in to the yard to report on the progress of a terrace of cottages at Kittybrewster, and to inspect the balustrade he had ordered for a coal merchant's mansion at Belhelvie. It was finished, but for the hand-polishing of the more intricate sections which could not pass under the polishing discs and equally could not be hurried. These stood in the inner yard, under a covering of protective sacking, awaiting the final touches. The yard was particulary busy, with a dozen different polishing jobs all needed urgently, and it might be another week, Wyness said, before the thing was finished. Tom had only to cast his eyes over the work-sheds and yard where upwards of four dozen men and boys were hard at work to see the truth of Wyness's words, but such delays were becoming increasingly frequent and the news had not improved Tom's temper.

'You may be right about the contracts,' he said now, 'but I doubt it. We'd be better completing the ones we have on time, than snaring

[42]

for dubious new ones at a wedding that will be social chit-chat, the parade of privilege, ostentation in every sickening shape and form, and little else. I wonder you can bear to associate yourself with it.'

'I can bear it, lad, because I haven't your baseless prejudices, nor the taste of such envious bile in my mouth.' Wyness steered the younger man away from listening ears – it did not do to let the work-force hear such discord – and towards the office. 'You should watch yourself, Tom lad. You are beginning to let personal animosity sour your judgement. We can't have that, not in a business where men's lives are at risk.'

'It's precisely because of men's lives that I feel as I do. Or rather, because of men's deaths. You may have forgotten Mhairi's husband Alex, but I have not. They killed him, for God's sake! Proof or no proof, all the town knows it. *And I want an eye for an eye.*' He kicked a chip of broken granite in his path with unnecessary force.

'And a tooth for a tooth, is that it? You had your "tooth" when Mungo Adam died. Or do you want them all to die before you're satisfied? Nay lad, I understand your feelings,' Wyness went on, more quietly. He put a reassuring arm around Tom's shoulder and felt the bones grow rigid under his touch. 'But nothing you do can bring Alex back again. Brooding is futile, Tom, and it was a long time ago. It's time to forget Old Testament retribution and move on.'

'Turn the other cheek, you mean?' Abruptly Tom shook free of the other's arm. 'And let the Adams do us down twice over?'

'Of course not, you fool,' said Wyness, loosing patience. 'But Mungo Adam is *dead*. How many more times do I have to remind you? There'll be no more crooked dealings from that quarter, more's the pity. Watching to see which way the old devil would move next did add a certain spice to life.' He sighed in rueful reminiscence. 'If they do try any tricks, they'll be no more devious or dangerous than from any of a dozen other business rivals in the town. You may refuse to admit it, but young Fergus Adam is not the rogue his father was, though he drives his men as hard, by all accounts, and strikes as hard a bargain. But with debts like his, who wouldn't?'

Wyness stopped, shouted a warning at a slurry boy to 'Look lively with that broom or you'll be out on your ear!' then resumed his progress, picking his way between half-finished headstones, plain polished slabs, others awaiting only lettering, yet others shrouded under sacking, his eyes darting this way and that, alert and watchful. George Wyness had not built up his prosperous granite yard from a mere square of bare ground over thirty grinding years to relax vigilance now.

'Besides,' he resumed as they reached the open patch in front of the office. 'Fergus Adam did not have to invite us. It was a generous gesture and should be recognized as such. It is time to forgive and forget, Tom.'

'Not for me it isn't. You do what you like, Mr Wyness, but don't presume to tell me when to forgive Alex's murderers or forget the best friend I ever had.'

'I can see I'll get nowhere,' sighed Wyness, torn between irritation and pity. 'You are hell-bent on hatred and willna be diverted. But you'd do a lot better to divert your venom from the personal to the practical and wage your war through business rivalry. That way at least we'd all benefit.' When Tom made no answer, but continued to glower at anything that came in his path, Wyness added, 'Just remember, hatred is a corrosive poison that can eat into a man's soul. I only hope you are not feeding my grandson a diet of such venom.'

'Georgie knows nothing about it, and if he did I . . .'

'See it stays that way,' interrupted the other. 'I have no patience with you. At least Mhairi has the sense to see the futility of such an attitude. She forgave long ago and a good thing too.' Before Tom could find a reply Wyness had slammed into the office, closing the door behind him.

At Rainbow Cottage, Tom found Mhairi in the kitchen, kneading bread. For a moment the sight of his sister, her black clothes hidden under a voluminous apron, with flour to her elbows and more of it on one cheek filled him with overwhelming tenderness, for her bravery, her dogged endurance and her unfailing love. Then he remembered his errand.

'Is it true?'

'Is what true, Tom? And please close the door behind you or the dough will not rise.' She brushed a stray hair off her brow with the back of a hand and left a streak of flour in its place.

'Is it true you are going to the Adam woman's wedding?'

'I . . . I had thought of it.' Mhairi concentrated on her lump of dough to hide her elation.

Elation was not too strong a word for the feeling which had swept through her when she first read the invitation, and which she still felt whenever she allowed herself to think about it. Fergus Adam had invited her to his sister's wedding. Mhairi Diack Grant, whose father had been a humble causeyman in Silvercairns quarry, and who herself had once stitched petticoats for Lettice Adam. She had carried them on foot, in a wicker basket, up the long drive to Silvercairns House. Fergus Adam had overtaken her, walked beside her, and ever since then Mhairi had known there was an unspoken bond between them, in spite of family enmity and grief. Once, he had kissed her and the forbidden memory was sweet. Too sweet, perhaps, for might she not have remembered more than there had really been? Substituted love for mere sympathy, good faith for a spur-of-the-moment urge? But whatever the truth of her memory, it was undoubtedly true that he had invited her to his sister's wedding when he had no need to do so, and where at last they would meet as equals: she a major shareholder of Wyness, Diack & Grant, granite merchants, with a quarry at Rainbow Hill and a polishing yard in town; he, sole owner and manager of Silvercairns, the biggest granite quarry in Scotland. At the thought of that meeting she felt her heart tremble with excitement, and knew it would show in her face. To hide it, she half-turned away and bent over the dough, slapping and pummelling it into shape with practised efficiency.

'You had thought ...' repeated Tom, scarcely above a whisper, then anger burst its banks in a roar of fury. 'You must have lost your wits, woman. Have you forgotten who Adam is? What he has done to us.'

'No, I have not forgotten.' Her brother's words doused the elation as effectively as a pail of water would a candle. She straightened and looked him steadily in the eye, the smears of flour on cheek and brow in no way diminishing her dignity. 'As to what he has done to us ... is he to suffer for his father's sins?'

'It wasna his father who sacked our Da, was it?' said Tom, jabbing an accusing finger at her, with an air of triumph which chilled her blood. He wore a tailored jacket of good worsted, waistcoat and trousers to match and a fresh linen shirt, with leather shoes you could see your face in and a pair of incipient side-whiskers, as darkly gleaming as his hair. Under the prosperous building contractor's exterior she could see nothing of the cheerful brother who had once set out from this very cottage, often before dawn, in a flannel shirt and workman's moleskin trousers, his quarryman's boots loud on the solid ground and his quarryman's tools in a battered leather bag

[45]

slung from his shoulder: she saw only a stranger of implacable hate. His eyes were as blue as when he was a young apprentice in Silvercairns quarry, but instead of smiling as they used to do, they were cold and accusing.

'Da would be alive today if it wasna for your precious Fergus Adam.'

'Hardly. His chest would have killed him within the year, Adam or no Adam. And you know it.' But in spite of her apparent scorn, Mhairi was trembling inside, all joy extinguished in a grey and spreading dread. She tried one last plea. 'Our enemy was the father, God rest his soul, not the son. It is neither Christian nor fair to blame Fergus Adam for his father's sins. They say he inherited dreadful debts,' she finished, as if that should be punishment enough.

'The deeper into debt that lot sinks, the better I'll be pleased, and so should you be, or you're no sister of mine.' He began to pace the room, restlessly and without purpose, now leaning forward to peer out of the small, curtained window, as if to check for enemies, now kicking the peat in the simmering fire.

Mhairi watched him, hoping his temper would burn itself out, at least before Annys came in from the back scullery, where she was scrubbing clothes. But when, for no apparent reason, he aimed a kick at the scullery door and set the plates on the dresser rattling she said sadly, 'Oh Tom, where is your spirit of Christian forgiveness? Poor Ma would turn in her grave.'

'And Alex would turn in his,' he retorted, 'to hear his widow speak of "forgiving" his murderer.'

'No, Tom,' said Mhairi with the firm patience of a mother trying to calm a difficult child. 'Alex was never blind to justice, as you seem to have become. Perhaps Mungo Adam was behind that fatal explosion, but Fergus had no part in Alex's death. In fact . . .' She had been going to add 'he was horrified when he realized and came in secret to warn me of his father's latest plan to ruin us' but she remembered her promise never to speak of it and stopped, just in time. Tom did not even notice.

'An Adam is an Adam,' he snarled, 'and don't ever forget it. Look how that villainous brother of his ruined Lizzie Lennox.'

'But Fergus has tried to make amends. Be fair, Tom. He and his sister have brought up Lizzie's son as if he were their legitimate nephew. All the town says so. What more would you have him do?'

Tom ignored the question. 'Oh it's "Fergus" now, is it? And what

[46]

does all the town say about Alex's death? That your precious Fergus should make amends there, too? By comforting the widow, perhaps, and warming her bed?'

'That was uncalled for,' said Mhairi quietly. 'You may be my brother, but that does not license you to insult me in my own home. You will apologize.'

'I will do no such thing. "Fergus" indeed. "Christian forgiveness". You fancy him, that's the plain truth of it.'

'Don't be ridiculous,' cried Mhairi, her face hot with anger and guilt. 'If you were not a grown man and twice as strong as I am, I'd put you over my knee and wallop you for wickedness and lies. Then maybe you'd see sense and ... and ... oh what's the use?' She collapsed suddenly into a chair, laid her head against the chair back and closed her eyes. When she spoke again it was calmly and without expression. 'You have said what you came to say, bullied and shouted and spread hatred everywhere. If you have not the grace to apologize, then at least get out of my house.'

There was silence in the room, but for the stirring of the fire and the slow ticking of the clock. Tom had given her that clock, she remembered, when he came back from Australia. Three years ago, or was it four? Long enough, anyway. There were faint sounds of splashing water from the back of the house and suddenly a fly, duped out of hibernation by the room's heat, buzzed and bumped foolishly against the window pane. She opened her eyes to see Tom still standing in the same place, staring at her. She gripped the arms of the chair and pulled herself briskly to her feet.

'You may have no work to do this morning, Tom Diack, but I certainly have. So for pity's sake leave me in peace to do it.' She pushed the hair back from her face, moved to the table and resumed kneading the dough, stretching and turning it with unnecessary vigour on the floured surface. Tom watched her in brooding silence.

'Well?' she challenged, her eyes angry. 'Are you going or not?'

'Not until I have your promise.'

'What promise?' though she knew before she asked the question.

'That you will refuse the Adam invitation.'

For a long moment blue eyes challenged blue, searching, defying. How dare he tell her which invitation she might accept and which not. How dare he bully and order her about as if she had no authority in her own home. But behind the blustering anger Mhairi saw the guilt which had tormented Tom ever since he had returned from

[47]

Australia to find his sister widowed and his friend dead. It was senseless, of course, but understandable, and something only Tom himself could overcome. Yet it still had power to twist her heart with pity and protective love. She remembered the long, loyal years since their parents' death, his unwavering help and support, remembered their mother's dying words, and Mhairi's own promise to look after the family for her and 'see wee Annys grows up right'. She had needed Tom's loyalty then, and still did. Whatever romantic dream she might have had of Fergus Adam and his sister's wedding reception, it was only a dream. Whereas Tom was her brother and, in spite of everything, she loved him.

With a long sigh of weariness and loss, she said, 'I do not agree with you. I acknowledge nothing. But I give you my promise.'

'Good.' Tom turned on his heel and strode for the door. In the open doorway he paused, the winter garden a withered backdrop of bare twig and grey earth. The snow had melted days ago and no more had fallen to take its place so that even the grass looked colourless and dead. In spite of the gust of cold air, Mhairi did not look up from her task, though the fire spurted suddenly high.

Slowly, reluctantly, as if ashamed, Tom came back into the room, leaving the door standing wide. Then, he put an awkward arm around his sister's shoulder and kissed her briefly on the cheek.

'Thank you, Mhairi. And ... I am sorry.'

A moment later the door closed behind him, cutting off the outside air, but leaving little warmth in its place. Tom's kiss had been cold, his apology graceless and brief. But it had been an apology.

'Has Tom gone?' asked a timid voice from the scullery and Annys came through into the kitchen, her sleeves rolled up above the elbows and her arms red from the wash-tub.

'Yes.' Mhairi did not look at her sister, but began to cut the dough into sections. She shaped the first into a round and slashed a deep cross on its top.

'Was he very angry?' Without asking, Annys took a section of the remaining dough and began to do likewise.

For a moment Mhairi did not answer. But Tom had been shouting at the top of his voice. Annys must have heard most of the conversation for herself. Why pretend otherwise?

'Yes. He thought I meant to accept the Adams' invitation.'

'And ... did you?' Annys looked at her with ingenuous eyes.

'I had considered it. It was courteous of Mr Adam to ask me, and it would have been equally so on my part to accept. However, Tom does not wish it, so that is that.'

'I am sorry, Mhairi. I know you specially wanted to go.'

'Whatever gave you that impression?' said Mhairi sharply. The memory of Tom's taunting words still stung her with shame. 'I merely thought it churlish to refuse. That is all. And if you are going to stand there squeezing that poor dough to a lifeless lump, then for pity's sake get back to the wash-tub and leave the baking to me.'

Afterwards, Mhairi was ashamed. It was not the fault of poor Annys that Tom had caught her on the raw, had forced her to confront her own motives and to admit that she had planned the tenderest of meetings between herself and Fergus Adam. Daydreams. Silly, girlish fantasies such as Annys might indulge in, but which she, Mhairi, should have grown out of long ago.

'I am sorry,' said Annys meekly. 'I came for more hot water.' She unhooked the heavy kettle from its chain over the fire and staggered out of the room with it, to return some five minutes later, still staggering, the kettle re-filled with cold water from the pump. She hooked it back on its chain, swung the sway into position over the fire, added another peat, and went out again.

In the back scullery, her arms immersed to the elbows in hot suds, Annys bore her sister no animosity. She knew how Mhairi must be feeling and was sorry for her. If to 'fancy' meant to think of often, to weave dreams around, to imagine meetings and intimate conversations with, to yearn for with longing and excitement, then if Tom was right, as Annys suspected he was, Mhairi must think of Mr Adam as Annys thought of Kit O'Brien. What would Tom say about Kit if he knew? Or Mhairi, for that matter? The thought brought a shiver of excitement and apprehension. But they did not know. No one did.

Annys scrubbed at her brother's heavy flannel shirt, Lorn's or Willy's, she had forgotten which, lifting its dripping bulk half out of the water every now and then to see whether the dirt was shifting, and thought of Kit O'Brien. He must have been chosen for the railway job in the Crimea. She was sure she would have seen him otherwise, in the Castlegate or the Green. There had been other men, morose and disappointed, ranging the bars of the city and railing at those who didn't know a good worker when they saw one. But Annys knew Kit had not been among them. He had been among the chosen and would be on his way to Balaclava at this very moment, in one of the twenty-three ships chartered for the purpose. Sailing the Black Sea perhaps, putting in to port on the Russian shore, even building the hutted camp in which they would live while they laid the line. They said the promised railway was the British soldiers' only hope, dug in as they were around Sebastopol, with no food, nothing but cold and disease for company and the only road between them and the British fleet impassable in the bitter winter weather. If any horse-drawn carts and litters of the wounded did manage to fight their way back through snowdrifts, over rutted ice and jolting, snow-packed tracks in temperatures that froze the drip on a man's nose and the toes off his feet, then most of them were dead on arrival. Kit's railway, when he built it, would carry food and medical supplies to the starving soldiers and bring back the wounded to the hospital in Balaclava. Kit's railway would save the British army from defeat.

And when it was built, thought Annys dreamily, hardly noticing that the water had grown cold again, her fingers raw and blue, Kit would come back to Aberdeen. She would be in the Green perhaps, at her market stall. Or walking on the Woodside road. He would see her, speak to her, call her his walking angel ... Smiling to herself in anticipation, Annys wrung out the first of the shirts, dropped it into a pail of clear water, and began on the next.

When Thomas Brassey and his partners contracted to build a supply railway between the British fleet at Balaclava and the starving British army at Sebastopol, they undertook to complete the twenty-nine-mile line by the end of April, and beat their own deadline by three weeks.

The progress of the railways which would connect Aberdeen and its commerce to the outside world was not so swift, albeit there were no soldiers' lives at stake and no wars depending on the outcome. Except perhaps the wars of the boardroom and the bank balance. In January of 1855, almost ten years after the royal assent had been given to the Aberdeen Railway Bill, tenders were invited for the construction of station works at the terminus of the branch line to the dock. Naturally, George Wyness and his young partners decided to apply, and equally naturally, Mhairi was given the task of delivering the sealed tender to the offices in Union Street on that snow-swept January morning. With the Adam wedding imminent, Mhairi was particularly busy with dressmaking and fittings, which required frequent visits to her clients' houses in various parts of town as well as frequent calls on the local haberdashers for supplies of sewing cotton, ribbons, pearl buttons and lace. Add to that the normal business of household marketing and Mhairi had enough reasons to be in Union Street anyway: one more errand was nothing.

So it was that, head down against the icy wind, one hand bundling her skirts to lift them clear of the trampled snow and the other, heavy basket on elbow, clutching the precious envelope against her breast so that no snow should smudge the ink of the superscription, Mhairi battled her way to the doorway of number 177, and collided violently with a gentleman coming out. She dropped basket and envelope and would have fallen, had his arms not come around her to hold and steady her. She felt her heart pound hard with shock against the firm strength of his chest, before she could collect her startled wits and regain her balance.

'I am sorry, Madam. My fault entirely. I do apologize...'

The voice, both courteous and concerned, brought her startled eyes to his face and she blushed a deep and burning scarlet.

'Not at all, Mr Adam. I was not looking where.. where I was going.' She pulled away from his enclosing arm, dusted down her skirts, and sank to one knee at exactly the moment when he did the same.

'Allow me, Mrs Grant,' he murmured, his gloved hands finding the basket and setting it upright without benefit of sight, for his dark eyes never left her face. As if mesmerized, she looked back at him, unable to look away, while her hands made similar, unguided efforts to collect her scattered merchandise. The marmalade oranges she had bought only five minutes ago had burst their paper packaging and lay scattered like golden baubles in the snow. Fergus picked them up, one by one, and dropped them into the basket.

'Why did you refuse my invitation?'

'I ...' Mhairi could no longer meet his gaze and looked instead at the trampled snow where all that remained of her scattered goods was a small packet of ribbons. From its open end strands of scarlet and blue spilt out, unnaturally bright against the grey. But he was waiting for his answer. 'I am afraid that family matters prevent ...' Her voice trailed into silence as she coiled the ribbon neatly round her fingers. She saw with annoyance that they were trembling.

'No one is ill, I hope?' There was genuine solicitude in his voice as

[51]

he straightened, her retrieved basket in his hand. Silently he held it out to her. 'Your sister, perhaps? Or one of your children?'

'No. It is just that ...' Bleakly she looked up at him, saw the concern in his eyes and, behind the concern, something more which made her discard her planned platitude and put truth in its place. 'My brother does not consider it fitting.'

'And you?' He looked steadily down at her, compelling truth.

'I wanted to accept, but ...' she shrugged, her smile bleak.

'I am truly sorry.'

'And I.' For a moment they regarded each other in silence, then through Mhairi's head rang those taunting words, 'You fancy him, that's the truth of it.' Abruptly, she broke the spell. 'Thank you for your help.' She turned away, her eyes checking over the trampled snow for any scattered item she might have missed. They found one. Swiftly she picked it up.

'Goodbye, Mrs Grant,' he said, with formal courtesy, raised his hat and stepped back to leave the entrance to the Railway Company Office free. 'I wish you well.'

'But not, I think, with this?' She smiled and tipped the envelope so that he could read the superscription, blotched now with snow but still legible. It was a valiant effort, acknowledging business rivalry, and the impregnable barrier that separated them.

He laughed. 'You must excuse me ... but business is business.' It was a warm laugh, without rancour, and Mhairi felt her spirits lighten. She nodded acknowledgement and stepped past him into the office. As she did so, she heard him murmur, 'I hope we shall meet again.' Before she could frame an answer, the heavy door closed between them, and though she finished her business with the Railway Company with all speed, when she stepped out into the street again, Mr Fergus Adam had gone.

'Would you mind, Tom dear, if I asked Annys to stay for a day or two?' said Fanny, some ten days later. 'You know how involved Mamma is with her comforts for the soldiers and if she is to have the boxes parcelled up in time to reach the London agent before the boats sail, she will need every help. Her hall is already piled high with mountains of warm clothing waiting to be dealt with and poor Papa can hardly step through the door without falling over a heap of knitted mufflers, or into a morass of woolly socks. I said she might

[52]

send the overflow here,' she finished, and before Tom could speak smiled sweetly, laid a soft hand on his and said, 'I knew you would not mind. They say the frost is bitter in the Crimea and those poor soldiers, so far away from home ... I felt so sorry for them.'

'No doubt,' said Tom, frowning at his drawing pad, his head on one side. 'You would feel sorry for anyone who asked you to, you soft-hearted little silly – and I love you for it.' He pulled her towards him and kissed her cheek. They had been sitting companionably on the sofa in front of the fire, she with her sewing, he with his notebooks and papers. He was sketching rough plans for a house to be built in the west end, a 'tappietourie' mansion which by its loud magnificence and spawn of unnecessary turrets would proclaim to the passing world the riches and social aspirations of its owner.

'You know, Fanny,' went on Tom, adding an extra turret and studying the effect, 'we might take a trip along Deeside one day, and see this new-fangled wonder of a castle for ourselves. We could take the train to Banchory, then a coach to Ballater. The children could come with us and we could make a holiday of it. In the spring, perhaps.'

'That would be lovely,' said Fanny. 'I have been on a train only once, and did not particularly like it, but that was because it was a formal opening, with crowds everywhere and speeches. With you and the children it will be different, especially when the new leaves are bursting and there is blossom everywhere. Georgie will be so excited. But he is still very young and will not understand why the engine is so loud and the smoke so dirty and thick. I fear he might be frightened, as I confess I was a little myself, and perhaps summer would be best? Or even spring of next year? Of course, if you wanted to go sooner yourself, I would not mind, Tom dear. You could take Lorn or Willy, or even Donal. He is so very good at drawing and would take a perfect likeness of the castle in no time at all.'

'Hmm, you may be right, Fanny. That is not at all a bad idea. In fact, I might not need to go myself at all, until wee Georgie is large enough, and brave enough, to come too. With his valiant mother, naturally.'

'Naturally,' smiled Fanny, content to have shifted the hazardous journey into the future, and without argument. 'And you don't mind about Mamma's parcels? I thought if Annys came to stay, she could help me with them, as well as amuse the children.'

'No, I don't mind. By all means ask her, as long as Mhairi can spare her. I expect Annys will be glad to have something more to do than sell vegetables in the market once a week and help run Mhairi's messages. After all, she will be sixteen before the year is out. When Mhairi was sixteen,' he said, suddenly thoughtful, 'Ma was dead and she was running the house, looking after Da and the rest of us, sewing for yon Ladies Working Society, mothering Annys, seeing Lorn and Willy did their lessons and didna skive off school. She was always the last to bed and the first to rise in the morning, and I have no doubt still is.'

Tom's conscience was not entirely clear where Mhairi was concerned: he had been absolutely right about that damned Adam wedding, there was no question of that, but he should not have spoken to her so harshly, should not have said what he had said. And though he had made token apology, they both knew it was only token. But the opportunity had not arisen to make a more genuine one, and it was too late now, the harm done.

'Poor Mhairi. She is the same age as I am and yet when I was sixteen I did nothing at all,' confessed Fanny, 'except go to dancing classes and drawing classes, both of which I hated. And stay at home with Mamma, being ladylike.'

'What a useless little madam you were,' he teased, but she took him seriously.

'Yes, I was, and I know it. But not any more. Annys is not useless,' she went on thoughtfully. 'She helps Mhairi with the children and the housework and with the quarry accounts too, on occasions. When Mhairi made marmalade last week, Annys helped shred the peel and that is a tedious enough task, Tom dear, for I have done it myself. Then Annys carried the marmalade into market to sell. But these are ordinary tasks which any housewife can do once they know how, and Annys is clever. She is far cleverer than I am, and don't try to deny it, Tom dear, for I know it is true. Perhaps she should be a governess? Or a teacher? There is a vacancy at the Female Industrial School, for I saw it advertised only yesterday.'

'I doubt Mhairi would allow it,' frowned Tom, 'even if Annys were brave enough to apply. Besides, whatever you say she is well enough where she is and Mhairi needs her. And so do you,' he teased, 'if not to keep that rascal Georgie in order, then for your precious parcels for the soldiers.'

'So I do,' said Fanny, pretending agreement, but resolving privately to sound out Annys about her hopes and ambitions. Mhairi

[54]

was her dearest friend, but at the same time Fanny suspected she could be overprotective, especially where her sister was concerned, and though Mhairi might think of her still as a helpless child, Annys was a grown woman. Old enough to marry, if she chose.

The thought was a startling one. Young Princess Vicky was Annys's age and already there was speculation around the nation's tea-tables and in the more dignified seclusion of the nation's Gentlemen's Clubs about a suitable royal husband for that young lady. But when the time came, no doubt Princess Vicky would meet a succession of young 'suitables' in a succession of social engagements arranged for the purpose: Annys would meet nobody.

'I will speak to Mhairi about it tomorrow,' she said aloud. 'And while Annys is staying with us, perhaps I will invite one or two friends to join us for tea, to relieve the tedium of tying up so many bundles and to make the time pass more agreeably.'

'Just so long as you do not expect me to hand round the teacups, or tie the knots on those blessed parcels of yours. I have enough to do as it is, with this folly of a house and the new railway contract. We did well to win that one,' he said, with a reminiscent grin. 'I know for a fact that Silvercairns put in for it, not to mention half a dozen others.'

Fanny made suitable congratulatory noises, but the mention of Silvercairns reminded her of the wedding. It was a pity Tom was so dead set against the Adams: for though her Mamma would tell her all about it afterwards, Fanny would love to have seen everything for herself. Even to watch the guests arriving in their finery would be better than nothing, though of course she could not go alone. Nor could she ask Mhairi to go with her because of Tom, and Mhairi's promise. Then she remembered Annys's projected visit. Annys had not promised Tom anything and if she and Annys could contrive to be passing in the street at the right moment, surely no one would notice them in the inevitable crowds? She would not want Tom to find out, of course, but she would so like to see.

Tom must have sensed something of what she was thinking for when he next spoke it was on that very subject.

'Met a fellow today, newly arrived from London, but nice enough on the face of it. Came in to the yard inquiring about a fountain. For his father's place down south. Donal sketched a few ideas for him on the spot. It was only when he was leaving that he said he was here for that wedding.'

'Oh?' Fanny's eyes brightened with interest. 'Who was he?'

[55]

'Some sort of cousin of the bridegroom's, several times removed. Name of Philip Drummond, which is why no one connected him with the Adams. Why should they? Especially as the first thing he said was that the Wyness yard had been recommended to him, by someone he met at that charity concert the other day. The one you wanted to go to.'

'The Haydn Society's concert in the Assembly rooms? I didn't really want to go, Tom dear, not without you. And I know you are too busy to waste time on such things. It was just that the proceeds were all to go to the Patriotic Fund and it is such a worthwhile cause.'

'Your parcels are just as worthwhile, Fanny. More so, because you do it for love, not merely in order to be seen in a "large and fashionable audience.".'

'Tom, that is not fair! I will not have you so sour and prejudiced. Why should people not pay to listen to good music if they choose to do so, and enjoy it the more because they know their money will help others? Who are you to say their motives are quite otherwise!'

'Darling Fanny, you are so naive and generous-hearted. I submit completely to your judgement.' He kissed her lightly on the forehead. 'On Mr Drummond's capacity for musical appreciation I make no comment, but I would be prepared to bet Niall Burnett has absolutely none.'

'What has Niall Burnett to do with it?' said Fanny, mystified.

'Apparently he was the gentleman who recommended us to Mr Drummond. "Don't touch Silvercairns" he told him. "They're overstretched and can be unreliable at times." Very clever, if you think about it, especially if he was not quite sure who he was talking to. Not exactly libellous, and not offensive enough to put a relative's back up, especially if said with apparently genuine concern. "Try the Wyness yard instead," Burnett told him. So he did.'

'And did he order anything?'

'Not exactly,' said Tom, frowning. 'Said that naturally he owed a certain loyalty to his cousin, remote though the connection was, and as the cousin was marrying an Adam, and he never made judgements on hearsay alone, he felt in honour bound to make inquiries there, too. But he did say that he never let sentiment stand in the way of business and was most impressed with Donal's preliminary sketches. Asked us to send the finished drawings to him at the Douglas Hotel and promised to talk over ideas with his father when he returned

[56]

south and let us know on his next visit. I gather he will be back for the shooting, in September.'

'And what is he here for this time? As well as the wedding, I mean, for it is a long way to come for a distant cousin's wedding, especially if you are obliged to stay in a hotel.'

'The fishing, I expect,' shrugged Tom. 'He did not say.'

Later, Fanny checked the columns of the newspaper for enlightenment, but all she found was, listed among recent arrivals at the Douglas Hotel, 'Mr P Drummond and Miss Henrietta Drummond, on their way north' and was none the wiser.

Lettice Octavia Adam, only daughter of the late Mungo Adam of Silvercairns, and the even later Charlotte Blackwell Adam formerly of Blairgowrie, Perthshire, was duly married, on 14th February 1855, to Dr David Stewart Marshall, whose antecedents were not considered worth noting, at St Nicholas kirk, with appropriate celebrations afterwards at the Adam town house in the Guestrow, which from this felicitous day forward was to be the commodious and comfortable home of the distinguished Dr Marshall and his bride.

Fanny Diack, unbeknown to her husband and with young Annys Diack, sworn to secrecy, at her side, happily watched the wedding guests' arrival at church from the concealing anonymity of an Aberdeen crowd.

'Doesn't Lettice look lovely,' sighed Fanny, with sentimental indulgence, and completely forgetting all that lady's barbed and hurtful comments over the years they had known each other. 'And isn't Fergus handsome?'

'Yes,' agreed Annys and added innocently, 'What a pity Mhairi is not here.'

'You must not tell her,' said Fanny in alarm. 'At least, not if anyone else is there. I would not want Tom to find out.'

But later, when Annys's visit to Tom's household was over and she was back in Rainbow Cottage with Mhairi, Annys described in careful detail everything she could remember, not only of the ladies' dresses, many of which Mhairi had sewed, but also of the gentlemen's appearances. 'There was a most handsome young man from England,' she finished earnestly, 'who could have modelled for a prince in one of your fairy tales. Tall, fair-haired, with perfect features and the true air of a gentleman about him. A cousin,

[57]

someone said, of the bridegroom who himself looked well enough, I suppose, though I doubt anyone would call Dr Marshall handsome. But Fanny and I agreed that no one in the entire company was more distinguished looking or more handsome than Fergus Adam.'

'What?' cried Mhairi, her astonishment at Fanny's daring conveniently hiding her excitement. For her sister's description had brought the principal figures vividly to mind and she was absurdly happy to hear Fergus so praised. 'You tell me that Fanny actually disobeyed her husband and took you to the wedding?'

'Not really,' defended Annys. 'We happened to be passing, that was all. After all, everyone said that the wedding might not even take place.' She looked solemnly at Mhairi who looked solemnly back at her, until suddenly both girls spluttered into laughter.

'Imagine Lettice Adam's face if he had jilted her at the altar,' gurgled Annys delightedly.

'Annys, that is not kind. I am quite shocked.' But Mhairi was smiling in spite of her words. Like most of Aberdeen, she had heard of the various wagers being laid on whether or not the gentleman would take flight at the last moment. Then another thought struck her. 'I wonder what will happen to Leo?'

Although, contrary to all gleeful prognostications on the townswomen's part, the bridegroom had not fled the country on the eve of the wedding and those rash pessimists who had laid money on it, lost, he did leave the country the day afterwards, though he had the grace to take his wife with him, for a protracted continental honeymoon.

Those who protested about the expense and speculated aloud where a mere country doctor got the money from (when the whole town knew it was *her* money or why would he have married her?) had to be content with the information that the trip abroad combined business with pleasure. It seemed that Dr Marshall was consulting colleagues, giving lectures, working at some hospital laboratory or clinic in Paris and would come home again when whatever work he had gone to do there was done, no doubt with a few more letters added to those he already had after his name. Whether his wife would stay the course throughout these working weeks only time would show, but if Lettice Adam arrived home again before the month was out no one would be in the least surprised.

In this, as in the wedding, the tea-tables of Aberdeen were disappointed. The wedding guests dispersed, dust-sheets remained in place in the Guestrow house where the servants were on board wages, and at Silvercairns that little Australian firebrand Leo Lennox, with no one to supervise his homework or keep him in check when the master was out from dawn till dark at the quarry office, led Mrs Gregor and her housemaids a merry dance with his mischief and his high spirits.

Which is why, on a certain Saturday in late spring, Fergus Adam gave in to the boy's persistent nagging, and to Mrs Gregor's pleas for 'a wee bit peace and quiet in the house so a body can get her work done', ordered a suitable hamper to be prepared for the two of them and promised Leo a ride in a train, a day in the country and a picnic, if in return he promised to stop tormenting the servants and be good. For Philip Drummond, before returning south, had given Fergus an introduction to a fellow in Banchory who was a surveyor with the Deeside railway and at present working on the extension of the line westward. As well as making himself known, so that when future contracts came up his name would be familiar, Fergus intended to pick his brains about the granite beds of Aberdeenshire. It was time he took positive action and what better cover for prying eyes than a picnic for a restless nephew? One day, before the year was out, Fergus intended to make the trip westward all the way to Balmoral, though when he did so it would be without young Leo's company.

For Fergus was as interested as Tom Diack and for much the same reasons in the building that was replacing the domestic jumble of the old castle. Rumour said the new edifice was a cross between an Austrian schloss, a Scottish baronial tower-house and something out of Grimm. All the materials for this architectural 'gingerbread' came from the estate, of course, so he had no personal motive on that score: merely a granite-man's interest in what could be done with the material. Especially, as seemed increasingly likely, the loyal burghers of Aberdeen intended to build their own copies. Fergus Adam's business was raw granite, more particularly the business of harvesting it from the ever-deepening chasm of Silvercairns. Once the blocks were blasted from the bed rock, squared and shaped enough to be loaded onto carts and dragged up the ever-lengthening zig-zag path to the surface, and thence despatched to their destinations, whether polishing yard, building site or quay, Fergus's work was done. But every now and then he liked to see the uses his precious

[59]

Silvercairns rock was put to, the shapes it could be made to take, and the delicacy of design or polish which his granite would sustain.

Half of Aberdeen, his father used to boast, was built of Silvercairns granite, and he was probably right. You had only to walk down Union Street to see building after building, pillar after pillar, balustrade, portico, gracefully curving arch, all of that particular shade of silver grey which only Silvercairns produced. On a grey day, the granite echoed the mood in shades as muted and delicate as a dove's plumage; in sunlight after rain, whole streets dazzled bright with silver stars. Churches, houses, offices, shops, all bore lasting witness to the wealth of Silvercairns, but, thought Fergus with the usual thud of foreboding, how long would it be before that wealth was exhausted? Already the quarry was close on 180 feet deep. Suppose the next time they blasted deeper they threw up not granite, but ...? Fergus shuddered at the familiar vision of the quarry floor cracking apart before his eyes, disintegrating and falling away into a black void which surged and roared and then welled up in overwhelming vengeance to consume everything in its path. With every blast he imagined the horror, with every blast successfully over, felt blessed relief that the quarry floor still held.

But with every ton of rock successfully harvested and despatched the question of an alternative grew more pressing. Though his father had not lived long enough to change his will, Fergus knew he had intended to leave Silvercairns to Leo Lennox, in place of Fergus, his legitimate heir. Though Fergus had no legal obligation to do so, he felt a moral one to see that one day Leo, together with any children he or Lettice might have, inherited his proper share. If that share was to be more than a pittance, it was time to expand; not this time the quarry they already had, for Fergus knew in his bones that they were near the edge of Silvercairns' limits, but in a new venture. A lease on a working quarry, or, better still, on a potentially rich piece of untapped land.

He had been half-looking for some time now, not mentioning it to anyone lest he alert the competition, and for the same reason not appointing agents to look in his place. But he went out of his way to make conversation with railway engineers or road surveyors, when he met them, even professors from the college, hoping to pick up a hint of where the richest granite seams might lie.

That cousin of Marshall's had been an informative chap, though nothing had yet come of his inquiry about a fountain. Fergus had told the fellow Silvercairns granite was ideal for the purpose, of course, that he would be honoured to supply whatever Drummond required, but that Silvercairns provided only the rock. He must look elsewhere for the design and the workmanship. Remembering his meeting with Mhairi Diack, he had recommended not Macdonalds, but the Wyness yard.

In return Drummond had mentioned geologists he knew and their interests, and given him the name of the fellow in Banchory. That settled, Fergus had dutifully looked at the Drummond sister with matrimonial eyes and within two minutes of their meeting, had conceded, with private relief, that Henrietta Drummond would be no mother for Leo. A pale, slight girl with no conversation to speak of, she was little more than a cipher, albeit an elegant one in what was, apparently, the latest idiocy of female dress – a crinoline skirt that required its wearer to take up the space of three. The idea of Miss Drummond and Leo in the same room was ludicrous enough: as mother and son, impossible. The matter safely settled in Fergus's mind, they had got on famously. Or rather, Drummond and Fergus conversed freely about the geological surveys necessary before a railway could be laid, discussed the choice between bridges, tunnels and cuttings and the relative costs, while Miss Drummond looked on, smiled vaguely now and then and said nothing. She was of delicate health, apparently, and intended to take the waters at Pannanich before she returned south for the summer.

Those conversations with Drummond had been helpful, but had left him no clearer in his mind as to whether to stick his neck out and make an offer for Willowbrae, or to look further afield. But if he did not hear of an alternative soon, he might have to take more positive steps. Meanwhile, a trip on the only railway in which he still held shares would both show him how his investment was progressing and give him the opportunity to see a different stretch of country from the immediate vicinity of Silvercairns and Aberdeen. More to his purpose, according to Drummond, one or two stretches of the railway line passed through what might be interesting granite country, about which the Banchory fellow would be delighted to enlighten him. If nothing else, the journey might amuse Leo – and at the same time help clear Fergus's head of the confusion of thoughts which had filled it since Lettice's departure: caused not so much by the unexpected emptiness she had left behind her, as by her parting words.

'If you have not managed to find a bride for yourself by the time I

[61]

return, brother dear, then I shall have to look about and find one for you. I have given some thought to the matter already, and have come to the regretful conclusion that you could do a lot worse than marry the Widow Grant.'

'The Widow Grant, as you choose to describe her, has no interest in me, as I have none in her,' he lied, pretending unconcern.

'Then I suggest you change your mind, Fergus dear, and set about changing hers. I believe our Widow Grant has a sizeable share in a quarry, with a foot in the door of a polishing yard for good measure. What better way to pay off that debt of yours? And maybe rebuild the west wing into the bargain?'

'Don't be ridiculous, Lettice.' Fergus had been furious with his sister for finding out his weak spot and attacking it with such a mercenary weapon. As if he would consider marrying any woman for her money, least of all Mhairi. 'You are forgetting Wyness severed all connections with Silvercairns long ago.'

'Maybe,' teased Lettice, greatly enjoying her brother's obvious discomfiture. 'But I'll wager anything you like that for all his pious bluster Headstane Wyness would be glad of the chance to do us a service. And you could hardly find a better alliance for Silvercairns if you scoured the whole of Scotland. Especially as Papa is dead now and there is no one to disinherit you for marrying into the servant classes.'

With that barbed reminder she had left him to his bachelordom and Leo.

'When will the train start, Uncle Fergus? Why is there different writing on the carriages? What is that man with the red flag doing? Why is that lady carrying her dog in a basket? Can't it walk on its own legs? Why are those people shouting and pushing? Where is our picnic basket? I'm hungry, Uncle Fergus, I want something to eat. Ma Gregor said there is chicken pie. I want a piece of chicken pie.'

'You will get nothing at all if you don't shut up,' said Fergus, exasperated beyond patience. In his plans for his nephew's outing, Fergus had omitted to check the calendar. Otherwise he would have known that on that particular weekend all seats on the Deeside railway were half price. In consequence the station was packed, the noise level high, and they would be lucky to find places, let alone a carriage to themselves. Already he was regretting his kindly impulse.

The whole idea was a ghastly mistake. Whatever had possessed him to plan to spend a whole day, voluntarily, in Leo's exhausting company? Moreover, if the cheerful loud-mouthed and exuberant crowds were anything to go by, on what seemed to be some sort of public holiday? Then he remembered that other Leo of the nightmares and the terror, felt the happy excitement which quivered through the already grubby hand that clutched his, and relented.

'Tell you what, Leo. You can choose the carriage for us. One with plenty of leg room for me – and space for the picnic hamper. And don't fall under the train!' he called after the lad, who was already racing up the platform, dodging in and out among the travellers, stopping only to peer inside an open carriage door before rejecting it and moving on. Suddenly Leo made his choice.

'Here, Uncle Fergus! This one has lovely red seats and a picture of a stag on the wall!'

Too late, Fergus realized he should have answered that question about the writing on the carriages. They had tickets for 1st class and Leo had chosen third. Moreover the carriage he had chosen was already crowded with passengers and their untidy luggage and only two narrow seats remained. Third class carriages provided seats for eight, while the same space in First was shared between a mere six. Looking at the small section of seat still unoccupied Fergus shuddered mentally with revulsion. To be pressed into that space and wedged there by the fatty folds of the vast, red-faced woman occupying the adjoining seat was more than imagination could stomach. He saw with horror that she had a faint moustache which already glistened with perspiration and he smelt in imagination the stifling acridity of armpits and worse.

'Not that one, Leo,' he said, avoiding the woman's eye. 'One that says "First" on the door. Come out.' When Leo made no move, but settled deeper into his seat and glared defiance, Fergus seized the boy by the collar and tugged.

But Leo had staked his claim to the corner seat and was not going to give up without a struggle. Especially as a boy of about his own age was watching the tussle from the corresponding seat on the far side of the carriage; a black-haired boy with blue eyes which seemed to be scorning Leo from a position of lofty superiority. The boy wore a neatly buttoned serge jacket and trousers, ornamented by a starched collar of dazzling whiteness and uncomfortable constriction. Leo's own collar had acquired a mysterious smudge and come adrift at the front, his hair was an untamed bush, his jacket unfastened, and his boots, which the kitchenmaid had polished for him specially only that morning were already smeared with coal dust and mud. In contrast, the other boy's boots were mirror-bright and he had a look of such scrubbed cleanliness that the carriage could just as well have been a pew in church on a Sunday, except for the air of pride and excitement which emanated from every inch of his body. He held a string-tied cloth bundle on his knee and seemed to be with the tall man opposite him, who was drawing squiggles in a notebook and occasionally making signs at the boy with his fingers.

'I said *come out*,' repeated Fergus through clenched teeth. 'Do as you're told, you little horror or I swear I will never take you anywhere again.'

For a moment Leo hesitated, weighing up the mortification of giving in in full view of that other boy who was watching the proceedings with virtuous enjoyment, against a future barren of all excitement. The future won. With a face of rebellious resentment and as much dignity as he could muster, Leo climbed down from the carriage, but not before he had seen a quick smile flit across the odious boy's face.

'Good,' said Fergus, with frowning relief. He had not enjoyed the tussle, the more so as it had been in front of a curious and no doubt gloating audience. Family disputes should be kept discreetly behind family doors. 'Now hurry up or there will be no seats left anywhere.'

Leo turned his head, saw the other boy still watching, and deliberately stuck out his tongue. Then, honour satisfied, he scurried up the train in search of an unoccupied first-class carriage.

As he watched his disreputable ward wrench open door after door, peer rudely inside, slam it shut again and move on until he made his choice, Fergus realized that for the first time he had thought of Leo, without reservation, as 'family'.

The journey to Banchory passed in less than an hour, but Leo, who had forgotten all grievance in the excitement of the moment, kept up a stream of non-stop chatter, commenting, questioning, demanding answers to everything from *why does the steam whistle?* to *why can't I put my head out of the window?* and *what makes the wheels go round?* with the regular refrain of *I'm hungry, Uncle Fergus, when can we eat our picnic?* For the first time Fergus realized just what Mrs Gregor had to put up with, and wondered whether an increase in her wages might be a wise investment.

Then the steady rattle of the wheels eased, the pistons laboured slower and slower until with a final grinding of brakes and a whistle of escaping steam, the train came to rest in Banchory station.

Doors banged, voices rose in chattering excitement and the small country platform filled with a motley assortment of passengers in holiday mood. Some dispersed quickly into the countryside, laden with picnic bundles that would weigh nothing on the return journey, or with gifts for friends and relatives with whom they hoped to spend the day before the evening train home to Aberdeen. But the larger number stayed, moving and swirling in endlessly changing patterns around the stationmaster's office and the waiting room, until someone marshalled them into suitable order for the next stage of the journey, which, when the Deeside Railway Company completed its track, would one day continue by rail, but which at present had to resort to more old-fashioned means.

The coaches which would take those who wished to venture further westward stood lined up outside the station yard, the horses harnessed and ready in the shafts.

'Which is our one, Uncle Fergus? Can I ride on the top?'

'None of them, and no, you can't,' but Fergus's attention was elsewhere. Then he saw what he was seeking. 'Unless I am much mistaken, ours is that horse and trap over there. The one with the red and gold paint. We will drive out to visit Mr Crawford before choosing our picnic spot, and if you keep absolutely quiet while I finish my business with him, then I might, just might, let you take the reins for five minutes on the way back.'

With a whoop of delight, Leo hurled himself towards the waiting vehicle and clambered straight up onto the box.

'I said on the way back,' Fergus called after him, then shrugged. What was the use? The boy was incorrigible. Worse than an untrained mongrel pup. No wonder Lettice had been so anxious to rid herself of the responsibility and unload it all onto Fergus instead. But, like it or not, and whichever side of the blanket he was born on, Leo remained his nephew. With a sigh of resignation, Fergus picked up the picnic basket and followed.

'Mr Adam? Mr Fergus Adam?'

At the touch on his shoulder, Fergus turned to see a man of about forty, clad in tweed plus-fours of a gingerish hue, with jacket and side-whiskers to match.

'Out early on the Alford survey. Heard the train whistle and thought I'd intercept you here.'

'You must be . . .'

'Crawford,' interrupted the newcomer and held out a firm, freckled hand. 'Alex Crawford. Drummond said you are interested in the geology of the area. Not prospecting for gold, I hope?'

'No, I . . .'

'Waste of time if you are. Australia's the place for that. Thought of going out myself more than once, but changed my mind. Too fond of the fishing here, and the shooting. Plenty of sheep to shoot in Australia, I suppose, and kangaroos, but not the same, not the same.' As he talked he steered Fergus towards the pony and trap. 'All ready and waiting, as you ordered. Reliable horse. Well-sprung bodywork. Take a rut in the track without the wheels flying off. Thought we'd go to my place first. Look at a few models and charts before we take to the open roads. What particular aspect interests you? Railways is it?'

'Well, I . . .'

'The future lies in railways, no doubt about it, but difficult terrain sometimes. Difficult terrain. Good land and the owner wants to hang onto it. Understandable, of course, but expensive. Not so good and you are talking of viaducts, cuttings, blastings and tunnelings. Just as expensive in the long run and then you have the shareholders to content with. Why didn't you make a detour, they say, and if you do decide to do that, you have all the residents from the avoided places thundering at your door to demand why the line did not go past their own front doors. This next stretch of the line is a headache, I don't mind telling you. You a shareholder?'

Before Fergus could answer, Crawford was off on another tack. 'Alford. They talk of a line to Alford. Who will travel on the line no one knows, but no one wants to be left out of the great expansion. Before we know where we are the land will be riddled with railway lines, the whole population constantly on the move. Stations everywhere. Railway cottages. Hotels. But you didn't say. What is your particular line of business?'

They had reached the vehicle and this time Crawford's pause demanded an answer. He stood, one hand on the polished door of the dogcart, his eyes on Fergus's face, waiting.

Fergus could not help a watchful glance to either side before admitting in a low mumble, 'Granite.'

[66]

'Granite?' shouted Crawford in delight and clapped Fergus heartily across the shoulders. 'Why didn't you say so in the first place? If it's granite you want I can show you the most pig-headed, obstructive, downright antagonistic rock you ever hoped to meet. And if you're a granite man, perhaps you can tell me in return the quickest way to shift the stuff? That's my horse there, by the way. I'll ride beside you. This yours?' He pitched the picnic basket into the dogcart and stood aside to let Fergus mount the step. Then he noticed Leo.

'Hey, you!' He reached up and took the boy by the ear. 'Out, if you know what's good for you. And quick, before I call the stationmaster.'

'Leo is with me,' said Fergus gravely, though not before Leo had seen the grin hastily smoothed over. 'Nephew,' he added, adopting Crawford's own clipped style of speech. 'In the back, Leo. With the basket.' Then he took up the reins in his gloved hands. 'Ready, Mr Crawford?'

At least one person in the lingering crowd had seen the exchange, and made no attempt to conceal his grin. But it was a brief rejoicing, soon lost in the wonder of watching the smart equipage swirl across the station yard in a cloud of dust and scattered hens. Gold paint flashed in the sunlight; red paint gleamed.

Hamish Diack noted the ginger-haired boy of the railway carriage in the back, saw him turn his head and put thumb to nose in an expression of derision. In return, Hamish tugged his own ear, rolled his eyes, jerked sideways and grinned horribly in a pantomime which said clearer than any words, 'I saw what happened and it served you right' but when the dogcart had turned the corner and disappeared, Hamish's expression changed to one of mingled envy and regret.

The gentleman in the glossy black hat, the immaculate frock-coat and buff breeches, the handmade kid gloves and handmade leather boots, was Mr Adam of Silvercairns. Uncle Donal had told him so. So the boy with the hair that was woolly as a sheep's pelt, but bright red, must be Leo Lennox whose mother lived in Australia and whose father no one mentioned. At least, not in Rainbow Cottage, where Mr Adam must not be mentioned either.

Donal had told Hamish the reason: the Adams owned Silvercairns and were their deadly rivals. Hamish's own father, Donal's brother, had died because of the Adams, which made them enemies as well as rivals. The Lennox boy had had nothing to do with that, but he was an Adam nonetheless. He rode in a first-class carriage and was met by a hired dogcart with red and gold paint. Which made his treatment, first at the hand of Mr Adam and later by the unknown gentleman, all the more satisfying. How dare he give himself airs when he was no better than Hamish himself? Worse, because though Hamish had no father either, at least his parents had been married. The whole town knew the Lennox boy was a bastard. Hamish was not allowed to speak the word, of course, but that did not prevent him knowing it. Leo Lennox was a bastard and had no right to give himself airs, to put out his tongue and thumb his nose at those who were every bit as good as, if not better, than he.

But what really upset Hamish was none of these reasons. It was the sight of Leo on the box of the beautiful red and gold painted dogcart, the reins in his hands. And though he had been cuffed off the box and relegated to the back, Hamish knew in his bones that before the day was out Leo would hold the reins again, this time with the dogcart in motion.

Hamish would love to drive a dogcart. Or a landau or a phaeton or a four-in-hand. Even a governess cart would do, to start with. But all he had yet been allowed to do was help with the quarry dray-carts and lead the horses on the tow-path of the canal, until it was sold to the railway and closed.

One day, he vowed, I will drive a carriage of my very own, pulled by two pairs of matching greys with jingling harness and dancing plumes. It will have a painted crest on the door, brass lamps front and back, and fur rugs for the ladies' knees. When I am of age and the quarry shares are mine.

Meanwhile, the coachman was calling for passengers to take their seats. The coach to Potarch was about to leave. Hamish tugged urgently at Donal's sleeve and they joined the press of people scrambling to secure the best seats.

His uncle Donal seemed impervious to all annoyance, content to take whatever seat fell to their lot. He did not need to explain that the weather was clement, the air dry and an outside seat gave much the best view anyway. Had it been raining and a near gale, Donal would still have allowed others to go first, except, of course, if Mhairi had been with them, or Annys.

Calm as always, with an inner strength that Hamish recognized and respected, Uncle and nephew were the closest of companions, and had been for as long as Hamish could remember. Now, side by side on the outside seat, with the countryside bowling past them on either side and the wind in their faces, there was no need for words. Later, over the simple lunch which Mhairi had prepared for them and tied up in a clean cloth bundle, they would talk a little, but for the moment it was enough to watch the unfamiliar countryside slip past them, trees and meadows and the wide silver sweep of the river. There were salmon in the Dee, Donal said, and where the river passed Balmoral, a special pool where the Queen's husband, with his guests and tenants, waded about in the water spearing the fish with leisters.

But they were not going to Balmoral for the fishing. He and Donal were on important business, emissaries from Wyness, Diack & Grant with a mission to undertake. There was little time for all they had to do and it was Hamish's task to see that everything went smoothly. But even the sense of his own responsibility could not quite banish envy: Leo Lennox, who had put out his tongue at Hamish and thumbed his nose for good measure, was going on a picnic, with a wicker hamper big enough for six, in a red and gold painted dogcart Hamish would have given his eye teeth for.

Sensing his nephew's restlessness, Donal laid a reassuring hand on the boy's knee. 'Soon,' he told him, shaping the words carefully. 'We will be there soon.'

'Potarch, Kincardine O'Neil, Aboyne,' recited Hamish, from memory. 'Three changes of horses before we reach Ballater, and then another for the last part of the journey.'

The last part was the important part. They were to hire horses, or a conveyance of some sort, to take them from Ballater to Balmoral and back in time to catch the three o'clock coach for the first stage of the long journey home. 'We will have little time,' Donal had told the boy, 'but enough.' Donal was to sketch the new castle as quickly and as accurately as he could, while Hamish acted as spokesman, kept watch, interpreted and generally guarded his uncle's welfare. For Donal, though in appearance well-built and personable and in intelligence brighter than most, had been deaf and dumb from birth. Those who did not know him took his silence, and the strange noises that occasionally passed his lips, for idiocy and treated him accordingly, though never if one of his family was on hand to take his part and for as long as he could remember, Hamish had been Uncle

[69]

Donal's self-appointed champion and defender. Donal was the Wyness yard's most accomplished draughtsman and the obvious choice to make clandestine copies of the Balmoral folly, for Tom to reproduce adorned with granite balconies, curleques and turrets in the richer parts of Aberdeen's West End. For Tom had had a request from a sea captain who had made a fortune in whaling for a house 'like yon castle at Balmoral. Smaller, mind, for I'm nay married to a queen wi' the money to pay for it, but wi' all the turrets and that, identical.'

'Identical,' Tom had agreed. The granite would not be the same, of course. Balmoral was built of stone from its neighbouring quarries, a whiter granite than their own quarry at Rainbow Hill produced, but the sea captain would not know that. Nor would he expect a tower a hundred feet high, or a ballroom. But if the house was to be remotely 'identical', the directors of Wyness, Diack and Grant agreed, they would need a scale model on which to work. Looking round the table at that meeting in the quarry office, all eyes had fixed on one person. After that, there was no question whose job it would be to take the copy, or who to send with him.

It was a weary collection of travellers who assembled that evening on the platform of Banchory station. The train was in a siding, having some vital final check to its insides, and even Hamish had not the energy to inquire further. The train would leave at seven as arranged and that was all they needed to know. He and his uncle found a convenient corner under the eave of the station building and prepared to wait, leaning side by side in silence against the wall.

It had been an exhausting afternoon: first the scramble, which they had lost, for a pony and trap, then the search for an alternative. The jolting journey by farm-cart westward, the arrival at Balmoral and the first, breathtaking glimpse of the new castle, luminous white against the green woodland background, what remained of the old castle crouching humbly in its shadow. The wondering awe and excitement. Then the laconic announcement from the driver that they'd need to turn around and set off back again in half an hour at the most, unless they wanted to miss the Ballater coach.

That brief time had been spent by Donal in frenzied sketching and by Hamish in questioning whatever workman he found willing enough to talk. Now he went over and over in his mind the details he

[70]

had gleaned: tower, 100 feet by 35 feet, ballroom 68 feet by 25 feet, dining-room 'small' for a country house, drawing-rooms and library ditto, building materials from the quarries of Glen Gelder, timber from the neighbouring woods, tartan upholstery and curtains everywhere, thistle patterns on chair seats. His mother would be interested in that particular detail, thought Hamish with satisfaction. There had been descriptions in the newspaper, but it was not the same as seeing for oneself, and some of the workmen had volunteered inside knowledge. For instance, Prince Albert, the Queen's husband, was not satisfied with the road and wanted to build a bridge at the castle gates to take it over the river instead of through the castle grounds as at present. Hamish wondered idly if they would use local materials for that too, when the time came, or whether Rainbow Hill could tender for the road metal, even for the bridge itself? He half thought of asking Uncle Donal, but for once the effort of sign language seemed too much. He would wait till they were on the train. Besides, he did not want to interrupt his uncle who had taken out his sketch book and pencil, and had resumed work on the last, unfinished sketch. He looked utterly absorbed.

Hamish watched him for a while, then lost interest He had seen the sketches already and knew them to be both accurate and good. He wandered to the end of the platform from where he could see the unfinished railway workings which would one day stretch all the way to Ballater, but there was little of interest. He was making his aimless way back again when he found it suddenly blocked by the red-haired boy of the pony and trap, sitting on a picnic hamper. The boy stood up, but made no attempt to move out of the way. In fact, when Hamish stepped to one side to go past, the boy did likewise, to bar his path. They were almost the same height, their eyes level. The red-haired boy's were brown and gleaming with devilment, Hamish's a cold and challenging blue.

'I've been a drive in the country,' the boy said, with taunting belligerence. 'To inspect the railways. Where've you been, neep-head?'

Ignoring the insult, Hamish said with lofty disdain, 'To Balmoral. To inspect the queen's castle.'

The boy looked taken aback by this rejoinder, but only for a moment. 'I could build a castle like that one any time I wanted,' he jeered. 'My uncle owns a quarry.'

'That's nothing. So does mine.'

[71]

'My uncle's quarry is the biggest in Scotland.' Before Hamish could dispute the fact, the boy went on quickly, 'And he's going to buy another one which will be even bigger. They'll both be mine one day.' He preened, this time convinced of victory.

'My uncle's quarry is half mine already. My father left it to me in his will.' Before the boy could counter this crushing claim Hamish added, 'and my other uncle is the best architect in the country. He could build another Balmoral castle tomorrow and you wouldn't be able to tell the difference. He's working on the plans now.' And Hamish waved a nonchalant hand towards where Donal still leant against the station wall, concentrating on his drawing.

'An architect? Him?' The Lennox boy gave a shout of derisive laughter. 'If he's your uncle, no wonder you're so daft. He's a dummie wi'only a halfpenny in the shilling and lucky not to be locked up.'

Forgetting eight years of Mhairi's gentle upbringing, Hamish hit him.

Fergus heard the commotion from the stationmaster's office, where he had retired for a quiet cigar and an exchange of news with that gentleman, and something in the quality of the disturbance told him that Leo was involved.

'Excuse me.' He stood up, tossed his half-finished cigar into the grate where the sulking coals eagerly snatched at it, and strode out of the office. On the platform a throng of people barred his path and he had to barge and thrust his way through towards the source of the noise. There he found the crowd had made a natural circle around two small boys who were rolling on the ground in a tangle of struggling limbs, but no one was making any attempt to part them. On the contrary, they were watching the progress of the tussle with interest, several of the menfolk offering cheerful advice and only one among the watching women making any protest and that on behalf not of the boys, but of their clothes. 'He'll tear that collar right off if he's not careful, and I pity the lass who gets the stitching of it,' she declared as Leo's fingers locked round the starched linen at Hamish's throat. When Hamish kicked out in protest, she clucked loudly in renewed outrage. 'Look at those lovely boots, all scratched. His ma will have something to say when he gets home, and that's a fact.'

[72]

But Fergus had finally forced his way to the front.

'Leo!' he bellowed above the general hubbub. 'Stop that at once or I'll tan you black and blue!'

In the momentary pause which followed a sound came from behind them and Fergus turned his head to see a tall, well-built man with dark hair alone by the station office. The fellow gave another strangled cry, then leapt towards them, plunged through the crowd with the single-minded purpose of a wild boar charging a thicket, and a moment later was at Fergus's side. Another and he had taken in the situation, seized the boys by their collars and swung them upwards, one in each powerful hand. Then he set them down on their feet, face to face, but still gripping each by the collar and holding them apart, and studied them in frowning silence. Leo's nose streamed blood, his once-clean shirt was dirt- and blood-spattered and his jacket torn. Hamish's left eye was rapidly closing, his lip split, his collar adrift, his clothes awry and similarly daubed with blood, though whether Leo's or his own was not clear. They glared at each other, unrepentant.

Still holding them firmly apart, Donal looked from one to the other and shook his head in wordless sorrow. Neither spoke.

'What is the meaning of this unseemly brawl?' Fergus Adam's cold words sliced the silence and triggered self-justification.

'He hit me first,' protested Leo, then, seeing his uncle's expression, added belligerently. 'For nothing.'

'It was not for nothing. You said . . .' Then, realizing his audience, Hamish stopped. He could not repeat the insult to his beloved uncle before anyone, least of all on a public railway platform and with Donal himself present. Fortunately for him, at that moment a train whistle split the air with piercing triumph and the first slow chug of grinding pistons followed. Instantly the crowd split up in the scramble to secure seats as the train eased its way into position at the platform and contestants and guardians were suddenly alone.

'Well Leo?' said Fergus. 'Are you going to apologize?'

'What for? He hit me first.'

'A gentleman does not brawl in the street. You will apologise for causing a public scene.'

But Leo's sense of primitive justice was outraged. 'Won't,' he said and clamped tight his jaw.

Donal Grant was similarly urging his nephew, in a series of increasingly agitated signs which Hamish steadfastly refused to see.

[73]

Out of his one good eye he glared unrepentant hostility at the Lennox boy who glared similarly back.

'Very well,' said Fergus, white with shame and anger. 'If you insist on behaving like a guttersnipe, you shall be treated like one. Guard!' he called, with an imperious anger worthy of his dead father, 'Take this boy and shut him in the guard's van.' He dropped a coin into the man's hand. 'See he does not escape. I will collect him when we reach Aberdeen.'

'But sir, there's pigs in the . . .'

'Good,' interrupted Fergus. 'He will have the company he deserves.' Then he turned his back on the group, mounted the step of the nearest first-class carriage and slammed the door behind him.

If he had looked out of the window he would have seen the final exchange of facial insults between the two boys before each was gripped by the upper arm and led firmly away, Leo to the guard's van and Hamish to an already crowded carriage where he had to stand for the entire journey, the object of much curiosity and whispered comment.

But Hamish refused to hang his head and to all Donal's silent questioning replied defiantly, 'I had no choice.' As to an apology, and he was very much afraid that his mother would require one, his mind was made up. On that point at least, he and the detestable Leo agreed.

'But why did you strike him?' said Mhairi with careful patience and for the twentieth time. As before she received no answer, only a stubborn tightening of the lips and a more determined set to her son's head.

Mhairi was close to tears. The sight of her precious son, bloodsplattered and with one eye rapidly closing, his lip split and swollen, neat Sunday clothes muddied and torn, had jolted her heart into terrified memory. She saw, with a vividness undiminished by nearly seven years of widowhood, her husband, blown half across the quarry by a rogue explosion, his clothes similarly blood-spattered, his body bruised and broken. She had wiped the dirt and blood from his dear face, though she knew it could do no good, and as she washed her son's face clean and dabbed healing lotions on the cuts and bruises she felt the anguish of that far-off day with undiminished pain.

[74]

Alex's accident had been fatal, and none of his doing. Hamish, in trivial contrast, had suffered mere bruises, but it seemed he had deliberately sought them, by picking a fight with the Lennox boy, on the public railway station. Hamish, who was a mild-tempered, kindly boy as a rule, and who knew his mother's attitude to fighting of whatever kind. Last night she had been too agitated to do more than clean the boy up and pack him off to bed with a soothing drink, but with the morning had come reaction and the overwhelming need to know every tiny detail of the encounter.

'Why?' she repeated now. 'You do not deny that you hit him, so tell me why?'

When he made no answer, but continued to stare at his boots, the look of unhappy obstinacy firmly nailed to his face, Mhairi felt tears of weary frustration threaten and for once made no attempt to check them. Instead, she sank into her chair and closed her eyes.

Donal, who had been standing unhappily by the table, made an awkward move towards her, but she waved him away. 'No Donal,' she sighed. 'It is no good. He will not tell me. How are we to know what to do if he will not tell?'

Donal had already given his story, brief though it was. He had been sketching, utterly absorbed, had sensed a change around him, why he could not say, but he had looked up and seen a crowd with something at its centre. He could see Hamish nowhere and had feared, with a dreadful terror, that an accident had befallen the boy. That the crowd was surrounding his body. Then he had found the boys fighting and parted them. That was all he knew.

If it had been any other boy but Leo Lennox Mhairi would probably have left it at that: some senseless private quarrel, too embarrassing to tell to adults. She would have punished the boy and forgotten the matter. But the Lennox boy was different. She blushed to admit it, even in her most secret thoughts, but it was because the boy's guardian was Fergus Adam that she needed to know exactly what had been at the root of the affair. In all probability it was nothing, and they could laugh about it together: but suppose it had been something more serious? Something personal? Or touching on the past?

The peats stirred in the hearth and in the sudden quiet Mhairi heard the faint singing of the big black kettle that hung from a chain over the fire. Soon Annys would be home, with the others. Mhairi had sent them to church, and allowed no excuses, for she had hoped the time alone with Hamish and Donal would have told her what she wanted to know. Instead, she had wasted hours in futile questioning. She ought to stir herself, make tea, put food ready, but she could not summon the energy to move from her chair. If Alex had been alive, he would have known what to do. Suddenly the years of loneliness, of bringing up her children with no husband to help her, of having to make every decision herself, were too much. Silent tears ran down her face and she had not the energy to raise a hand and brush them away.

Donal pushed Hamish hard in the small of the back and nodded towards Mhairi with unmistakable meaning.

'I am sorry, Ma,' said Hamish in a small voice. Donal glared at him, urging him to go on. Hamish stepped to his mother's side, took her limp hand in both his and, his back to Donal, said, 'Don't cry, Ma. I will tell you, if you send Uncle Donal away.'

Mhairi jerked open her eyes. 'Send him away?'

Hamish nodded.

'All right. I will ask him to fetch me more peats. Will that do?'

Again the boy nodded, and though there was a fair supply of peats waiting beside the hearth, she indicated to Donal that he should fetch more.

'Well, Hamish?'

'He was boasting,' began Hamish, his eyes still not meeting hers. 'He said he would own his uncle's quarry one day. He said Mr Adam was going to buy another quarry and he would own that too.'

'And you hit him for that?' Mhairi sounded incredulous.

'No. I was boasting too, a little. Then I said my uncle was a brilliant architect. Then he said ... he said ...' and blushing with shame on Donal's account, Hamish mumbled the odious words.

To his astonishment, Mhairi threw her arms around him and laughed and wept together. When she could speak again, she said, 'You did right, Hamish, to defend your uncle. Absolutely right. Your father would be so proud of you. He would never let anyone, however strong, torment Uncle Donal and it was wicked of the boy to say such things, but I don't expect he meant them. He is thoughtless and silly, that is all. And really, my love, fighting is not the answer to such ignorance. So next time, promise me you will not pick a fight?'

'But ...'

'Promise?'

Before her son could answer, Donal returned with the superflu-

[76]

ous peats and dumped them in a heap beside the hearth. Then he straightened and looked a question at Mhairi, passing her the notepad he always carried. She scribbled:

'The argument was about nothing. A silly boast, that is all, and Hamish and I are friends again.' She smiled, her arm round her son's waist. 'Isn't that so, Hamish?'

'Yes, Ma.'

But I didn't promise, he reminded himself later that night as he lay curled up in bed in the attic room he shared with his Uncle Willy. Uncle Lorn and Uncle Donal had the other, across the wooden landing where the stair led down into the darkness. Sometimes, faint light would come up through that square, if his mother was working late at her sewing or his aunt Annys was reading, but tonight his Ma had doused the last lamp and the household had settled down for the night. The only light came from the small skylight overhead which framed a rectangle of night sky, blurred in one corner with cloud, but patterned here and there with stars. An owl called from a distant wood and somewhere a fox barked. Comforting, familiar sounds which he had known all his life.

Usually, Hamish went to sleep the moment he pulled the blanket up to his chin, but tonight he lay watchful, long after his uncles slept. If he strained his ears into the darkness, he could hear their breathing, slow and regular, and from downstairs the slow tick of the clock.

His lip hurt where it had split against his tooth, and if he turned his head to the wrong side by mistake, his bruised eye throbbed against the pillow. But these minor troubles were not what kept him from sleep. It was the memory of his mother asking for his promise, and, he was almost certain, believing he had given it. But he had not promised. Uncle Donal had come in and he, Hamish, had not spoken a word. The trouble was, if his mother believed that he had promised, what happened if Hamish had to fight Leo Lennox again? And he might have to, whatever his mother said. The Lennox boy had deliberately barred his path, deliberately provoked him, and had gone to the guard's van rather than apologize. That sort of boy was capable of anything. Besides, wasn't he an Adam, and an enemy?

Across the black hole of the stair well, Donal too lay awake, looking through a similar skylight at the same patch of cloud and the same stars, though the silence which surrounded him was patterned not with owl call or fox, but with the blanketing void he had known all his twenty-eight years. Tonight he felt bitterly the loneliness of that barrier. He, who could hear nothing, had been sent from the room at the boy's request, so that Hamish could confess to his mother. That could mean only one thing: the fight had been on Donal's behalf. The thought was at the same time poignant and mortifying. The boy's father, Donal's brother, had been the same, leaping in with fists flying on Donal's behalf at the slightest provocation. But Hamish was only eight: he should be under Donal's protection, not the other way round.

Going over and over in his head the events of the last two days, Donal came once more to Mhairi's explanation. 'The boys were boasting. Hamish said he would own a quarry one day. Leo said he would own two. Why two? Because his uncle was going to buy another one. Idle boasting, to annoy each other. That is all.'

Donal had not believed her then, and he did not now. It was not 'all'. But for the first time Donal looked more closely at that boast about the quarries. Was it possible that Adam was planning to buy another quarry? Or had that been merely Leo's embroidery? He remembered the man who had met Adam on Banchory station and driven away with him. The absence of one of Donal's five senses had sharpened the others beyond the ordinary and given him a near photographic memory which he called into action now to replay that scene in the railway station yard. The two men had been standing beside the pony and trap, Adam with his back to Donal, the other facing him. Adam had said something and the other man had shouted aloud before slapping Adam on the back in obvious pleasure. Donal strained to remember the man's face, the shape of his mouth, the formation of the shouted word. *Gran-ite*. It could have been. Must have been. And if it was . . . Silvercairns was already by far the biggest quarry in the north-east: if there was indeed to be a second Silvercairns, then the competition would be truly formidable. Wyness and his young partners would need to look about them, and plan accordingly.

Perhaps young Hamish's escapade could be turned to their advantage after all? On that optimistic thought, Donal closed his eyes and slept.

Mhairi was alone in the cottage on an afternoon some days later, when she heard the sound of hooves in the lane. Not the regular plod of the dray horses, but a lighter, crisper sound. She was instantly transported back in memory to a day four years ago, when Annys lay in the grip of a raging fever and the fortunes of the Wyness yard hung by a thread. He had come to her, given her the information which had saved them from his own father's planned disaster, bound her to secrecy, and left again. But not before he had kissed her. The memory brought a piercing, shameful longing which she thrust quickly away. Why should she imagine it was his horse? Why should he visit her, after all that had happened, after all this time? The idea was preposterous.

Perhaps it was Tom, on one of his increasingly rare trips to Rainbow Hill? But Tom came usually in the company of a prospective client, or with Mr Wyness. If he was visiting the cottage, he came with Fanny and the children. Never alone, and certainly not on a gentleman's high-stepping thoroughbred. She listened more carefully, heard the sound of wheels and felt an instant's disappointment. It was her sister-in-law Fanny, that was all. Come on one of her usual afternoon visits. Then she listened again and detected a much lighter sound than Fanny's carriage made on the hard-packed earth of the lane. As of two wheels rather than four. A dogcart, perhaps? Or a gig?

Her heart began to thump unnaturally loud and she looked quickly about her, checking automatically that the room was fit for visitors. But there was no reason why the vehicle should call at the cottage. It might just as well be going to the quarry office, further up the lane. It did happen, after all. Though much of the business was handled in the main office in town, there were clients who preferred to deal direct with the quarry. Mhairi had met them herself, on the days when she helped with the wages. That pleasant Mr Drummond, for instance, who was inquiring about a fountain and wished to see the colour of the natural rock. He had driven his sister in a cabriolet, she remembered, because it had threatened rain and Miss Drummond had insisted on having the hood raised. The Drummonds had returned south months ago, but had promised to come back again, in the autumn. Perhaps they had come back earlier than expected?

But whatever soothing explanations her brain came up with, her heart still thumped too quickly for comfort. She smoothed her skirts, put a quick hand to her hair, then clasped her hands firmly together to still their trembling while the horse's hooves came inexorably closer.

Suddenly, she could bear the suspense no longer. She crossed the

[79]

room and risked a glance through the small-paned window. What she saw brought the blood rushing to her cheeks, then drained it as swiftly. She drew back out of sight, momentarily paralysed by shock and excitement in equal measure. He had come to her house, where she was alone, unchaperoned and undefended. But she must not panic. She was a grown woman, a widow and mother, mistress in her own home. She was equal to any situation, even this.

The horse stopped, there were steps on the path, a pause, then a firm rap at the door.

For a long moment she considered ignoring it, pretending she was out, anything rather than face him. Then she straightened her back, took a deep and steadying breath, and lifted the latch.

It had not been an easy decision to make. Fergus Adam had debated the propriety of such a visit long into the night, on every night since that abortive railway outing: on one side remembering her brother's hostility and the history of enmity between Adam and Diack; on the other, considering family honour, grace and courtesy, the necessity if not for an apology, then at least for an inquiry into the boy's health, not by a mere note, but in person. Surely it was the least a gentleman could do? And whether he liked it or not, Leo must learn to behave like a gentleman.

And yet, behind all these intellectual arguments, Fergus was uncomfortably aware of a motive unrelated to any considerations of good manners: he wanted to see Mhairi. That was the plain and shameful truth of it. The fracas between a pair of boisterous boys was merely the hook on which to hang his excuses. Leo would apologize, he would do the same, with suitable noises of concerned regret, but the real purpose of his visit would be to ... But here imagination shied and doubt set in. Suppose she were to take the bruising of her child as a personal assault and slam the door in his face?

He drew in his horse to the sedatest of paces on the last stretch of the track, while beside him Leo alternately sulked, or bounced up and down in excitement demanding to be allowed to take the reins, 'Just for five minutes, Uncle Fergus. I know how to do it, honest I do.'

'I said, on the way home,' said Fergus for the dozenth time, 'and then only if you behave as I told you to do and apologize properly.'

'Won't,' muttered Leo, again for the dozenth time, but there was an element of ritual repetition in the exercise and a moment later he was demanding yet again to be allowed to take the reins, 'Just for one minute. Please?'

'One more word out of you and you will be forbidden all contact with horses for the rest of the summer,' said Fergus, with feeling. 'Moreover, you will walk all the way home. Now remember what I told you. We are nearly there.'

Past the rowan tree, the wicket fence, until, too soon, they reached the garden gate, while memory flooded through him to set his heart pounding with hope and apprehension. Even then, he might have changed his mind and turned back, had he not seen a shape at the window, her face, quickly withdrawn. But that glimpse had set his heart pounding again, this time with resolution.

He looped the bridle of his horse over the gatepost, clamped a hand onto Leo's shoulder, for he was taking no chances, and walked up the short path to the door. He took a final steadying breath and raised his hand to knock. Silence. For an empty, desolate moment he thought she was going to snub him, keep the door barred against him until he slunk away, defeated. Then with relief and joy, he heard the soft click of the latch and the door swung wide.

'Good afternoon, Mrs Grant.' He regarded her gravely for a moment in silence, taking in her thick dark hair, the unruly twists which had escaped their pins to curl delightfully across her pale forehead, the eyes which were even bluer than he remembered. Cornflower blue against the sombre background of her widow's clothes. 'I must apologize for intruding, unannounced, on your...'

But under Mhairi's steady gaze the carefully rehearsed speech deserted him. Instead, after a moment's tongue-tied, blushing pause, he said simply, 'May we come in?'

He thought she was going to refuse, but she stepped back, said 'Please do,' and indicated the family kitchen. The entrance hall was so small that he could not help brushing against her as he passed and the contact sent disturbing shivers to his very fingertips. Had it not been for the presence of Leo, still firmly clamped under his hand, he might have forgotten self-control, snatched her against this chest and kissed her there and then. Instead, he walked sedately into the family kitchen, pushing Leo in front of him, and stood in the middle of the room, waiting. He heard the door close behind him, the rustle of skirts, then her soft voice at his back.

'May I take your hat, Mr Adam, and your riding crop?'

Startled, he realized that with his free hand he was clutching both like a shield against his chest.

'Thank you.' He handed them to her, his eyes following her as she moved away, laid them neatly on a chair near the door, came back again. She moved with grace and, he realized with sudden revelation, with a self-control as rigid as his own. The knowledge filled him with joyful hope, though he revealed none of it in his carefully expressionless face.

'This is Leo,' he said unnecessarily, and gave the boy a warning shove.

'Good afternoon, Mrs Grant,' gabbled Leo. 'Uncle Fergus says to say I'm sorry or I won't get to ride a pony again all summer, so "I'm sorry".' Then he muttered with lingering resentment and in a whisper quite loud enough to hear, 'But I'm not really because he hit me first.'

Fergus drew in his breath on a smothered oath, then he saw Mhairi's expression and his own relaxed. She seemed to be having the greatest difficulty keeping a straight face.

'Good afternoon, Leo. I am afraid Hamish is out or you could have apologized to each other. But perhaps you would like a drink of stone ginger and a scone instead?'

'Is it fizzy?' asked Leo with interest and earned himself another shove and a furious whispered warning to 'remember your manners'.

'Yes-please-and-is-it fizzy?'

'Very,' said Mhairi, straight-faced. 'It has already blown the stoppers out of three bottles and shattered a fourth.' Then she turned to Fergus. 'Will you take tea, Mr Adam? Or perhaps a dram?'

'No thank you. I ...' But she was not quite quick enough to hide the flicker of disappointment. 'Tea would be most welcome,' he amended, smiling. 'The day may not be hot, but the road is dusty nonetheless and my horse will persist in kicking up his heels with most unnecessary vigour.'

'It may be necessary to him,' pointed out Mhairi, with the hint of a smile, quickly gone. But it was enough. It told him that hostilities were over: the truce begun. What that truce might lead to, he did not know, but suddenly, jubilantly, he believed anything was possible. She moved to the dresser. 'Please sit down Mr Adam, and excuse me for a moment.'

Fergus watched her quick, competent movements with quiet

[82]

pleasure as she set out cups, saucers, teapot, on a neat chequered cloth.

'You will forgive my not using your tablecloth,' she said, not looking at him, 'but it is put away in the kist, for special occasions.' Then realizing the interpretation that could be put on her ingenuous remark she added quickly, 'I did not mean . . .'

'What is that chain for?' demanded Leo, pointing to the sway over the fire.

'For the kettle,' said Mhairi, with relief. 'Like this,' and she replaced it on its hook and swung it over the hottest part of the fire.

'The fire in our kitchen is much bigger than your one,' boasted Leo. 'We could hang ten kettles over our fire all at once. Twenty if . . .'

'Be quiet, Leo!' warned Fergus, then went on gravely, 'I am flattered that you remembered the cloth at all, Mrs Grant. A wedding present from a mere acquaintance, so many years ago.' But it was not flattery that set his heart singing. She was blushing most delightfully and he was almost sure the cause was nothing to do with social embarrassment, or the heat of the fire.

'"In friendship",' corrected Mhairi, quoting the card which had accompanied that long-ago gift and the last shred of caution fled.

'It was in friendship that I came,' said Fergus, his voice warm with an intimacy that set the cup trembling in her hand. 'And to apologize on my nephew's behalf. As you see, Leo is not the quietest or most biddable of boys.'

'I am quiet now,' protested Leo. 'I am waiting for my stone ginger.'

'If you go into the back scullery and look on the floor under the sink, you will see a bottle,' said Mhairi. 'But carry it very carefully so as not to shake it up, and bring it to me here.'

'Tea, Mr Adam?' she said, when the boy had gone. She handed him the cup, her hand steady again. He was relieved to see no trace of censure in her face.

'I trust your son has suffered no ill effects from his ... er ... meeting with my nephew, Mrs Grant?'

'Young bruises heal quickly, as I see they have done in Leo's case, but the causes of them are not so quickly forgotten.'

'No.' After one glance at her face, grave with private sorrow, Fergus subsided into silence. He was wondering how best to proceed in order to get the business of Leo out of the way so that they might talk of more personal things, when she took matters out of his hands.

'Leo should not have said what he did. Hamish should not have struck him. The blame is equal. Let us leave it at that.' She smiled, and the whole irritating business of two squabbling boys fell into proper perspective. 'It would be far better, Mr Adam, if we were to forget the matter and talk of other things. For instance, no one has told me yet about the train journey, or the progress of the Deeside line. How long will it be before it reaches Balmoral, so that the Queen may travel in comfort by railway, all the way from London to her own highland front door?'

'How long indeed. With every section to be argued over before the route can be settled it may be years. But I doubt our sovereign lady will allow an internal combustion engine to disturb the peace of her new Balmoral. They say Prince Albert plans to move the road to give them greater privacy, so what chance has a railway track? It will stop a discreet distance away, out of sight and earshot. If, that is, it ever moves beyond Banchory.'

'Why have you got a dead rabbit out there?' interrupted Leo, wandering in from the scullery, a thick stoppered bottle in his hand. 'Tied up by its feet?'

'Because I am going to cook it in a stew,' said Mhairi, unruffled.

'Can I have it's feet? Leckie says rabbit feet are lucky and . . .'

'Remember what I told you, Leo,' warned Fergus.

'But I've done all that.' protested the boy, stamping his foot with annoyance. 'I said what you told me to say didn't I? Didn't I, Mrs Grant?' and he turned to Mhairi for confirmation.

Mhairi looked down at the boy whose shock of fiery red hair reminded her poignantly of his mother, who had once, long ago, been her friend. How could Lizzy have parted with him? Her own son? If he was the unruly, foul-mouthed handful the whole town said he was, then was it any wonder? Behind all the rudeness and the boasting was an ordinary eight-year-old boy, like her own Hamish, only Leo had no mother to love and teach and guide him, as Hamish had.

'Yes, you said you were sorry.'

'Uncle Fergus promised I could drive the gig home if I said it, and I did.' He glared belligerently at first Mhairi, then Fergus.

'I am warning you, Leo,' began Fergus ominously, but Mhairi interrupted him.

[84]

'I don't know what else Mr Adam told you to do, but I expect it was good advice, Leo,' she said gently. 'You see, if you say you are sorry, you must try and mean it too, even if it is difficult to do.'

'Why? I said what Uncle Fergus told me.'

'Certainly you did. But suppose I said to you "Have a bottle of stone ginger" and then took it away from you, like this?' She deftly removed it from his fingers, and held it out of his reach. 'You expect other people to mean what they say, don't you?'

'Yes, but...'

'But you are only a child and can do what you like?' she finished softly and watched the flush spread across his freckled face till face and hair were two shades of brilliant red. Then she unstoppered the bottle, poured the frothy liquid into a large mug and handed it to him. 'This was my father's mug, so please take care of it. And if you look in that tin with the flowers painted on it, you will find biscuits. Unless you would rather have bread and cheese? The bread crock is in the scullery.'

Without a word, Leo went out into the back regions and Mhairi turned to Fergus with a smile. 'You were talking of Banchory, Mr Adam. You did not continue the journey from there, I understand? Is it a pleasant area in which to spend the day?' Her voice was quiet and soothing, conducive to conversation and to confidence.

'Oh yes. The surrounding countryside is delightful and my companion was most informative.' Before he realized, Fergus found himself telling her all about Mr Crawford's findings, his own fears for the safety of Silvercairns and his plans to develop a new quarry to replace the old. If he paused, Mhairi prompted him with a pertinent question or sympathetic comment, so that he hardly noticed when she re-filled his teacup, twice over. Once, Leo came in, put down his mug, and wandered out again, muttering something about making sure the horse and trap were all right. Once, Fergus caught himself up short, aware that he was giving away thoughts and plans he had confessed to no one.

'I am afraid I have been indiscreet, Mrs Grant. I hope I may trust you to regard what I have told you as of the strictest confidence?'

But when she smiled and murmured, 'Of course,' he forgot caution and resumed without restraint. They talked of the countryside and, by natural progression, of Mhairi's life at Rainbow Cottage.

'Are you never lonely?' he asked her.

'With my brothers and the children to look after? How would I

[85]

have time to be lonely?' But when he looked at her searchingly with dark, compassionate eyes she admitted quietly, 'A little. Now and then.'

'I wish I might be allowed to ...' Fergus stopped abruptly. It was too soon. What would she think of him? He put down his cup and stood up, before his tongue might lead him into further indiscretion.

'Might be allowed what, Mr Adam?' She spoke lightly, as of nothing in particular, but she did not meet his eyes.

'To ...' Through the window he saw Leo on the front seat of the gig. 'To give young Hamish riding lessons,' he improvised on the spur of the moment. 'Leo greatly enjoys his and perhaps the two fatherless boys could patch up their differences and learn together?'

'Thank you.' Was it imagination or was there a trace of disappointment in her voice? Even anger? 'But I fear it will not be possible. When he is not at school, Hamish helps in the family business, as he is doing today. He has little free time. And I have even less.' She stood up and preceded him to the door. 'You forget he is of working stock, Mr Adam. Not a gentleman of leisure.'

'That was unkind,' said Fergus quietly. 'And uncalled-for. A boy may ride whether his father be king or beggarman, and to ride well is an advantage to any man. As to gentlemen of leisure, I number few, if any, among my acquaintance. Though there is widespread belief to the contrary, even a gentleman has to pay his debts.'

There was a small silence in which a blush of embarrassment rose slowly to engulf Mhairi's face. She endeavoured to hide it by turning away to pick up his hat and riding crop from the chair, but when she held them out to him, the blush was still there.

'I am sorry, Mr Adam. You are quite right. It was petty and small-minded of me to speak as I did. Please forgive me?'

'I think I could forgive you anything,' he said, very quietly. 'As to being petty and small-minded, you could never be either. It was I who was thoughtless and obtuse.'

He took a step towards her. Then, before his courage could desert him, he laid his hands on her shoulders, bent his head and kissed her gently on the cheek.

Whether she made the first move or whether he did, neither of them ever knew, but the next moment his arms were tight around her, her lips found his, and they were kissing with all the tenderness and hunger of their dreams, while hat and riding crop fell unnoticed to the floor.

'Darling Mhairi,' he murmured, holding her head against his chest and caressing her hair with long, gentle strokes. 'If you knew how many years I have longed to do this...'

'And I ...' she confessed, unashamed. It was as if the barrier which had separated them for as long as she could remember had suddenly vanished, shrivelled into dust which the wind had caught up and tossed away. For ever, she vowed. Nothing should ever separate them again.

'I think I fell in love with you the day you ran, distraught, across my quarry yard, all those lonely years ago...'

'When poor Ma was dying...'

'And you had come to fetch your father home. You looked so frightened, and vulnerable and beautiful. You have lived in my heart ever since. Even when you married, and I thought you were lost to me for ever...'

Perhaps I am? said a warning voice in her heart and she could not suppress a shiver.

'My father was a ruthless man, God rest his soul,' murmured Fergus, still cradling her head against his chest. 'He was responsible for so much enmity and hate. Sometimes I think his shadow threatens even now, looming ominously over Silvercairns, always watching...'

'Don't say that,' she said quickly. 'The dead are dead.' And yet, when she visited the churchyard and the family grave, she felt her husband's presence there, sensed her mother's tender solicitude and her father's love. Why should not evil linger on as well as good? The thought made her shiver again and Fergus looked down at her in concern.

'You are cold?'

She shook her head. 'It was the thought of the past, that is all.'

'Forget the past. Forget rivalry and enmity and revenge. I love you, Mhairi. That is what matters to me. And, dare I hope, to you?'

For answer she kissed him, obliterating doubt, fear, everything in the wonder of new love.

Then in the distance a whistle sounded and Mhairi stiffened, her eyes suddenly wide with alarm. Suppose, on their way home past the cottage, the quarry workers were to see and recognize the vehicle? Suppose Tom were to find out?

'You must go,' she said, with sudden urgency. 'It would not do for anyone to see your horse tied at my gate.'

[87]

'Your brother?' Mhairi nodded. 'Is there nothing I can do to make my peace with him? I would like that more than all the world.'

'Nothing,' said Mhairi in a flat voice, all joy drained out of her. 'Or if there is, I don't know what.'

'I refuse to give you up,' said Fergus, with quiet intensity, taking both her hands in his. 'Remember that.' He bent to kiss her again, but she pushed him away.

'Please go, I beg you.'

'Not until you say I may visit you again.'

'Not here, cried Mhairi in growing alarm. 'You must not come here.'

'Then you must visit me at Silvercairns, or we must contrive to meet on neutral ground.

'Yes, yes,' cried Mhairi in agitation. 'Anything, as long as it is not here. But please go!'

She thrust hat and riding crop into his hands and pushed him towards the door. He opened it and gave a low whistle, as to a well-trained dog. Instantly, Leo jumped from the gig and came at the run.

He thrust out a grimy hand, gabbled, 'Goodbye Mrs Grant and thank you for having me,' then with hardly a pause turned to Fergus. 'There. I said it without you telling me, Uncle Fergus, and I know I said it right. So can I take the reins like you promised?'

Fergus raised eyes to the heavens on a sigh of resignation. 'I suppose so, but wait for me!' he called after him as Leo sped back down the path and leapt up into the gig. Then he turned to Mhairi, with a shrug of helplessness. 'You see how it is?'

'I think, perhaps, you had better not keep Leo waiting,' she said gravely. 'Not unless you plan to go home on foot.'

'No.' He reached out and took her hand, she thought to shake it in farewell as Leo had done. But instead he held it for a moment so that she felt the soft flesh warm against her own, then, before she realized what he meant to do, raised it to his lips. 'Goodbye, Mrs Grant.'

'Goodbye, Mr Adam.' She expected him to loose her hand, but, still holding it, his eyes looking deep into hers, he turned her hand gently over and kissed it, softly, in the palm. He closed her fingers over the place and then, at last, released her.

It was both a declaration and a promise.

Inside the cottage, Mhairi leant against the closed door and let happiness fill her to the fingertips, to the very roots of her hair. Fergus Adam had declared his love, more clearly than in any words. Fergus Adam of Silvercairns, who was as handsome and courteous and kind as any prince in her childhood daydreams. She clasped her hands around her waist, closed her eyes and rocked gently to and fro as memory wrapped her round with joy.

Then into her happiness intruded the murmur of men's voices, the vibration of distant trudging feet. The quarry workers were going home. Suddenly, the impossibility of the situation washed through her, dousing her joy. Tom would never countenance such an alliance. Look how he had stormed at her over the wedding invitation. And if she quarrelled with Tom, the family would be split down the middle. The family which she had promised her mother on her deathbed to protect.

From the past, as it had done in so many times of trouble, came her mother's soft voice saying, 'Never give up hope, Mhairi. Hope makes all things possible.' And her mother was right. Somehow, surely, they would find a way to soothe Tom's antagonism? To make him accept Fergus for what he was: not Old Man Adam's tyrannical successor, but a good and honest man? Smiling once more and humming softly to herself, Mhairi moved about the room collecting the tea-things and heaping them onto a tray. They would need to be washed and put away before she tackled the first of the many tasks necessary if that precious family of hers was to be fed. She picked up the tray, turned towards the back scullery, and stopped dead in the doorway.

Annys was standing at the board beside the sink, unpacking a basket.

'How long have you been back?' demanded Mhairi, her mouth suddenly dry.

Annys looked up, her eyes a little too innocently wide. 'Not long. Trade was slow today, but I managed to sell everything. Catriona wanted to stay longer at the farm so I said she could if she watched for Donal passing and came home with him. Oh and Mrs Macrae sent these.' She indicated a pair of fowls, still unplucked and with their stiff, yellow claw legs tied together with string.

'That was kind of her.'

Mrs Macrae often sent such presents home with Annys who, for some unaccountable reason, had become the family's expert on the

[89]

war in the Crimea. She visited the reading room whenever she was in town and read avidly anything she could find on the progress of the conflict. Often Mrs Macrae would waylay her on her way home and ask for news, then Annys would go into the big farm kitchen, sit at the scrubbed deal table, dutifully eat the scones or bannocks provided and give Mrs Macrae such details as she thought suitable for the mother of a young soldier caught up in the conflict: Lord Raglan's latest conference, the arrival of new munitions, the successful tackling of a storehouse fire. She did not mention the smallpox in the fleet, nor the hand-to-hand fighting with hatchets, pickaxes and staves which took place when Russian and British working parties accidentally met. For Annys worried enough on Kit O'Brien's behalf to know how such information would haunt poor Mrs Macrae. Now she took an apron from the back of the door, tied it round her waist and cut the string on the first of the fowls.

Watching her, Mhairi felt her first alarm ebb a little. If she had not yet had time to put on an apron, surely Annys could not have been home more than a minute? Though how could she have failed to see the gig in the lane?

'They are only boilers,' said Annys conversationally, as she began to pluck the feathers. 'Old birds that had stopped laying, Mrs Macrae said. But with long, slow cooking, they will make a fine stew. I thought I'd best start on them straight away.'

Mhairi did not answer, but began to unload the tray of tea-things, suddenly aware that there were two cups, two saucers, two teaspoons. Suppose Annys were to notice? 'Has Mrs Macrae heard from her son?' she asked, a little too loudly, as she filled a basin with water and fetched hot from the kettle. 'It has been a long time.'

'Oh yes. She had a letter today. That is why she called me in. Otherwise I would have been home much earlier.'

Was it imagination or was there really a knowing look in the girl's eye? 'Oh?' said Mhairi carefully, adding soap to the water. 'And is Willy well?'

'He says he is. Since the railway was completed things are much better, he says. Stores and ammunition can get through to the troops and the wounded can be transported to the hospital in safety. He says he has made friends with some of the labourers, many of whom are from Aberdeen.' Annys paused, and Mhairi was surprised to see a secret smile on her face, before she resumed, 'Willy says the labourers are doing a splendid job and now that the line is finished they are building a road and extra huts for the Sanitarium.'

There was a small silence as Annys tugged away at the feathers and Mhairi attempted to dispose of the damning evidence of the teacups behind her back.

'He is very handsome, isn't he?' said Annys suddenly. 'Like a prince in a fairy-tale.'

Mhairi's heart lurched. 'Willy Macrae?'

'Of course not.' Annys gave her a conspiratorial smile. '*Him.*'

'I haven't the least idea who you are talking about,' said Mhairi, pushing past her with the tray of incriminating china, though she knew it was already too late.

'I mean Mr Adam, of course. Especially in that beautiful riding jacket, with that cream brocade waistcoat and...'

'Mr Adam called with his nephew to apologize for his nephew's behaviour and to ask after Hamish,' said Mhairi, a little too quickly. 'That is all. And for pity's sake stop mauling that hen about. You'll rip the skin to shreds. If you can't pluck a bird properly at your age I don't know where I went wrong. Get out of my way and let me do it.'

'Yes, Mhairi,' said Annys, unperturbed. She watched her sister in silence as Mhairi began to strip the breast feathers, with neat, angry hands. After a moment Annys added, as one woman to another, 'It's all right, you know. I will not breathe a word to Tom, I promise.'

Then began a time of secret enchantment for Mhairi. She had forgotten what it was like to be in love, to think of someone every waking hour and fall asleep embracing the dream. To feel young again and pretty, every sense alert to the world's beauty. During her seven years of widowhood, she had schooled her body to deny desire, but now that carapace of ice cracked into splinters and she felt her blood stir once more into lusty life.

At first, she was decorous and circumspect, met him only as if by accident, in the coffee room of the Royal Hotel, in the reading rooms, in St Nicholas' kirkyard, where she went regularly to tend her parents' and her husband's graves. Then, as she emerged from her widow's chrysalis, they grew less circumspect and took to meeting on the riverbank, or in the woods of Persley Den. In the softness of the summer woods, it became harder and harder to refuse him anything. Afterwards, whenever she thought of woods, she saw the shielding canopy of tender leaves, felt the softness of the grass beneath them, layered as it was with moss and last year's leaf mould, heard the birdsong when she closed her eyes against the sunlight, felt the touch of his lips on her eyelids, then, more sweetly, on her lips. She remembered every passionate curve and strength of his body with a longing she had thought forgotten for ever, and instead of feeling shame, her heart sang within her, drowning out the voice of warning. It was high summer and she was in love.

Annys was true to her word. If she noticed any difference in Mhairi she made no comment. If Mhairi disappeared for several hours and came back smiling, pink-cheeked and dishevelled, though the day was calm, Annys pretended not to notice. Most important of all, she said nothing to Tom.

But Tom, like everyone else that summer, had things on his mind. Yard and quarry alike had more work than they could handle and when he was not riding about the countryside checking up on the progress of this building or that, Tom's full attention was taken up with work sheets and contracts, estimates and schedules. Since Donal had returned from that Deeside trip with a sheaf of full and accurate drawings, they had acquired firm orders for several similarly turreted mansions, two in the country and three in the better part of town, as well as serious inquiries for as many more.

Meanwhile, the building which was their inspiration steadily progressed and though the new castle would not be complete in time for the queen's autumn visit, the tower and adjoining rooms being still only half built, the main rooms were ready, splendidly carpeted with Clan tartan and equipped by a London firm with furniture of African ash. The queen herself was in Paris.

'Dressed in plain Scotch plaid,' as Mrs Wyness complained to her daughter in a mixture of disapproval and astonishment. 'With a white bonnet and white lace mantelet. Very unprepossessing for a queen. And they say the French set such store by the clothes a person wears. What must they think of her?'

'That she is a sensible housewife who does not throw away money unnecessarily?' teased Fanny. 'I wonder if she will come across Lettice Adam in Paris?'

'Why ever should she?' snapped Mrs Wyness who, as usual, had had a tiring day. What with those endless "comforts" to be dispatched to Balaclava and charity concerts and the like to be organized for the Patriotic Fund as well as the usual local soup kitchens and relief of the poor, she had hardly a minute to herself, let alone any time to spend with her grandchildren. Only two so far, thank the Lord, but no doubt there would be more. Fanny never had been blessed with sense. 'What has Lettice Adam got to do with the Queen?' she grumbled, 'And this tea is cold. I cannot abide cold tea.'

'I am sorry, Mamma,' soothed Fanny, in whose house they were. 'Let me pour you fresh. It does get cold rather quickly in these particular cups.' Especially if you are too busy grumbling to drink it, she added under her breath, but was far too good-natured to say so aloud. 'As to Lettice Adam,' she went on when her mother's cup had been emptied and refilled, to her grudging satisfaction, 'You will remember she and her husband were to spend some months in Paris, while he worked at a special hospital there. It is very possible that their paths might have crossed.'

'Why? Is the Queen ill?'

Fanny suppressed a sigh before saying patiently, 'I sincerely hope not, Mamma, for you know that preparations are already in hand to welcome her here in September, less than three weeks away now. And you are quite right. Paris is a big place and it was silly of me to suggest such a thing.' Then, to divert her mother from further argument, she said quickly, 'I wonder when Lettice will come home again and whether the doctor will come with her?'

'Now it is extraordinary that you should say that,' said her mother, irritation forgotten and a gleam of new interest in her eye. 'Mrs Macdonald mentioned the subject this very morning. You would not think it possible, but she told me that she has it on the best authority, the very best, that Lettice Adam is a *changed woman*.'

Fanny raised an eyebrow. 'Really? In what way?'

'In every way,' said her mother portentously and Fanny had the greatest difficulty suppressing a smile.

After a moment she said brightly, 'Well, very soon we shall see, for Jessie told me that her sister told her that the dust-sheets have been put away in the house in the Guestrow and all the chandeliers untied.' Jessie was the kitchenmaid. 'She did not know whether food had been ordered for the kitchen yet, but she said the whole house was to be aired and the brasses polished.'

'Really, Fanny. I have told you a hundred times not to gossip with the servants,' frowned her mother. Then curiosity got the better of her. 'Were the beds to be aired, too?'

[93]

'I believe so. And Jessie said the cook had orders to hire an extra scullerymaid.'

'Well, well. Mrs Macdonald made no mention of it, but you can be certain someone is coming home, and soon. I wonder which of them it will be?'

Annys Diack could hardly contain her excitement. Fortunately most of Aberdeen was in similar turmoil and the girl's bright eyes and air of joyful expectation were put down simply to the imminent arrival of the Queen, with all the attendant junketings and celebrations. They were not to know that her patient combing of the newspaper columns had trawled up a pearl.

In all the long descriptions of the siege of Sebastopol, the disposition of troops and munitions, the digging of trenches, the transport of supplies, the movement of the wounded from battlefront to hospital, Annys sought only the mention of those valiant labourers who had sailed out to brave the Russian winter and build the railway lifeline between Sebastopol and the port of Balaclava. In spite of her sister-in-law Fanny's involvement in fund-raising, even Miss Nightingale's work in Scutari was of little interest to her. Naturally, out of consideration for his mother, she kept a dutiful eye open for word of Willy Macrae's regiment, but, that aside, her interest was concentrated solely on tracing the movements of those labourers hired by Thomas Brassey and the firm of Peto & Betts.

The line had been finished, she knew that. Many of the labourers had come home, or gone to work elsewhere. Others had stayed on to maintain the line, or to help build the Sanitarium on a hillside above the port. Already Dr Jephson's hospital, she read, had the appearance of a curative village. Lord Raglan himself had inspected it and approved the new plan of ventilation for the little huts that would be built on the plateau five hundred feet above the sea. There was to be a reservoir, too, and gardens, and already the workmen had built a good, firm road up the sides of the ravine to the hospital. Kit O'Brien had worked on that road, she was sure of it. Willy Macrae's letter had mentioned a 'Kit'. For in all the hundreds of navvies in the Crimea there might be more than one 'cheerful Irishman who had worked on the laying of the Aberdeen railway', but there could be only one 'Kit'. 'I'll miss the fellow when he leaves,' Willy had written, 'but I've told him to call on you, Ma, and give you all my news.' Willy had not said

[94]

when this would be, but the implication had been that it would be soon.

Then Annys, after sifting through the reports of Lord Raglan's death and the latest news of the siege of Sebastopol, had turned to the local shipping news and found, among the sailings and arrivals, notice of a ship from Balaclava, on its way home, and knew it to be the one. Kit O'Brien was coming back. The ship was bound for London, but that did not matter. He would come to Aberdeen somehow, sometime, and when he did ... She gazed dreamily into the tiny mirror, wondering if he would see a difference in her, see the woman instead of the gauche and inexperienced girl? She slipped a hand into her pocket and felt the reassuring polish of that pebble he had tossed to her, was it really only a mere nine months before? It seemed as if it had happened years ago, in another lifetime. But she had been a schoolgirl then, with no understanding of love. Now, she was more mature.

'Annys!' called Mhairi from the scullery. 'Will you be long?'

'Coming!' Annys sighed with pity. Poor Mhairi. She had looked so happy when Mr Adam kissed her. He was like a medieval courtier, handsome, courteous and strong. The picture of the pair of them, in that loving embrace against the simple backdrop of the cottage kitchen, was burned indelibly into her mind. They had not heard her, of course, and she had sped on silent tiptoe back into the scullery to wait until the door closed behind him. But she had seen, had heard him murmur words of love. It was so romantic. The prince and the goosegirl. Not that Mhairi was a goosegirl of course, amended Annys with a blush at her own disloyalty. Perhaps Romeo and Juliet would be a more appropriate analogy: star-crossed lovers divided by family enmity. Except that they were both too old. Mhairi was *twenty-seven*. As for Mr Adam, he was positively middle-aged. Thirty at least and probably more. But they were so right for each other, Annys dreamed, and why should they not be happy together for ever, as they had been for the past sweet weeks of summer. Annys had guarded their secret well. Though she knew when Mhairi set out 'to do a little marketing in town', smart and spruce and with an air of suppressed excitement about her, that she went to meet her lover, Annys had not breathed a word to anyone, and especially not to Tom. She understood the need for secrecy. For, remembering that dreadful scene when he had forbidden Mhairi to go to Lettice Adam's wedding, she knew that however happy Fergus Adam and Mhairi were together, their love was doomed. Her brother Tom would never countenance it. Never, she repeated sadly, till the end of time. Poor Mhairi . . .

'Annys! Did you hear me? For pity's sake hurry up or we'll never find a place.'

'Coming!' She took a last look in the mirror, patted her hair into place, and bit her lips to make them pink.

'If you are not ready in *one minute*, we're going without you.'

With a sigh, Annys hitched a plaid over her shoulders and closed the bedroom door. It was a pity love made some people so irritable.

The message came by electric telegraph that the royal party had passed through Stonehaven, fifteen miles down the coast, and was approaching Aberdeen. They had hardly time to digest this thrilling news when, to the delight of the waiting crowds, the guard's signal announced the train's imminent approach and the royal engine and eight carriages steamed into Ferryhill Station one minute ahead of time, at precisely nine minutes past two.

The Queen had travelled by railway all the way from London, staying overnight at Holyrood Castle in Edinburgh before embarking on the final stretch of the journey. She had graciously agreed that her train should stand three minutes in the station so that her loyal subjects of Aberdeen might welcome her with due ceremony, and two companies of royal militia were drawn up as a guard of honour on the platform while the band played appropriate music. The provost and other dignitaries of the town had assembled in a specially constructed enclosure, together with directors of the Deeside Railway and a large number of invited ladies and gentlemen, and the station had been lavishly adorned with greenery, loyal banners and appropriate emblems of welcome.

George Wyness had a seat in the garlanded enclosure, with his wife in voluminous mazarine silk beside him. He had offered to procure seats for Tom and Fanny, and for Mhairi too if she wished, but, like her brother Tom, Mhairi had declined, though for different reasons. Tom had work to do, he said, and better ways to spend his time than loitering about on a station platform for hours on end in order to shout 'hurrah' at a train. As to patriotism, he could show that just as well and better by the honest pursuit of his trade.

Fanny, out of wifely loyalty, had refused to go without him, whether into the enclosure with her father, or onto the platform with

Mhairi, though she would dearly like to have seen the royal arrival from either place. As for Mhairi, she had thanked Mr Wyness but explained that she really had nothing suitable to wear and anyway the children would much prefer the freedom of the common platform, especially as Hamish hoped to speak to the engine driver. It would be unfair to expect Annys to watch her children for her, with so much else to occupy her eyes and interest, so she would do so herself.

In truth, she could not accept Mr Wyness's offer because she had already refused Fergus.

'Sit with me openly, for all the town to see,' he had urged, when he had tracked her down unexpectedly in St Nicholas kirkyard, on one of her regular visits to tend her parents' and her husband's graves. He stood looking down at her, his athletic outline clean-cut against the August sky, his face in shadow, and Mhairi felt love flood through her in a rush so strong it took her breath away. Only by looking deliberately at those bleak words carved into the stone did she prevent herself rising from her knees and kissing him in full view of the town. *Alexander Grant died September 1848 aged 23.* Her husband.

'Afterwards we will drive home to Silvercairns and you shall stroll about the gardens with me before I give you dinner,' Fergus was saying, his voice low and vibrant with love. 'Bring your children, too, if you wish, and your sister. All who are dear to you are dear to me and there is room enough for all. But we will escape them for a little while, to be alone together.'

Mhairi had felt longing rise inside her like a thirst. To spend a day with him, a whole, blessed day, would be paradise. Then she had remembered Tom.

'I am sorry, Fergus, but I dare not. Not yet. Please let us keep our love secret a little longer? If I came with you to Silvercairns, even if some helpful busybody did not report it to Tom, the children would be so excited they would talk about nothing else for days and it would filter through to him that way.'

'Does it really matter what your brother thinks? He is not the one I want to sit beside me in the special enclosure. Sometimes I think you do not love me at all. You will not come to the theatre with me, or out to dinner. You will not even drive home with me, to my own house, with your family as chaperones. I begin to think you are ashamed to be seen in the company of an Adam.'

'Ashamed? How can you say such a thing when I am awed and

[97]

proud and ...' But as Mhairi had looked helplessly around the sombre churchyard the words had died in her throat. Fergus was right. They were not criminals, had nothing to be ashamed of, were both free to meet who they chose, where and when they chose. So why was she so hesitant and afraid? It was not the thought of Alex, dear though he was to her. Alex would be glad that she had found happiness at last, and Fergus was a good man who would bring up Alex's children as his own.

No, she confessed with an inward shudder. It was Tom. The memory of his cruel taunt 'You fancy him' still rang too raucously through her mind, with the cold insult of his apology and the lingering hurt. In truth she was afraid that if they moved too soon Tom's anger would shatter her happiness, soil the rainbow colours of their secret love and destroy the bloom for ever.

She was crouching over Alex's grave, arranging a posy of flowers in a jar, and she had looked up at Fergus with eyes that begged for understanding. 'I long more than anything to stand beside you before the whole world, Fergus, but not yet. You see, I am afraid. I need time to soothe Tom's prejudices, to reconcile him to the idea of amnesty, even, one day, to actual friendship. Otherwise ...' but she could not expect him to understand the strength of family loyalty which bound the Diacks tight in unity, and which would be irretrievably shattered if she were to marry Fergus against Tom's will. Although he had not said so in as many words, she did not doubt that marriage was what Fergus had in mind. Anything else would be an insult, both to her and to him. But Fergus's own family had not been renowned for unity: why should he understand?

'Please Fergus?' she said, sitting back on her heels in an attitude of unconscious grace. 'Bear with me just a little longer? Until I can be sure that Tom will not mind.'

'And what about my minding? I am not sure how much longer I can bear to wait.' He had looked at her with such passionate eyes that she had blushed, then looked hastily to either side, lest someone see.

'Nor I,' she confessed, and saw his expression soften. They kissed and made up in the shadow of the church porch, whispered loving reassurances and kissed again, until they were interrupted by a party of mourners preparing for a funeral. Not a good omen, thought Mhairi with a stir of foreboding, as they said their decorous goodbyes at the kirkyard gate.

But on that September morning of sunshine and excitement, Mhairi forgot all anxiety for the future in the jubilant pleasures of the present.

'Although you refuse to take my arm in public and sit beside me to welcome our queen,' Fergus had teased her, 'Promise you will wave to me? Or at least send me a smile across the crowds? Otherwise my day will be desolate.'

And she had kept her promise. She had shepherded Annys, Catriona and Hamish to a suitable vantage point on the platform and, under the guise of seeking out Mr Wyness and his wife, had scanned the flamboyant ranks of the special enclosure until she found what she was looking for. Her wave and radiant smile could as easily have been for the elderly, top-hatted gentleman with the grisled side-whiskers and the portly wife in blue, as for that other, slimmer figure on the row behind, with the red-headed boy beside him. But every time she looked across the packed station platform to that special, flag-decked enclosure and his handsome figure, straight-backed and correct in dark suit and gleaming top hat, diamond sparkling from immaculate cravat, she saw him looking at her and read the love in his caressing eyes. Happiness filled her with a secret, overflowing joy which seemed to be echoed all around her in the cheerful expectation of the crowd.

'Everyone who is anyone in the town seems to be here,' said Annys, with apparent innocence. 'And isn't that Mr Adam in the enclosure, sitting just behind Mrs Wyness?'

'Is it?' Mhairi shrugged with feigned unconcern. The incident of Annys in the scullery and her seeing, or not seeing, Mhairi and Fergus embrace, had not been mentioned since. If Annys knew more than she implied, she concealed it well and Mhairi, for her part, preferred to ignore the whole affair. Officially, Fergus Adam was of no more concern to her now than before. Officially, Annys accepted this. It was a charade they were both, for different reasons, content to play. 'I did not notice, Annys. But whether he is or not, it is surely no business of ours. Look Catriona,' and she hoisted the child up by the armpits the better to see, 'The train is coming into the station.'

Annys opened her mouth to pursue the point, but before she could speak, saw something that stopped the words in her throat.

'Watch how the wheels go slower and slower,' Mhairi was saying beside her, while in her arms Catriona wriggled with excitement and

[99]

Annys felt Hamish's hand tugging in hers as he struggled to break free. '. . . until they stop . . . just . . . here.'

The train ground to a triumphant halt in a sigh of escaping steam and all eyes turned to the windows of the royal coach where the queen herself could be clearly seen. All eyes, that is, but those of Annys Diack. Her astonished gaze had been caught by a movement at the rear of the train where, one foot on the step and hanging from the rearmost coach by one hand, was a figure in tattered moleskin trousers and work-worn jacket, cap rakishly askew above weather-tanned face and wind-tousled hair.

A great cheer lifted from the crowd and was redoubled as Her Majesty rose and bowed graciously through the train window, and it was at this precise moment, when all attention was focussed on the royal coach, that Annys saw the figure jump neatly to the platform, adjust the canvas bag on his shoulder, and stroll nonchalantly towards her, a familiar swagger in his step. Then the shifting crowd closed ranks and he was lost to view, leaving Annys white with shock and trembling with astonished joy.

Kit O'Brien had come back.

In the royal carriage, someone was attending to the windows so that both passengers and spectators might have a better view. More cheers greeted the lowering of the window glass while the band played and the royal children waved. The scheduled three minutes came and went with no sign of departure. Apparently there was some sort of trouble with an over-heated axle and the train would rest in the station till the fault was righted. But from what they could see through the open windows, everyone agreed the royal carriages were very elegant and comfortable.

Princess Victoria was clearly visible, a sketch-book in her hand.

'I believe she is drawing in it, to pass the time,' said Mhairi. 'Imagine, Annys. She is almost exactly the same age as you are.'

When Annys made no answer, but seemed to be staring dumb-struck into space, Mhairi added, 'I wonder what her subject is.'

'Us, of course,' said Catriona and Hamish added, 'Or the train.'

From Ferryhill, the royal train was to travel on to Banchory on the Deeside line. Here, another crowd was already assembled, under a splendid arch proclaiming 'Victoria and Albert, welcome back to your Highland Home,' and with a stretch of Crimea carpet ready to lead from train to Refreshment Room and the elegant lunch which awaited the royal party there. Mhairi had heard it from one of her customers over a dress fitting. The lady in question had a married sister in Banchory who was to be among the welcoming group and had given her sister all the details, down to the three vases of exquisite wax flowers, though not, unfortunately, an invitation to the ceremony. Hamish, however, was not interested in flowers, wax or otherwise. All he wanted to see was the train, for since his trip on the Deeside line he had talked of little else. So when Hamish begged to be allowed to push his way to the front of the platform and look at the engine, Mhairi agreed. 'But take care, now. Mind you do not go too close. And come back here, to this pillar, the moment the train is ready to go. Annys and I will walk about a little, with Catriona, to see who we can see.'

'No,' cried Annys, jerking suddenly awake. 'I will wait here alone. So that we do not lose each other.'

'But we are far more likely to lose each other that way,' said Mhairi in surprise. 'It would be foolish to separate. However, if you do not wish to stroll about, we will stay here until Hamish comes back. Oh look!' she cried, interrupting whatever protest Annys was about to make. 'Isn't that Lettice Adam? The fair-haired lady in the pale blue dress and white straw bonnet, standing with her back to us by that open carriage door? The third carriage from the back. Though the gentleman with her is certainly not Dr Marshall. It looks more like ...'

'Mr Drummond,' said Annys. She was blushing and her eyes and her attention seemed to be wandering all over the crowd.

'Are you looking for somebody?' asked Mhairi, curious.

'No, no,' said Annys hastily and added, before Mhairi could question her further, 'And the lady is not Lettice Adam at all. She is far too short. You will see when she turns her head. There, what did I tell you. It is Miss Drummond. Miss Henrietta Drummond. She came to coffee with Fanny while I was staying there and though she said very little, she was very charming and pleasant.'

'Why, so it is. Of course. I remember when she and her brother visited Rainbow Hill in the spring. Her brother is quite a personable gentleman,' went on Mhairi thoughtfully. 'Wasn't he the gentleman you mentioned seeing at Lettice Adam's wedding?' She looked sideways at Annys who, she noticed for the first time, looked decidedly bright-eyed and agitated, her cheeks charmingly pink.

[101]

'Like a prince in a fairy-tale,' she teased, 'with that golden hair and handsome, straight-nosed profile. Did you meet him, too, when you were staying with Fanny?'

'No.' But when Mhairi looked closely at her sister, she blushed even more.

Then perhaps it is time such a meeting was arranged, thought Mhairi, with dawning interest. There and then the germ of the idea took hold and blossomed. It was not completely impossible, after all. Annys was young, of course, but obviously much struck by the gentleman or she would not be blushing as she was, and Mr Drummond, though his father did have some sort of an estate in England, did not give himself airs. He was connected with the railways, Mhairi understood, in an advisory capacity as a surveyor or an engineer. She was not sure which, and it did not matter: what mattered was that he was unmarried, and though a gentleman was not one of Tom's scorned 'idle rich'.

'Look after the family for me, Mhairi,' her mother had begged her on her deathbed. 'See Annys grows up right,' and Mhairi had done her best. Annys was a daughter her mother would have been proud of: virtuous and honest, beautiful and true. Mhairi's younger brothers were grown men now and could take care of themselves. All that remained for Mhairi to do was to see Annys wed, then her job would be over, her debt to her mother paid, and, she thought with new excitement, she herself would be free.

But she did not want Annys to marry into poverty as she had done. To be sure, they were not poor now, though not rich either, but if Alex had lived, she might have had half a dozen children by now instead of merely two. How far would the money have stretched then? How would her health have stood up to the childbearing and the constant struggle to make ends meet? How would their love have survived? That, Mhairi would never know. But she did not want Annys to run that risk. Annys must marry into a better life than that of a quarry-worker's wife.

Annys was shy and beautiful, with gentle manners and a graceful bearing. She had met Miss Drummond on an equal footing in Fanny's drawing-room. Moreover she was well educated and the cleverest of them all. Why should she not marry well? Mr Drummond had made inquiries at the Wyness yard about a fountain for his father's estate. That would provide the perfect opening, and when he met Annys he could not fail but be charmed by her, thought Mhairi

[102]

with a mother's partiality, the more so as Annys herself had obviously fallen already under his spell. She wanted Annys to be as happy as she was, in love with a good man who loved her in return. Mhairi resolved to confide in Fanny at the first opportunity and enlist her help.

'I assume they have come north for the season,' said Mhairi now. 'Or perhaps for Miss Drummond's health. I wonder where they will be staying?'

But before the day was out, the tea-tables of Aberdeen were buzzing with that very news. Word had come from Paris that Lettice Adam's husband had offered his services to the nation's wounded in the Crimea, and was already on his way there. Lettice Adam had gone with him. 'To be at her husband's side in his hour of peril,' said the more sentimental, touching handkerchief to moistened eye. 'To make sure he doesn't escape,' said the more brutal. 'Or take up with a dark-eyed Muscovite beauty and go native.'

As to the house in the Guestrow which had been so thoroughly dusted and aired, the patriotic couple had let it, dust-sheets, chandeliers, new scullerymaid and all, to Philip Drummond and his sister Henrietta.

Fergus found the letter waiting for him when he returned from the day's celebrations and carried it into the library, to read in peace in front of a relaxing wood fire, while he awaited the dinner gong. He lit a cigar, settled into his favourite chair with the day's newspapers within reach, and, unsuspecting, took up the letter and broke the seal.

Unfolding the stiff paper, Fergus thought to find a short note from Lettice, written in her usual peremptory style, ordering him to oversee whatever instructions she had given to her housekeeper in preparation for her return, to chivvy up the dressmaker, see the game was well hung, check the contents of the cellar. She would also no doubt tell him where and when to meet her in order to have the privilege of driving her and her husband home, for, contrary to the general opinion of the town, Fergus still believed they would return together. Lettice might, if she remembered, append a warning to 'young Leo' not to forget his lessons and to behave, but Fergus expected little else.

Instead, he found a closely written page in which his sister

[103]

informed him that David, in the course of his researches in Paris into post-operative sepsis and the infection of wounds, had caught the notice of a military man and in consequence had been approached by the War Department to go to the Bospherus to assist the Sanitary Commissioners in carrying out the instructions they had been given. In short, he was to lend his knowledge to the Barrack Hospital at Scutari in the great fight against avoidable suffering and death. *As you will have seen, brother dear (if ever you raise your worthy nose sufficiently above the rim of your precious quarry to read a newspaper) she they call the Lady-in-Chief, the Lady Florence, Miss Nightingale, is fighting her own battle to bring about a radical change in the running of our military so-called hospitals and by so doing to reduce the figure of unnecessary deaths. Already it is down from over 3,000 in January to just over 1,000 this month.* Fergus glanced to the top of the letter and saw to his surprise that it was dated June, three months ago, from an address in Scutari, though why it had taken so long to reach him he did not know. The hazards of war, no doubt. With new attention, he resumed reading.

But the fight is not yet over. Of course, dear David had no hesitation (no choice, more likely, commented Fergus) *and we travelled to the Bospherus at once, delaying only long enough to collect as many necessary supplies as we could carry with us. There are still hospitals where the sick and dying have no shirts to their backs, where medical supplies are barely sufficient for a hundred let alone a thousand patients, but fortunately David knew what best to take.*

At first, David urged me to go home to Aberdeen (he fears I might catch a virulent fever or the cholera which is distressingly rife) but if Lady Florence can survive, I told him, so can I. Besides, in the hearts of thousands of our people there is a yearning to be able to share the toil and hardship, the danger and distress of caring for our sick and wounded soldiers who lie in so many endless ranks of hopeless misery and why should I not feel something of the same? A diet of opulence and entertainment has its limits and there is a boredom in the parade of the latest crinoline or so-called witticism which can become insupportable. I do not pretend to any medical skill, and you, dear brother, will no doubt be the first to say my patience is not all it might be, nor my compassion. But I am strong-willed and determined. Some may call these faults, but they are positive virtues in the morass of bureaucratic muddle which still bedevils our military hospitals and I have no doubt I can turn them to good use on behalf of both David and the Lady-in-Chief. So you may tell Fanny Wyness and her worthy

[104]

mother, if you happen to see them, that their efforts on behalf of the Barrack Hospital at Scutari will be much appreciated, especially if they send twice the amount of help, twice as fast.

I am growing used to the sight of suffering, Fergus, but it does not become easier to bear, either for the victim or for the nurse. Be grateful for peace and good health. I think of you and Silvercairns more often than I should, but when this war is over, which pray God will be soon, we will come home again to Aberdeen. Tell young Leo that I will bring him a Russian Officer's helmet if he has behaved himself, and possibly a sabre as well. Your affectionate sister. Lettice Adam Marshall. Post-script: The Guestrow House will be occupied by Philip Drummond and his virtuous sister until our return. See they do not steal the silver.

Thoughtfully Fergus folded the letter, only to open it again and re-read it, twice over. Behind the brittle exterior of the old Lettice, which was still apparent here and there, was a new, more thoughtful and compassionate side which he had not suspected. Reading between the lines of that last paragraph, Fergus divined that Lettice was not merely hectoring the administrators to do this and that, but herself was actually nursing the sick and dying. She was also, unless he was woefully mistaken, homesick. Lettice had never been one to express affection, and Fergus was touched by her thoughts of home, and by her promise of gifts for Leo. Not only had she remembered the boy, but had selected just the presents to send him wild with joy. Though the prospect of Leo in a Russian helmet with a Russian sabre in his hand was not a reassuring one. Fergus only hoped the sabre would be blunt.

'What's that?' demanded the boy himself, bursting into the library as if summoned by a genie's lamp. At Fergus's frown of warning, he skidded to a halt, and shot out again, slamming the door behind him, only to give it a token knock and burst in again with scarcely a pause.

'You are supposed to wait until I say "Come in",' sighed Fergus. 'How many more times do I have to tell you?'

'Sorry,' said Leo, unrepentant. 'What's that paper? Ma Gregor says you've had a letter from Aunt Lettice. Is that it? Ma Gregor says . . .'

'Mrs Gregor to you. And speak properly if you expect me to answer.' But he spoke without rancour. To pour manners into Leo Lennox was like trying to fill a sieve. He would have given up trying long ago had his conscience permitted, but he felt responsible for the orphaned lad. Had the boy had a mother, of course, she would have taught him from the cradle the rudiments of courtesy and he would have been spared the effort of this long-running and fruitless battle.

Then, with a stir of unease, Fergus remembered that Leo did indeed have a mother, somewhere in Australia, though he doubted whether good manners featured high on her list of priorities. With that disturbing memory came another: his sister Lettice saying *Suppose that dreadful mother of his has made a fortune in the gold diggings and comes home to claim him?* It was not long since a ship had arrived from Sydney with more than a thousand ounces of gold and nearly two thousand sovereigns, all the product of those wretched diggings, which had lured too many hopefuls half across the world in the expectation of gain. Though most of them would be disappointed, some undoubtedly would make a fortune, and some of those fortunate ones would come home again to boast and parade their wealth before their envious townsfellows. Remembering the pert young scullerymaid who had fled to Australia with her 'buying-off money' and a handful of Lettice Adam's jewellery, Fergus thought sourly that it was just the sort of thing Lizzie Lennox would do. The thought fuelled his conscience and his strength of will.

'This, Leo, is indeed a letter from Aunt Lettice. But you will not hear one word of it until you remember your manners and speak as a gentleman should.'

Leo opened his mouth to say 'Won't' but changed his mind, though his face was pinched tight with rebellion. He rubbed the back of one leg with the boot of the other in hesitation, then as Fergus folded the letter and tucked it away in his inside jacket pocket, curiosity won.

'Please Uncle Fergus, read me Aunt Lettice's letter? And I know it is Mrs Gregor really, but everyone else calls her Ma behind her back and ... Sorry.' When Fergus still said nothing, but took up the newspaper from a sidetable and opened it, Leo said carefully, 'Mrs Gregor said you had had a letter from Aunt Lettice. I would like to know what is in it, Uncle Fergus. Please?'

'I suppose that will have to do,' sighed Fergus, folding the newspaper again and laying it down. In reality he was delighted with the progress he had made. At least the boy was beginning to know what he ought to do and one day he might actually remember to do it without prompting. Fergus was reminded of how Mhairi had dealt with Leo on that visit to the cottage and marvelled afresh at her calm

[106]

and friendly handling of the lad. She would make an ideal mother for him, one day.

One day. The memory of her holding back and the reason for it brought a momentary frown, but the doubt passed. She had no need to ask her brother's permission to marry: she wanted only his approval, so that family harmony should not be broken. She loved Fergus. He had not the smallest doubt of that. And her loyalty towards her family was an essential part of her and one he would not wish to change, even supposing he had the power. She was strong and straight and true and there was no other woman he wanted for a wife, to cherish him as he would cherish her, and to bear his children. Past enmities could not be obliterated, but they could be forgiven and forgotten. As to business rivalry, the town was big enough for both of them. Besides, Silvercairns presented no challenge to the Wyness Polishing Yard: in fact, Silvercairns could provide the yard with the highest quality granite it could wish for for those monuments and fountains and similar triumphs of the granite polisher's art. At least, for the foreseeable future.

With a jolt Fergus remembered the 'dead' half of the quarry, the unknown quantity of harvest still to be reaped. But already he was working on a plan for a future should that harvest fail, and there was no need to let such a remote possibility colour his hopes today. Or to mention the matter to Tom Diack. Mhairi knew of his doubts, of course, and of his plans for Willowbrae, but she would keep his confidence. Firmly he thrust doubt aside.

He would marry Mhairi Grant and by so doing cancel out past differences and forge a new and beneficial link between the two camps: Silvercairns Quarry and the Wyness Polishing Yard. It was a link Fergus's own father had angled for, years ago, to no avail. But his father was dead and things were different now. Once the brother realized what financial advantages the marriage would bring, his antagonism would vanish, and he would give Mhairi his blessing.

'Please, Uncle Fergus?'

Fergus had forgotten Leo in the thoughts the boy's presence had called up. Now he smiled, drew out the letter and said, 'Shall I read it to you? Or would you prefer to read it yourself?'

'You please, Uncle Fergus. My eyes are tired today.'

This was Leo's usual excuse to avoid the effort of reading, but for once Fergus let it pass.

'Very well. And if you listen quietly, without interrupting every

[107]

second word, we might take the horses out together later. I've been meaning to investigate the land on the west of the quarry for a long time and it is a beautiful evening for a ride.'

During the long summer months Tom had fallen into the habit of coming home late, for when it was daylight till after ten at night, why not make use of it? The only exception had been on the night of the celebrations for the fall of Sebastopol: bonfires, fireworks, singing and celebrations way into the small hours. The stationmaster at Banchory got £50 reward for conveying the news to Her Majesty at Balmoral, where everyone from Prince Albert to the lowest ghillie climbed the hill behind the house to light the celebratory bonfire, in a salvo of gunfire and bagpipes, before drinking and dancing the night away.

Even Tom had not had the face to refuse his workmen leave to celebrate with the rest of the country and, work out of the question for the day, he had offered to take Fanny and the little ones into town to watch the fireworks and the pipe bands. When Fanny suggested that Mhairi and her family join them, Tom had raised no objection and for a brief time they had forgotten friction and disagreement in an evening of relaxed celebration. But September would soon be over, the leaves turning on the trees and a nip of autumn in the air.

On an evening some two weeks after the Sebastopol celebrations, Tom was home later than ever. It was nigh on eleven when Fanny heard the front door close and when Tom came into the room he collapsed into a chair, stretched out his legs and closed his eyes, without a word.

Fanny set aside her sewing, rose quietly and went to stand beside him. She laid a cool hand on his forehead and he opened his eyes briefly to smile at her before closing them again with a sigh of exhaustion.

'You work too hard, dear,' said Fanny. 'I worry for you.'

'I work for you,' he said, without opening his eyes. 'And for our children.'

Who you never see, thought Fanny with rare bitterness. Aloud, she said, 'I know you do, Tom, and I am grateful. But ...' She stopped, uncertain how to go on. She knew the slightest criticism of his work sparked him to anger, knew how touchy he was on the subject of money, especially hers. Even her shares in the company

[108]

were a potential source of anger, for he persisted in denying himself all right to them.

Now his eyes jerked open, instantly on the defensive. 'But what?'

'But I miss you,' she said, with bleak simplicity. 'Sometimes I feel almost as lonely as I did when you were in Australia.'

For a moment she thought he would explode into anger, but the moment passed. Instead he pulled her down onto his knee and held her in his arms, in silence, his cheek against her hair. She was shocked, and deeply moved to feel a tear-drop slide across her forehead and knew it to be his.

'I am weary, Fanny,' he said at last. 'Weary to my soul.'

She knew better than to suggest he take a holiday. 'Is it the building work?' she asked gently. 'Or the quarry?'

'Everything. The business is grown too big, like a child's foot in last year's shoe. We ought to expand with that growth, take on more men, lease a new quarry perhaps, but it would be a gamble, in the beginning, and George Wyness is a cautious man. I know he is your father, Fanny, and I mean no offence to him or to you, but I must say it. He has no foresight. He gathers more and more custom, as any good businessman does, but with no thought of how the extra work is to be done. We are expected to welcome and deal with it, without extra manpower and without any lack of skill or efficiency. It is not humanly possible, Fanny. Lorn and Willy agree with me, and even Mhairi complained the other day that young Hamish was working too long hours. Too long hours, at the age of eight, and after a day's schooling. We are a family business, Fanny, not a sweat shop.'

'I think you should tell my father exactly what you have told me,' said Fanny, kissing him gently on the eyelids. 'Because if you do not do so, then I promise you I will. I do not want my husband worked into the grave before I have had the enjoying of him. You must tell him tomorrow.'

'If I do, what reward will I get?'

'My undying devotion, of course, and,' she teased, murmuring against his ear, 'perhaps a little ... enjoyment?'

'Do you know, I believe I am not weary after all.' He pushed her from his knee and stood up. 'Though it is certainly time for bed.' They doused the lights, took a candle from the hall table, and, arms round each other's waists, went up the darkened stairs together.

The meeting was called for Saturday of the following week, in the yard office, all shareholders to be present, and all working members of the family, including Hamish.

'Never too young to start learning,' Wyness had told her when Mhairi protested. 'And the school's closed Saturdays so you've no excuse there. Besides, the lad might have something useful to say, and he'll have his own stake in the business one day. Don't forget that.'

Mhairi had not forgotten, as she had not forgotten the husband who had earned his son that stake. How could she ever forget Alex? she asked herself now, with a twinge of guilt, as she looked round the assembled company: Tom, Fanny, her brothers Will and Lorn, Donal with Hamish beside him, and George Wyness himself in the chair. *What would they think of her if they knew?*

She had seen Fergus only twice since the Queen's arrival, but each time had been an occasion of happiness the more piercing for its brevity. Fergus was busy not only with quarry work, but, since the arrival of the Drummonds, with shooting parties, excursions to inspect the progress of the Deeside railway, and other, more secret investigations of his own. But they had managed to meet once in the Royal Hotel coffee rooms, where he joined her, as if by accident, at her table; once in St Nicholas' church, which Mhairi preferred, for should anyone see her, what more natural than that she should say a quick prayer after tending her husband's and her parents' graves? If she felt any shame it was lost in the joy of Fergus's company, his arm at her waist, his lingering kiss in the shadow of the porch. On the last occasion he had told her he must go to Glasgow for a while, on business, but when he returned, she knew he would seek her out somehow. Her heart glowed at the thought and she lowered her eyes, lest anyone should guess her secret. She, Mhairi Diack Grant, mother of two and seven years a widow, was gloriously in love.

Surely Alex would not grudge her her happiness? He would not want her, as Tom did, to be lonely because of a memory, however dear. Besides, surely it was no disloyalty to the dead to love again? Not if the dead were still held precious? Yet, looking at the faces assembled at the table, she feared that one at least would not see it so. She had hoped to soften Tom's heart before now and certainly before the end of the year but, looking across the meeting table at his sombre face, her spirit faltered. How could she hope to bring about such a momentous change in a few short weeks?

'Well,' growled Wyness, frowning round the company. 'All present and correct? Then we may as well begin. This young stirk here has had the impudence to tell me my job. Aided and abetted, I have no doubt, by my own daughter. I am moribund and behind the times, a slave-driver, extortioner and heartless, grinding bully. Would you say that was a fair summing-up of the situation, Tom?'

Deliberately, Tom said, 'Yes.'

For a second Mhairi thought her brother had gone too far, then Wyness threw back his head and gave a shout of laughter. 'Well I'll be damned,' he repeated over and over. 'The brazen cheek of the lad.' Then, as suddenly as it had begun, his laughter stopped. 'Exaggeration aside, Tom has made a serious point, and one which must be seriously discussed and seriously dealt with. Agreed?'

The company nodded.

'Right. First complaint. Tom's says we've too much business for the men to deal with. What's on the order book, Tom lad?'

'There's the station works to be completed at the Branch line terminus; that tappitourie mansion for my whaling captain, a terrace of eight houses in Ferryhill, the new Free Church at Rayne, cassies for the New Town in Edinburgh and that load of road metal still promised to London, a reformatory at Oldmill, four more houses in ...'

'Hold on, hold on. Not so fast. You've got the order book by rote by the sound of it. And a full order book, no denying that. Nicely full. That means the quarry's nay lying idle.'

'The quarry's running at full speed, just to stand still,' said Tom. 'Isn't that right, Will?'

'Aye. And as often as not we leave ourselves behind. We're a month out with yon order for cassies as it is, and two, maybe three weeks with the ashlar for the Ferryhill job.'

Wyness frowned. 'What about the yard?'

'Three weeks' backlog,' put in Lorn quickly. 'Maybe four. Monument for London, promised for last month, still awaiting final polish. Double tomb for yon Perthshire gent, needing a granite block eight feet by four. The first one was cracked, remember, by some careless fool in a hurry. They're waiting a new one from the quarry. Then there's balustrades needed for Tom's mansion and a plinth for ...'

'That reminds me,' interrupted Wyness. 'I've one piece of good news for you. Though maybe I should more rightly say, good news and bad. You remember that fellow Drummond?'

Mhairi stiffened with interest: she had not forgotten her plans for Annys's future happiness, but had not yet found the right moment to mention it to Fanny. Besides, the Drummonds had disappeared somewhere into the country and there was little point until they came back. But Tom was speaking.

'With a sister? Came north for the Adam wedding and again, maybe a month back, for the shooting?'

'Aye, that's the one. Living in the Adams' Guestrow house when he's not wriggling on his belly through the heather, taking pot-shots at anything that moves. Well, he's ordered his fountain. Had a note today. He said Donal's design was far and away the best he'd seen the length of the country. Well done, Donal lad,' and he slapped Donal genially on the shoulder. 'There's only one flaw. He insists on granite from Silvercairns, for the colour.'

Tom drew in his breath on a hiss of annoyance.

'Nay, Tom, it's no use you getting on your high horse about it. The money's in the polishing and carving of the thing and if Drummond wants Silvercairns granite, then he shall have it. There's no denying it's a paler colour than our own and if you can't bring yourself to do business with the man, then you're not the fellow I took you for. I told you way back to sink your personal differences in honest to goodness trade rivalry, and now's your chance to sink them once and for all. If we're really as pushed to the limits as you say we are, then an alliance with Silvercairns might be just what we're needing. So I suggest you swallow your so-called grievances and get down to it.'

Tom opened his mouth as if to protest, then closed it again.

'Well Tom? Will you do it? Or would you rather I spoke to Adam myself?'

'I'll do it,' said Tom with reluctance, then shrugged and even managed a grin of sorts. 'If I must.'

'Fine. We can't afford to turn down good business.'

'And we can't afford to take it, Papa,' said Fanny, seeing her opening and snatching it while she could. 'At least, not unless you will consent to make the changes Tom suggests.'

'Changes? What changes?' glowered Wyness. 'I thought it was extra workers he wanted, so we can all go to bed early and sleep late.'

But Fanny's interruption had successfully diverted Tom's attention from Silvercairns and the future, to the present and Wyness himself.

'Aye, I do want extra workers,' cried Tom, striking his fist on the

[112]

table and half rising from his seat. 'And yes, I'd like to get home at nights before eleven. Who wouldn't if he had a wife and children he never saw? But that's not why I want more men. I want them so that we can complete our orders on time, like we used to. So we can hold our heads high with the best of them and concede superiority to none. Not Silvercairns nor Macdonalds nor Fyfes nor anyone. When did we last win a bonus for early delivery?' He jabbed an accusing finger in Wyness's direction. 'I'll tell you when. Three years ago. There was a time when the name Wyness guaranteed the quickest and the best. Not any more, by God. You've heard what Willy and Lorn have to say. Now, it's all we can do to scrape through at the last minute and we'll be late with that Bon Accord contract even if we work round the clock for an eight-day week. Weeks late. Ye canna sell what ye havena got and granite doesna quarry itself.' His accent broadened as his anger increased. 'It takes time and strength in the getting of it and one quarry canna supply the stone of two. Neither can one man do the work of two, however willing. Not without dropping dead from the strain of it. Or causing an accident through sheer exhaustion. This time it was only a cracked slab and no one nearby to suffer. Next time . . . '

But Tom's anger was burnt out, leaving him suddenly drained and weary.

'What's the use? I've said my piece. Now it's up to you.' He collapsed into his seat and held his head in his hands.

Mhairi saw Fanny lay a reassuring hand on his knee and whisper something in his ear. Suddenly she felt unbearably alone. That mention of accidents had reminded them all of Alex's death and Tom could not have thought of a better way to carry his point. But it was not Alex's arms she longed for to comfort and sustain her. Alex belonged to the past and it was the present that concerned her now. And the future. Remembering Tom's promise to negotiate with Silvercairns, she felt the first small ray of hope: surely when the men met face to face, on equal terms, Tom would realize that all Adams were not as black-hearted as Mungo Adam had been?

But George Wyness was speaking. With an effort she brought her attention back to the meeting and the airless, crowded room: by long tradition, windows and doors were kept closed for such policy meetings, for one never knew where a spy might lurk.

'. . . time to expand,' Wyness was saying. 'Tom is quite right. It would never do for word to get around that we canna meet our deadlines. Old Man Adam would be laughing in his grave. I've been thinking over the matter for some while now, and I'm grateful to Tom here for bringing things out into the open.'

Mhairi saw her opportunity. Now, quick, before she lost her nerve. 'You mentioned an arrangement with Silvercairns, Mr Wyness,' she said carefully. 'For the Drummond fountain. Would it not be possible to make that arrangement a permanent one, and ensure for ourselves a second source of granite, without the expense of quarrying it?'

She had expected an outburst from Tom, but after the first strangled grunt, none came. Instead it was Will who said, half facetiously, 'Anything's possible. Why not a pact with the devil himself while you're at it?'

'Don't listen to the loon, Mhairi. His wits are wandering,' frowned Wyness. 'That's a perfectly sensible suggestion of yours and worth considering. At the right price, of course,' and he winked at the company in general. 'I mind a time when Old Man Adam came round here with that same suggestion, thumping the table and bellowing when I didna fall down and lick his boots. But all he offered was the privilege of his name over my door and the use of my own canal boat when he'd finished with it. Grasping old devil.' Wyness sighed with what sounded like genuine regret. 'So if we do decide to do a deal, it'll be on our terms, all the way. And it might be the most sensible solution to Tom's problem, as well as having a kind of poetic justice. I can just see Old Man Adam writhing in his grave and gnashing his teeth with frustrated fury.'

'Just so long as he doesna climb out of it and haunt us,' said Lorn with a grin and earned himself a frown from Mhairi and a warning glance in Hamish's direction.

'Of course, there is another possibility,' said Wyness. He paused, sweeping the assembled company with his eyes to gather their attention. 'I reckon taking the lease on Rainbow Hill was about the smartest move I made, one way and another, and I've been thinking it's maybe time we repeated the exercise.'

'Lease another quarry?' said Will. 'Aye, I like the sound of that.'

'As long as we can find another as good,' said Lorn beside him. 'Waste of time quarrying rubbish.'

'And we'd need to find the right men to work it.'

'That goes without saying,' said Wyness. 'It'd take time, mind, and you'll maybe think we haven't the time to waste if Tom's backlog is to be cleared. It might be best to approach Silvercairns, as Mhairi says. We'd have to pay, of course, but we'd save on manpower and quarrying costs.'

'I think that would be best,' said Mhairi bravely. 'For the time being anyway.'

'Mhairi's right ...' began Fanny, but Tom had recovered.

'The day we go cap in hand to Silvercairns to help us run our business is the day I ...' He caught Wyness's warning eye and stopped short, drew a deep breath and when he resumed, it was in tones of quiet reason. 'You said yourself, Mr Wyness, that any deal would be on our terms. If we approach Silvercairns now, we do so from a position of weakness. The fountain is one thing: plain expediency. But to say "We are behind with our orders so can you please help us" is quite another. We would be in no position to dictate terms, even supposing Adam was prepared to consider them. I vote we start with the fountain arrangement, see how it goes and work from there.'

'Tom's right,' said Will. 'It'll be all round Aberdeen, else. They'll say Rainbow Hill's asked Silvercairns for help, and that'll be us finished.'

'I don't see why,' began Mhairi bravely. 'The fountain arrangement is perfectly legitimate and there is no reason why anyone should...'

'No reason?' interrupted Lorn. 'And us telling the world we canna...'

'Enough!' Wyness banged his fist on the table to collect their attention. 'We've a business to run in case you've forgotten, and better things to do than blether round a table all day. Ifs and buts and maybes will get us nowhere. It's facts we must deal with and the plain fact is that we've too much work for our resources. So, step one: we take on more men. That's straightforward enough. Step two: we expand. I take it we're all agreed so far? Good. Then the only question is, how. Do we look around for a new quarry venture of our own, or do we approach Silvercairns for some sort of an arrangement? And before anyone says things they'll regret,' he went on as there was a rumble of discord, 'we'd best take a vote on it. Those in favour of a deal with Silvercairns?' Mhairi's hand was the only one raised until Fanny, with a sideways glance at Tom, added hers. 'And those favouring a new quarry of our own?' All the men raised their

[115]

hands, including Donal. Even Hamish, after a glance in his mother's direction, added his.

'Not much doubt about the number of hands' said Wyness, 'but if we take shares in the company into consideration, there's a formidable number against.'

'Fanny's don't count,' growled Tom. 'Leastways, they count as mine.'

Wyness raised an eyebrow. 'Is that so? And there's me thinking that on your wedding day you vowed my daughter should keep control of her own shares. I must have misheard. But if I'm deaf, I'm certainly not blind and I saw what my daughter voted for and what she voted against.'

There was an awkward silence, which Fanny broke. 'I voted as I did, Papa, not because I don't want a new quarry of our own, but because I want the quickest solution to the problem. I know it is selfish of me, but I want Tom to come home at a reasonable time in the evenings and with the energy to talk to me and play with the children, instead of falling asleep at the table before he's finished his meal. Remember what it was like when you took on Rainbow Hill? You all worked twenty-five hours a day till it was running smoothly and I do not want that to happen all over again.'

'Aye, well . . .' This compendious statement conveyed acceptance of her reasons, consideration of their value, and the promise of an imminent decision. It came.

'It seems to me,' said Wyness, 'that the best thing we can do is take on more men immediately, keep a good eye on them, and note the best of them for future use. That way we can catch up a bittie with the work in hand while we look about us, take our time, ask the right questions, and choose how and where we want to expand our business. If we decide on a new quarry, as we seem to have done already, one way or another, then we want a source of good granite rock, in fine big blocks, granite that'll take a polish like glass. We want a quarry with promise, not a scraped out hole with the goodness gone, nor a useless piece of scrubland fit for nothing but roadmetal.'

There was a pause while everyone considered his words, and the possibilities the locality offered.

'Mr Adam is going to buy another quarry,' announced Hamish into the silence.

All eyes looked at the boy in surprise, though Mhairi, after the first shocked glance, lowered hers lest someone see the horror in them and the fear. How did the boy know, when Fergus had confided his plans to her in secret? But *however he knew, dear God, don't let him tell.*

'How do you know that?' asked Tom, a strange look in his eye.

'Leo Lennox said so,' admitted Hamish uncomfortably. 'On the station in Banchory.'

He expected someone to refer to the fight and to tease him accordingly, but before they could, Donal who had been busily writing on a note-pad, finished with a flourish and pushed the pad to Tom.

Tom studied it for a moment, then looked up. 'Are you sure, Donal?' he mouthed.

Donal nodded.

'Well, well. Donal says Adam was inquiring of the railway geologist about granite. In Banchory.'

'But that's eighteen miles from Aberdeen,' protested Will. 'I wonder which particular piece of land he has his eye on?'

'Perhaps none,' said Mhairi, a little too quickly. 'Is he not a shareholder in the Deeside railway? You mentioned it yourself the other day, Mr Wyness. Perhaps he was merely investigating the route the line will take?'

'It'll not go through Silvercairns land, so why should he?' said Will, before Wyness could comment. 'There'll be no compensation to warm his pocket, whether he's a shareholder or the King of Siam.'

'Unless he plans to use his inside knowledge to buy the land on the sly and line his pockets that way?' grinned Lorn. 'The Adams were aye a devious, swindling . . .'

'That's enough of that, lad,' cut in Wyness. 'Remember we've business to do with Silvercairns and slander will win you no discounts.'

There was a moment's silence, which everyone expected Tom to break, but Tom seemed deep in private thought, and it was Fanny who spoke.

'But if Fergus Adam really was looking for more land to quarry,' she said brightly, with some idea of diverting criticism from Fergus and easing the pain which she read in Mhairi's face, 'Why ever should he choose Banchory? Surely it would be more sensible to look for somewhere nearer home? Willowbrac for instance.' At these words the shock on Mhairi's face was, if anything, worse, and Fanny elaborated, with a hint of desperation in her voice, 'After all, though now it is only grazing land and scrub I am sure someone told me that

[117]

once, years ago, there was a little quarry there. Besides, it is practically next door to Silvercairns.'

'So it is,' said Tom thoughtfully, and added, 'Doesn't it belong to Ina Dickie's brother?'

'Who would have sold it years ago if he could have got good money for it,' said Will. 'Grasping old devil.'

'Old Mackinnon always said whoever started scratching away there shouldna have given up so easily,' offered Lorn, a wary eye on George Wyness for signs of irritation. 'Mind you, I wouldna relish it myself. You could dig yards deep for days on end and likely find nothing.'

'Not if you knew what you were doing,' said Tom. 'Took expert advice, maybe, so you knew where to start.'

Suddenly George Wyness chuckled. 'Can you just imagine his face if we took over the place and . . .?'

'If it was worth the trouble,' interrupted Mhairi quickly, 'it would have been worked long ago. Mungo Adam would have seen to that. So if Fergus Adam is inquiring in Banchory, there must be a good reason for it.'

'There's the new railway,' offered Fanny and Mhairi siezed on the idea with relief.

'Of course! There's no railway at Silvercairns, so Mr Adam goes to Banchory. But we don't need to do that. We already have Donside.'

Tom looked at her in surprise, but before surprise could change to outright suspicion she hurried on.

'For the railway access. Tom has told us how behindhand we are in every part of the business. What use would a piece of undeveloped land be to us? We need access roads and railways. We need a working quarry, one we can take over and use to capacity with no time wasted on development. Speculation is all very well in its place, and splendid in the future, but for the present, didn't Tom say he needs a second. Rainbow Hill? A Donside quarry would be ideal. A working quarry with direct access to the railway. Persley Den, perhaps, or Sclattie. I am sure we could buy over a lease, one way or another. And if it was close enough to Rainbow Hill we could even use the same dray horses.'

Please God they would see the logic of her argument. Please God they would forget Willowbrae and leave Fergus alone.

'Hmm,' said Wyness, frowning. 'Mhairi may have a point.'

[118]

'We'd get undeveloped land for less, and make a bigger profit,' pointed out Tom, wearyness, over-work, broken deadlines all forgotten, and a new gleam in his eyes. 'And if it was in the right place, say in the same seam as Silvercairns, we might even get a granite white enough for that Drummond fellow's fountain.'

'That is not the point, Tom dear,' said his wife gently. 'Mr Drummond wants his fountain now, not in five years' time. What help would it be to any of us to have a piece of untapped land? I thought the point was to clear the backlog of overdue commissions as fast as possible, so that wee Georgie might see you for five minutes between one Sunday and the next. When we have done that, then we can think of speculation. But for the present, I am on Mhairi's side. The side of practical common sense.'

'It was a nice idea, Tom lad,' said Wyness with a sigh, 'but it looks as if we're out-voted. For the moment, and no doubt for the best. But our day will come, I promise you that. And when it does ...' He grinned in gleeful mischief. 'I've nothing against the man, mind you, but I've missed Old Mungo's competition and, to liven things up a little, I'd fair like to see a few Adam feathers fly.'

'Aye,' agreed Lorn. 'Mhairi's always fancied living in the big house, haven't you Mhairi?'

But relief had left her faint and trembling. Mhairi pushed back her chair and stood up, holding the table edge for support. 'I'm sorry, Mr Wyness. I need air.' She almost ran from the room and when Fanny hurried anxiously after her she found her sister-in-law leaning white-faced against the outside wall of the building with her eyes closed.

'What is it, Mhairi? Are you sick.'

Sick with relief, thought Mhairi, and with fear. Aloud she said only, 'A little. It is so airless with the windows closed and so many people. I will be fine again in a minute or two.'

But it would take more than minutes to obliterate the memory of the chasm which had threatened to open between Fergus and herself. She had fought off disaster for the moment, but how long would it be before that dreadful idea surfaced again? He would think she had betrayed his confidence. And if, by some wild mischance, they were to outbid him for Willowbrae ...

'Take my smelling salts,' urged Fanny beside her. 'They will make you feel much better.' She unscrewed the little silver cap and offered the phial.

[119]

As she felt the acrid fumes prickle her nostrils and startle her senses into life again, Mhairi remembered something else. Tom had agreed to conduct business discussions with Fergus Adam. At least, she thought with the first flicker of reviving hope, Tom's antagonism seemed to have dwindled. He had been thoughtful and uncommunicative, but he had not joined in the sneering or the teasing. Perhaps everything would be all right after all? In a few short weeks, Christmas would be upon them and the end of the year. Surely by then Tom would accept that she and Fergus loved each other, the last of his animosity would die away and with it any lingering idea of revenge.?

Clinging to that small hope, she obediently breathed in when Fanny told her to, and felt the last grey shreds of cloud disperse.

'There, I am quite recovered,' she said, smiling. 'Shall we go back inside?'

'What was the matter with Mhairi?' asked Tom, when the meeting was over and he and Fanny were on their way home.

'Nothing.' Fanny tucked her arm under Tom's and snuggled closer. It was a gusty day of bright sunlight and tossing leaves, but there was a chill edge to the wind and she was glad of her fur-trimmed woollen mantle and bonnet.

'At least,' she amended, hurrying her steps to keep up with his, 'she only needed air. It really is very stuffy with all the windows closed tight and if the fire is smoking too, I sometimes wonder we don't all asphyxiate. And then Mhairi is used to the country air. Also,' she added, when Tom made no comment, but continued to stare ahead of him as if in brooding thought, 'I know it is naughty of me to say so, but I suspect she had laced her stays too tight in order to emphasize her waist. You may not have noticed, Tom dear, but Mhairi has begun to take more notice of her appearance lately and high time too. She has been drab and mournful for far too long.'

'Stays?' said Tom, turning his head in puzzlement. 'What are you talking about?'

'I declare you have not heard a word I said,' pouted Fanny and withdrew her arm in pretended pique. 'I shall walk home alone and talk to myself instead.'

'You will do nothing of the kind.' He seized her by the waist and drew her close. 'People who talk to themselves in the street get locked up in asylums, and then what would I do for a wife? So tell me about these mysterious stays before we walk another step.'

[120]

Fanny giggled. 'I am not at all sure it is a proper subject of conversation between a lady and a gentleman, but if you insist. I merely said Mhairi felt faint because her stays were laced too tight, and I know exactly how she feels.'

'You do not feel faint?' said Tom in alarm. 'Because if you do ...'

'Of course not, Tom. I only meant ... oh never mind. This is a silly conversation. Let us talk about something else.'

'By all means, wife. I entirely agree.' But though he drew her hand once more under his arm and kept it there, in companionable warmth, Tom walked the rest of the way home in silence. The morning's meeting had left him with much to mull over as gradually the full implication of his father-in-law's words took hold. *Sink your personal differences in honest to goodness trade rivalry*, George Wyness had said and ever since the germ of an idea had been growing and strengthening, filling Tom with a secret excitement he had not felt for years. Not since the day he had known he must go to Australia. But that revelation had been tinged with sorrow, involving as it did a three-year parting from the girl he loved. This idea had no such drawbacks, but was gloriously, splendidly right.

Trade rivalry. Open and above board. And to the death. It was the perfect solution, the perfect atonement for Alex's death. He was amazed he had not realized the possibilities before, instead of wasting his energies in futile personal resentment. At one end of the scale of retribution, he could punch the fellow on the nose, as Hamish had punched young Leo: at the other, he realized with slow wonder, he could ruin him, utterly and completely, while extending the hand of business friendship with a smile on his face. All that was needed was patience, careful planning, and time.

Annys was alone in the cottage that bright October morning. Already she had made the beds, cleared away and washed the breakfast things, and prepared the vegetables for the day's broth pot. Then, as it was a clean, fresh morning with sunlight and a crisp breeze, she had hung out the day's washing to dry. As she stood admiring its flapping cleanliness and fresh, damp smell, she had remembered the hens, and collected what eggs she could find from hedgerow, garden and yard. She carried them carefully in her looped apron into the scullery where she wiped them clean and set them with the others in a basket on a high shelf. If she found as many tomorrow, they would have enough to take to market. Dreamily she remembered the first time she had gone to market alone and had met Kit O'Brien. She had told a lie to Mhairi that day, and, though it had been a sin, she did not regret it. The lie had kept Kit secret.

She wondered what he was doing? Working, most probably. On the railway, perhaps, as he had done before. There was still plenty of railway work around for a man with determination and a strong arm. Unless he had gone on across the water to see his family? Her heart faltered for a moment at the thought. But only for a moment. If that had been his plan, surely he would have jumped the train at Glasgow, if it came through Glasgow, or in Edinburgh. Instead, he had come to Aberdeen. And unless he had made a fortune in the Crimea, which judging from the clothes he wore seemed unlikely, he would be looking for work.

But the thought of work reminded her of the instructions Mhairi had reeled off as she left the house that morning. Hadn't sweeping the kitchen been somewhere on the list? She'd better do that next. She tied her hair up in a kerchief and fetched the broom, while she tried to remember any other task she might have forgotten.

When the children had been sent off to school and her brothers to work, each provided with lunch packets appropriate to their needs, Mhairi had gone up to the quarry office on Rainbow Hill, as she did from time to time, to inspect the books, cast her eye over the quarry yard and generally satisfy herself that all was well. Since that meeting in George Wyness's office they had hired more men in both polishing yard and quarry and it was as well to keep a check on the new arrivals. Any man with obvious aptitude or exceptional skill was to be noted and marked down for possible promotion. Any man who did not pull his weight, or who bungled a job through incompetence, was to be paid off on the spot.

'We canna afford to carry dead weight,' Wyness had pointed out. 'Sickness is a different matter and no one can accuse me of heartlessness on that score. If one of my workers falls sick, he's taken care of till he's fit again, always supposing he's worth the money, eh?' and he had winked with pretended greed, but Annys knew, as Mhairi did, that Wyness rewarded loyalty with loyalty, and paid generously for excellence wherever he found it. Look at the widow's pension he had paid Mhairi on Alex's death, and still paid her in spite of her protests.

I wonder if he will continue to pay it when Mhairi marries? thought Annys as she carried the rug from the kitchen into the back yard and

[122]

began to beat it with a firm and regular thwack. Annys would like Mhairi to marry again, then she would not feel guilty when she, Annys, married and left home. Mhairi must marry Fergus Adam and live in Silvercairns. It would be much the best solution to everything and if only Tom would stop being so obstinate, he would see it too. Thwack! That was for her brother. To beat the sense into him. Thwack! And another, for good measure.

But the dust clouds had dwindled to almost nothing. She gave the rug one last resounding whack and looked searchingly around her to check the air was truly clean. Only then did she notice the washing, its once white surface speckled with a layer of new grime.

Bother, she said under her breath. Mhairi had told her over and over to beat the mat before she put the washing out, but in the dreamy inconsequence of her thoughts she had quite forgotten. But if she hurried, she would have time to rinse it out again before Mhairi came back. She carried the rug back inside, laid it carefully in front of the hearth and swung the kettle further over the flames. She would need hot water if she was to get those shirts clean, and there were so many of them. With a sigh she set about filling the wash tub all over again. But she did not really mind. A girl could think and dream whatever her hands were doing.

Ever since the Queen's arrival at the railway station platform when she had glimpsed him for one glorious moment through the crowd, Annys had expected each new day to bring her news of Kit O'Brien and though almost a month had passed since his arrival, with neither word nor sight of him, her hope had not flagged. He would come one day. If ever she doubted that the figure she had seen on the station platform was him, she had only to turn over the pebble in her pocket to feel faith flooding back. It was because the likelihood of his arrival grew stronger with every day that passed, that Annys had chosen to stay in the cottage today. She would not want to be out when he called, or when Mrs Macrae sent to tell her that news had come of Willy, via a friend.

She was singing softly to herself, lost in her dreams, as she hung up the twice-washed clothes in the back yard, and heard no approaching step. So the voice at her back made her heart lurch with alarm. Until she turned her head and saw him.

'Well, well, if it isn't the Pretty Dancer herself, unless I'm still asleep and dreaming. Kit O'Brien, home from the wars and at your service, ma'am.' He bowed with a theatrical flourish and grinned.

[123]

Annys had planned over and over in the months since his departure for the Crimea what she would say to him when he returned; had composed endless speeches of welcome, planned whole conversations in which he would say this thing and she that. But when it came to it, she could only stare into his weather-tanned, cheerful face, her eyes wide with wonder and her tongue tied with shock.

'Are you thinking you've seen a ghost? I thought I saw one on the railway station a month back, the ghost of a lassie I'd seen on the highroad a winter ago, a winsome slip of a lassie with fine blue eyes too shy to meet mine when I paid her a compliment. As they are now.'

Annys bit her lip and blushed. 'I saw you on the station, Mr O'Brien. At least, I thought I did and then ...' She stopped, confused.

'Then you wondered what was a tink like Kit O'Brien doing riding on the royal train? But riding where I'm not wanted is a speciality of mine, remember?' and he winked. 'The skill lies in choosing your moment. Remember that, little Dancer, if you ever plan to jump a train. A fine ride I had too, though maybe not as elegant and comfortable as Her Majesty's. But we travelled through the same countryside, and saw the same view. Though the food I had to sustain me over the long miles was maybe not the same. Unless the Queen has a fancy for cold bacon and a hunk of bread?'

But the mention of food had jerked her into social consciousness. 'I am sorry, Mr O'Brien. I should have offered you refreshment. Would you care for a glass of milk, or of ale? I cannot offer bacon, I'm afraid, but I have eggs ...' Her voice trailed into silence as she saw his face.

'You cannot know, Miss Traveller, how enchanting you look, with your hair tied up in a bundle, clothes pegs in one hand and wet washing in the other. The end is trailing in the mud, by the way. You may not mind, but I felt it only polite to draw it to your attention.'

'Oh *bother*!' cried Annys, tears of exasperation blurring her eyes. Then she blushed and said, 'I am sorry. But you see, I have washed it twice already. It is too bad.'

'It'll brush off when it's dry,' said Kit cheerfully, 'and what's a muddy shirt-tail in the vast and intricate splendour of God's universe? A thing of no importance. Here, give me those pegs and we'll have the rest of your linen flapping in the breeze in the whisk of a cat's tail.'

[124]

'Oh no,' protested Annys, blushing. 'It would not be right.' Her brothers had never pegged out washing in their lives.

'And why not? Two pairs of hands are better than one. Besides, the sooner you finish, Pretty Dancer, the sooner you can make that cup of tea you were about to offer me and weren't you going to say something about buttered scones, with strawberry jam?'

'Was I? Oh yes, of course. I mean ...' Blushing with mortification at her own gaucheness, Annys dropped a peg, retrieved it, fumbled the shirt somehow onto the line, and snatched up the next, all the time conscious of Kit O'Brien's solemn gaze as he stood beside her and handed her the pegs, one by one. But at last she was finished. She picked up the empty linen basket and made for the scullery door, only to find her way barred.

'Before you go back inside, little house mouse, I have something to show you. Would madam care to take my arm?' and he offered it in a flamboyant parody of a high-born gentleman.

Intrigued, Annys put down her basket in the yard and put her hand timidly in the crook of his arm. He led her round the side of the cottage towards the quarry track. 'You were preoccupied, Miss Traveller, and singing, or you would have heard the noise of our approach. There!' He stopped and flung out his arm in pride.

Lazily mouthing the autumn offerings of the grass verge, stood a sturdy dray horse, yoked to a farm-cart whose sides were newly painted brilliant green with, in scarlet letters outlined in gold paint, the words 'Kit O'Brien, Carrier'.

'Well? What do you think?'

Annys was lost for the right words of praise. Instead, she said insanely, 'Is it yours?'

'And would I be painting my name on the side if it wasn't, woman? And each letter alone taking me the best part of an hour to do. That's why I settled for "Kit" the second time round. It's "Christopher O'Brien" on the side you can't see. But maybe folk will think I've two carts to my name? For that's what I aim to have a year from now, if ... but you'll not be wanting to hear my plans. You've work to do, I can see that.'

He sounded suddenly deflated and Annys was ashamed and at the same time afraid that he would leave before she had heard the half of what she wanted to know.

'I want to hear everything,' she said firmly. 'About Peto & Betts and the railway and Balaclava and how you came by that elegant cart,

[125]

with such a beautiful horse to pull it. But not until I've made you tea and buttered a plate of scones. You must be hungry. What is his name, by the way?'

'Whose name? Oh, my horse. He's a she, and she's called Merry. After the Merry Dancers who were lighting up the sky on the day you first crossed my path.'

'I will boil a kettle,' said Annys, blushing, and hurried back to the scullery door and inside.

Kit O'Brien followed.

'I did consider walking up the garden path and knocking on your front door,' he said, 'but I know my place in life. It's the back door for Kit O'Brien, leastways until he's made his fortune. Which, he assures you, he intends to do.'

'You have started already, by the looks of it,' said Annys, pouring water from the kettle into the teapot and setting it on the hearth, to keep warm. 'Last time I saw you, you had nothing but a canvas bag, and that half-empty.'

'Ah. You noticed that, did you, and me thinking you were too shy to notice anything, even the admiration in a stranger's eyes. But to save your blushes I'll tell you. You were right. All I had was a change of shirt to my name and a pair of my father's breeches. But they fitted us out with working clothes on the Russian railway. They had to, or we'd have frozen solid in our tracks and if they'd wanted their railway they'd have had to use us, laid in rows, for sleepers. But they paid us well for speed, and speed helped to keep the frost out of our bones. Some folk squandered their pay on vodka or whisky or any other spiritous liquor they could find, but I saved mine, every last penny. Kit my boy, I said, if ever the temptation took me, remember the lassie on the Woodside road, and how proud she'll be when you come back a rich man. So I saved every last penny of the railway money and the hospital money and the roads money that followed, till I reckoned I'd enough to come home and set myself up.'

'With a cart?' prompted Annys, pouring him tea and offering scones. Mhairi had baked them specially for when Fanny Wyness came, with her children, to tea that afternoon, but Annys did not care. Kit's need was greater.

'Aye. I've always liked horses and I've worked long enough for other men, with nothing much to show for it. Now, I'll be my own boss. It took me a while to find the right cart and the right animal to pull it. There's horse-thieves and villains everywhere, lass, and I've met my fill of them. But when money's as precious to a man as mine was, he'll not be taken in by the first rogue he meets, however smooth-tongued and persuasive.'

'Was?' repeated Annys. 'Have you nothing left?'

'Only my wits and the strength of my arm,' he grinned. 'That's why I came calling. I heard tell at the farm that the quarry's expanding and I'm hoping for carrier work.'

So he had called at the farm already. Knowing Mrs Macrae, she would have filled him to the ears with milk, cheese, bread, ham, bannocks and oatcakes and all the manifold riches of her farmhouse kitchen, and if he brought her news of her son Willy, as he must have done, then she would have fed him twice over. Annys smiled.

'I think you are something of a smooth-tongued rogue yourself, Mr O'Brien. Hungry indeed. How you found room for even half that poor scone after feasting at Mrs Macrae's table I just don't know. Unless it is sheer greed.'

For a moment he was taken aback, then had the grace to look shamefaced.

'I confess it freely. But how else was I to wheedle my way into your charming company, Miss Annys? Miss Annys Diack, I believe? And before you wonder how I found out your name, Mrs Macrae told me. Though if she had not, it would have made no difference. It was branded on my heart for ever, when that churlish crofter whisked you up into his cart and carried you away.'

'And you,' dared Annys, and Kit laughed.

'If you could have seen your face, little frightened mouse that you were. I could have kissed you ...' He stopped, suddenly embarrassed.

Annys blushed scarlet and busied herself unnecessarily with the teapot. She could think of nothing to say.

After a moment, Kit cleared his throat and said, 'It was the thought of Mr Dickie's cart that gave me the idea.'

Into the awkward silence which followed, came the creak of the garden gate, the sound of light steps on the path and before either could speak again, the door opened and Mhairi hurried in.

'Annys, there is a strange horse and cart in the road and...oh.'

Kit put aside his teacup and stood up. 'Kit O'Brien, ma'am,' he said, offering his hand. 'And the equipage is mine. I hope Merry is not eating your flowers?'

Mhairi ignored his hand and turned a questioning look on Annys.

'Mr O'Brien was sent by Mrs Macrae,' she explained, embroidering freely. 'He is a friend of Willy's, come all the way from the Crimea to bring news of him to Willy's mother. Mr O'Brien is looking for carter's work and Mrs Macrae thought he might find it at Rainbow Hill. He called to inquire,' she finished, her voice trailing into silence as Mhairi continued to regard their visitor with sharp suspicion.

'The quarry office is the place for that.'

'So I explained, Mhairi, but as I expected you back at any moment I thought it polite to offer tea and let Mr O'Brien speak to you here, himself.' She laid only the smallest emphasis on the word 'polite' but it was enough.

'I am so sorry, Mr O'Brien,' said Mhairi with an effort at welcome. 'I do not mean to be inhospitable, but with the roads as they are and so many strangers about, and my sister alone in the house ... you know how it is.'

'You mean I might be a black-hearted villain with wicked designs upon a defenceless maiden?" he said, solemn-faced. 'And so I might be, though, God strike me dead if I tell a lie, I am nothing of the kind.'

'No. Well,' said Mhairi, flustered. 'All the same, it would be best if you asked at the quarry office. Straight up the lane and the first building on the right. Ask for Will Diack and tell him I sent you, though whether there is any carter's work today I could not say.' All the time she was talking, Mhairi was edging him towards the door. 'You'd best go now,' she said firmly. 'Before the office closes.' She opened the door and stood back to let him pass.

But Kit O'Brien stood his ground. 'If it's all the same to you, ma'am, I'll go out the way I came in, by the back door. I'll be needing all the luck I can get if I'm to make that fortune, so I'll not be after blighting it by tempting fate.'

In the doorway of the scullery Kit O'Brien turned. 'Goodbye, Miss Diack,' he said to Annys, with a courteous dip of the head. 'And thank you for your gracious hospitality.' He winked, grinned, then he was gone. A moment later Annys heard his cheerful 'Come along there, Merry my lass. Move a hoof,' from the lane outside.

'Good riddance!' said Mhairi with feeling. 'Really, Annys, I credited you with more common sense.'

'I don't know what you mean,' said Annys, moving to the window in the hope of glimpsing Kit's horse and cart in the lane.

[128]

'You know perfectly well what I mean, and come away from that window. He might see you.'

'Would it matter if he did?' Annys could see the top of Merry's head through a gap in the hedge, then Kit himself on the seat of the cart, cap pushed to the back of his head. He looked as if he was whistling.

'Of course it would matter. I will not have you gawping out of the window at strange young men, like a common scullerymaid. Try and be a little more ladylike. And what on earth possessed you to invite a perfect stranger into the house when I was away? Anything might have happened.'

'But he is not ...' Annys stopped herself just in time. If she confessed to a previous acquaintance with Kit O'Brien she would never hear the end of it. 'He is not a complete stranger,' she amended. 'Mrs Macrae knows him and sent him on to us. Otherwise, of course I would not have asked him in, Mhairi,' she finished, widening her eyes in artless innocence. 'But you have always taught me to offer hospitality to visitors.'

There was a small silence before Mhairi said, with an effort, 'You are quite right. It is just that I worry about you, Annys. I would not want you to come to any harm.' She moved to the small mirror above the dresser and began to take the pins from her hat. Annys remembered a time when Mhairi had been content to cover her hair with a plaid, but for almost a year now, since the winter anyway, her sister had worn a bonnet like Fanny did, or a little straw hat. It had not occurred to her before. And the bonnet Mhairi was removing now was new.

'Is that why you would not let me apply for the schoolteacher's job?' she said, made brave by the discovery. 'Or the position as lady's companion or nursery governess?'

'Of course not,' blustered Mhairi, 'It is just that ... that there is no need for you to work. After all, you can always help Fanny if you need a change of scene, and then one day you will meet someone, someone like Mr Drummond perhaps, and marry. Until then, I need you at home. I would miss you and so would the children. Who would supervise their homework?'

'You would. After all, you are their mother.' Annys moved with dignified grace towards the table and began to collect cups and saucers together. 'But you are not mine. And one day, I would like a life of my own.'

[129]

Mhairi was shocked and shaken by the antagonism in her sister's voice. Annys, who had always been so docile and obedient. After a moment she said carefully, 'I understand that, Annys dear, but there is no need for you to go out to work in order to find it. You have freedom here, and space, the time to read and study as you choose. Where is the oppression in that? Until you marry and have a home of your own, we can manage well enough as we are.'

'We could manage better if I earned my share.' If Kit O'Brien was saving every penny he earned, the least she could do was the same. Suddenly Annys was filled with a raging jealousy towards Mhairi. How dare she buy new clothes, meet her lover in secret, come home warm with love and private smiles, and then tell Annys off for giving Kit O'Brien an innocent cup of tea. 'And I do not mean going to market once a week to sell an egg and a cabbage leaf.'

Head held high, Annys picked up the tray and turned towards the scullery. Then something about the two cups, two saucers, and the plate of scones stirred her memory. 'Moreover,' she said with scathing dignity, 'If I wish to offer hospitality to a gentleman caller, then I see no reason why I should not follow your example and do so.'

With that crushing remark she carried her tray triumphantly into the scullery.

She returned some ten minutes later, to replace the best china on the dresser. Mhairi watched her in silence till she had finished, then said quietly, 'I know you are restless, Annys. It is natural at your age. But you are not yet sixteen.'

'Ina Bain is my age and she has a job.'

'Yes. As a scullerymaid. But you are an intelligent girl, Annys, and I want more for you than that. Don't you see, my love,' she pleaded suddenly, reaching out and clasping Annys's hand. 'I want you to be a lady. Ma wanted that so much, for both of us . . .'

'Ma is dead,' cried Annys, snatching her hand away and facing her sister with furious eyes. 'What does it matter what she wanted? She has been dead for years and I don't even remember what she looked like. As to you wanting me to be a lady – why must I always do what you want? Why can't I do what I want for a change? Like you do? I know who you've been seeing all summer, but I haven't followed you about, hemming you in, telling you to do this and that, have I? *So don't do it to me.* Or I swear I'll go straight to Tom and . . .' Annys stopped, drew breath, and said with quiet intensity, 'Why can't you leave me alone, for pity's sake? I am not a *child*.'

She flung from the room, slamming the door behind her.

Mhairi stood in the middle of the floor, her face white with shock. Annys had never shouted at Mhairi in her life, never thrown a tantrum and certainly never slammed a door. Whatever had got into the girl? And all because Mhairi had reproved her for offering a stranger tea.

Perhaps Fanny was right. Fanny had said long ago that Annys should have a job, a responsible, educated job which would use her talents to the full. She had offered to find her one, through her mother's various contacts, but Mhairi had refused. Now, however, with Annys's outburst still ringing in her ears, she took out the idea and examined it more closely. It might be what the girl needed. Rainbow Cottage was certainly isolated, the neighbours, though friendly enough, on a different intellectual plane from Annys. The Macrae boys were good, loyal working men, the Bain girls strong and tough. Mr Dickie's brood were the same, but, thought Mhairi with a sinking heart, the girls would be married at sixteen, mothers at seventeen if not before, and by twenty-five would be middle-aged women, shapeless, work-worn, worried, with a gaggle of hungry children clamouring to be fed. Their husbands would be grey-faced with exhaustion and morose with care.

She did not want that for Annys.

As it was, Annys spent too much time alone, reading, or staring out of the window, or merely lost in daydreams. With a thud of alarm, Mhairi realized that she had no idea of the content of those dreams. Perhaps she was dreaming of love? Perhaps even of Philip Drummond, her fairy-tale prince? After Annys's accusation of oppression, she could not possibly ask. Mhairi herself had moved in a private dream for so long now that it was hard to hawl herself back to reality and face the problem of her sister's future.

I have been selfish, thought Mhairi, so concerned with my own happiness that I have given no thought to hers. I have been so caught up in my own dreams, worrying over the problem of Tom and Fergus and how to reconcile them, that I have neglected poor little Annys. No wonder she turned against me. But I will talk to Fanny about it this very afternoon.

In the turmoil of her own anxieties, Mhairi had pushed the Drummond idea aside. Now she took it out again for serious consideration. The connection was there, without undue manipulation. Mr Drummond had ordered a fountain from the Wyness yard and would undoubtedly check now and then on its progress. Fanny already had some small acquaintance with his sister. What more natural than that brother and sister should be invited together, to some suitable social occasion at Fanny's house? Or if Tom objected to that, then to the Assembly Rooms or a concert? Annys had been to stay with Fanny on several occasions, to help with the children or keep Fanny company if Tom was away. Fanny must invite Annys to stay again.

Unaccountably, Annys refused to go.

'I am sorry for what I said, Mhairi dear, and I did not mean it. You are the best sister in the world and the only mother I ever had. At least,' she amended in the interests of truth, 'the only one I can remember. This is my home and I will stay here with you.'

To all Mhairi's arguments she returned the same answer: she was not bored, not hemmed in, had not meant what she said about taking a governess's job, was perfectly content to help Mhairi in the house, supervise the children's homework, darn shirts or socks as required and go to market once a week, as before.

'If Fanny or one of her children was ill and needed me, then of course I would go,' she assured Mhairi, innocent eyes wide and earnest. 'But they are not and she has Jessie to help her. You have no one but me.'

Exasperated, baffled and strangely touched by Annys's dogged loyalty, Mhairi gave up the struggle. If Annys was to meet Mr Drummond it would have to be by different means, and certainly the girl seemed happier than for a long time. She was eager and willing to do whatever Mhairi asked of her, sang about the house when she thought no one was listening and looked prettier every day. Perhaps she had needed her outburst to clean the system and make everything right again?

Mhairi puzzled over the matter, not entirely convinced the explanation could be so simple, yet unable to come up with another. And whatever Annys said to the contrary, one day things would inevitably change. Mhairi dare not frame the thought in as many words, but she was thinking of the day when she herself would marry. When Tom would smile and give his blessing, shake Fergus Adam's hand and say 'I could not hope for a better brother-in-law.' The day when she and Fergus would stand before the world as man and wife.

There had been a time when Mhairi had feared that her brother would never be reconciled to an Adam as a brother-in-law. That she would be forced to choose between Fergus and her family. That she would not have the strength of mind to choose aright. But as the weeks passed, she began to hope, at first tentatively, then with strengthening joy. For, as old Wyness had instructed him to do, Tom sought a meeting with Fergus Adam to come to an arrangement about the Drummond fountain. The bargain was struck, in apparent amity and to their mutual satisfaction, and sealed in a dram. They parted if not exactly as friends, as new and well-intentioned business acquaintances.

'I think you are mistaken in your brother,' Fergus told her, when they next met. He had been again to Glasgow and she had not seen him for more than two weeks. 'He was most civil and accommodating. He could not have been more so had I asked him for your hand in marriage.'

'You didn't?' cried Mhairi, aghast. Then looked quickly about her in consternation lest any of the clientele of the respectable hotel coffee room had heard her. All it needed was one of Mrs Wyness's friends to see her and the news would be all over town: *that widow woman Grant was having coffee with Mr Adam. In the morning, and tête à tête. And him a bachelor. Do you think there could be anything in it?* Tongues would wag nineteen to the dozen and in no time at all Fanny would hear about it. Much as she loved her, Mhairi had no faith in Fanny's discretion. She would tell Tom, as she told him everything. And quite right too, between husband and wife.

'Would it be so dreadful if I had?' asked Fergus, reaching across the table and taking her hand in his. She made a half-hearted attempt to withdraw it, then gave up the struggle. Warmth flowed from his hand to hers, filling her body with quivering pleasure and when he looked at her as he was looking now, with dark and passionate eyes, she was powerless to resist.

'Not dreadful,' she managed. 'Only premature. And a little impertinent. I am quite capable of deciding for myself who I will marry and it is really no business of his. All the same, I want him to be happy when he hears the news ...'

'He will be. At least, if he has any feeling for you, he will. Don't worry, my darling,' he murmured, leaning across the table till their faces were almost close enough for a kiss. 'Your brother and I are acquaintances already. Soon we will be relatives, and friends.'

[133]

'I hope so.' Mhairi bit her lip, her eyes large with longing and shadowed with doubt.

'I know so,' he said, and before she realized what he meant to do, he had pulled her towards him across the table and kissed her on the lips. Then he fell back into his chair, smiling at her confusion. 'There. Let the town pussies report that to their tea-tables.'

'Would you like more coffee, madam?' asked a waitress at Mhairi's side. The woman's voice was carefully expressionless, even slightly reproving, but Mhairi knew from the look in her eye that the moment she reached the back regions, gleeful outrage would bubble forth into ribald speculation and smothered sniggers. Mhairi did not care.

'Thank you,' she said with admirable dignity. 'I think I would.'

The diversion gave her time to arrange her turbulent thoughts and to harness the hunger which his sudden kiss had sent racing through her blood. In a public restaurant, she thought with shame and threatened laughter. Whatever would her mother have thought of her? Then she looked up and saw Fergus watching her, his eyes alight with teasing and something more. Suddenly she did not care who saw them together; let the whole world shout about it if they chose. She loved Fergus Adam and he loved her. That was all that mattered.

As for Tom...

'It will be all right, Mhairi darling. I promise you.' Fergus's voice was low and warm with love. 'Only trust, and wait.' There was a strange excitement in his voice now and after a moment's obvious struggle, he said, 'I had meant to wait till Christmas, but I am as bad as Leo with a parcel and I find I cannot wait another moment. I want to tell you...'

'Cream, madam?'

This time the waitress's arrival was less than welcome, but the moment she had gone again Fergus resumed.

'...what happened in Glasgow. I have at last paid off that rapacious old money-lender and on top of that, I think I have found a bank which might be prepared to finance my new plan. I know you will not breathe a word to anyone.' He paused, glanced quickly to either side as if to check for eavesdroppers, then continued in a low and eager voice, 'I have spoken to the farmer at Willowbrae. He's a canny fellow, with the light of greed in his eyes and I think he took the bait. As long as no one else gets wind of it and outbids me, I believe

[134]

I'm home ... And when I am, Mhairi darling, our future will be assured, and our children's future.'

Mhairi could not speak for the joy which welled up inside her, but there was no need for words. Her eyes said everything Fergus could have wished for.

'I brought something else back from Glasgow, too,' he began, smiling, then stopped and shook his head. 'No. Leo's impatience can be excused, but I am old enough to know better. I will save that particular surprise for Christmas after all.' And though Mhairi pleaded and begged, saying it was unfair to tantalize her so, he merely smiled.

'You have tantalized me for long enough, Mrs Grant. Surely you do not grudge me my turn?'

'Tantalize? Whatever can you mean, Mr Adam?'

Oblivious of coffee cups, customers and even the hovering waitress, Fergus told her. When they left the restaurant together a short while later, they did so hand in hand. Mhairi did not notice the elderly lady in black at the corner table, with her disapproving lorgnette, nor the expression on their waitress's face. If she had it would have made no difference. Why should it, when soon the whole world would know that Fergus Adam loved her and wanted her for his wife. For once, she had forgotten Tom completely.

By early December, the backlog of work at both quarry and yard had noticeably dwindled. The extra men proved more than worth their wages and Tom was well pleased. Another month and they should have caught up with the work and even be a little ahead.

'Then we can look around us,' said Wyness, beaming round the office table where the men had gathered for an impromptu meeting. Mhairi was at Rainbow Hill and Fanny at home, but from the ease with which the men talked together it was obvious that the female shareholders were not missed.

'I haven't forgotten that expansion idea,' went on Wyness, 'and I've put out my spies. I'll hear soon enough when anything comes on the market. Meanwhile, I keep my eyes and my ears open. As you should be doing.' He caught Tom's eye across the office table and winked. 'But I don't need to tell you that, Tom lad, do I? That was a shrewd contract you drew up with Adam, by the way. Very neat. I liked the touch about Donal choosing the rock himself.'

[135]

'So did Donal. You know how particular he is when he gets an idea into his head and it'll save a lot of time if he picks out the stone on the spot. He had his first look yesterday. Hamish went with him.'

'Did he indeed?' Wyness's eyes gleamed with expectation. Hamish was a bright and observant lad.

'Aye, he did. And came back with an interesting story to tell. Half the quarry floor roped off and out of bounds and the other half, Donal reckons, just about scraping the bottom. No wonder Adam is looking around for another hole to dig.'

'As we are, eh lad?' and Wyness winked.

'I met Farmer Dickie today,' said Tom after a moment. 'Mhairi's neighbour, remember. Dour fellow with too many children. Said he'd heard there might be a quarry going at Sclattie come Candlemas.'

'I heard that too,' put in Will, 'but I havena' had time to say. I was down at the railway, seeing to the loading of that ashlar for the Bon Accord job with the new carter O'Brien – a good lad, that one, and strong – when up comes this chappie. "Mr Diack?" he says, real deferential. "I heard tell as how you was looking for labour." Not any more, I tells him. We've all the men we need meantime. He looked real disappointed. Turns out he works at Sclattie and had just heard the London firm that owns it is giving up the lease at Candlemas. No telling who'll take the place over, he says, with only a year left and no saying what'll happen after, and I reckon I'd rather work for someone whose reputation I know. That's us.'

'But only a year to go,' repeated Lorn and shook his head. 'Nay worth it. Besides, I reckon Mr Wyness is still hankering after something Silvercairns way. Isn't that right?'

Wyness grinned. 'Maybe, lad, maybe. Though there's no word yet of anything coming on the market. But if Sclattie's ripe and for the picking, and the granite's good...'

'Aye, the granite's good enough,' agreed Will. 'Fine, heavy beds of rock, with a good line to the posts. More upright than our own, I reckon, but a shade darker colour. It maybe doesna take a polish quite as well as ours does, but it's nay bad and perfect for mason's work.'

'But it has been worked for years already,' pointed out Lorn. 'It could be worked out by now. Maybe that's why yon London firm is giving it up?'

'Maybe,' conceded Will, 'but it'll nay be scraped clean in a year

[136]

and a year'll give us time to get the feel of the place. It's nay a hundred feet deep yet and I reckon we can quarry it another forty at least and still find rock worth the taking.'

'Aye, maybe. But the deeper you go, the greater the cost of bringing the stuff to the surface. Look at Silvercairns. And with only a year ...'

'There is another possibility,' said Tom and waited till he had everyone's attention. 'I told you I met Farmer Dickie. Well, we got talking and he happened to mention ...'

When at last Tom finished, Wyness gave a long sigh of satisfaction. 'Well, well. I reckon that's worth investigating, don't you, lads? See to it, Tom. But softly, and carefully. It must be honest and above board, mind. Nothing underhand. And don't make any move without consulting me. When we buy, we want value for money. Remember that. And not a word outside these four walls,' he finished, looking round the table. 'We dinna want to alert the competition.'

Tom felt more genially inclined than he had done for months. The business was doing well and all set to do better. Whenever he thought of Farmer Dickie's news he positively glowed with excitement and the necessary secrecy of his delicate negotiations merely added to the thrill. Besides, with the shorter days and longer, darker evenings, he was home in time to see something of his children before they went to bed, and to spend time with his wife.

Though he usually spent the evenings studying this or that plan for whatever building work he was engaged in at the time, that did not matter. He sat in a comfortable chair at one side of the fire to do it, while Fanny sat with her sewing in another. He had only to look up to see her a mere few feet away across the hearthrug, to see the firelight touching her dark hair with light, and the calm expression on her sweet face. He knew that expression so well: at first he had assumed it meant unquestioning compliance in all things and complete submission to his wishes. Gradually he had realized this was not the case. Her calmness came not only from her unwavering love for him, which he never doubted, but from an equally unwavering knowledge of what was right and wrong. If ever there was conflict between these two certainties, as there had inevitably been in three years and more of marriage, Tom had discovered that her love for him did not

[137]

necessarily take precedence. Or, if she allowed it to do so against her natural instincts, then that calm expression that he loved became overlaid with trouble and doubt. She would say nothing, yet his conscience would grow restless until inevitably he would admit to himself that he was wrong. Sometimes he admitted it to Fanny, too, but not always. He suspected she knew it anyway, and a man had his pride.

But tonight there was no trace of trouble in her face nor in his own heart. The order books were full, the business prospering, plans for the future well in hand and his family in good health. Moreover the boiled mutton that Fanny had produced for his supper had been the finest he'd ever tasted. Even Mhairi could not have produced better.

The thought of his sister brought the first frown of the evening, but he smoothed it firmly away. That business of the Adam invitation was long past and forgotten. Mhairi had given her promise and had kept to it. Perhaps he need not have spoken to her quite so roughly, but he had apologized, and after all, he had spoken to her for her own good. She had been a little remote with him for a while, as was only to be expected, but the rift was healed over now, and it had all been for the best. Young Hamish was turning into a fine lad and Catriona seemed a bright and biddable lassie. With Annys to keep her company of an evening, what more could Mhairi want? Besides, if things went as Tom hoped they would, Mhairi, like all of them, would have other, more important things to think of. The excitement of that particular idea gave rise to another.

'I've been thinking, Fanny. The work's going well and come Christmas, I thought I might celebrate and take a wee holiday.'

Fanny looked up in astonishment. 'But Tom, you've never ...'

'Just for a day or two, mind,' he interrupted. 'I can drive you out a bit. See friends, maybe even go to the theatre or one of those concerts you're always talking about. What do you say?'

'That would be lovely, Tom. I know there is to be a Grand Concert in the County Rooms when little Arthur Napoleon will be the piano soloist. Just think, Tom, he is only twelve years old and such a genius. I do not know the programme, but I am sure it will be lovely and yes, I would dearly like to go. Unless, that is, you would be bored?'

'If I am, I shall fall asleep, and snore loudly all through the performance.'

'You will do no such thing, Tom, or I will ...' then seeing his

[138]

expression she laughed. 'But it will be your holiday, Tom dear, so you may do what you like. We could even take that railway journeyyou talked of. Georgie is older now and would not be so frightened, and there are sure to be special offers for New Year. We could ask Mhairi and the others and make up a pleasure party. There are special rates for that, too.'

'What a thrifty little housewife you have become,' teased Tom. 'Or don't you think your husband can afford the full price of a railway ticket?'

'There is no sense in throwing money away, however much you have. Tease me if you must, but when we have another child to feed as well as our two precious darlings you will be grateful that we did not squander all the family fortune before the little mite was born.'

'I will be grateful for more than that, Fanny,' Tom said quietly, suddenly reminded of the deadly hazards life held in store to spring on the unsuspecting, especially during childbirth. Suddenly, vividly, he saw in his mind the picture of his mother dying, of his father's helpless grief and despair . . . He closed his eyes, not speaking, till the fear that had gripped him receded into the shadows. Then he shook his head to rid it of such terrors, put aside his papers and stood up. With his back to the fire, like the proud head of the household that he was, he said, 'I know how careful you are with the housekeeping and how little you spend on yourself, Fanny, but if I am to have a holiday, which, as you know, is rare enough, then you must have something special too.'

'But I don't want anything, Tom. I . . .'

'Then I am sorry, but there will be no holiday. If you refuse the smallest indulgence, even though it is Christmas, then I have no option but to refuse too. I shall go to work as usual.'

'That is not fair, Tom. It is blackmail.'

'Yes.' He resumed his seat and took up his papers. 'Now if you will excuse me, I have to finish this estimate for the Ferryhill job.'

There was silence in the room as Tom frowned at his diagrams and columns of figures, and Fanny watched him in increasing uncertainty.

'I do so want you to have your holiday,' she said at last, in a small voice. 'And there is one thing I would like.'

'Good.' He smiled at her in triumph. 'Whatever it is, you shall have it, my love. You have only to say, and it is yours.'

[139]

Fanny looked at him, trying to assess the depth of his conviction. 'Anything?' she repeated doubtfully.

'Anything at all and I solemnly promise, hand on my heart, that, if it is in my power to give it, it shall be yours.'

When she did not speak, but still looked at him in hesitation, he said, 'Another servant, perhaps?'

She shook her head. 'I have all the help that I need. In fact, I am truly blessed, Tom dear, and I spoke the truth when I said that I can think of nothing that I lack. Except . . .' She bit her lip in indecision. 'You will be angry with me if I tell you.'

'I shall certainly be angry if you do not. So tell me at once. What is it?'

'I would like you to invite Fergus Adam to the house, when Mhairi is here.'

There was a long silence in which Fanny watched her husband's face in growing apprehension. He was not only frowning, but all the genial bonhomie that had been there a moment ago had vanished, leaving fuming resentment in its place.

'It would be only civil,' she said nervously, 'now that we have a business arrangement with him. Besides,' she went on, gathering courage, 'Jessie said that her cousin saw them having coffee together in the Royal Hotel and, to use her words, they were talking "intimately" across the table. Jessie's cousin is a waitress there and she told Jessie that he actually held Mhairi's hand.' Here Fanny gave a nervous giggle which, as she saw her husband's face, dried instantly in her throat.

'I knew you would be angry,' she said into the silence. 'I was afraid you did not really mean what you said.'

'Of course I meant it, woman. But I thought you would ask for a fur tippet or a wee muff or some other feminine falderal. Something solid, damn it. Something I can buy you in a shop.'

'Something easy,' said Fanny sadly. 'Yes, I thought you meant that. Even though you did say "anything at all". But you see I do not want a fur tippet and I have a muff already. I want you and Mhairi to be at ease together, as you used to be. I want Mhairi to be happy. That is all.'

'All?' exploded Tom. He leapt to his feet and began to stride around the room, thumping a fist now on the back of a chair, now on the mantelshelf or table. '*Happy*. With that fellow? Someone whose father murdered Alex?'

'He cannot help what his father did and when you met him, Tom, you said he was surprisingly courteous and straightforward to deal with. You know you did.'

'Business is one thing. Besides I mean to . . . Oh God! Did you say he was actually holding her hand?'

'Yes. I have suspected for some time that they have grown fond of each other . . .'

'Fond of her money, more like.'

'But Mhairi has no money, Tom dear . . .'

'Shares are money, aren't they? And Mhairi has a thirty percent share in our company. Ours, Fanny. And I mean to keep it that way, not hand over thirty percent of it to an Adam!'

'I think you do Fergus an injustice,' said Fanny quietly, and the expression Tom knew so well came over her face. 'He is a gentleman, who would not dream of taking what is not his, nor of depriving Mhairi's children of their due. He is an honourable man, with honourable intentions. I did not say anything, because it is not my business, but he and Mhairi have been seen together more than once. That is why I wanted you to invite him here, Tom. For Mhairi's sake. Please?'

'I can't, Fanny. You don't understand.'

'Yes, Tom, I think I do. And please do not thump the furniture so hard. I am afraid you will break something. It all stemmed from that invitation to the Adam wedding, did it not? Mhairi wanted to go out into the world again, to look about her and find a little enjoyment after so many years of loneliness and grief. You did not wish it. You forced a promise out of her by emotional blackmail and ever since have been ashamed of yourself, but too obstinate and proud to admit it.'

'Have I indeed? Then it is most kind of you to tell me.'

But having found the courage to say as much as she had, Fanny was not going to stop now. Tom was angrier than she had ever known him: whatever more she said could hardly make it worse and there was a small possibility that he might listen to her. To give her greater courage, she too stood up and faced him bravely across the room where flickering firelight picked out the cheerful reds and blues of the patterned hearthrug and cast leaping shadows across the wall behind them. The heavy curtains were drawn against the winter night, the lamps lit, and in other circumstances the room would have been a comforting cocoon to bind them close. As it was the cocoon

[141]

seemed to Fanny more like an arena where two antagonists faced each other in battle.

'I understand your anger,' she said carefully, making the first delicate move. 'You are angry on your friend's behalf. Because the man Mhairi has chosen is an Adam you are doubly angry, for no other reason than his dead father's crimes. Is poor Mhairi to spend the rest of her life without a man to love and care for her, her children without a father, just because you cannot find it in your heart to forget or forgive? It is unfair, Tom, and cruel. If I died I would not want you to be lonely and unhappy for the rest of your life. I would not want my children to lack a mother.'

'Don't say that!' cried Tom, shocked out of anger into fear.

'But I must say it, Tom. It is a possibility, after all. If I died and you met a good woman – and whatever you say to the contrary you know and I know that Fergus Adam is a good man – a good woman who would love my children as her own and with whom you could live content, then I would entreat all the angels in heaven to bring such a marriage about. Not straight away, of course,' she said, with a tentative smile, 'for my nose might be a little out of joint unless you waited at least a year. But if you had not remarried after seven years, then I would begin to think I had made marriage so unpleasant for you that you were glad to be single again.'

'Unpleasant? Oh God, Fanny . . .' He snatched her to him, holding her tight against his chest and burying his face in her hair. After a long moment, he said, very quietly, 'Do not talk of dying ever again, do you understand me?'

Then he led her to the sofa and pulled her down beside him, cradling her close, her head against his chest, his hand caressing her hair. After a while, Fanny heard the last of his anger leave him in a long breath of capitulation.

Then he said, very quietly, 'Tell me what it is you want me to do.'

The invitation took Mhairi by surprise, especially as her brother Tom rode all the way to the cottage expressly to deliver it in person. A concert party was surprise enough, for Tom was renowned for his scorn of all such evening entertainments, especially for working folk 'who have better things to do with their time', but supper afterwards at his house for herself and Annys, with a bed for the night so they need not travel home in the black cold of the winter small hours

[142]

showed a consideration that brought a smile of genuine gratitude to her face. When she had asked who else would be of the party, he had been evasive, but when she had pressed him he had elaborated his original 'various friends and business acquaintances' into 'Philip Drummond and his sister, among others'. He had added, not looking at her, 'Mr Adam was invited, too, but unfortunately has a prior engagement.' Mhairi suspected her brother was glad of it, but no matter. The first conciliatory move had been made and at least Annys was to meet her fairy prince at last. Mhairi could hardly contain her excitement both on her sister's behalf and on her own for though she knew Fanny's manipulative hand was behind the enterprise, Tom had agreed to it and that was victory enough.

Perhaps after all he had thawed towards her? For in spite of that cold kiss of apology all those months ago Mhairi had been aware of the draught of disapproval which still blew in her direction on the rare occasions when they met. Now, however, she felt the first real hope she had allowed herself since Fergus extracted his promise. The quarry was working smoothly again, there had been no further talk of Willowbrae, and now she was to be included, as of old, in Tom's family circle. Could it be that all this time she had feared for no reason?

Annys noticed the change in her sister and could not fathom the cause. It seemed to stem from that invitation of their brother's, but Annys could not imagine why the prospect of an evening in the company of Tom and Fanny, who they could visit whenever they chose, and Mr Drummond and his sister, who they hardly knew, should bring that light of suppressed excitement to Mhairi's eyes and set her singing when she thought herself unobserved. And though the Wynesses might be there too, that did not explain it. Baffled, Annys decided that the excitement must stem from the prospect of the concert itself, unless it was merely the opportunity it presented for dressing in one's smartest clothes and going out into company.

Though Annys herself had smiled obediently, said 'How lovely' and tried to sound enthusiastic when Mhairi had told her, she had little interest in the evening. She knew, from the number of times his name came into the conversation, that Mhairi hoped for something to develop between Annys and Mr Drummond, but Mhairi could hope as she chose. Annys would be polite to the gentleman, of course, but she had interest only in Kit O'Brien. After Mhairi's embarrassing behaviour when she had practically thrown him out of the house, Annys had the sense not to admit as much to her sister, but her ears strained for the sound of cart wheels on rutted track, a frequent occurrence when the quarry was working full tilt as it was now, but only one of those carts was accompanied by the distinctive 'clop' of Merry's hooves and Kit's inimitable whistle. Whenever she heard that, she contrived to be at the window, or in the yard outside to watch him pass.

But, as he had told her himself, he was his own boss and though he did carting work for Rainbow Hill, he also worked for anyone else who would pay him well, including Silvercairns. He moved household belongings, took cabin trunks to the railway station, delivered parcels. 'Though I steer clear of the harbour, so as not to step on the Shore Porters' toes, and I draw the line at coal. Granite dust plays havoc enough with my precious paintwork, no matter how much straw and sacking I cover it with, but at least granite is clean.'

Pigs were not so clean, nor crates of hens, nor turnips, and even sea-sand had its drawbacks. But no matter what load Kit conveyed in his precious vehicle, it was always spotless the following day, paintwork touched up and wheel spokes gleaming. He had even bought a pair of splendid carriage lamps so that the shorter daylight hours of winter need not cramp his style.

'Next, I'll be looking for that second cart I mentioned, then I'll be needing an assistant to drive it for me, eh lad?' and he had ruffled Hamish's hair, to the boy's proud delight. That had been on an occasion when he stopped the cart at the gate to drop off Hamish and Catriona, after picking them up on the road from school.

Unfortunately, Mhairi had seen and disapproved. The Irish 'tink' might be a good carter, as her brothers said he was, but he slept, like his horse, in one of Mrs Macrae's outhouses and hadn't a penny to his name. She knew nothing to his actual detriment, but she knew nothing of his family background either and he made her nervous. After that, Kit had had the sense to drop any passenger he might have collected well out of sight of the cottage window.

So it was a surprise one morning in December to hear the familiar whistle, run to the window, and see Kit O'Brien on the box of the cart with a strange boy at his side. The boy held the gathered reins in one hand and a whip in the other and looked inordinately proud of himself. It was even more of a surprise when the vehicle drew up at the gate and Kit O'Brien jumped down, a covered basket in his hand.

[144]

'Special delivery, ma'am,' he said with a wink when Annys opened the scullery door.

'Who is it?' called Mhairi from the kitchen.

Before Annys could answer Mhairi came through from the front of the house, a pinned and tucked garment in shimmering yellow taffeta in one hand and a threaded needle in the other.

'Mr O'Brien is delivering this basket,' said Annys, blushing at the smile in his eyes. 'There is a note, addressed to you.'

'From Tom, I expect. Put it on the table, Annys. Thank you Mr O'Brien. I am sorry I cannot offer you refreshment after your journey, but as you see I am rather busy.' She indicated the sewing. 'An order that must be finished by this afternoon.'

'Would you like ale?' said Annys quickly. 'And perhaps the boy would like milk, or ginger cordial?'

'What boy?' said Mhairi. She moved swiftly back into the kitchen and to the little front window, a flurry of pins and yellow thread drifting after her across the floor. If the carter was on his way to Rainbow Hill, as seemed more than probable for Tom would hardly send him all this way with a mere basket, then she wanted to know which particular scallywag was riding with him. They had had too much trouble with mischievous lads in the past to take any chances.

But what she saw set her heart beating suddenly faster. The lad was about Hamish's age, with an unmistakable shock of bright red hair: Lizzie Lennox's son, from Silvercairns.

What was the boy doing on Kit O'Brien's cart? Unless he came as messenger, from Fergus? For the first time the incongruity of the relationship struck Mhairi, hard, and with it the realization that whoever married Fergus would have to accept Leo too. It was a thought she had deliberately suppressed until now, as she had suppressed the thought of marriage: the latter out of superstition, but the former out of sheer cowardice.

She had no doubts about Fergus's relationship with her own children, should the heavens bless her with such a husband, nor about her own ability to cope with Leo. It was the havoc the boy might cause in the family nest that struck her now, with cold foreboding, as she watched him flick the whip experimentally above his head, then at the branch of a nearby birch, bare but for a flutter of tenacious leaves, like well-worn yellow coins, which even the winter winds had not dislodged. The whip cracked short of its target and Leo, frowning, prepared to try again.

[145]

At that precise moment, by some mischievous quirk of fate, Hamish himself rounded the corner from the direction of the quarry, where Mhairi had sent him on a message, and stopped dead in his tracks. Mhairi had time to see the Lennox boy forget mischief and preen himself with importance on the box of the cart, the triumphant expression on his face swiftly followed by a rude, protruding tongue before she looked swiftly back at her son, dreading the worst. Then she bit her lip in amused relief. For instead of retaliating with fists flying as she had feared, he was solemnly squinting, tongue lolling out like some hideous gargoyle, while his ears, she saw with astonishment, were definitely moving up and down. The Lennox boy's own face lost its derisive look and instead took on one of wondering admiration. Then Hamish suddenly became his old self again, hitched the mason's bag into a position of prominence on his shoulder and turned in through the garden gate, ignoring cart and Lennox boy, and with a jaunty swagger in his step.

''Morning, Kit,' he called, as O'Brien appeared at the side of the house. Hamish touched his cap in a gesture of manly comradeship. 'If that's blasting powder in the back of yon cart and you're on your way to the quarry, you'd best hurry. Uncle Will's nay in the best of tempers, with the bore holes ready and waiting and nay powder to pour into them. Leastways, nay powder that's dry. But you can tell him I'll be back to help out, just as soon as I've had my piece. Oh, hello Ma. I didna see you there. Anything to eat? I'm starving.'

'Aye,' said Mhairi, suppressing a smile. 'There's bread newly baked, and cheese. But you'll have to get it yourself, for my hands are full.' She looked again out of the window, then at the basket which Annys, for some reason, still held in her hands.

The girl's cheeks were pinker than usual, though it could have been the heat of the fire and the baking. 'And perhaps you'd like to take some out to the Lennox boy. As a peace offering.'

'And for Mr O'Brien,' said Annys quickly. 'I will carry it out to him at the gate.' Before Mhairi could speak, Annys put down the covered basket at one end of the scullery table and began to cut bread at the other.

Mhairi sat down again in the family kitchen, her sewing in her lap, but though the needle was threaded and the seam only half stitched, she did not attempt to complete it. Instead she waited, her heart thudding with excitement, till Hamish and Annys had gone, each bearing gifts, to the gate, then she walked into the empty scullery and

[146]

stretched out a hesitant hand towards the basket. It must be from Tom, she told herself over and over. Just because the Lennox boy was in the cart did not mean ... But she had best hurry, before Annys came back. Annys's eyes were too sharp for comfort and she had not forgotten her sister's hysterical threat to tell Tom. Now, when they were almost reconciled, she dare risk nothing that might jeopardize success.

She peeled back the crisp linen cover and saw three brace of pheasant, trussed ready for the table, a jar of ginger preserve, another of pineapple, and three bottles of what looked like excellent claret. There was also a sealed note. Trembling, she slit the seal.

In friendship, and in the hope, very soon, of something more.

Swiftly she thrust the note deep into her pocket. The words were brief, correct, even unromantic, but she read the joyful intensity and passion behind them as clearly as if Fergus had been here in the room with her, his arms around her and ... Abruptly she pushed aside the thought. Soon, very soon, there would be no more need for secrecy: she could entertain Fergus here with open welcome and ride over to Silvercairns to call whenever she chose. Until the day when she became Mrs Adam and Silvercairns became her home, for ever. It was almost too wonderful to believe: she, the daughter of a humble quarryman, miraculously changed, as by a fairy wand, into the lady of the manor.

For a moment her faith faltered. What would Lettice Adam say when she came back from the war and found her brother promised to a girl who had once been her own dressmaker? What the world in general would say she had little doubt: but it is Fergus I love, and would still love if he were penniless and homeless. The thought drove the warmth from her heart and left her suddenly cold with dread. She had been reared in poverty, was used to it and could face it again, if need be, with fortitude and faith. But Fergus was different. For him it would be hard, especially for his pride. Dear Fergus was a gentleman, upright and honest, with such innocent hopes: please God let him buy Willowbrae before someone else takes it from him. Please God let Tom forget business as well as personal rivalry and leave Silvercairns alone. Please God ...

'Who is it from, Mhairi?' said Annys, bursting in from the garden on a gust of cold air. 'Hamish has gone with them, by the way. Kit ... I mean Mr O'Brien is showing him and Leo how he can control the horse with the reins in one hand – so he can eat bread and cheese with the other.'

But Mhairi seemed hardly to be listening.

'Is it really from Tom?' Annys peeled back the cloth which Mhairi had replaced and peered into the basket. 'Tom would never send *claret*. I doubt he would send pheasants either unless he had too many himself.'

'Annys, that is not kind,' said Mhairi automatically, her mind still with Fergus. He had sent his gifts out of eager impatience, at the same time a reminder and a pledge. But at least he had had the delicacy not to embarrass her with anything personal, she reflected, as Annys inspected the contents. After all, anyone might send a friend a brace of pheasant and the world would think nothing of it. Yet at the same time, she confessed to a vague disappointment. It was rash and foolish of her, and the basket of food was both generous and welcome, but if, in his loving impatience, he must send her presents, she would have liked something, however trivial, just for herself.

From the saddle of his favourite horse, Fergus Adam surveyed the stretch of winter scrubland in front of him with a mixture of apprehension and faith. This was the land for him. Unprepossessing enough at this time of year, with colourless grass, dead heather, tufts of withered this and that, but scattered among the rabbit warrens and the bracken, surface rock which even at a distance was full of promise. He had checked with Crawford at Banchory, with every book on the subject in his father's library, and finally with his own foreman and all agreed. There was no reason why this land, which abutted his own at Silvercairns, should not produce the same fine-grained, blue-grey mixture of mica, felspar and quartz. The quarry workings at Silvercairns had thrown up stone of a progressively richer colour the deeper they had quarried and the fact that what tentative scratchings there had been in the past on this unlovely scrubland had produced nothing but inferior 'barr' meant nothing. Or rather, it meant that a better bargain might be struck over the price.

If he could bring the farmer to the negotiating table. The man had made ominous rumblings on the subject of railway compensation, but as the railway in no way abutted his land, Fergus had interpreted this merely as toe-in-the-water bargaining and had answered accordingly.

'If you feel that you might find a better price with the Deeside Railway, then I shall quite understand, Mr McPhee. They go by the book, of course, with no consideration for particular circumstances, and often it is wiser to sell to a private individual, but naturally the choice is yours. I will not detain you further.' He had walked a good three steps away, before saying, as if on an afterthought, 'Of course, I might still be willing to consider the land, even if the railway company reject it, but not for much longer. I have a business to run, Mr McPhee, as I am sure you understand, and yours is not the only piece of land under consideration. In fact, I have no doubt I shall find the ideal place for my not inconsiderable investment before the year is out. Good day to you, Mr McPhee.'

He had spent an agonized five days wondering whether he had overplayed his hand and waiting for the wretched man to make a move, before the expected note arrived. Mr McPhee had been thinking things over and might be willing to come to an agreement, for the right price.

The fish was nibbling.

Fergus had written back, suggesting a date in three days' time It would not do to appear too eager. But he had not been able to resist the ride out to the edge of Silvercairns land and on to the wasteland which, if all went well, would soon be his. He had brought Leo with him, on the pony which had been Fergus's summer indulgence for the lad, not so much to keep him happy as to keep him out of Fergus's hair. Leo had taken to the saddle like a duck to water and Fergus had no fears for him on that score, provided he keep within Silvercairns limits except by prior permission. As the penalty for disobedience was to be instant removal of the pony, for ever, Fergus had no fears on that score either. After Lettice's departure, he had early established in his relationship with Leo that he meant what he said.

Now, looking sideways at his unlikely companion, he felt a stir of real affection for his dead brother's bastard son. The boy was as disreputable in appearance, as uncouth in speech and as unreliable in behaviour as he had ever been, but there was a core of simple loyalty somewhere in the lad, an enthusiasm and vigour which, if channeled in the right direction, could work wonders, and the boy seemed genuinely interested in the work of the quarry.

Fergus himself had enjoyed the business of quarrying rock from

[149]

the deepening bowl of Silvercairns for as long as he could remember: ever since the day his father had first taken him, at the age of five, down the spiral path onto the floor of the quarry. It had been a mere seventy feet deep then, and over the years he had watched it deepening, while Old Mackinnon, his father's foreman, had initiated him into the wonders of blasting, boring, hewing and shaping. Fergus would have welcomed Old Mackinnon's advice now, for the challenge of starting a new quarry from the first surface scratch was both daunting and exhilarating. His father's brooding shade still hovered in the shadows of Silvercairns, which, after all, was both the old man's triumph and his tribute. But the new quarry would be Fergus's alone. A new start, for a new life. He would buy it as a wedding gift for Mhairi, work it as a livelihood, for her and for their children. It would be the symbol of their life together, and their hope for the future. The thought swelled his chest with pride and challenge.

'You see that rock over there,' he said to the boy beside him, pointing with his finger. 'The one beside the gorse bush? I think we'll make our first diggings there.'

'Can I light the first fuse, Uncle Fergus? I'll be careful, truly I will. Please, Uncle Fergus? I promise I'll do exactly what you say.' The pony, feeling its rider's excitement, shifted restlessly on the earthen track and with a 'Whoa there' and a smack, Leo brought it firmly to order.

'All right,' said Fergus, leaning down from the superior height of his own mount and ruffling Leo's already ruffled hair. 'I accept your promise. But we haven't got the land yet, remember.'

'But you've got it nearly, haven't you, Uncle Fergus? And no one else wants it, do they?'

'I sincerely hope not,' said Fergus with feeling. 'So I would be grateful if you would keep this information to yourself, Leo. No shouting the news at the top of your voice in the Castlegate, or boasting to your friends. Remember the quarry may one day be yours – but only if no one takes it from us first.'

'Silvercairns will be mine anyway,' said Leo, sitting easily in the saddle and narrowing his eyes into the distance as he measured the extent of this new piece of land. 'Grandpa said so, before he died. Hamish Grant has a quarry, but he only has a piece of one. And however many other quarries they get, he'll still only have a piece. I have a whole one, all to myself, Grandpa said so, and when we get this one I'll have two. Won't I, Uncle Fergus?'

Fergus did not answer, suddenly aware of the obligations to posterity. When he married and had children, then Leo must take his turn with the others. It made the acquisition of Willowbrae all the more vital: Silvercairns might last Fergus's lifetime, but it could not hope to provide for the next generation.

'Won't I?' persisted Leo at his side and Fergus sighed.

'You will have nothing at all if you boast about your prospects to all the riff-raff of Aberdeen, as you are boasting to me now, because they will join together out of sheer greed and plot to take the whole lot away.' Even as he spoke the words Fergus felt a cold hand at his heart and added, as much for his own spirits as for Leo's, 'Why don't you ride on home and see if there's a letter from Aunt Lettice? She is sure to write to us for Christmas even if she is in the wilds of Scutari and I will catch you up in a moment.'

When the boy had gone, digging his heels into the pony's fat flanks and scudding off in a swirl of dust, Fergus turned back to the prospect laid out before him. It was winter land, dry and sparse, but please God it would be fruitful.

'Do I really have to come, Mhairi?' pleaded Annys on the morning of the Great Day. 'I would really much rather stay here with the others.'

'I know you would. But Tom and Fanny have invited you, most particularly, and it would be rude to refuse, especially at this late date.' Mhairi was folding a particularly pretty shawl prior to packing it away into a travelling bag. 'I have put in your night clothes and your best stockings.'

'But I would be much more useful here, Mhairi. It is a lot for Catriona to do. She is only seven and ...'

'The food is all prepared and ready. All the child needs to do is serve it and the boys will help her.'

'Nevertheless, I ...'

'You will come with me,' said Mhairi firmly. It had taken long enough to arrange a meeting between Annys and Philip Drummond and she was not going to let the opportunity slip by because of an attack of shyness on Annys's part. And it was shyness, Mhairi was certain of it. Annys had been alternately curious and reluctant ever since the invitation had arrived: she was unused to going out into any sort of company, and to go to the concert with a supper party afterwards was no doubt a daunting and overpowering prospect,

[151]

even though the host and hostess were her own brother and sister-in-law. But Annys must not be allowed to back out of it now.

Then, remembering the girl's extraordinary outburst and not wishing to sound too domineering and parental, she added gently, 'Quite apart from politeness to Fanny, I need your company. You know how stern Tom as been towards me and I will feel braver with you beside me.'

'Truly?' Annys looked at her in amazement. The idea of Mhairi needing moral support was astonishing enough, especially where the family was concerned, but that she should need it from Annys . . . It made her feel suddenly mature and womanly, as if she and Mhairi were almost equal.

'Truly,' said Mhairi.

'Then perhaps I will come, after all. If you really need me?'

'I do.' Mhairi kissed Annys lightly on the cheek and smiled her approval. 'You are looking particularly pretty today, Annys. And I know you will enjoy the music. It is to be in the Round Room and Fanny said she has taken the best seats in a little group so we will all be able to sit together. I expect Tom will fall asleep in the shadows at the back and not be noticed!'

'And you can sit beside Fanny in the front, with your lovely lace shawl,' said Annys, her eyes shining, 'so that all the audience can see how smart and elegant you look. As it is a special performance, I expect all sorts of people will be there.' She looked meaningfully at Mhairi, who averted her eyes.

'Yes.' Mhairi made great play of tying the ribbon bow at her neck. 'After all, it is a charity performance.'

In fact, the evening's entertainment had been organized by the Florence Nightingale Fund committee, of which both Mrs Wyness and her daughter Fanny were members, and Mhairi knew that, had not Fanny secured their acceptance first, the Drummonds would have made part of the party from Silvercairns. Fergus had told her himself that he owed it to his sister Lettice to support the event, 'though with Austria's ultimatum to Russia and so many rumblings of peace in the air, that wretched war should soon be ended, and the need for military hospitals ended with it, at least in that part of the world.' He would be with his own party, but had promised to look out for her during the evening, and however large the audience, she knew that he would find her.

The Assembly Rooms were glittering with the collected wealth of town and county for the charity performance. Diamonds added their sparkling light to that of the central chandelier and gold and jewels flashed from the ranks of solid citizens assembled in their public-spirited finery to support the efforts of the musicians on the raised dais in front of them, and, by their patronage, of the devoted nurses who laboured night and day to relieve the suffering of the nation's sick and wounded soldiers, far across the sea.

'Our Queen is very moved by the plight of her loyal soldiers,' murmured Miss Drummond to Annys, during the first interval. Annys had been placed between the two Drummonds, on the second row of chairs, with her brother Tom on Miss Drummond's other side, though when the lights were turned off, except for a single chandelier above the musicians, Annys had noticed that Tom drew his chair further back into the shadows and, though she did not look directly at him, she was almost certain he had slept through the entire first half. However, when the lights went up again, he and Philip Drummond, with Fanny's father, had gone in the direction of the supper rooms in search of liquid refreshment, leaving the ladies to study the audience, wave to friends, stroll up and down if they chose to do so, and generally entertain themselves.

'We were taking the waters at Pannanich, Miss Diack,' explained Henrietta whose voice at the best of times was little more than a breathless murmur, 'and were privileged on one occasion to be invited to Balmoral. The Queen was very gracious...'

Annys made suitable conversational noises while she tried to see past Mrs Wyness's ample shoulders into the elegant promenade area of white-domed ceilings and elegant, fluted columns where the more restless of the audience moved to and fro in a shimmer of diamonds and rustling silks and where she was sure she would see Fergus Adam, if she searched hard enough. She did so want Mhairi to marry him and be happy.

'... attended the church on Sunday. Such a beautiful service, and a truly uplifting sermon. *Not slothful in business; fervent in spirit; serving the Lord.* The hour flew past in the sheer beauty of the words as the minister expounded the meaning of his text. From Romans, chapter twelve. True religion, he explained, is not a thing only for a Sunday, but should colour every action of our lives. True religion is being and doing good. I do hope you agree, Miss Diack?'

'Certainly,' said Annys and then, as manners required something

[153]

more than that, added, 'You must have heard many interesting sermons in your travels.'

Miss Drummond had.

'I do declare I see Amelia Macdonald,' said Mrs Wyness, peering through her lorgnette at the doorway into the Square Room. 'And as thin as ever.' Amelia had been married for eight years and still no sign of children. 'She is with, let me see, her husband, Niall Burnett. And isn't that the provost? Talking to old Archie Burnett, there, standing behind her. And unless I'm much mistaken, that is . . . no, he's gone. Or it wasn't him at all.'

'Who, Mamma,' said Fanny, not really listening. She had been telling Mhairi about her infant daughter's teething problems and comparing the benefits of baked crusts and ivory. 'Georgie always chewed on an ivory shoe-horn, but Vicky insists on a bone, just like a dog,' she confided, in a giggling whisper. 'Mamma thinks it very vulgar, but Tom said the time to worry would be if the little thing started barking! I think Mamma thought that vulgar, too, but . . .'

'Good evening. I hope I am not intruding on a private party?'

The voice set Mhairi's heart pounding with joy and agitation, and she knew before she turned her head who she would see. Mrs Wyness moved her heavy crimson bulk with slow dignity to peer behind her, lowering the lorgnette and blinking to adjust her eyes to closer vision. Annys stared in wide-eyed silence and Miss Drummond did nothing at all. It was Fanny who took charge.

'Good evening, Mr Adam. And you are not interrupting anything, except a shameless inspection of our fellow concert-goers. I am afraid the gentlemen are not here, having gone in search of refreshment, but if you do not mind a company of defenceless ladies, please join us.'

'I cannot imagine more charming company,' said Fergus, bowing with formal courtesy. 'I confess I took the liberty, like you, of studying our fellow music-lovers and when I saw that Miss Drummond was among your party I ventured to come and pay my respects. And, of course, to Mrs Wyness, if you will allow me, madam? And Mrs Grant?'

His eyes met and held Mhairi's for only a moment, but a moment of such intensity that she knew without words what he had come to say and the passionate, if silent, declaration set her heart dancing and her blood singing in her veins.

'Well, Fergus,' said Fanny with uninhibited friendliness. 'Now that we have disposed of the formal courtesies, we can relax into informality again. I am sorry you could not join us for the evening, but I quite see why not. You, like all true patriots, were required to do your bit and if the size of your party is anything to go by, you are doing it splendidly.'

'As you are, Fanny,' smiled Fergus. 'I only hope Florence Nightingale will be grateful.'

'I am sure she will, and so will the poor wounded soldiers. But it is a lovely evening, is it not? Arthur Napoleon is truly a genius. His mother must be so proud of him.' Then, remembering Tom's martyred tolerance, she added anxiously, 'I trust you are enjoying the concert, Fergus?'

'I could say, not as much as I am enjoying present company,' he said with a twinkle which managed somehow to include all of them, though he spoke directly to Fanny, 'but I doubt you would swallow such outright flattery, true though it might be. And the performance is certainly very good. You will forgive me for not doting on the Infant Prodigy to quite the extent of the ladies, but I grant you that Piatti on the violoncello is tolerable.'

'Tolerable?' cried Fanny, then blushed. 'You are teasing me, Fergus, and it is not fair. I think the concert is lovely!'

Amid general laughter, Fergus, at Fanny's invitation, took the vacant chair beside Mhairi and there followed a rash of small talk in which Miss Drummond, although the ostensible purpose of his visit, took no part, and Annys little more. Then a bell rang somewhere in the depths of the building.

'It seems I must go,' said Fergus, with a sigh of regret. But before he stood up, he lent towards Mhairi and, under cover of retrieving her programme, murmured, 'A beautiful setting, for a beautiful woman: the perfect pairing. As I hope to find, with you.'

Mhairi opened the programme to hide her blushing elation, but she need not have worried. All eyes were on Fergus Adam's handsome face as he said aloud, with a neat bow in Miss Drummond's direction, 'I hope we will meet again, very soon. It has been such a pleasure.' With similar courtesies to the other ladies of the party, he made his departure and disappeared.

'Mr Adam is a perfect gentleman, do you not agree, Miss Diack?' whispered Henrietta Drummond. 'To make his way through those dreadful crowds in order to pay his respects ...'

Annys thought she finished her breathless sentence with the

words 'to me', but fortunately was spared the need to answer by the arrival of her brother Tom and the others.

Supper at the Elmbank house was a pleasant enough affair. Philip Drummond made himself agreeable to everyone with an ease of manner which was both courteous and friendly. In spite of the fact that her heart was, as Annys put it in her private daydreams, given to another, she found him pleasant company, and it was no effort to be friendly in return. Kit was dark and weather-tanned, his eyes dancing with mischief and humour, and with magic on his tongue. But Annys would be the first to admit he was not suave or elegant or even particularly civilized. Philip Drummond was all of these, as well as being golden of skin and hair, with the pale blue eyes of the Saxon. He was taller than Kit, too, with an elegance of dress and manner which Kit could never hope to achieve, were he to make his fortune ten times over. But Kit had hitched a ride, undetected, on Mr Dickie's hay cart and had thrown her a pebble as a keepsake. Kit had ridden on the tail-board of the royal train and painted his own name on his own, hard-won, cart.

Mr Drummond, she remembered, had also ridden on the royal train, but in one of the elegant saloon carriages, with his delicate sister beside him. The idea of either of them riding illicitly in the guard's van brought a smile to her lips and she had difficulty suppressing a giggle.

Then she realized that the delicate sister was speaking to her.

' . . . so glad you think as I do, Miss Diack. So we will sit on those little chairs, over there in the corner, and I will tell you my plan. But first, if you would be so good as to fetch me a dish of tea? And perhaps a tiny biscuit?'

Dutifully, Annys did so and when Miss Drummond motioned her to the chair beside her own, Annys took it. Mhairi was talking with the Wynesses and Fanny, and Tom and Philip Drummond were deep in consultation about the progress of the fountain. Annys wondered whether they had managed to get the right stone from Silvercairns, and whether Tom had finally swallowed his enmity in the cause of business co-operation and profit. She hoped so, for Mhairi's sake.

'We get on so very well together, don't you think Miss Diack?' her companion was saying and, without really listening to what appeared to be the usual inconsequential meander, no doubt about her brother and herself, Annys said 'yes'.

[156]

'I am so glad you agree, Miss Diack. But may I call you Annys as we are already such friends? And you must call me Hetty. That is my brother's pet name for me and always has been, as long as I can remember. We are orphans, you see, Annys dear. My mother died when I was born.'

'Mine died when I was four, but I can hardly remember her.'

'There. I knew we were soulmates. We have both suffered, Annys dear, but whenever I find myself grieving for poor Mamma, I think of her in heaven, looking down upon me and spreading her angel's wings to shield me from harm. Do you do the same? I knew it. You are so sympathetic and understanding. Annys dear,' and here she laid her soft paw on Annys's arm. 'I want to ask you a great, great favour, and when you hear what it is, I hope, no I *know*, you will say yes.'

Annys half rose from her seat, expecting a request for more tea or another of Fanny's ratafia biscuits, but Miss Drummond caught her hand with a small cry of alarm.

'Don't go. That is, not unless ... unless you do not wish to hear ...' Her voice trailed into woebegone silence and she looked at Annys with reproachful eyes.

Annys subsided into her seat again with a bright smile of encouragement. 'I am sorry Miss Drummond ... Hetty. I only stood up because I thought you wished for your shawl, perhaps, or a glass of water.'

'Dear girl,' murmured Hetty, tranquillity restored. 'I want to ask you for something much more precious than that. When my brother goes away again, as he does too often, alas, on tedious business trips to tedious places, I wish you would agree to come and keep me company? Just for a little while, Annys dear? I feel so vulnerable, you know, without a friend beside me and this evening you have been so very sweet and understanding. We have talked of so many things, and I know you feel and think as I do on all of them. Please say you will come?'

'I ...' Annys hesitated, her eyes darting around the room in search of Mhairi. Mhairi would have to be consulted, asked for her permission.

'Please?' said the soft voice at her side.

Annys smiled. After all, why should she consult Mhairi? She was a grown woman, perfectly capable of making her own decisions. Besides, she knew Mhairi liked the Drummonds, even had ideas for pairing her with Philip Drummond one day. It would be her secret joke to go voluntarily into the Drummond household, knowing her heart to be impregnable, her hand as good as promised. Though Kit had never said as much, she knew he felt as she did, knew she was the only girl for him. Hadn't he called her his Pretty Dancer, taken her arm and led her like a lady to admire his horse and cart, talked of the fortune he would make one day, and looked at her with smiling eyes which told her clearer than any words could do that the fortune was to be for her? It would take a year or two, maybe even as many as five, but she would wait. And while she was waiting, what harm would there be in taking a job? Mhairi would manage without her.

Annys supposed she would be some sort of paid companion, though naturally money had not been mentioned, but paid or not, she would enjoy living in the Adams' Guestrow House. And for a man who thought nothing of riding, uninvited, on the royal train, the Guestrow fortress would present no obstacle. Kit would find her out and visit her, just as he always did, and without having to run the gauntlet of Mhairi's watchful eyes.

'Thank you, Hetty,' she said. 'Of course, I must ask my sister whether she can spare me, but I am sure she will agree. And I will be honoured, and delighted, to keep you company whenever you wish.'

'Oh how lovely!' Miss Drummond clapped her little hands in a spurt of delight and when her brother turned his head in surprise, called out, 'Philip, dear. Such delightful news. Miss Diack has consented to be my companion next time you are so disagreeable and cruel as to leave me all alone.'

'Has she indeed? Splendid, splendid,' and he resumed his conversation with hardly a break.

'You see, Annys dear, how unsympathetic men can be? Always caught up in their tedious world of business? I could not possibly tell my brother the things I will be able to tell you. About Mr Adam, for instance,' she confided, dropping her voice even lower. 'You must have noticed how he looked at me. A little indiscreet of him, perhaps, but understandable. And did you not think it most courteous of him to seek me out like that in the middle of the concert? Courteous and perhaps, dare I say it, something more?'

It was the last day of the year and a Monday. Sunday was always a day apart, a day of rest, relaxation and enjoyment which families could spend together, but yesterday had been doubly special in that the

[158]

holiday had spread to include Hogmanay, too. For old Wyness had seen the difference a week's rest from work had made in Tom and though there was work still unfinished in the yard which he was itching to see tackled, he declared a universal holiday for quarry and yard alike. Besides, Mrs Wyness had been nagging him lately to 'take things easy' and a holiday would keep her happy and maybe quieten her tongue. It was good practice to tie up ends and clear what could be cleared before the end of the year, but the Drummond fountain alone needed weeks more work and what difference would one day make?

Since the hiring of so many more men at quarry and yard, the backlog had dwindled anyway, the tension eased, and when the work force resumed for the new year, they would do so, Wyness confidently expected, with renewed vigour and enthusiasm. There might, of course, be the odd sore head as a result of too many liquid toasts, as families and friends gathered to watch the old year out and the new year in, but fresh air and exercise would soon cure that.

Children would stay up late, unreproved; neighbours would call, drink, gossip, leave again to call on other neighbours; old grievances would be set aside for the moment, old quarrels be swept away with the dust of the old year, and general good will would prevail.

'Well, lass?' said Wyness, beaming at his wife who was adjusting the strings of her bonnet at the looking-glass in the hall. 'When you've finished fiddling with yon ribbon things, we'd best be going. Mackie has been waiting at the door this five minutes or more and you know we promised to call in at Fanny's on the way.'

'Fuss, fuss, fuss,' grumbled his wife good-naturedly. 'Knowing my daughter she'll not be ready anyway, what with Georgie to spruce up and little Vicky. As for Tom, he'll be "working", like as not.'

'No one is working today, remember?' He pulled open the heavy front door and felt the winter wind cold on his cheek. 'Brr. Hurry up, for pity's sake, afore we freeze solid where we stand.'

'Work?' repeated Fanny in dismay. 'But it's a holiday, remember. Mr Wyness said ... '

'I'll not be long,' interrupted Tom. He pulled on his Sunday overcoat, kissed her on the cheek and strode for the door. 'Just a spot of business I want to settle before the New Year. You go on to Rainbow Cottage with your parents and I'll see you there.'

[159]

'You will come, Tom, won't you?' cried Fanny, hurrying after him to the door. 'You know you promised.'

'I'll come, you little silly.' He looked down at her with a strange expression which she was to remember afterwards and understand, when it was too late. 'Now go back into the warm before you catch a chill. And don't worry. I would not miss it for the world.'

He went out of the house, whistling.

Fergus Adam stood in front of the pier-glass in his dressing-room and checked his appearance for the dozenth time. Not naturally a vain man, he nevertheless felt the need for reassurance on today of all days. For he had promised himself that the end of the year would see the end of secrecy. Whatever the differences in background, whatever the enmities and rancours of the past, whatever the antagonisms of their respective families, Mhairi Diack Grant was his choice and, in spite of her evasions, he knew that he was hers. All that remained was for him to make his formal declaration, and then, her hand in his, to tell the world. Thinking of that world and Mhairi's deep-rooted loyalties, he saw a flicker of doubt cross the face in the oval glass, but it was quickly gone. She loved him and he loved her. That was all that mattered. He straightened his shoulders, flicked a speck of dust from a sleeve, adjusted his cuffs.

But even the most nervous of eyes had to acknowledge that his linen was spotless, his jacket and trousers of impeccable style and execution, his boots like mirror glass, his cravat, tied for the fourth time, as neat as it was possible for it to be.

He checked one waistcoat pocket for watch and chain, then the other for the small, velvet-lined box which he took out and opened yet again. Yes, it was as perfect as he remembered, elegant, beautiful, utterly appropriate.

He did not hear the door open behind him, nor the boots on the muffling Indian mat.

'What are you doing, Uncle Fergus? Why are you looking at yourself in the mirror? What is that box in your hand? When are we...?'

'Out! How many more times do I have to...'

'But I did!' cried Leo in indignation. 'I knocked and you didn't hear.'

'Then get out and knock again, till I do,' roared Fergus and was instantly ashamed: his nervousness was not Leo's fault. So when the knock came a moment later, threatening to splinter the door panel and loud enough to wake the dead, all Fergus said was 'Come in.' When Leo glared at him in mutinous defiance, he added, in the interests of discipline, 'I said "knock", not "kick",' but the rebuke was a mere technicality, without rancour.

Honour satisfied, Leo relaxed and began to range the room, picking up things and dropping them, opening drawers, waiting for Fergus's patience to snap. It did.

'Well, now that you are in, what do you want?'

Leo was instant eagerness. 'When are we going, Uncle Fergus? Can I drive the gig? I can drive with one hand now, Kit showed me how. He showed Hamish Diack too, but I can do it best. Can I drive all the way there and all the way back?'

'No.'

'Why not, Uncle Fergus? And you've tied that already. Why are you undoing it again?'

'For pity's sake, Leo, will you . . . Look, just go downstairs and wait for me in the hall. I will be down in one minute.'

'Then I'll wait and go down with you, Uncle Fergus.' He picked up one of the silver-backed brushes from the dressing chest, peered close into the glass and attempted carefully to brush the red tangle of his hair.

'Put that down,' said Fergus, with dangerous quiet. 'Go out of my room and downstairs. Stand absolutely still in the middle of the hall until I come. Because if you do not, you will not come with me to Rainbow Cottage. You will go to bed and stay there, till the day after tomorrow, when all the celebrations will be over. Do you understand?'

'Yes, Uncle Fergus,' said Leo in a small voice. With exaggerated care he replaced the brush, tiptoed across the floor to the door, opened it and closed it soundlessly behind him.

Fergus let out his breath in a long shudder. The boy had been no more irritating than usual, and had Fergus's nerves not been stretched taut already, he would have found the patience to deal with him. But Leo needed more than patience. He needed a firm and gentle hand to guide him, a 'mother's' hand. Suddenly Fergus realised that the encounter had banished any lingering nervousness and left in its place a new and confident resolve. Mhairi would take the boy in hand, would steer him with loving kindness along the right

[161]

path. If he had had the smallest lingering doubt, which he had not, then Leo's behaviour would have settled it. As it was, Fergus saw the future with an even rosier tinge than before: when he married Mhairi, all would at last be well with his world.

Fergus resisted the temptation to take one last reassuring look into the pier-glass, replaced the little box in his waistcoat pocket, and made purposefully for the door.

Kit O'Brien gave one last rub to the brasses on his horse's harness, stood back and smiled with slow satisfaction.

'I reckon you'll do, Merry my lass. I've never seen a finer mare, nor a finer cart behind her. And however many more I buy, and I mean to buy several, you'll always be the best, my old Merry.' He stroked her gleaming flank with affection and when she turned her head towards him, nuzzling his pockets for titbits, he stroked that too before finding a lump of sugar to feed her on the flat of his hand.

'That's your treat for the day, my lass. Now for mine.' He looked across the cobbled yard to the farmhouse door, which stood open to the snatching wind, and called, 'Are you ready, Mrs Macrae?'

Straw danced in whirling eddies above the yard, a gaggle of hens scratched and foraged as best they could on the leeward of the barn, their feathers outraged by the ruffling wind, and somewhere an outhouse door banged rhythmically on creaking hinges. The sky was heavy to the north, with the grey weight of threatening snow, but there was no heaviness in the spirits of the farm folk. Since the fall of Sebastopol the news from the Crimea had been encouraging and even Mrs Macrae had shaken off worry for her son. Soon there would be peace talks, everyone said so, then the war would end and Willy would come home. Meanwhile, today was a holiday, a day for relaxing with friends and neighbours, for singing and laughter, food and drink, a day for forgetting troubles.

'Aye, I'm coming, lad,' called Mrs Macrae, slamming the kitchen door behind her. She handed Kit a covered basket, which he stowed away in the cart, then he helped her onto the seat beside him and tucked a rug over her knees.

Mrs Macrae swelled with pleasure. 'Fancy me riding in style, when I've still the use of my own two feet. But I reckon I could take to the life, nay bother. The others are not long set off so we'll maybe catch them up on the road. But we'll nay let them climb aboard, eh Kit?' and she gave him a wink and a nudge. 'I want my coach all to myself. And my coachman.'

'I am honoured, madam,' said Kit, with the best bow he could manage while negotiating the rutted track so that his cart suffered the least damage to its axles. 'I and my trusty steed would happily drive you to the ends of the earth, even to the borders of heaven itself, where you, illustrious madam, would be welcomed with open arms. Though I doubt the Almighty would be letting an Irish tink through the pearly gates, not to mention a farm cart like mine, however bright the brasses.'

'Away with ye, lad. What nonsense you talk, but the Irish always were smooth-tongued liars.'

'Now it is funny you should say that, Mrs Macrae,' grinned Kit. 'Only the other day ... ' But he stopped in mid-sentence. What passed between himself and Annys was not to be used in public jest. 'Look!' he cried, seizing on the excuse. 'Isn't that your lord and master on the road ahead?'

'So it is. With my no-good lazy sons. Tell your Merry to run them down and trample them underfoot. They trample me for the rest of the year so why not make the most of today?'

'Certainly, madam. Hold tight,' and to the accompaniment of Mrs Macrae's shrieks of mingled laughter and alarm, Kit urged Merry into a swaying trot which grew faster and faster until, with a shout of 'Watch out ahead!' they ploughed straight through the group of trudging men, scattering them like a bow wave into ditch and hedge-row. Mrs Macrae shrieked with merriment.

'Did you see their faces, lad? And their behinds? I'll suffer for it after, but it was worth every minute. My but I've been looking forward to today, Kit lad. The best day of the year ... '

'Aye,' agreed Kit, with a private smile.

'Take an old woman's advice and make the most of it while you can.'

'I intend to,' said Kit, thinking of a certain assignation already made. 'Old woman indeed. If it were not that your old man is following behind us and his eyes green with jealousy already, I'd be taking you in my arms, Mrs Macrae, and giving you the kiss your youth and beauty deserve.'

'The bare-faced effrontery of the man! And you young enough to be my son. It's not me you should be kissing, you impudent young

[163]

stirk,' but she was laughing, and Kit laughed with her. There was laughter in the air that day and tomorrow would come soon enough.

In the kitchen at Rainbow cottage Mhairi felt the same elation, the same sense that today was not only a holiday, but a day set apart for happiness. A timeless day of joy and love when all would at last be well and when dreams would come true ... Though a stern voice at the back of her mind reminded her that normality would resume with the first working day of 1856, she sang as she worked and refused to let sober reason douse her happiness.

For before that dreary day, in that magical time when geniality reigned, and all the world was, however briefly, friends, Mhairi hoped to see Fergus and her brother Tom at ease together in Rainbow Cottage. There would be no need to tell the assembled company of her love for Fergus and his for her, for it would be plain for all to see and in the happy companionship of the moment, family and friends would give their blessing. Mhairi was as certain of it as superstition would allow.

For the co-operation between Silvercairns and the Wyness yard over the matter of the Drummond fountain had worked without acrimony and without dispute. A fair price had been set, specifications given, and the stone had been delivered as ordered and on time. Mhairi hoped it was a co-operation that could be continued on a permanent, and family basis. If Tom had lingering reservations, which would be only understandable, even they should vanish under the obvious practical advantages of an alliance between Fergus and Mhairi. Tom was no longer a raw stonemason, but a businessman, shrewd and resourceful, who aimed to go far. She knew he wanted to provide for Fanny as well as her father had done, and better, and that the coming of children had only strengthened that resolve. With a third little one on the way, how could he resist the practical advantage of allying Silvercairns with Rainbow Hill?

So Mhairi sang to herself as she baked bread and cakes, boiled a ham to be sliced and served cold, made broth and oatcakes, directed Annys and Catriona to do this and that to help her make the house ready for company, sent the boys on errands concerning peat for the fire and drink for the guests and was happy from the roots of her hair to the soles of her feet.

Tom had been friendly towards her ever since the night of the

[164]

charity concert and they had talked and laughed together almost like old times. He approved of Annys, approved of her new relationship with Henrietta Drummond, even congratulated Mhairi on the way she had brought up their young sister. He approved of Hamish and Catriona, too. In fact, Tom seemed to look on the world in general through benign and tolerant spectacles.

Perhaps it was the result of his holiday? For during a whole week and for the first time in family memory, Tom had done nothing but spend his time with Fanny and the children, and he had promised to bring them all to Rainbow Cottage to spend Hogmanay with her.

But the clatter of wheels on track, the whinnying and 'Whoa there, steady now' proved to be Mrs Macrae arriving in style with the lad Mhairi still thought of, with suspicion, as the Irish tink. Today, however, she made a special effort to be friendly, urged him to come in with Mrs Macrae and take a drink, but he declined.

'Thank you kindly Mrs Grant, but I'll be seeing to my horse first. Though that's not to say I'll not take up the offer later.' With that convoluted refusal he tipped his bonnet further back on his head and went down the path, whistling. Soon after that the Macrae menfolk arrived, with much jostling and laughter and demands to Mhairi to produce that 'racing devil of a carter that nigh killed us on the road.' 'And dinna say he's not here because his horse is tethered to yon tree on the corner.'

'He is not here,' said Mhairi serenely. 'See for yourselves.'

'Yes he is.' 'Ma's hidden him.' 'He's hiding, more like, terrified.' 'It's disgraceful. Chasing young men at her age.' 'Look under the table.' 'The bed, more like.' 'Wait till I get you home, you checky young puppy, and it's the belt for you.'

In the banter and laughter that followed while Mrs Macrae and Mhairi handed round drinks and her brothers did the same, no one listened to Catriona who was following her mother round the room, tugging at her arm, until in a momentary pause the child's voice came clear and high. 'Kit is not hiding. He's in the kitchen, with Annys, and they are ...'

'Here,' interrupted Kit from the doorway. 'Am I wanted?' In the mingled roars of 'No' and 'Yes' no one noticed the particular brightness of Annys's eyes or the tell-take pink of her cheeks as she slipped into the room behind Kit and busied herself with the dishes on the table.

When the next carriage arrived it was Annys who answered the door, to Fanny and her children, with Mr and Mrs Wyness. Then, astonishingly, to Fergus Adam and the red-headed Lennox boy. Annys did not hesitate. She opened the door into the bedroom (transformed today into a second parlour) said, 'Wait here, if you please, Mr Adam,' and closed the door again. She grabbed Leo's hand and dragged him through the throng in the family kitchen to where Hamish was talking to Kit. Then she found Mhairi, whispered in her ear, 'In the bedroom. He's waiting for you,' pushed Mhairi out of the room, across the tiny hall, and closed the door behind her.

After the heat and crowded noise of the cottage kitchen the silence was cool and calm, and suddenly, piercingly intimate. Fergus took a step towards her and stopped, his eyes searching hers.

'Well?' he said, very softly.

Mhairi found she was trembling so hard she could not speak. Instead she looked at him with brimming, joyful eyes.

He moved as if to take her in his arms, then checked. 'First, my pledge.' His eyes still holding hers, he felt in his waistcoat pocket and drew out a small, square box. Then he took her unresisting hand and placed the box on her palm. 'Open it,' he prompted as still she did not move.

Slowly, she opened the lid to reveal, in a bed of rumpled white satin, a ring with a single stone.

'A sapphire, Mhairi. Blue as your eyes are blue. Blue as hyacinths, as cornflowers, as summer skies.'

'It is beautiful,' she breathed in awe.

'As you are, my love. My life ... and soon, I hope, my wife?' He slipped the ring onto her finger and in almost the same movement, clasped her close and kissed her, long and deep. Suddenly he broke away and said, with fierce intensity, 'You have not answered. Say you will marry me.'

'I ... will ...'

'Say it.'

'I will marry you.' The words irrevocably spoken, she added with jubilation, 'Tomorrow. Today. Now, this very minute, if you wish it. Oh Fergus, I love you so very much.'

'Good. I have waited far too long for you to say it, you tantalizing woman. Say it again, and again.' He held her by the shoulders and looked down at her, with an expression that melted her very bones and set her blood racing.

'And if I do, what reward will I get?'

'This,' he said, sweeping her suddenly up into his arms and cradling her like a child. 'And this.' He swung her round so that her skirts flew in an arc of rustling petticoats, her arms came up round his neck and she clung to him, laughing and crying out to him to stop. Suddenly he did. Her arms were still round his neck, her face flushed with laughter, her hair dishevelled and her eyes looking up into his. There was a moment's absolute stillness before he murmured softly, 'And perhaps even this?' He bent his head to kiss her.

Simultaneously, the door burst open and a gaggle of squealing children erupted into the room with Kit O'Brien, growling like a bear, on their heels.

Instantly, Fergus set her feet on the ground and stepped back while Mhairi straightened skirts and hair with agitated hands, but in spite of their confusion something of love and laughter lingered around them like a halo and Kit O'Brien had to fight to keep the smile from his face.

'Tis sorry I am to be disturbing a private conversation, Mrs Grant,' he managed with tolerable solemnity. 'But we'll be leaving you alone again the moment I can chase these wee varmints into the kale yard where they belong,' and he lurched after the children with a terrifying growl which set them shrieking with delighted terror. Wee Georgie scrambled on all fours under the bed, Catriona catapulted into her mother's skirts and clung there, squealing while the rest of them swirled round the room, evading Kit's outstretched arms, until they dodged past him and out into the hall.

'You can come out now, Georgie,' said Mhairi, lifting the edge of the quilt to reveal the child crouching in the shadows. 'It's all right, the bear has gone and Catriona is here.'

'But I wanted the bear to find me,' wailed Georgie.

'So did I,' said Catriona, holding out her hand. 'Come with me and we'll find the bear instead.'

A moment later the room was empty again. Fergus took both her hands in his and said, 'Now, where was I when we were interrupted?' But she twisted free.

'No, Fergus. There will be time for that later and I am the hostess,

[167]

remember? Besides, I want to introduce you to everyone. Give me your hand.'

Her eyes bright with love and joy, she threw open the doors so that both rooms and the tiny hall were one happy space filled with noise and laughter.

'Listen everybody,' she called. 'Please, just for a moment. I want to tell you . . . '

But at that moment the house door burst open on a gust of winter air and Tom stood on the threshold, shaking the first flurries of snow from his greatcoat and stamping his feet. He doffed his hat and dusted that, too, shaking his head at the same time to dislodge the snowflakes from his hair. His cheeks were pink from cold air and exercise, his eyes ice-blue and startlingly bright.

'Am I too late?' he said, beaming round the company. 'Or is there still whisky enough for everyone to toast our good fortune in a dram? Here, take my coat, lass,' he went on, tossing it to Annys, 'and my hat, Georgie lad.' He put his hat on his son's head, where it slipped down over his eyes and sat precariously on his ears, to the boy's proud delight. 'Well, what's the matter Mhairi? Aren't you going to ask your own brother in, to celebrate Hogmanay?'

'You are in, Tom,' pointed out Mhairi, smiling with nervous excitement. 'And you have arrived just in time to hear my announcement.' She took Fergus's hand and pulled him forward, but before she could go on, Tom interrupted.

'And just in time to make an announcement of my own.' He pushed his way through the throng to the centre of the family kitchen and looked around him, gathering attention. 'Well, where's that whisky?' Lorn thrust a glass into his hand. 'Thanks, lad, and about time too. Has everyone a drink in his hand? Right. Then listen all of you. I want you all to raise your glasses to Diack, Grant and Wyness and our newest venture.'

'What's that, Tom?' called Willy, and Lorn added, 'I didn't know we had one.'

Wyness said nothing, but the frown on his face alerted Mhairi as nothing else had done. Even so she was unprepared.

'Nor we did have, until tonight,' beamed Tom. His eyes swept the company, deliberately including Fergus Adam in his bonhomie. 'But I've just come from Farmer Dickie's house where his brother-in-law is visiting, and McPhee and I have come to an arrangement, shaken

[168]

hands on it and sealed the bargain with a dram. So I ask you all to raise your glasses to our newest venture: Willowbrae!'

George Wyness's incredulous 'What?' was drowned in the chorus of cheers and questions which greeted Tom's words. Beside her, Mhairi heard Fergus Adam gasp, saw the blood leave his face and cold fury take its place. She clutched his arm in pleading, but he shook free and with a smothered oath slammed out of the house.

Mhairi pushed her frantic way after him, but by the time she had fought through the glass-clinking crowd to the door, he had already reached the garden gate.

'Fergus!' she cried, stumbling and running to catch him up. 'Please ...' He turned his head and the fury in his eyes was like a physical blow. Nevertheless, she tried.

'I told no one, Fergus. On my honour and as God is my witness, I did not speak a word. Not to anyone. Please, Fergus. You must believe me. I love you.'

She clung to his arm, and looked up at him with tear-filled eyes. For a moment she thought he was going to strike her, but instead he wrenched his arm away with such force that she stumbled on the uneven ground and would have fallen had he not put out a hand to catch her. She thought he would withdraw it again the moment she regained her balance, but instead the fingers dug into her arm with the force of his grip and his eyes burned with frightening passion.

'If you love me, prove it.'

Behind them the door of the cottage opened wide and a shaft of light fell across the path.

'Ma?' called a child's anxious voice. 'Are you there, Ma?'

'Prove it,' repeated Fergus in a voice that stopped her heart. 'Come away with me now, this minute, and marry me, if we have to ride as far as Gretna Green to find a minister. I'll buy you clothes, anything you need. Only come with me, *now*.'

She opened her mouth to speak, hesitated, and through the throbbing silence came the child's voice, calling. 'Ma! Where are you, Ma?'

'I will ask you once more, and for the last time,' he said, with deadly quiet. 'Will you come away with me?'

'I ...'

With an oath, he flung her away from him and leapt up onto the footboard of the gig. He swung the animal round, lashed its flank with cruel force and sent the vehicle careering down the lane at

[169]

terrifying speed while the horse's hooves pounded out his accusation
... *traitor, traitor, traitor* ...

'Fergus!' Mhairi's despairing cry was lost on the wind, as Fergus himself was lost in the swirling darkness of the night.

For the snow clouds had at last loosed their burden, in thick flakes which whirled and danced in an increasingly frenzied measure, but Mhairi saw only the emptiness where Fergus had been; heard only the hatred in that one, smothered oath.

'Has Mr Adam gone?' asked Catriona's timid voice behind her.

'Yes.' Mhairi continued to stare into the darkness of the empty lane while snowflakes fell unnoticed on her bare head and drooping, unprotected shoulders.

'But he didn't have any of the cake or the whisky or ... Are you all right, Ma?' Catriona slipped her hand into her mother's and looked up at her with anxious eyes.

'Yes.' Mhairi did not look at her.

'Then why are you standing in the snow without your plaid, Ma? Your best dress will get all wet and ... You're not crying, are you?'

With a huge effort Mhairi turned her head and managed a smile. 'Of course not. It is the snow, that is all.' She shook her head this way and that, brushed at the settling flakes on breast and skirts. 'And I am perfectly all right. Why shouldn't I be, when it is Hogmanay and I have my family around me?'

Smiling with relief, her daughter took her by the hand, led Mhairi back into Rainbow Cottage and closed the door.

Part 2

The new year dawned with promising news from the Crimea. Russia finally yielded to growing pressure and agreed to discuss the possibility of peace. There would be conditions, of course, delicate manoeuvrings to and fro on the diplomatic front, discreet bargaining and, when the occasion demanded, sheer, bone-headed obstinacy until an acceptable Peace Treaty could be drawn up and signed. The first, preliminary, bargaining took place in Vienna, in February. The Peace Treaty was signed in Paris, at the end of March.

Mrs Macrae, in company with all mothers of soldier sons, was delighted and talked of nothing else but her dear Willy's imminent homecoming. But, the Treaty signed, others, too, would come home. Lettice Adam, for instance.

'And I do not know what we shall do then, Annys dear,' whispered Henrietta Drummond, touching a lace-edged handkerchief to her eye. 'For you know how very fond I have grown of this dear place. These walls, these painted ceilings, these dear, embracing shutters. What happiness they have enclosed within their tender confines. What trembling joy...'

Annys suppressed a sigh of impatience and, as she had learnt to do in the weeks of her incarceration with Miss Drummond, switched off her listening faculties and retreated into private thought. It was strange how so short a time with Henrietta Drummond had knocked the infant bloom off her own daydreams and replaced it with more sober common sense.

She had not wanted to come to the Guestrow house. After that dreadful scene in Rainbow Cottage when her brother Tom had destroyed Mhairi's happiness, Annys had wanted only to stay at Mhairi's side, to shield and comfort her as best she could. But Mhairi had rejected her help, as she had rejected all help in the days that followed. Calm and cold as a granite statue from the Wyness yard, she had said, 'You will go, Annys. You have given your word.'

[173]

Nothing Annys said could change her mind. Mhairi had withdrawn into an impregnable shell of control, her face colourless, her eyes blank. She had spoken to Tom, when it was necessary to speak to him, with politeness, but as to a total and unwelcome stranger, and he, for his part, had had the grace to flush and look momentarily ashamed.

But only momentarily. Annys knew he boasted of the coup he had pulled off, snatching the Willowbrae deal from Fergus Adam's grasp at the last minute. 'All it took was an extra twenty pounds,' she heard him crow, over and over. 'I never spent a better twenty pounds in my life. Just to see the fellow's face!'

Fanny, like Annys and all who loved Mhairi, had said nothing. At least ... Annys remembered a particular day when she and Miss Drummond had called on Fanny and encountered a red-faced and angry Tom on the steps going out. Fanny herself had been white-faced and unnaturally self-controlled. But if she had told Tom a thing or two, it was a wife's duty and privilege to do so and no more than he deserved. Poor Mhairi ... Annys's own eyes brimmed at the thought of her sister's broken heart, for that it was broken she had no doubt. And, unless she was totally mistaken, so was Fergus Adam's heart, though that was sheer male pride and entirely his own doing. He might behave as though nothing had happened, give dinners, go to theatres and assemblies, but Annys was not deceived. She had seen Mhairi and him together. No man who had loved as he had, could forget so easily.

Kit O'Brien agreed with her. For that momentous day which had ended Mhairi's hopes, with the year, had begun Annys's secret life with Kit. He loved her, had told her so, if not in as many words, then as nearly so as made no difference. 'In a year or two,' he had said, stumbling over the words. 'When I have made my way in the world, I wonder if ... I mean, when I am in a position to support a wife and ... do you think you might ...' Then, his customary fluency deserting him, he have given up all attempt to state his intentions and had kissed her instead. But she had understood. Since then he had sought her out in the Guestrow, whistling in the yard outside till she came down to speak to him. Once, when she had time off to visit Mhairi, he had given her a lift in his cart almost all the way, though prudence had made him put her down just out of sight of the cottage door.

'We'll not be wanting to remind the poor woman of her own

[174]

sorrow,' he had said, kissing Annys goodbye. It was a discreet kiss, on the cheek, for none knew better than Kit how gossip flew from hedgerow to hedgerow in the beat of a crow's wing. But there was more than plain discretion behind his caution. Annys knew that he had not forgotten Mhairi's hostility when he first called at Rainbow Cottage and he was running no risks. 'Tis not the time to be telling her now,' he warned Annys, 'with her heart sore and her mind a turmoil. She'll likely not see things as we do.'

Remembering Mhairi's hopes that she should be 'a lady', that her stay in the Drummond household was the first step up the social ladder, Annys knew he was right. Especially now that Mhairi's own hopes had been so cruelly destroyed. How could Tom have done it? How could Fergus?

'... but I see you are frowning, Annys dear.'

Miss Drummond's soft voice penetrated Annys's thoughts and brought her back to the present and the stifling intimacy of the overheated room. The shutters were closed, the fire banked high, the lamps lit and lest any impertinent draught find its way inside to discommode the occupants, a roll of heavy felt had been laid across the foot of the door. Suddenly, Annys longed for the cold wind of the hillside behind Rainbow Cottage, the gusty, salt-laced air of the open market on the Green. She had not been to market for two months and more. As soon as Philip Drummond returned from whatever business was keeping him away, however hard Miss Drummond tried to dissuade her, Annys would insist on going home.

'I hope it is not on Mr Adam's account that you are frowning, Annys, for I assure you he has been the soul of discretion, the purest, whitest soul ... like a medieval knight, courteous, respectful and gentle, yet at the same time so strong and manly and ... and ...' The last word was little more than a breathless murmur. 'Adoring...'

Adoring? With a shock, Annys jerked back to full attention. Choosing her words with slow care, she said, 'I do not quite understand you, Hetty dear. Naturally I would not wish you to tell me anything you do not wish to tell, but I am a little, just a little unclear ... has Mr Adam ...?' She trailed deliberately into modest silence, her eyes lowered.

'Oh no. Nothing like that,' breathed Hetty with maidenly virtue. 'He is a gentleman of delicacy and breeding. But you must have noticed yourself, Annys, how he looks at me? Ever since that evening at the Assembly rooms when he, by his own confession, sought me out, I have *known*. And then, the other evening, at the Assembly? *Two* dances? And now, to be invited to Silvercairns, to dinner? You must see, as I do, Annys dear what it means? And my brother and he are such friends.' She sighed with a happiness that set Annys's heart thumping with doubt and alarm.

Suppose the silly, simpering girl was right? Miss Drummond was of the right age and status, no doubt with a suitable dowry too, and all Aberdeen was saying that the best way young Adam could retrieve his fortunes now was by a rich marriage. Marriages of convenience were nothing to folk like that and even Annys had to agree that an Adam–Drummond marriage would be 'convenient' if nothing else. At least, on the surface.

'Of course,' Miss Drummond was confiding, 'there are difficulties. I do not wish to be uncharitable – in fact, I strive constantly against such a straying from the path of virtue. But truth is also a virtue, is it not, and in the interests of truth, Annys dear, I must say it. The sister is quite dragon-like.' She shuddered prettily, in mock fear. 'I confess I felt positively faint when I met her at the wedding, though fortunately I was not required to speak to her more than once. So arrogant and overbearing. Not at all like her brother.' Miss Drummond paused to allow a dreamy look to wander over firelight and shadow.

Annys kept her face determinedly expressionless while her thoughts raced in mingled horror and disbelief. But if there was the smallest substance in what Henrietta Drummond was saying, then Annys must give up all thoughts of home and stay firmly where she was, to watch and wait. As she waited now.

'Then there is the child,' resumed Miss Drummond with a sigh. 'Such an undisciplined and tiring child. I doubt one could find a boarding school to take him, though of course it must be done. Dear Mr Adam is too soft-hearted, but one cannot, one really cannot be expected to share one's house with a ... with a *person* who is little better than a gypsy. Can one?'

Annys made the non-committal murmuring noises which she had learnt were all that Hetty required while her first anxiety receded. Men who were suffering from wounded pride and public humiliation were capable of any idiocy; there was little to be done on Fergus's account. But if anyone could send Miss Drummond packing, it would be Leo. Annys made careful note of the fact. She had found the boy exasperating, infuriating, could cheerfully have walloped him on more than one occasion, yet she liked him for all that. He was making a valiant effort to defy life and all the disadvantages it had dealt him and he would defy Hetty Drummond too, if required.

But surely, whatever Miss Drummond's daydreaming, such help would not be required? However large the dowry, however deep the humiliation, surely no man who had loved Mhairi could willingly take in her place a self-deluding and utterly selfish nonentity like Henrietta Drummond?

'The best twenty pounds you ever spent, was it?' glared Wyness across the office table. 'The worst damn-fool waste of other people's money, more like. Because it wasn't just twenty, was it? You forgot to mention the hundreds that went with it – straight down the drain.'

'But you said yourself you'd like a bit of competition again,' protested Tom. 'To beat Fergus Adam at his own game. You said . . . '

'I said you were to make no move without consulting me,' roared Wyness. 'An instruction you conveniently forgot, you bone-headed, self-seeking fool.'

'Self-seeking?' cried Tom, shooting to his feet and leaning forward, hands on the table between them. 'I'll thank you to take that back. I did what I did for the business, for us dammit!' He thumped the table so hard that the papers on it shook, then swept the assembled company with furious eyes.

'Rubbish. Balderdash. Bare-faced and outright lies. You did what you did out of revenge, pure and simple, and to hurt Mhairi.'

Tom's face flushed crimson. 'That's a lie! If you were not my father-in-law and twice my age I'd throttle you for that.'

'Throttle away, but what I say is the truth for all that. And you know it. Why the paroxysms else? No, don't bother to defend yourself. I know what you'll say. You did it purely in the line of business. But it's a queer sort of businessman who doesna check his facts first. A daft sort of businessman who buys a bit of land without inquiring first how he's going to get to it. And a downright dishonest businessman who spends other folk's money on a folly merely to settle an old grievance and boost his own precious pride.'

'I'll not take this from anyone,' began Tom. 'I'll . . . '

'What will you do, you blustering, bubbling nincompoop? Ram my

[177]

teeth down my throat? Because if you try, whether you're Fanny's husband or not, I promise you I'll ... I'll ...' He stopped, as if to catch his breath, one hand clutching his chest.

'Are you all right, Mr Wyness?' asked Willy, pushing back his chair.

Wyness waved a hand towards a side-table and mouthed something.

'Water?' When Wyness nodded, Lorn reached the jug before Willy and had a glass of water in the old man's hand before anyone else could move. They all watched anxiously as Wyness drank, waited, let out his breath, and eventually said, in apology, 'Aye well, some of us are not as young as we used to be.'

Tom bit his lip, mumbled some sort of apology.

Wyness jerked up his head and fixed him with a relentless eye. 'Are you still here? I thought you couldna "take" home truths when they were offered. I thought you wanted things all your own way and couldna brook reminders that you were not the boss you thought you were. I thought you were leaving.'

'You forget I am a partner in this firm, Mr Wyness, with a say in how the firm's run. And – '

'And you forget, Tom Diack,' interrupted Wyness with fury, 'who it was that built up this firm from nothing when you were a penniless apprentice in Old Man Adam's yard. Where you'd still be now if it wasna for me. I'll thank you to remember that, Tom Diack, when you're thinking how important you are. And while you're at it, you can also remember that marrying my daughter doesna give you the right to run the place!'

If Wyness hoped for any sort of retraction, Tom's glowering face told him the hope was vain.

'Oh what's the use. I can talk till I'm blue in the face and you'll not listen.' He closed his eyes as if to draw strength and patience. When he opened them again, his voice was quieter, but no less effective for that. 'Well, get out if you're going. Walk out and leave us to clear up the mess you've landed us in. And before you say you've a stake in the firm just remember it's a mere ten percent, and don't count on my daughter's share to boost your own. Fanny has more sense in her little finger than you have in your whole bog-rotten turnip of a head and more loyalty with it. She'll not support your mean-spirited vendetta any more than I will. Or anyone else in this room. Am I right?'

[178]

There was silence as old Wyness looked from face to face. Tom did the same: Lorn, Willy, Donal, young Hamish. Mhairi had declined to attend and Fanny was indisposed. Remembering that indisposition Tom's heart lurched, but he refused to acknowledge fear. She was ill merely because he had refused to see things her way, had stuck to his principles over the buying of Willowbrae. Whatever she said to the contrary, there had been nothing underhand in the deal. And if Adam chose to think he had been betrayed, then that was his pigeon. At least he would not get his hands on any of their shares. As to Mhairi, she had been a fool to consider such an alliance and Tom had done her a favour, shown her the fellow in his true colours, saved her from disaster. One day she would be grateful. And yet . . . the memory of his wife's white, appalled, despairing face rose up to haunt him with doubt. A doubt which grew as no one spoke up in his defence.

'Well?' challenged Wyness. 'Has nobody a word to say?'

'I have,' declared Tom. 'Sentiment has no place in the world of business and Willowbrae is good land. Potentially, a second Silvercairns. Why else would Adam have been after it, ask yourselves that?'

'Perhaps because it's next door?' sneered Wyness, 'and he could drive to it up his own lane, through his own yard, with his own horses and his own gear? Not make a five-mile detour and pay through the nose for the privilege.'

Tom was silenced. Not so his nephew.

'I don't understand, Mr Wyness. What does "pay through the nose" mean?'

'It means pay too much,' said Willy.

'With no choice,' added Lorn.

'Because,' said Wyness with weary sarcasm, 'your precious uncle was so eager to buy that land before Adam could get hold of it that he forgot to ask how we were going to get the men and the carts and the horses near enough for them to find the blasted granite or shift it when they found it.'

'But there's a road past Silvercairns. Leo said so and – '

'Aye, there's a road, lad. A private, Adam road. And Fergus Adam has had the good sense to refuse us access. And quite right too. Why should he let us churn up his road with carts carrying the granite he wanted himself? We'd have done the same, in the same circumstances.'

[179]

'Which means,' explained Will, 'that the only other way in is from the farm side, an extra five miles round by public road.'

'Then either build our own track,' said Lorn, 'or pay McPhee to let us use his.'

'Through the nose,' repeated Hamish and nodded. 'I see.'

'And no doubt you all see,' growled Wyness, 'Tom excluded, just what a bargain we've been landed with. A piece of barren land and no way to get to it. Ill-will in the Adam camp, just when the co-operation was working smoothly. And to crown all, long faces among the ladies.'

There was silence until Hamish said, in a small voice, 'What do we do, Mr Wyness?'

'We? We do nothing, lad. Tom got us into this mess and Tom can get us out of it, because if he doesn't, and the company loses by the deal, I promise you there'll be more than fireworks at the next meeting. There'll be a full scale explosion – with Tom in the middle of it.'

Tom turned on his heel and slammed out of the room, leaving a cold draught behind him.

'Shut the door quickly, dear, and come over to the fire,' said Mrs Wyness, pulling her shawl closer about her shoulders. 'There is such a chill in the air tonight.'

'Aye, in more places than one,' muttered Wyness. He stood with his back to her, holding his hands out over the fire to warm them.

'Mrs Macdonald's drawing-room was like an ice house this afternoon,' complained his wife. 'We might as well have been sipping our tea in the kirkyard, for all the warmth that miserable fire of hers gave. Talk about comforts for the soldiers. We could have done with a few comforts ourselves, certainly in the way of warm underwear and mittens. Mrs Farquharson told me afterwards that she reckons Mrs Macdonald counts the coals one by one, morning and night, and frets if there's more than three burnt in a day.'

But her husband did not make his usual joking comment about the widow's mite. In fact, he seemed not to be listening.

'George? Are you sure you are all right, dear?'

'Aye lass, I'm fine,' he said with a sigh. Then he turned and she saw the drawn lines of his face and the unnatural colour.

'You are nothing of the kind,' she cried in alarm. She scrambled to

[180]

her feet and hurried to his side. 'Take my arm. Sit here, in your favourite chair. There. I'll put this rug over your knees and you are not to move until Dr Marshall comes.'

'I'm not needing a doctor, woman,' grumbled Wyness, though he allowed himself to be tucked up into the chair and fussed over. 'I'm a wee bit tired, that's all. Yon meeting at the yard was more than I bargained for, with Tom ranting and raving, but five minutes' peace and quiet and I'll be fine.'

'Fine or not, I am going to send Mackie for Dr Marshall and while we wait for him to come, you are going to sit quietly and drink a cup of hot tea. Or something stronger, if you think it will do you more good.'

'You do me good, lass,' he said, reaching out a hand to take hers, and though her heart thudded hard with fear, she managed a smile. 'But send for old Marshall if it will make you happy. At least we can drink a dram together and talk over old times.'

'Was the meeting very trying?' asked his wife when she hurried back from issuing her domestic orders.

'Aye. Leastways, young Tom was. I've not been happy in my mind about Tom since that business at New Year. He used to be a fine, clear-headed quarryman, but now I reckon he's lost his way, somehow.'

There was a small pause before Mrs Wyness said, 'Do you think there really was anything between Mhairi and Fergus Adam? Fanny seems to think so, and there was certainly gossip...'

Wyness shrugged. 'If there was, there isn't now. Poor Mhairi. She's a fine-looking lass.'

'Was,' corrected his wife. 'Fanny was saying only yesterday, and I quite agree with her, that Mhairi has lost her bloom since New Year. She does not take the trouble she used to do with her clothes, and looks quite wan and thin. I know we are none of us growing any younger, but there is really no need to hurry things along as she is doing.'

'Mhairi? Ill?' Wyness looked at her in alarm. 'We can't have that. Why didn't you tell me before, woman. She must come here to stay, at once.'

'No, no, dear, don't distress yourself. I did not say she was ill. Merely a little depressed and out of sorts, as can happen to any of us, especially in winter. But you will make yourself ill if you carry on like this, dear. Be calm.'

[181]

'How can I be calm when Mhairi's ill and Tom acting like a fool and . . . and . . .' With a sigh, he lay back in his chair and closed his eyes. "The trouble is, I'm weary, lass.'

The words shocked his wife as nothing else had. But before she could think what best to do, there was the sound of a vehicle outside, the slam of a distant door, footsteps in the hall, and the doctor was announced.

Wyness opened his eyes. 'Dr Marshall, come in, come in. You'll have had a wasted journey, right enough, but you know what women are, aye fussing for no reason. You'll take a dram?'

'Where is Papa?' asked Fanny in surprise as she took off her shawl and looked round the empty drawing-room. Young Georgie was already demanding 'Grandpa' and tugging at Mrs Wyness's hand. Usually on a Sunday afternoon the old man would be sitting in his particular chair at the fireside, with the open newspaper in his hands. He would deliberately lower it, peer over the top and raise it again, then Georgie would hurtle across the room and smack small hands into the offending newsprint, before scrambling onto his grandfather's knee. Now, however, the chair was empty, the newspaper folded neatly on the table.

'He is not very well, dear,' said her mother, signalling to the maid to remove the children to the old nursery. When the door closed behind them, she gave up all pretence, clasped Fanny tight in a rare embrace, then said, between her tears, 'He hasn't been right since that meeting when he and your Tom quarrelled. The doctor said to take things easy, but you know your father. Then this morning he had another wee turn. At breakfast it was. He looked at his kipper and he said "I dinna just fancy a kipper this morning, dear," then he made a sort of gasping noise and clutched his chest and I rang the bell quick for Ina.'

'You should have sent for me at once, Mamma,' cried Fanny. 'You know I would have come.'

'The doctor said a day or two in bed was what he needed and not to worry you yet awhile, especially in your condition, and then I knew you would be coming today anyway. I thought he'd be better and . . . oh Fanny, I'm so worried.'

'I must go to him.' Fanny pushed past her mother and out of the room.

'You'll see a change,' warned her mother, hurrying after, but Fanny paid no heed.

Upstairs she found her father, propped about with pillows and lying in the matrimonial bed, his face suddenly mottled and old against the white linen, his cheeks sunken and his hair whiter than she remembered. *He is an old man*, she thought with shock and immediately afterwards, *he is dying*.

'Hello, Fanny love.' George Wyness stretched out a hand and his daughter took it, her eyes brimming tears. 'Nay lass, there's no call to cry. I'm nay dead yet, and I want no long faces till I am and canna see them. There's your ma not letting me out of bed and the doctor blethering on about over-straining the system till I feel like a prisoner in my own house. Or a naughty boy, sent to bed with no supper.' He winked and Fanny managed a small smile.

'Does Mamma not feed you?'

'A dish of slops not fit for a baby? I mind a time when I got a pair of good cutlets to my dinner, and not so long ago neither. Cast me off, she has, like an old shoe,' and he smiled affectionately at his wife who bit her lip and turned her head away. Suddenly his spirits left him. He closed his eyes and Fanny felt his fingers tighten briefly over hers.

'I'm glad you came, lass.' After a moment, he opened his eyes again and looked at Fanny with sudden intensity. 'Is that man of yours with you?'

'No, Papa, he . . .'

'Gone to Willowbrae, has he?'

'I believe so. He did not say.'

'No, well he wouldn't, would he? Not after the damage he's done. I don't know what there was between Mhairi and young Adam and it's none of my business, but Mhairi is a good lass and I'm fond of her. I dinna like to see her unhappy. As for yon Fergus, he's not a bad lad, for an Adam.' He attempted a grin and Fanny had to fight hard to keep back the tears.

'I'm telling you this, lass, because I want you to understand. Your Tom's not a bad lad, neither. I wouldn't have let you marry him if he had been. But he's lost his way lately. This Willowbrae business. I'm all for competition, beating the opposition, snatching business from under their noses – just so long as it is good business and not a pig in a poke, bought out of malice and spite.'

'Tom thinks it is good land,' said Fanny, loyalty compelling her to

[183]

speak on his behalf. 'A trained geologist is going to inspect it, in order to find the best place to start blasting.'

'He'd do better hiring a ferret to find the best rabbit holes. Rabbits fetch ninepence a head in London and that's more profit than any geologist mannie will make for him. But you're quite right to stick up for your man, though he doesna deserve it. You're a good wee lassie, Fanny, and always were.'

He closed his eyes briefly and Fanny took the opportunity to brush hers quickly with the back of a hand.

'I'll not pretend I didn't want a son, and maybe sometimes I was a wee bit harsh with you in consequence.'

'No, Papa, never. You were always the dearest, kindest ... oh Papa, I do love you so.' She hugged and kissed him, her tears wetting his cheeks and the pillow behind his head.

'There, there, lass,' he soothed. 'What did I say about long faces? Besides, my next wee grandchild will be seasick if you carry on like that, and the poor mite not even born. And here's your Ma, glaring at us for ruffling up her clean bedclothes.'

'I'm sorry, Papa.' Fanny straightened, brushed the hair from her face and attempted a smile.

'That's better. Because I haven't finished what I want to say. Where was I? Oh aye. I always wanted a son and maybe I said as much sometimes, but that time is long past. I couldn't have had a better daughter than you, lass, and when you gave me my wee grandson, well, as I said to your Ma, my heart was that full of happiness I could have cried with the joy of it.'

'Georgie is here, Papa. Shall I fetch him in to see you?'

'Later, lass. Later. I've nearly done. It's because of Georgie that I'm telling you this. Is your Tom here?'

Fanny exchanged a glance with her mother. 'No, Papa, I told you, he – '

'It doesn't matter. It's all in the letter anyway. He can read it when he comes. But tell him it's no good him shouting and swearing. Yon lawyer drew it up himself, all signed and sealed. It's not that I've anything against Tom, but after that Willowbrae nonsense I got to thinking. Mhairi's always been a good sister to him and he'd no call to be that high-handed. Mhairi's loyal and true, with a sensible head on her shoulders. You and she always got on fine, didn't you?'

'Yes, Papa. She was my friend and still is. But you were talking about Georgie.'

[184]

'I am, I am,' he said testily and Mrs Wyness crossed to the bed and laid a calming hand on his brow.

'There's no call to agitate yourself,' she said, smoothing his hair back from his brow. 'Remember what the doctor said. You'll only make yourself tired.'

'Fuss, fuss. Can't I talk to my own daughter without . . . ' His voice trailed away into silence and the women looked at each other in alarm. But a moment later he spoke again, faint, but lucid.

'Mhairi has always done the best for her Hamish and I know you'll do the same for Georgie. And for his brothers and sisters. This house will be your mother's, for as long as she wants it, with a wee legacy for her to live on, and I know you'll look after her when I'm gone. As to the rest, it's all set out in this letter. I thought it best for Tom to know at once, so he can get his shouting and swearing out of the way in private.'

'But why should he swear, Papa? What have you done?'

George Wyness told her.

Later, they brought the children in to see him, lifted them onto the bed so he could hold them, one on either side. He caught Fanny's eye and smiled with a depth of love and commendation and fulfilment which was to stay with her a lifetime.

'Kiss Grandpa goodbye now,' she said, with a steady voice. Then she too bent to kiss him.

'Goodbye, Papa, and thank you.'

'I won't come down with you, Fanny dear,' whispered her mother in the doorway. 'Ina will see you out. I will just sit here, with your father.'

'Would you like me to stay, Mamma? I will willingly do so.'

'I know, dear. But your father and I have things to say to each other, in private.'

Mrs Wyness closed the bedroom door.

George Headstane Wyness was buried on the 1st of May 1856 in the kirkyard of St Nicholas with all the ceremony befitting a town councillor, director of railways, giant of the granite trade and self-made man. But he was also an honest and fair-minded employer, repaying loyalty with loyalty, and a staunch friend. Consequently, the church was full to overflowing for the ceremony.

Mhairi, correct in mourning black, sat with Annys and her brothers in the second pew from the front, behind poor Mrs Wyness, Fanny and Tom.

Fanny was white-faced, her eyes red with weeping, but Mhairi noticed with surprise and some alarm that Tom was not supporting her, as she would have expected, with a hand at her elbow, or even a solicitous glance. Poor Fanny, six months pregnant and devastated by her father's loss. But perhaps Tom, too, was devastated? Rigid with the effort of control and afraid to move, lest he break down and weep? Mhairi felt her own tears hot on her cheeks as the service progressed, remembered George Wyness's cheerfulness and generosity, his brusque good sense, his unfailing kindess to her and her family, especially after Alex's death. Beside her, Will and Lorn were wet-eyed and Donal too, though he had a look on his face which Mhairi recognized at once: he was fighting his grief in the best way he knew – a design for a monument which would be a fitting memory for such a well-loved man.

It was as they stood grouped at the graveside that she saw Fergus Adam, through the black veiling gauze of her hat. There had been a formal note of condolence, of course, to Mrs Wyness and another, equally formal, directed to the company office, but she had not expected him to attend in person and the sight of him, immaculate in black, a white silk stock at his throat, set her heart racing with shock and pain. She lowered her eyes, but not before she had met the full shaft of his eyes across the space between. Against all resolution, she looked again and saw a young lady and gentleman join him, saw the lady slip her gloved hand under his arm and look up into his face. Saw him put his hand briefly over hers and withdraw it again. Henrietta Drummond, with her brother. Jealousy stabbed with a pain which mingled with her grief for George Wyness and brought fresh tears to her eyes.

'Don't cry, Ma,' said Hamish at her side. He stood, shoulders squared like the man he hoped to be, and who would one day take his father's place on the board of Wyness, Grant and Diack. Leo Lennox, for all his boasting, had not been allowed to come to the funeral. 'It will soon be over.'

She had thought it was over already, thought she had stamped out love. But looking across the bare space of kirkyard and the open grave, she realized that she had deceived herself. Henrietta Drummond might be vapid and silly, but she was a lady, with a dowry and

[186]

connections in the right places. The railways, for instance. Now that Fergus's ambitions for Willowbrae had been thwarted he might well turn his attentions elsewhere.

Willowbrae. She wished to God they had never heard of the place. George Wyness had not wanted it, might even have traded it back somehow if he had lived. But now Mr Wyness was dead and Tom would have a free hand.

She heard the soft thud of earth on the coffin lid. Hamish was right: it was over, for ever.

The bore-holes were ready, blasting powder weighed and fuses measured.

Fergus Adam surveyed the quarry floor through narrowed eyes His foreman beside him did the same. The dark-shadowed northern part, roped off for safety and long disused, green fronds of fern and weed growing from dusty fissures in the rock, self-seeded broom and gorse clothing the jagged remnants of Old Man Adam's last abortive blast. In contrast, the raw southern half, scoured white and scraped almost to the bone, but clean-cut, still productive, and at its edge on either side a rugged strip of weathered rock, patched here and there with green. The two men conferred, nodded agreement, parted, the foreman to instruct the blasting team, Fergus to stand aloof, at a point on the upwardly spiralling path from which he could watch proceedings. He knew by long practice which stretch of path afforded the best view of which rock face. Knew where the rock would fall. What he did not know, and therefore feared, was how each fresh explosion would affect Silvercairns House.

Now, as he waited, a solitary watchman on the empty path, he knew he had taken a decision from which there was no going back. For the roped off area had been diminished, the margin of safety narrowed and, if today's blasting was successful and the house survived, he would do the same again. And again. He had banished caution, with Mhairi Grant, for ever.

Wincing, as at a touch on an open wound, Fergus steeled himself for the pain and touched again. Every time he expected it to be less: every time expectation failed him. Damn the woman. Damn her to everlasting hell. But imprecation was no help, just as memory was none. Even the memory of her treachery served only to remind him of her eyes as she looked up at him, imploring. *Please, Fergus ... I*

[187]

knew nothing of this ... nothing ... I swear to you I did not breathe one word to Tom or to anyone ... please ... He felt the clutch of her hand on his arm even now, heard the rush of air as he wrenched his arm away and her gasp as she stumbled. Heard his horse's hooves pounding, pounding, with the blood of fury in his brain, and later, when recollection pierced the scarlet rage, heard his own voice, ice-cold and arrogant, at the forge. 'Urgent business which cannot be delayed.' In memory he felt the hard edge of coins against searching fingers, the rough skin of the blacksmith's outstretched palm. 'Find that carter fellow, O'Brien. Tell him to bring my nephew home. Immediately.'

Once in the open road, he had braced his feet, like a charioteer, against the board and given his horse full rein, heedless of wind and weather, ice or snow, while wheel shafts creaked and strained, wheels bounced and spun, and the pounding hooves drove nail after nail after nail into the bitter coffin of his love. By the time he reached Silvercairns House, his horse was lathered in foam, its flanks quivering and steaming into the grey sleet of the evening. He had spoken not a word to the stable lad who came running, merely jerked his head towards the animal and turned his back, before leaping the steps, thrusting past the servant who had hurried to open the great front door, and flinging his way into the library. He could still hear the lingering resonance of the door as he slammed it behind him, feel the sudden balm of silence which enclosed him, with the whispering comfort of the fire. In memory, he saw firelight on gilded bindings; soft, familiar shadows. He saw the headlines in the open newspaper, *The War*, *The Allied Armies* and *Grand Crimean Steeplechase*. He could even smell the wood-smoke. It had been pinewood, resinous and soft.

He had been a fool to try to change his life, a fool to think of marriage to anyone, let alone to Mhairi Grant, a fool to lay himself open to such betrayal, ridicule and pain. The memory of Tom Diack's triumphant face still had power to set his blood churning, but he would pay the man back one day, milk him and grind him and thwart him at every turn until he regretted the day he heard of Willowbrae. As to that contract between the two firms, it had not long to run: and when it expired, there would be no renewal. With George Wyness's death, the last moderating influence had gone: from now on, it would be outright war. Already Fergus had put in for, and won, three major contracts which Tom Diack had thought were

[188]

in the bag. Already he had drawn up tenders for four more. If his foreman ventured to suggest caution, Fergus brushed him aside. Win the contracts first, then worry about the granite. For the first time, he began to understand his father: to feel something of the same murderous rage for which Old Mungo Adam had been renowned. Though in his father's case that rage had too often been turned on Fergus himself, it had its roots in the same ground: the granite seams of Silvercairns.

From now on, Fergus vowed, with a frown which would not have disgraced his notorious father, he would think only of himself, his quarry, and young Leo, who promised to be the only family Fergus was likely to have. And if the house must be sacrificed, stone by stone, to feed the quarry's hunger, so be it. He had no need of a house, had no son to follow after, and as for Leo, he would be happy to live in a cave if need be, as long as the quarry survived.

Remembering Leo and the boy's capacity for mischief, Fergus cast another searching glance over the quarry floor. Leo, who had been ordered to stay at home, was quite capable of disobedience, foolhardy enough for trespass and pigheaded enough to go where he chose, when he chose, including the forbidden areas of what he called 'his' quarry.

'Grandpa said it was mine,' he would shout, if corrected. 'Ask Aunt Lettice. She was there and she heard him.'

'One day,' Fergus would say, with weary patience, 'it *might* be yours. When you are older and more responsible. But as long as you argue and shout and behave like an ill-disciplined child you will not be allowed near the place.'

Not that such a veto would stop the boy, thought Fergus with a sigh. He wondered yet again why he had not packed the lad off long ago, to the servants' quarters, to his Lennox relations in their Aberdeen tenement, even to his dreadful mother in Australia. Why, against all arguments of common sense, did he persist with his futile efforts to 'civilize' his nephew, to educate him whether he liked it or not, and to teach him quarry lore for all the world as though Leo were his legitimate heir? Unwilling though he was to admit it, even to himself, perverse and foolish though it sounded, it could only be because he felt a degree of affection for the lad. More than affection, he realized, with a start which jerked his eyes wide with shock and set him searching the quarry floor yet again, this time with the anxious care of a father for a beloved, straying son.

[189]

But there were no suspicious shapes or shadows, only emptiness, bare and waiting. He gave the signal for the fuses to be lit.

'What a bang,' breathed Leo in awe. 'Did you see the rocks fly high as the moon?'

'There isn't a moon,' muttered Hamish, but it was a routine contradiction, without belligerence. He shifted position in the undergrowth where the boys lay hidden, prone and side by side. He scratched a knee where a bracken stalk was sticking into him before whispering, 'Did you feel the ground shake? I thought the cliff was going to break off and drop us into the pit.'

'If it did, we'd easy climb out again,' boasted Leo. 'Leastways, I would. But it didn't break off, did it? I told you it wouldn't. When they've finished waiting for the rocks to settle and are busy clearing them up and sorting them, we'll creep down and I'll show you. Then you'll know it's not a lie.'

'You said you had two quarries and you havena,' pointed out Hamish. 'That was a lie.'

'Only 'cos your uncle stole one.' Leo spoke without rancour. Stealing was nothing special: if you wanted something, you took it, whatever Uncle Fergus said. If the owner was smart enough to stop you, it was your bad luck. If he wasn't, it was his.

'He did not steal it,' whispered Hamish fiercely. 'He bought it.'

'Same thing, when you do it behind someone's back. Bare-faced theft, Uncle Fergus said. He said if anyone from Tom Diack's band of brigands so much as set one toe on Adam land he'd horsewhip them to kingdom come and back again.'

Hamish gulped, but Leo did not seem to have made the connection between Hamish and the 'band of brigands' and Hamish was not going to remind him. He had hitched a lift with Kit to the edge of Adam land, dodged through the bushes to the back of the quarry yard where Leo was waiting for him, then on again together to their secret vantage point where Leo had promised him 'the biggest explosion you've ever seen.'

Hamish was awed by the blasting he had witnessed, and still shaken by the fear that had overtaken him when he and Leo first squirmed their way into their bolt-hole, under the palisade of tangled gorse, villainous with thorns, to the patch of flattened bracken and mingled winter grass which, Hamish had realized with alarm, was not only on the very rim of the quarry, but on the forbidden, northern side. As they wriggled into position, russet fronds of bracken had crumpled and crushed beneath them, giving off puffs of pinkish dust which stung Hamish's nostrils with intolerable irritation. Only a finger jammed firmly across the base of his nose had kept back the sneeze. Now, he was reminded again that all that stood between them and the scene on the quarry floor was a screening fringe of puny yellow grass. Ma would be horrified if she knew. But before he could suggest they forget the idea and go home, Leo spoke again.

'My Uncle Fergus said "Next time I set eyes on Tom Diack," that's your uncle, "I'll skin him alive for a thieving bastard" and then that silly Drummond woman pretended to fall over. I hate her,' he added, with venom. 'I have to eat in the kitchen when she comes.'

'I thought you liked that. You said ... '

'I do. When *I* choose. It's different when I'm sent there as a punishment. And when I'm let upstairs again I have to be "seen and not heard". Or else. You can hear her, though,' he said, with a sudden grin. '"La, Mr Adam, look at the boy's boots and in the *dwawing-woom*"' He mimicked Henrietta Drummond in a mincing falsetto which set Hamish snorting with glee. 'She can't even speak proper, daft woman. Your Ma's much nicer.'

There was silence as both boys studied the scene below them and followed their own thoughts. When Leo spoke again, it was with a hint of puzzlement in his voice.

'Ma Gregor says the Drummond woman is setting her cap at Uncle Fergus.'

'What does that mean?' said Hamish, intrigued.

'Dunno. It's a stupid cap anyway. Soppy lacey stuff with ribbons When Aunt Lettice comes back, she's going to bring me a real Russian helmet and a sword.'

Hamish was silenced by a boast for which he could find no equal. While he was searching his mind for comment, Leo suddenly grabbed his arm with one hand and with the other pointed through the screening bracken to where, far below them on the quarry floor, men had appeared, small as lead soldiers, among the fallen rocks. Caps, helmets, women all forgotten, the two boys peered through their grassy screen in excitement.

'Look!' breathed Leo. 'They've come out again. That's Uncle Fergus and the foreman.'

[191]

There was a whistle, a shout. A flag waved from the quarry floor and was answered by another from the quarry yard on their left, somewhere beyond the screening brambles. There was a stir of voices, the thud and shuffle of many boots, a shout. Men began to move down the spiral path in a ragged string of twos and threes. Then, near the top, where the track dipped under the rim of the quarry, the first of the horse-drawn carts appeared and began its descent towards the rock-strewn floor of the quarry. Here and there dust still hung in dove grey clouds, but through the haze the surface of new rock flashed and gleamed.

'Bet our rock's better than your rock,' breathed Leo, his eyes on those distant pinpoints of light.

'Bet it's not.'

'It is so better. Uncle Fergus says it's the best in the world and he's going to bag every contract going from under your uncle's thieving, poxy nose.'

'Well, my uncle says your quarry's finished. One more blast and the bottom will crack open. Then there'll be nothing but earth and rubble.'

'Your quarry's nothing but earth and rubble already,' jeered Leo, then, rivalry suddenly forgotten, he peered again at the devastation below. 'Look at all those boulders. Big as houses, some of them. What a splendid explosion!'

Remembering his dry-mouthed terror as the ball of light danced along the fuse towards the hidden catalyst in the rock, and his relief now that normality had settled, with the dust, on the scene below, Hamish whispered, in some sort of explanation, 'My Da was killed in an explosion like that.'

Not to be outdone, Leo countered, 'My Grandpa was squashed flat. A bit of the house fell on him. And on me, only I wasna flattened.' After a moment, he added, with less bravado, 'I hope it hasn't blown the house down this time.'

Together they turned their heads to look behind them, but gorse and bracken together succeeded in blocking out all view except one or two shreds of greyish sky.

'We'd have heard it,' said Hamish in reassurance.

'Aye,' agreed Leo, regaining confidence. 'Sure to. But I reckon it's time to go. They'll not see us, because of the bushes and that, and being too busy themselves. Now, this is the difficult bit,' he went on, wriggling into position. 'There's a rope I've tied, only it's over the

[192]

edge, a wee bit down the cliff. When we get to it, we climb down the rock face to the place I said. Easy as pie.'

Hamish looked unconvinced.

'I've done it hundreds of times, no bother,' jeered Leo. 'You'll manage fine. But no noise, mind. No kicking pebbles and that or they'll hear and look up to see what's happening. Ready?'

With a gulp of fear, Hamish nodded. All he wanted was to turn tail and run for home, where his ma would be waiting, with the comfort of a wooden broth bowl and a slab of home-made bread. She thought he was 'helping Uncle Donal' as he often did when there was no school. Remembering the lie, Hamish felt a twinge of guilt. But it was not really a lie. Hadn't Donal wanted him to 'find out about Silvercairns' and he was finding out.

'Don't look down,' warned Leo, swinging round and over the rim of the quarry, till only head and clutching arms remained.

Naturally, Hamish did and promptly reeled with terror.

'Scaredy-cat.' The taunting words came up from somewhere out of sight, but close below him. 'You're scared, just like the others. I knew you would be. Even Leckie Bruce didna dare and his da's the foreman.'

'I'm not scared,' protested Hamish, white-lipped. He looked helplessly to either side, praying for someone to appear and stop them. He even half-rose to his feet on the skyline, inviting a shout of warning. None came. Only that taunting voice from somewhere under his feet.

'Scaredy-cat. Scaredy-cat.'

Shaking with terror, Hamish dropped to his knees again, then onto his stomach. He lay there petrified and praying. But no help came. He had no choice but to squirm his way backwards to the edge of the cliff-face, wind his fingers tightly into the grass tussocks on the verge, clamp his eyes shut and edge his feet over and down, into the quarry's waiting maw.

'Just feel with your feet,' came Leo's disembodied voice. 'There's a wee ledge you can stand on, but mind and don't miss it or you'll fall.'

'Hamish!' cried his mother in horror. 'Where have you been? You've dust in your hair and why are you holding your hand like that? Have you hurt it?'

[193]

Hamish evaded her eyes and shook his head. He edged towards the fire, his back carefully turned.

'Come here.' The voice was quiet, but Hamish knew better than to disobey. He stopped, turned and came reluctantly towards her, his eyes lowered.

'Hello, Hamish. What have you done to your hand?' It was his sister Catriona this time, coming in from the scullery with an armful of clean washing.

'Nothing.'

'Yes you have, you've got blood on your sleeve.' The child heaped the washing onto the scrubbed deal table, caught a shirt before it could fall to the floor and pushed it back again. 'Shall I do the ironing now, Ma?'

'Thank you, dear,' said Mhairi with careful calm. 'But mind and don't burn yourself. Now, Hamish?'

Slowly, the boy held out his closed fist, palm upwards. Mhairi steadied it with her own hand and waited, rigid with control, until the grubby fingers uncurled and she saw.

Throughout their childhood, whenever one or other of her children was hurt, even the smallest scratch, she had had to fight to stamp down hysteria, to keep a hold on sanity, to appear calm and reassuring, when her brain was churning with a hundred imagined tragedies, her heart thudding with unknown terrors and her blood threatening to fail her, as it had done once, long ago.

And as it threatened to do now.

'Are you all right, Ma?' said Catriona, looking up from the hearth, the flat iron in her hand.

'Yes, I . . .'

'Sit down, Ma,' cried Hamish in alarm. Catriona dropped the flat iron and scrambled to her feet, just in time to help him support Mhairi into the nearest chair where she fell back, eyes closed and face white as the newly-washed linen on the table.

'We must do something,' urged Hamish, looking wildly about him for inspiration.

'What?' Catriona regarded him with helpless, frightened eyes. 'I wish Aunt Annys was here.'

'Well she's not, so shut up. And for pity's sake, don't cry. I know,' he said, remembering. 'You fetch cold water, for her forehead, while I find a feather to burn.'

[194]

There was water on her face, running down her cheeks, reaching cold, wet fingers inside her collar and down between her breasts. And an acrid smell which stung her nostrils and made her shudder. Smoke. Not wood-smoke, though. Or pipe-smoke. More like wool, or feathers. Oh God! The house was on fire. Mhairi jerked suddenly into full consciousness, looked wildly round the ordered, comfortable kitchen, then, as her children said together, 'Hush, Ma. You're all right,' closed her eyes again on her despair.

'I'm sorry,' she moaned. 'I did not mean . . .'

'Lie still, Ma. Catriona is making you a cup of strong tea.'

'But your hand, Hamish. I . . .'

'I'll wash it myself. Properly. Then Catriona will tie a bandage. Don't worry, Ma. It's nothing.'

Nothing. When you have been led to the door of happiness, have seen it open for you with loving promises, only to have it slammed shut again in your face, hear the key turn and the bolts ran home, for ever. The sight of that small, peeled-back triangle of flesh on the boy's palm had brought vividly to mind the day she first met Fergus Adam. She had cut herself as Hamish had. Running to fetch her father to her mother's deathbed, she had fallen on the quarry path, almost at Fergus Adam's feet. He had taken her into the quarry office, been kind and gentle. And when she had opened her hand, as Hamish had, and the blood had welled up, as his had done, she had fainted and woken again to find Fergus Adam bending over her with tenderness and love. Yes, love. Though neither of them had realized it then. And now it was too late.

At last the tears which she had refused to shed on that dreadful New Year's eve welled up and overflowed.

'Don't cry, Ma.' Her daughter's timid voice broke through her grief, with the chink of china cup on saucer. 'Look, I have made you tea in the best cup. Drink it up and you will soon feel better.'

Gratefully, Mhairi drank. 'There. I am better already,' she said, with her first attempt at a smile. 'And thank you. Both of you,' she added as Hamish offered her biscuits on a plate, then took one himself. 'How is your poor hand?'

'All right. It was only a scratch,' shrugged Hamish, embarrassed. He had remembered the turbulent events of the morning and was

[195]

afraid that any minute now his Ma would remember too and begin to question him.

'I bandaged it for him,' said Catriona proudly. 'Now I am going to look after you.'

'We are going to look after you together,' said Hamish, with an air of new responsibility. 'Till Aunt Annys comes.'

'Annys?' Mhairi shot upright with shock. 'You have not sent for Annys?'

'No, Ma,' soothed Hamish. 'We did not need to. It is Sunday tomorrow, remember? She will come anyway, then we will ask her to stay.'

'You will do no such thing,' said Mhairi, with almost her old authority. She put down her cup, stood up and brushed the creases from her skirt. 'I don't know what came over me, but I am perfectly well again.'

It was the truth. At least, the pain and the loss were still there, as she feared they would always be, but the weeping had both cleansed and strengthened her. She felt in control of her life once more. If it was to be a barren, lonely life from now on, then so be it. She had her children, and her work, and, since George Wyness's death, her new responsibilities. Thinking of the cheerless future ahead of her she quite forgot to question Hamish further about his mishap: besides, falls were commonplace enough in childhood.

But her children were watching her. Seeing their anxious faces she realized what a shock her momentary faintness had given them and was filled with protective love.

'There is no need to look so worried, my pets.' She put her arms around their shoulders and drew them close. 'I will be fine. Besides, Annys has a job now. She cannot just come and go as she pleases. She is Miss Drummond's paid companion and must do as Miss Drummond wishes.'

It was on the tip of Hamish's tongue to say 'Leo hates Miss Drummond' but fortunately he remembered in time that he was not supposed to have any contact with Leo, or with anyone else at Silvercairns, and said nothing. Later, in the scullery, where Catriona was washing up the dishes, he told his sister what Leo had said about Annys's employer. She giggled delightedly over his falsetto imitations, but she did not understand the bit about the cap either.

'Perhaps Aunt Annys knows?' she said, wiping dry the china saucer with particular care.

[196]

'When she comes, we'll ask her.'

Catriona heard the carriage first and ran to the door, only to turn back again, disappointed.

'It's not Auntie Annys at all. It's only Kit's cart.'

'Kit's cart? On a Sunday?' Frowning with suspicion, Mhairi put down her sewing and hurried to the door, only to stand there, mouth open in astonishment. For stepping out of Kit O'Brien's cart, with all the airs of a duchess, was a creature with bright red hair and a bright yellow dress, the latter with the biggest hooped skirt Mhairi had ever seen. Over this construction she wore a green velvet cape with brown fur trimmings and sported a brown velvet hat with a curved rim and a huge white ostrich feather which dipped up and down like foam on a wave as she moved.

'What is it, Ma?' called Hamish and when she did not answer, put down the piece of wood he had been carving, under his uncle Donal's tuition, and joined her at the door.

'Thank you, my good fellow,' said the creature, pressing something into Kit's hand. When he raised one eyebrow and turned the coin over, inspecting it, she added, 'That's good money that is so you've no call to bite it, though I reckon it's you as should pay me to ride in that bone-rattler. I'll be black and blue all over come tomorrow, and it's a wonder I've a tooth left in my head.'

'I'll be on my way then,' said Kit, with a flick of the whip.

'And leave me stranded in the middle of nowhere? What do you think I'm paying you for? You'll wait in the yard till I've finished my business here, then you can run me back to the smithie. If I'd have known that villain of a coachman wouldna bring me right to the door, for fear of his blessed wheels falling off, I'd never have hired him in the first place and me in my best clothes. But it's only a social call, so I'll not be long. Twenty minutes, the gentry stay, though to my way of thinking, ye canna have much of a blether in twenty minutes and I've a deal of catching up to do. Well, what are ye gawping at? Away with you till you're wanted.'

Then the vision turned, saw the group of astonished onlookers in the doorway, and, with a simpering smile and mincing, kid-booted steps, came swaying towards them, her skirt lifting and bobbing like washing in the wind. Catriona saw the frilled cuffs of the lady's pantaloons and smothered a giggle. Hamish saw the yellow stuff

[197]

catch on a bush and pressed his lips hard together so as not to smile. Mhairi merely stared, with dawning recognition and dismay.

'Lizzie? Lizzie Lennox?'

'It's Elizabeth now, as you'd have seen if you read the papers. "Newly arrived at the Douglas Hotel, from Melbourne, Mrs Elizabeth Faraday." That's me. Wi' seven cabin trunks and five hatboxes. You should have seen their faces. The doorman was one of they Henderson laddies from up the stair. "It isna Lizzie?" he says, his mouth dropping that far open I thought he'd swallow himself whole. "No, it isna," I tellt him. "It's Mrs Faraday to you," and I clipped his ear. I don't stand cheek where I come from. One word out of place and they're out the door. But you can call me Lizzie if you like. For old time's sake. Well, aren't you going to ask me in, and me travelling half round the world to see you? Or do I have to stand on the doorstep all day?'

'I am sorry, Lizzie,' said Mhairi, recollecting herself. 'Please come in.' She stepped back to let Lizzie enter and Lizzie's skirt hoop promptly stuck fast in the doorway and could not be unwedged without a display of Lizzie's pantaloons almost to the waist. After much swearing and loud laughter, she finally manoeuvred herself into the family kitchen and sat down on the nearest chair so that the yellow skirts bounced up and showed her knees before she beat them down into submission. Mhairi whispered to Catriona to make tea.

'My what a pokey place you've got here, Mhairi,' said Lizzie, looking around her with complacency. 'No wonder you can't wear fine clothes like me, but have to go about dressed like a fish wifie. You used to be a fine-looking lass and I hadna expected you to look so old and drab. But that's married life for you. You'll maybe not be able to buy yourself clothes like I can, what with Alex being only a quarryman.'

'Alex is dead,' said Mhairi quietly. 'He died seven years ago.'

'That's a pity, that is,' said Lizzie, momentarily deflated. 'I didna know. But at least you'll not have too many kids, whining and moaning and driving you mad. Some husbands are worse than animals the way they...'

'Two children,' interrupted Mhairi. 'Hamish and Catriona.'

Lizzie eyed them briefly and looked away. 'Aye, well. Two's more than enough. But you're nay looking as well as you used to, Mhairi. Nay life about you. I reckon you're needing a man in your bed, to liven you up, like.'

[198]

'Have you visited your parents yet?' said Mhairi, speaking with strained politeness. Only good manners prevented her pushing Lizzie bodily out of the house.

'Are ye daft? I'm nay visiting that stinking tenement, not in my best clothes. If they want to see me, they can come to the Douglas Hotel. There's carpets there that thick you could lose your feet in them and not find them for a week. You wouldna be able to afford to stay there, Mhairi, but the cost's nothing to the likes of me and Lord Dougan. He's staying there too, with plenty other county folk. We gets our tea in a silver pot.'

Mhairi poured boiling water from the iron kettle into the earthenware teapot on the hearth, then swung the kettle back over the fire.

'You know what you should do, Mhairi?' said their visitor into the silence. 'You should marry again. Someone rich, nay like your Alex who was a nice enough lad, I grant you that, but what did he leave you with? Two bairns and nay much else by the look of things. Tell you what. You buy yourself a few clothes, smarten yourself up, like, till you look more presentable and come to Australia. I promise I'll fix you up with a husband before a week's out. Some of they farmers are right rich, they are. Like me.'

'Thank you for your offer, but I am perfectly content where I am.' At that moment Catriona staggered into the room, carrying a tray laden with tea-things which Mhairi gratefully took from her and together they set out plates, cups and saucers, china dishes of jam and butter. Finally Mhairi poured tea, offered scones and while Lizzie was helping herself, said, 'You said "Mrs Faraday". Is your husband with you?'

'That bastard?' Lizzie threw back her head and laughed, with a sound that made Mhairi cringe. 'Died of a swamp fever, he did, and good riddance. But the crafty devil struck it rich first.' She winked at the company and grinned. 'I've done well for myself, I have. See this velvet cape? Thirty pounds that cost in London and this brown fur stuff is sable. Real expensive. I've three more in ever such pretty colours and real ermine on one of them, just like a queen. And you should see my jewels. I'm nay wearing them all, with it being vulgar to show off, like, but I've great chests more of them at home. Leastways I did have, though there's no saying one of they Originals won't have pinched the lot while my back's turned. Or someone from the diggings. There's plenty scum around these days, hangers-on, beggars, parasites and the like. But I reckon I can spot them a mile away, the ones with no money to pay.'

She took a mouthful of scone and while Mhairi was trying to think of a suitable comment, the door burst open and Willy came in, with Lorn behind him, only to skid to an embarrassed stop.

'Well, well,' said Lizzie, raising her eyebrows. 'What a fine pair of lads to find in the backwoods.' She looked them slowly up and down before giving them a coquettish look. 'Would you like to introduce me, Mhairi, so as we can get better acquainted.'

Mhairi took a long breath before saying carefully, 'Surely you remember Will and Lorn, my younger brothers? This is Lizzie Lennox,' she added in explanation, 'Leo's mother.'

Hamish gasped and clapped a hand over his mouth while Catriona's eyes grew large with wonder.

'Will and Lorn,' cried Lizzie, 'would you credit it, and you no more than this high when I last saw you. You'll be married, likely?'

They shook their heads.

'Still tied to your sister's apron strings? A pair of grown lads like you? You should be in Australia, making your fortunes. A fine place for working lads is Australia. You'll be rich in no time, with all the lassies buzzing round you like flies and begging you to marry them.'

'Rich?' said Will.

'How?' added Lorn.

'Easy. There's the diggings, for a start. And if you dinna fancy that, there's land for the taking, and folks is crying out for skilled workmen to build them houses and that. Two years out there and you'll be millionaires. Then if you was wanting a Scottish lassie for a wife, you could come home and look around. Like I'm doing.' She winked.

While Lizzie was speaking, they had heard the sound of wheels in the lane and now Annys appeared in the doorway.

'I am sorry I am a little late, Mhairi, but Miss Drummond ... oh.' She stopped and stared in astonishment, her mouth open.

'You must be Annys,' said Lizzie. 'My, what an elegant gownie, and how you've grown. You're taller than Mhairi and twice as pretty.'

'I am sixteen,' said Annys, blushing and not looking at her sister.

'Then you'll be wed afore we know it, and by that secretive look in your eye you've a lad already. Dinna tell Mhairi, though, or she'll maybe stop you, her being strict and that. Or maybe just jealous?'

There was a sound from the shadows near the fire and Lizzie

turned her head. 'Is that your Donal, skulking in the corner? I didna see him, him being so quiet. But he would be, wouldn't he?' She laughed.

No one joined in.

'It's a pity he hasna a tongue in his head, for he's a handsome enough lad. A waste, really. Now if he was a lassie, I'd fix him up, nay bother, in Australia. They're that desperate for women out there they'll marry anything in skirts, even a dummy.'

Catriona ran to Uncle Donal, climbed up onto his knee and put her arms round his neck, while Hamish faced their visitor and squared his shoulders belligerently.

'Only rude and ignorant people speak like that. Ma says so, and she's right.' Then he too joined Donal in the corner and began some long explanation on his fingers, at the same time mouthing silently. For once, Mhairi did not rebuke her son for ill manners. No one else spoke.

'Donal's not the only one who's lost his tongue, seemingly,' said Lizzie with a false laugh. 'I reckon it's been a shock to you all, seeing how well I've done for myself and you still where you was ten years ago, with nay two pennies to rub together. Jealousy, that's what it is. But I was telling yon carter-laddie if he wants to get on, he should emigrate. There's special terms, seemingly, for laddies like him, strong and with a skill to offer. Only £1 passage money and he'll easy find that. Two years in Melbourne, I tellt him, and he'd have a whole fleet of carties and so much money he wouldna know what to do with it.'

'What did he say?' asked Willy, with interest.

'He said, first thing he'd do would be to buy a bunch of roses for the lovely lady what first directed his feet along the path to riches. Real poetic. I tellt him if he thought to get round me that way, he'd another think coming, cheeky young devil, and to save his blarney for the lassies in Melbourne.'

'What are they like?' asked Lorn with a wink at his brother. 'If there's money to be made that easy, and only £1 to pay, we'll maybe consider this emigration business ourselves.'

'The lassies? Nay enough of them and the best-looking snapped up afore they even set foot ashore. But your Annys is right pretty,' she said, studying the girl with her head on one side. Annys, looking embarrassed, busied herself with the tea-things. 'Tell you what, you was a good friend to me all those years back, Mhairi, so now I'll be a

[201]

friend to you. I reckon you'll not budge for love nor money, but when I go back to Australia I'll take Annys with me, if you like. Pay her fare and that so it'll not cost you, and as to that country laddie of hers, she'll forget him in no time when the men come swarming. I guarantee she'll have the pick of a dozen millionaires afore she's been in Melbourne a week. I can't say fairer than that, now, can I?'

It was Annys who answered her.

'No. And thank you for your offer.' But in spite of her apparent composure, she had two pink spots in her cheeks and she avoided Mhairi's eye.

'Think about it,' said their benefactress airily. 'I'll be staying a whilie in Aberdeen so there's nay hurry.' Lizzie picked up her teacup, little finger carefully outstretched. She drank, replaced her cup, looked around her at their watchful faces and said, "How's that old devil Mungo Adam? I thought I'd best ask afore I went round there, knowing his temper, like.'

The tension snapped as everyone spoke at once, then Mhairi said, 'Didn't you know? Mungo Adam died four years ago.'

'But what about my Leo?' cried Lizzie, her face red with indignation. 'I should have been told, I should. What with me being the lad's Ma. It was Mungo as wanted him, for a grandchild.' Then a thought occurred. 'What did he leave Leo in his will?'

'Leo is well cared-for,' said Mhairi, ignoring Lizzie's question. 'Fergus Adam and his sister took charge and brought him up as their nephew.'

'That Miss Carrot? What right has she to bring up my Leo? I'll soon see about that, I will. I'm nay having my Leo brought up by a pair of peely-wally, long-nosed freaks.'

'I doubt you have any say in the matter,' said Mhairi, an edge of satisfaction in her voice. 'You sold him, remember. You forfeited your rights.'

'Forfeit nothing. I lent him, that's all. Lent him to his grandpa as a comfort in his old age. Now the old bastard is dead, I'll have my Leo back, with the money he was heired, and he can be a comfort to me for a change.'

'But Lizzie, you really cannot...'

'Says who? I've money of my own now, and position. I'm an important lady, I am, with my own hotel. They canna tell me what to do, like I was still their housemaid. Oh no. And I'll tell that Miss Carrot so to her face.'

'You will have to go a long way to do so,' said Mhairi. 'She is with her husband, in Scutari.'

'She hasna taken my Leo?' Lizzie eyed the company with suspicion, as if they were banded together in a plot against her.

'No. Leo is at Silvercairns, with his uncle.'

'With Fergus Adam?' Suddenly, her face cleared. 'Then I reckon I'll pay a call on Mr Adam. An afternoon call, so as I can take tea in the drawing-room and do it proper. And if he's not in, I've got visiting cards and that. Had them printed specially, just like the gentry. Then he can ask me to dinner. He's not married, too, is he?'

'No,' said Annys. 'Not yet.'

'Then I'll maybe look him over, while I'm at it. I always fancied living at Silvercairns and with my Leo being there already . . . well, it would be kind of right, really. Mrs Elizabeth Adam of Silvercairns. Aye, I like the sound of that, and it isna as if I've no money. I can easy buy myself a real gent for a husband and have plenty left for clothes and that.' She settled further into her seat and beamed at the company.

When no one commented, she said, 'I reckon I havena stayed my twenty minutes yet, so I'll take another cup of tea. Besides, I want to see your Tom. Will he be long?'

'Tom?' With difficulty Mhairi brought her attention back from the turbulent thoughts which Lizzie's words had stirred.

'Aye, your brother. He was the best-looking of the bunch, was your Tom. I always had a soft spot for the lad.'

'He is married to Fanny Wyness and has a house of his own in Elmbank.'

'Married to Headstane Wyness's daughter? The crafty young devil,' cried Lizzie, laughing delightedly.

'And before you ask, Mr Wyness is dead and the family still in mourning.'

'Old Headstane dead? My, but your Tom's done well for himself, hasn't he? Well, well, he wasna so daft as I thought him. Not with Fanny being an only child. I'll not take that extra cuppie after all.' She attempted to rise to her feet, only to fall back again, pantaloons exposed. 'Drat these blessed skirts. I canna seem to manage them, with the room being so small. Give me a hand, will you, Lorn? And Willy can tell that carter fellow to bring the trap to the door. I'll be passing Elmbank on my way back to the hotel and there's just time to call afore the light fades, to offer my condolences.'

[203]

With the departure of Lizzie Lennox (for Mhairi did not believe in the husband, dead or otherwise), the calm of Rainbow Cottage lay in shreds. Will and Lorn talked enviously of Australia and the money to be made there, Annys seemed low-spirited and preoccupied and even Donal was restless, until the menfolk suddenly announced they were going out, to visit the Macraes at the farm. Hamish went with them.

'Don't worry, Ma,' he called from the doorway, 'We'll be back in time for our tea.'

Left alone with Annys and Catriona, Mhairi put the flat iron to heat at the fire and fetched a pile of ironing from the bedroom while the others cleared the table and carried the teacups and saucers into the scullery, to wash and dry them.

They did so in subdued silence, until suddenly Catriona remembered something. 'What does "setting your cap" at someone mean, Auntie Annys?'

'Trying to attract someone so that they will marry you, I think. Why?'

Whispering, so that Mhairi should not hear, Catriona told her.

When Annys returned, to replace the clean china on the dresser, Mhairi was ironing one of their brothers' shirts.

'Why don't you ever go into town, Mhairi?' said Annys, conversationally. 'I don't mean for marketing, but to visit friends or the shops. You could buy material, make new clothes for yourself, instead of always for other people. I would, if I were you.'

Mhairi did not answer, merely compressed her lips, took another shirt from the pile and resumed ironing.

'Or take a drive into the country, with the children.'

'In May? Catriona would catch a chill.'

'No she wouldn't. And you should not be ironing,' she went on, deliberately to provoke. 'What would the Sabbatarians say?'

When Mhairi continued to move the flat iron to and fro, to and fro, with no expression on her pale, drawn face, Annys's patience snapped.

'If I truly loved someone,' she cried, 'I would not let him go so easily. I would fight and fight until I got him back.'

'I don't know what you are talking about, Annys.'

'Yes you do. You love Fergus Adam and he loves you. But because of some silly business deal of Tom's you are not speaking to each other and I think it is stupid. Someone else will get him if you are not

[204]

careful and it will be your own silly fault. You don't even wear your pretty hat any more, but droop and drear under your plaid like . . . like some old fish wifie on the Green! Lizzie Lennox was quite right. You look like my mother instead of my sister and you don't even brush your hair properly any more. What would Ma say?'

That brought Mhairi up short, as nothing else could have done. From as early as she could remember, her mother had taught her to brush her hair a hundred strokes a day without fail.

'Ma would be ashamed,' said Annys into the silence. 'And so am I.'

'You have said enough.' Mhairi slammed into her bedroom in blushing fury, but Annys was satisfied. Smiling to herself, she took up the flat iron and resumed where Mhairi had left off.

There was silence in the Diack parlour. Fanny sat, head bowed over her sewing, the black of her mourning emphasizing the paleness of her face. As well as the voluminous folds of black paramatta which covered her pregnancy, she wore a small black lace-trimmed cap, which Tom had called demure and disgracefully provocative when he first saw it, on the morning of her father's funeral. But that was before he had read her father's letter and heard the will.

The money had been disposed of straightforwardly enough, with due regard for the needs of his widow, but the company was a different matter. 'I leave my thirty percent share in the firm of Wyness, Grant & Diack to my grandson George . . . to be held in trust until his maturity . . . said trustees to be his mother Frances Wyness Diack . . . and his aunt, Mhairi Diack Grant of Rainbow Cottage in the parish of Woodside.'

Tom had not sworn and shouted, as George Wyness had feared. Instead he had stood a moment in terrifying silence before saying, 'So. Your father did not trust me to look after my own son's interests.'

'It was not that, Tom. He did trust you, until you quarrelled. But that upset him.'

'Because I stood up for my opinions and he didna like it, I killed him? Is that it? Everyone else is saying so, so why not my wife, too?'

'No, Tom,' said Fanny quietly, though her hands were clenched so tight her knuckles were bone white. 'I do not say so. If you choose to think so that is between your conscience and yourself, but my

father told me, and I believed him, that he was worried about your ...
your professional judgement. After your differences over ...
over ...'

'Willowbrae? I might have known it. I have you and Mhairi to
thank for this. But if you think you can run the business between you,
you can think again. I'm nay having womenfolk poking their noses
into men's affairs and telling me what to do. When you married me,
whether your father liked it or not, your property became mine, to do
with as I please.'

'But not Georgie's.' Fanny did not realize, she had spoken her
thoughts aloud, but it was too late.

'That, Mrs Diack, must make you very happy.'

Those were the last words Tom had spoken to her, except for the
formal currency of daily life and after more than four weeks of it,
Fanny was not sure how much longer she could endure. To go to her
widowed mother's house, as she had been tempted to do more than
once, would, under the circumstances, give rise to no gossip, but
Tom would see it as one more betrayal and for herself, it would be to
admit defeat.

Now, when she had offered her daily olive branches of conversation: inquiries about the yard, comments on the children's doings,
even questions as to his opinion of the King of Prussia and of his
son's engagement to the Princess Royal, which had met with such
universal disapproval, and had received the usual monosyllabic 'Yes'
or 'No,' she kept her eyes on the infant garment she was sewing and
fought to keep back the tears. But in spite of her efforts the white lace
edging blurred, she fumbled her stitching, pricked her finger and
drew blood. Once, Tom would have kissed it better for her, teased
and cajoled her into smiles and then, perhaps, they would have gone
to bed together, in loving comfort. She was more than seven months
pregnant and cumbersome, but that had not turned him from her
bed before. Perhaps, when the child was born, he would come back
to her? *Please God*, she prayed and this time, despite all her efforts, a
tear welled up and spilled over.

Tom saw and ached, with love and rage and pity. But the knot of
pride and resentment was too firmly tied. It was her father who had
humiliated him, he knew that in his head, but her father was dead
and beyond haranguing, while Fanny was here, in his own house,
meekly going about her housewifely tasks, uncomplaining, solicitous, and a daily reproach. They should have fought it out at once,

through pain and recrimination to tearful reunion and love. Instead, they had done as the world expected, outwardly composed and calm, and if the world remarked a sombre edge to their composure, it was put down to their recent bereavement. Now, the pattern was set, and could not be broken.

Looking at his wife across the hearth, seeing her tears and the way the tiny scrap of cambric rose and fell on the mound which held their unborn child, only pride prevented him going on his knees beside her and begging her forgiveness. But pride held his heart in its inexorable grip and he could not find the power to shift it. He stood up, saw the hope leap in her eyes, and turned away. Instead of going to her, as he had wanted to do, he crossed to the table, picked up a folder at random and spread out its papers on the table. They were the plans for one of his town mansions in the West End, all calculations completed and approved, but he pulled out a chair, sat down and, with his back to the fire, pretended to study them just the same.

There was silence, but for the slow ticking of the clock on the mantel and the occasional stirring of the fire. Although it was almost June, they still kept a fire in the parlour, particularly on a Sunday, when Mrs Wyness visited, but she had gone home an hour ago and they were left in misery together.

Fanny was gathering courage to ask whether Tom wanted the lamps lit yet, when she heard carriage wheels in the street outside followed by some sort of commotion in the hall. Then there was a knock at the parlour door and Jessie appeared, looking flustered and irate and with some sort of card in her hand.

'There's a person at the door, asking for Mr Tom Diack,' she said. 'She tellt me to give you this, sir, and said you'd know who it was.'

Tom stretched out a hand, took the card, and read aloud, 'Mrs Elizabeth Faraday, Faraday's Hotel, Ballarat, South Australia?'

'That's me,' said a voice from the doorway. 'Your skivvy wasna going to let me come in, but I knew you'd be wanting to see me, what with me coming all this way to pay my respects and offer my condolences.'

Tom who had risen to his feet at her first words, took a hesitant step towards her. 'Lizzie? Lizzie Lennox?'

'You must be going blind in your old age, Tom Diack, if you don't recognize your old friend Lizzie, and us living on the same stair all those years ago and going to the same school. You came to Australia to visit me, remember, and right glad I was to see you, too.'

[207]

At her words, memory flooded through him. A night in Melbourne. He had been walking the town for hours, searching for her. At the back of Tom's mind, even when he was persuading Fanny's father to send him to Australia on quarry business and to make his fortune, had been the idea that he would seek out poor Lizzie Lennox, the friend of his childhood, and ... and what? He knew Hugo Adam had betrayed her, used her for his pleasure and cast her aside. Knew the villain had died of a fever and was beyond retribution. Knew Lizzie had borne a child. In his anger and compassion Tom had visualized a brave woman, beautiful in sorrow, ill-used and poverty-stricken, too ashamed to ask her family for help, but lavishing unstinting love on her innocent little baby. He had imagined himself finding her, holding out the hand of Christian friendship and forgiveness, perhaps even taking her home to Scotland and the bosom of her family. Instead, as he walked wearily through that stinking Melbourne night, he had seen a gaudy creature in a bright green dress who had called to him from her verandah. 'All alone are you, laddie? Wouldn't you like company?' Then, as the moon touched his face, she had cried out in recognition. But that Lizzie Lennox had not been the innocent of his imagination. Remembering the tawdry wooden shack, Lizzie's painted friend with the gentleman 'visitor', the unmistakable nature of Lizzie's own invitation before she realized it was Tom, he shuddered with remembered revulsion and dismay. As for the precious baby, Lizzie had pretended it was dead – until her painted friend told Tom that Lizzie had sold it. She had even boasted of the bargain she had struck with Mungo Adam. Laughed ... and he had turned and fled for freedom and clean air before he choked on the stench of such squalor and betrayal. And now the creature was here, in his own house, dripping cheap jewels and expensive vulgarity.

'There's no call for you to stare at me like a dummy, Tom Diack,' said Lizzie now. 'I havena changed that much, have I? Though it's maybe the clothes, what with me coming up in the world since I last saw you. Real smart, aren't they?' and she turned slowly round so that the yellow crinoline swung like a gilded bell under the sable-trimmed cloak. 'Well, aren't you going to offer me a chair and maybe a dram?'

'Yes, of course,' said Tom, recollecting manners. He sent Jessie for glasses and the decanter, then indicated his own chair beside the fire. 'Fanny, you remember Lizzie Lennox, do you?'

'I remember you,' said Lizzie, before Fanny could speak. 'You was Headstane Wyness's daughter and used to go around with that Miss Adam afore your father and his father quarrelled. Fancy you marrying Tom Diack. Folks always said you had your eye on Fergus Adam, but maybe he got away?' Lizzie laughed delightedly at her own humour, then suddenly stopped. 'I'm sorry. I shouldna be laughing, should I, not with your father being dead and you in mourning. Black doesna really suit you though. I wouldna wear it long if I was you, not with it making your skin look so sallow. Though it's maybe good for covering you up when you've no waist left. Is it your first?'

'No,' managed Fanny. 'Our third.'

'You sly old lecher, Tom Diack. And you pretending you was all virtuous that time you visited me in Australia. But I made him right comfortable, Fanny. You don't mind if I call you Fanny, what with you and me being nearly of an age? Though you was older than me, I remember, and then I've kept myself smart, not like some.'

Fanny was saved the necessity of comment by the arrival of Jessie, with whisky, water and a plate of biscuits. 'And I brought the madeira as well, sir, for the mistress.'

'Thank you, Jessie,' said Fanny. 'Perhaps you would pour it for me?' She knew she could not bear it if Tom ignored her in front of this dreadful creature who, apparently, he knew.

'I remember fine when we last drank whisky together, Tom,' said Lizzie, settling back into her chair and spreading her garish skirts. 'It was that time you came all the way to Australia, looking for me, remember? Then you found me, and what a rare night we had together. That was in Melbourne,' she said to Fanny, 'when he was on his own and lonely. But I made him right welcome, didn't I, Tom? What a blether we had, talking of old times and that, and then, well ... but I'd best not say any more, eh Tom?' She winked and grinned, before emptying her glass and holding it out for a refill.

Tom cleared his throat and said, 'Will you be staying long in Aberdeen?'

'Well, now, that depends, doesn't it?' She looked archly at Tom, as if Fanny was not there. 'I was just coming for a visit, to see old friends, like. But I might just decide to stay now I'm here. I might build a house for me and my son. A big house, wi' turrets and that, like the Queen's building herself at Balmoral. Yon carter laddie was telling me about it. He said you was building houses now. Is that right?'

'Yes. In fact,' said Tom, snatching at the opportunity, 'I have one or two plans here on the table. Perhaps you would like to look at them and see if it's the sort of thing you had in mind.'

'Come and see my outlines, is it?' Lizzie laughed suggestively. 'And on a Sunday, too. But seeing as your wife's here to chaperone us I reckon it's all right. Dinna worry, Fanny,' she called over her shoulder. 'With this dratted crinoline, he'll not be able to get near me anyway. Maybe you should wear one, then you'd nay have so many children.' Fanny did not answer but bent her burning cheeks over her sewing and Lizzie turned her attentions to Tom. 'How much would one of they houses cost, Tom? One with turrets and all? When I've got my Leo, I reckon one of they houses would do us fine.'

Fanny at last found her voice. 'Are you thinking of reclaiming Leo, Mrs Faraday?'

'Reclaiming? He's mine already. He was maybe lent for a while, to Old Man Adam, but I'm still his ma. No one can deny that. And now I've made a bit of money for myself, I've come to see how he is and maybe take him back again.'

'And what does Fergus Adam say about it?' asked Fanny. 'Or Leo, come to that?'

'My Leo'll do as I tell him or he'll soon know about it,' said Lizzie cheerfully. 'As to Mr Adam, well I havena just mentioned it yet. We'll maybe be able to come to an arrangement.' She jabbed Tom in the ribs and laughed. 'Then I wouldna be needing a house of my own, would I? But if I do, I'll be happy to have you build it for me, Tom. Special rates, of course, for an old friend?' Again the nudge and suggestive wink.

Tom straightened, bundled up the plans and put them away. 'May I offer you another drink, perhaps?'

'Aye, I will take one, for my strength. I was up visiting your sister Mhairi earlier, but all I got there was tea.' Lizzie resumed her chair and accepted a third glass. 'My but it's grand to see you, Tom, after all these years, and you a family man, with a wife and bairns. Who'd have thought it all those years ago in Melbourne, when you was young and free. I can remember it now, with the moon shining and the dingoes howling and you and me, all cosy in my little room.' She drank, smacked her lips and drank again. 'Aye, that was a night. It was morning afore you was gone, I remember, and the dawn so romantic.'

Abruptly, Fanny stood up. 'Excuse me. I must see to the children.'

She half ran from the room and a moment later a door slammed upstairs.

'She's nay looking well, your Fanny,' said Lizzie, spreading her ample bulk complacently in the chair. 'But pregnancy does that to some folks. Wears them out till they're old afore their time and then afore you know it, they're dead, like your ma.'

'Goodbye.' Tom crossed to the door and rang the bell. 'Jessie will show you out.'

'But I havena finished my visit...'

'Yes, you have.' Tom took the glass from her hand and slammed it down on the table. 'If you decide on a house, let me know.' He propelled her into the hall, through the front door and outside. The moment the door closed behind her, he bounded upstairs to the landing and the bedroom door. 'Fanny, my love, you are not to take any notice of...' But the door was locked.

'Fanny?' He heard muffled sobbing inside, but though he rattled and shook the door, cajoled and pleaded, she would not open it and eventually he turned away, defeated.

It was Kit O'Brien who brought the note, to the tradesmen's entrance of the Guestrow house, on Friday afternoon. *Fanny unwell. Come at once*

But to all Annys's anxious questions he could say only, 'Mrs Wyness is in her bed and the doctor summoned. That's all I know, except that she's wanting the company of the Prettiest Dancer in all Scotland to lift her spirits and warm her heart. As it does mine ...' Then he said other, more personal things which brought the blushes to Annys's cheeks, and lit her eyes with happiness. Had it not been for her anxiety about Fanny, she would have sung aloud. Instead, she went straight to Miss Drummond, who lay listless on a *chaise longue* in the drawing-room, an open magazine unread beside her. At the sound of the door, something like animation touched the fragile figure.

'Is it an invitation for me, Annys? To Silvercairns perhaps?' It was a week since she had dined there and no word from Mr Adam since, though she had sent such a pretty little note of thanks the very next day, suggesting he call on her, for tea.

'I am sorry, Hetty, but I am afraid it is not. No doubt there will be a note for you tomorrow, but today the message is from my brother,

[211]

summoning me to poor Fanny's bedside. Fanny is ailing and the doctor sent for.'

'Then really there is no cause for you to leave me, is there Annys dear? The doctor will see to everything and I need you here, beside me.' She waved a small, helpless hand towards the chair which had been drawn up beside the *chaise longue*. 'You know how disconsolate I have been these last, tedious days.'

'My brother wants me to go at once,' said Annys, her voice quiet, but firm. 'So you see I must do so. He would not send if Fanny were not ill.'

'But I am ill!' cried Henrietta, a small frown of petulance creasing her brow. 'See how pale and wan I am. I cannot possibly be left alone.'

Miss Drummond was certainly pale, as anyone would be who shunned sunlight as assiduously as she did. Annys had even been required to hold a sunshade over her in the drawing-room, in March. Anxiety and irritation gave an edge to Annys's usually gentle voice.

'You know your brother will be back tomorrow, so you will not be long alone and I shall order the carriage to take you for a drive when I am gone. Fresh air and a change of scene will work wonders.' Before Miss Drummond could protest, Annys added, with an air of sweet innocence, 'I am sure Amelia Burnett would be delighted to keep you company. You can talk about Silvercairns together. Mrs Burnett has known the family since childhood, I believe, though I do not think she and Mr Adam's sister were ever particular friends.'

Thus feeding jealous dislike and romantic attachment in one skilful sentence, Annys added, 'You are so sweet and understanding, Hetty, and with such a generous heart that I know you would not want to keep me away from my poor sister-in-law's bedside one single minute more than necessary.'

Having thus neatly deprived Miss Drummond of all further argument, Annys made her swift farewells, bundled together a few necessities and sped down the back stairs to the kitchen regions and the yard, where Kit O'Brien was waiting for her, with his brightly painted cart.

It was unfortunate that it was market day, that Kit turned out of the yard and into the Guestrow just as a farm-cart came labouring up the incline of Netherkirkgate, unfortunate that Kit was too busy demonstrating his ability to drive with one arm round his passenger's waist

[212]

to acknowledge the farmer, or to give him right of way, and disastrous that Kit's cart was not only gleaming with new paint, but bearing, as well as that shameless baggage of a passenger, a collection of neatly tied boxes and bundles for delivery in the better parts of town.

Farmer Dickie saw and fumed. His own farm cart was encrusted with poultry droppings, old feathers, mouldering hay and the stinking detritus of the day's market offering – an undersized and ailing pig for which he had received half what he had asked – and its only contents were a bundle of fence-posts and a roll of wire, for which he had bargained hard but, in his opinion, paid too much. And O'Brien had not even had the manners to rein in his horse and let his elders and betters go first. But if that thieving tink of an Irishman thought he could charm the wits out of George Dickie, as he seemed to have bamboozled too many honest townsfolk already, not to mention most of their women, he'd soon see his mistake. George Dickie wasna fooled by all that honeyed talk and bits of poetry. Bits of lies, more like. Aye, yon fellow'd soon see he couldn't drive about the streets, flaunting and boasting and forcing honest folks into the gutter because he hadna the manners to take his turn. He'd soon learn he couldna lay his filthy paws on an innocent, God-fearing Scottish lass and get away with it.

Farmer Dickie had always been on neighbourly terms with the Rainbow Hill folk, it was no more than common sense in the country, but since that deal of his wife's brother's, with Tom Diack, he had felt an even closer bond. Especially as, once Willowbrae got into operation, Tom had promised to find jobs for two of the Dickie sons.

He had meant to stop off at the Lemon Tree to soak his sorrows in a pint or two of soothing ale before taking his miserable purchases home, but envy and righteous spite produced a better idea. Mhairi Grant kept a generous table, with ale every bit as good as he'd find at the Lemon Tree and without the pain of paying for it. Besides, she was an honest, hard-working woman who did her best for her family: she had a right to know what was going on behind her back.

On that Friday afternoon, Mhairi was alone in the cottage. Since that turbulent visit of Lizzie Lennox, Mhairi had overhauled her small supply of clothes, laid aside some for alteration, others for embellishment, and taken from its camphor her newest gown, a deep blue dress of the finest woollen material which she had worn last summer, during those enchanted months with Fergus Adam. This

[213]

she had donned today, intending to go into market, not to sell, but to buy. However, she had changed her mind and spent the morning in the quarry office instead, checking the books. She did not admit it to herself but the sight of Lizzie Lennox, flamboyantly rich and boasting of her hotel and her jewels, had caught her on the raw. Mhairi also had status and position: she might have lost her lover, but the granite business remained. She owed it to her son, and to the memory of George Wyness, to do what she could to prosper the enterprise.

Now, however, though her hair still shone with brushing and she wore a brooch at her throat, she had tied a large and serviceable apron over those deep blue skirts while she prepared the evening meal. But the apron was newly starched and sparkling white. Mhairi had taken Annys's comments to heart and, now that her first anger had faded, was grateful to her for them. Annys was a dear, affectionate and honest girl with the courage to speak the truth.

The preparations over, Mhairi had just taken up her sewing when she heard a cart draw up at the gate. She laid aside her work and stood up, but expecting some message from the quarry, she did not hurry, and the door opened before she reached it.

'Nay lass, there's no cause for alarm,' said Farmer Dickie as she started back in surprise. 'Leastways, there's been no accident, if that's what you're thinking. But I've a piece of news I reckon you'll want to hear.'

'Then you'd better come in, Mr Dickie,' said Mhairi, recovering poise. 'Will you take a dram?'

'Kit O'Brien and *Annys?*' Mhairi looked at him in startled horror. 'Are you sure?'

'I've eyes in my head, and nay call to doubt them. I should have whipped the fellow way back, first time I saw him and your Annys together. "Only carrying my basket, Mr Dickie" she said and there's me believing her. I reckon they was carrying on even then. You should thank your stars he went off to the Crimea and a pity he ever came back if you want my opinion. She'd be in the family way, else, like my Jessie. Daughters.' He spat expertly into the fire and drew long and appreciatively on the mug of ale with which Mhairi had supplied him. 'My, but this ale's good. You could give yon wifie at the

[214]

Lemon Tree a lesson or two and that's a fact. Aye, daughters ... ' He sighed. 'Who'd have them?'

'You said "way back", Mr Dickie,' managed Mhairi while the first shock and disbelief turned to a slow and burning anger. 'Do you mean Annys had met him before he went to Russia? Before last autumn?'

'That's right. It would be, let me see, when was it now? They was signing men on to build yon railway at Sebastopol and there was that many men pushing and shoving a body couldna get near Waterloo Quay without fear of being shoved into the harbour. That'd be December maybe, a year back. Saw your Annys on the Woodside road, wi' yon Irish tink. Gave her a lift. Not him, though. Whatever your Annys said, I'd seen him fooling with the lass. Carrying her basket, she said. Molesting, more like. You want to watch your Annys, Mhairi lass. I'd lock her up if I was you, leastways till she's a ring on her finger.'

December, a year back, thought Mhairi, appalled. Almost sixteen months ago. That would have been the day Annys first went to market alone, the day the invitation came. The wonder of that invitation had blotted all else from her mind at the time, but now Mhairi made a huge effort to remember. She was almost sure that Annys said she had met no one – she recalled her own relief at the time – and Annys had never lied in her life.

Slowly Mhairi remembered other occasions: when she had found O'Brien and Annys alone together at the cottage, and Annys had been so hysterically angry. Annys's eagerness to take food to the carter when he called with that basket. Deliberately Mhairi remembered the occasion, her own secret joy, the note, the careful words. Deliberately plunged the knife until pain had run its course. Then turned again to Annys. Suddenly, with spreading horror, she knew that Farmer Dickie was right. Peel away all his spleen and spite and envious embellishments and the stark fact remained: he had seen them together on the Woodside road and Annys had told her a lie. Had continued to tell it until now, today, when Annys should have been safe at Miss Drummond's house and Farmer Dickie had seen them together in Kit O'Brien's cart, his arm around her waist.

'Not that it's any use ... ' Farmer Dickie grumbled. 'All the same is lasses. All the same.' He stared morosely into his mug, absent-mindedly upended it to let fall a single drop onto the clean-swept floor, and righted it again. Moving as in a trance, Mhairi rose from her chair, re-filled his mug from the flagon on the table and resumed her seat.

'My Jessie now. Many's the time I've belted her, threatened her, locked her in the hen-house, and what good did it do me? I tellt the wife she shouldna have let her take that town job, but no ... an opportunity, she said. A good wee job for the lassie and one mouth less for us to feed. One mouth more, more like. She'll be lucky if she gets yon lecherous soldier lad to marry her at all, let alone afore the bairn's born, and him safe in the Crimea where I canna get at him. I reckon he got himself sent there deliberate. Why else would he go, with the war ending and all?'

'He might come back now that the Peace Treaty has been signed. I know Mrs Macrae is expecting Willy to arrive at any minute.'

'Volunteer for India, more like.' Farmer Dickie glared into the fire, drew noisily on his ale-mug and glared again. 'Lassies. Nothing but trouble. At least your Tom's going to see my lads do all right. Any word yet of when you'll be starting at Willowbrae?'

Mhairi shook her head. She did not trust herself to speak even such a small, innocuous word as 'No.'

'It'll be soon enough, likely, with the days getting longer and the weather nay so bad. My lads are right looking forward to it.' He paused, drank, then said, with ponderous solemnity, 'The wife and I, we're real grateful to your Tom, and we'll not forget it. Dickie, I says to myself, Tom Diack's been a good neighbour to me and I'll be a good neighbour to him and his family in return.'

'You are,' managed Mhairi, and with an effort added, 'And always have been.'

'And will be again. So I'm telling you this, lass.' He laid an unsteady finger against his nose and winked in a pantomime of secrecy. ''Tween you and me. I've seen what I've seen. You've been good as a mother to yon lassie and a right fine job you've done of it, but you take my advice, Mhairi. Grown lassies is not the same as wee ones. Dinna let your Annys out of your sight till she's wed.'

'Thank you, Mr Dickie. I'll remember that. But hadn't you better be on your way? Mrs Dickie will be worrying.'

She steered him firmly towards the doorway and outside. When the cart had creaked off down the lane again and out of sight, she still stood where she was, staring out of the window into the tranquil evening, seeing nothing but Annys's innocent, guileless face, while in her breast the anger swelled and swelled till she thought her chest

[216]

would split open with the pain of it. Annys had lied to her, deceived her, pretended to admire Philip Drummond, her 'prince from a fairytale', and all the time the scheming little vixen was meeting that Irish gypsy fellow behind her back. A rootless nobody who slept in a barn and hadn't two halfpennies to rub together. How could Annys be so devious and so ... so ... stupid. Mhairi could have wept with frustration and fury. She had not brought up her sister, loved and nurtured and guided her, groomed and educated her into a demure and graceful young woman whom any gentleman would be proud to marry, to see her throw herself away on a ... a beggar with nothing to offer but a hay loft and a touch of Irish blarney.

A hayloft. Mhairi swallowed in horror. Suppose he had already lured her guileless sister into that loft with him? Beguiled her with honeyed words and then ... Oh dear God, what was she to do?

Should she go straight round to the Guestrow house and summon Annys home? But Farmer Dickie had seen them driving out together. There was no saying where they were going or for how long. She could send a note? Uneasily Mhairi remembered Annys's outburst: 'I am not a child ... I want to live my own life ... you are not my mother ...' What right had she to interfere in her sister's love affairs? Then she remembered her own mother's injunction to her to 'see Annys grows up right' and knew that, whatever the consequences, she must speak out.

When Annys came for her usual Sunday visit, all innocence and sisterly solicitude, Mhairi would confront her with it and see what she had to say for herself. As for O'Brien, if Mhairi had any say in the matter, he'd find no more work at Rainbow Hill.

She was still turning the matter over and over in her mind when Hamish burst in through the door, a crumpled note in his hand. 'Lorn said to give you this, Ma. It's from Tom.'

'Tom?' But as she read, the frown which came whenever she thought of her brother was quickly replaced by a look of shock and alarm. Fanny was ill. There was no cause for undue alarm. He had sent for her mother and Annys who were with her now and would stay as long as circumstances required.

She had just time to think *So that is where Annys was going* before relief was replaced by anxiety. Seven months pregnant and 'ill'. Poor Fanny.

[217]

'How is she?' asked Mhairi, hurrying into the parlour of the Elmbank house the following morning. 'I came as soon as I could.'

Tom looked up from the plans spread out on the table in front of him and Mhairi was shocked by the change in him. Tom looked haggard, tormented, his eyes burning with inner suffering. 'Her mother is with her, and Annys. Dr Marshall came two hours ago and is still upstairs.'

'If it is the child,' began Mhairi gently, 'then she is in good hands. Try not to worry.'

'Not worry?' cried Tom. 'Have you forgotten our ma? Besides, it is not only the child.' Suddenly his shoulder slumped and he bowed his head, with a desolation which tore at Mhairi's heart. She forgot the stranger who had denied her happiness, who had plotted to snatch Willowbrae from Fergus Adam's grasp, and saw only the brother of her childhood, whom she loved. She took a hesitant step towards him, then stopped as he began to speak.

'Things have not been right between Fanny and me since her father died,' he confessed, his voice strained and scarce above a whisper. 'And then the other day, when Lizzie Lennox came...'

Mhairi's heart sank with dread. 'So she came to you, too. I was afraid she would. What did she say?'

'It was dreadful. She ... she flirted with me in front of Fanny and I did not stop her.'

'It is not easy to stop Lizzie, especially in her new prosperity.'

'Prosperity? Do you know how she got that money, Mhairi? And don't tell me she owns a hotel, because I know better. She may call it "hotel" but I call it "brothel". I saw her, Mhairi, all those years ago. It sickened me then, and it sickens me now. *And I did not stop her.* Fanny was sitting there, quiet and pure and ladylike and instead of putting the woman out of my house, as I ought to have done, I gave her whisky and let her talk.'

'Politeness,' soothed Mhairi. 'I did the same.' Though she told me how old and plain I looked and filled the boys' heads with envy.

'Then ... Oh God.' He covered his face with his hands and shuddered.

'Did she perhaps comment on Fanny's clothes?' suggested Mhairi.

'Worse than that. She said that all those years ago I went to Australia because of her. She insinuated that I ... that I spent the night with her.'

[218]

'Surely Fanny did not believe her?'

'I don't know. She ran from the room and I have not spoken with her since.'

'WHAT?' Mhairi was appalled. 'Not spoken? But surely ... ' Her voice trailed into silence.

'She does not want me near her. Not even now. Oh God, Mhairi, what am I to do?'

'When the baby is born, it will be different,' soothed Mhairi, while her thoughts raced and her heart ached for Fanny. She had seen Lizzie in action, been on the receiving end of her hurtful comments, but Fanny was not as strong as Mhairi. Fanny was timid and vulnerable, especially now. She was searching in her mind for some sort of comfort to offer, when the door opened and the doctor came in.

'The child is born,' he said, without preamble. Tom and Mhairi both let out a sigh of relief but before either could speak, Dr Marshall went on, 'A girl-child and feeble, which is only to be expected with a premature birth. However, it might survive. I will send round a wet-nurse as soon as possible. I think I know a girl who will suit – strong, healthy, plenty of milk and in need of money. I have told your mother-in-law to expect her.'

'But ... a wet-nurse?' faltered Mhairi. 'Cannot Fanny ...?'

'Have you any reason to believe that your wife is troubled in her mind?' said the doctor abruptly, fixing Tom with a frowning stare.

'No.' Tom blushed and avoided Mhairi's eye. 'At least ... perhaps she has been a little depressed lately.' He turned his back and busied himself with the whisky decanter. 'Will you take a dram, Doctor? To celebrate my daughter's birth?'

'I'll take a dram, but it will be no celebration. If nothing was troubling your wife before, something is certainly troubling her now. Her mind is wandering, Mr Diack. Unless you can explain why she should talk of "Balarat" and "diggings"? There is also a slight fever.'

'Oh God,' breathed Mhairi, her face white. 'Childbed fever?'

'I may be wrong, of course,' said the old doctor, taking the glass from Tom, whose hand was shaking. 'But I have done what I can for the moment.' He raised the glass in a silent toast, emptied it in one, wiped his mouth on the back of his hand and said, 'Thank you. I needed that. Now I must be on my way. Half Aberdeen seems to be ailing today: if it isn't scarlet fever, it's typhoid and I'm rushed off my feet. You would think that blessed nephew of mine would come home and help now the war's over, wouldn't you? But not a word. I

[219]

suppose measles in Aberdeen hasn't the same lure as war wounds in Scutari. Good day to you, and to you, Mrs Grant. I will send round that girl I mentioned and I'll look in again myself this afternoon.'

Tom saw him out, then came back into the parlour and closed the door. His face was ashen, his whole frame shaking.

'Sit down,' ordered Mhairi, leading him to a chair. 'Drink this.'

When he had emptied the glass she gave him, he held his head in his hands and groaned. 'Oh God, Mhairi. Childbed fever. Fanny might die.'

'Yes.' There was no point in pretending otherwise. 'But she might recover.' She put into her voice as much hope as she could muster. 'It has been known.'

'But she may not want to ... I made her so unhappy these last weeks. I could not help it and now ... oh God, Mhairi. What will I do if Fanny dies?'

Mhairi laid a compassionate hand on his shoulder. The last of her animosity drained out of her, leaving only the protective love she had felt for her brother for as long as she could remember. After a moment she said quietly, 'It may not come to that. But if it does, then you will learn to live with sadness. You will find comfort in your children, as they will find it in you. And you will endure.'

Tom straightened, brushed a hand across his eyes and said, 'I am sorry. It was crass of me to ask you, of all people. Please forgive me?' He added humbly, in a voice she could hardly hear, 'For everything?'

'Of course, Tom.' They both knew what he meant.

'And now I must go upstairs and see my new daughter. And ask whether my own wife can bear to see me. Will you come with me?'

His eyes echoed the fear in her own heart: suppose Fanny was beyond recognizing who came near her? Suppose the fever had already tightened its inexorable grip?

She too dreaded any reminder of their mother's deathbed, but she nodded. 'Yes, Tom. I will come.'

The matter of Kit O'Brien quite forgotten, Mhairi and Tom went out of the room together, and upstairs.

On the whole it had been a pleasant enough afternoon. Sundays for Fergus had always been a frustration, custom requiring one thing of him and inclination another. In his father's day, he had had no choice, but the long hours of Sunday which church attendance and

[220]

leisurely mealtimes did not fill had passed easily enough in reading and private study. Since his father's death, however, and his sister's marriage, with the increasing pressures on him since the loss of Willowbrae, he found that his one wish was to work, not quietly in his study with a book, but on the quarry floor. He grudged every minute spent away from the quarry, would have snatched his meals standing up had it not been for the necessity of setting Leo a good example, and lately had hit upon the useful habit of giving Leo his driving lesson on a Sunday afternoon, ostensibly to teach the boy how to handle a dogcart or a gig, but really as an excuse to inspect the policies, and check the boundaries of his land.

He used the exercise, as the boy drove sedately along the pathways of the estate, to cast an eye over the terraces, the dovecot, the outbuildings; to note any signs of cracking or subsidence; to watch for the inevitable. For since his decision to scrape and scour the quarry to the very edges of his land he knew his days at the big house were numbered, though whether in hundreds, tens or single figures he could not guess. All he knew was that a crack had opened up again in the terrace which Tom Diack had mended all those years ago when he was a mere apprentice in Silvercairns quarry, a large crack, pointing like the finger of doom straight towards the house.

Tom Diack had come far, but Fergus intended to see he climbed no further. If possible, to topple him back where he came from, and for good. If ever he found his thoughts turning to Tom's sister Mhairi, he slammed the door on them, hard. That part of his life was over. He had allowed sentiment to overshadow common sense and in consequence both he and his business had suffered. It would not happen again.

His first step had been an inspired one: he had forbidden the Diack camp access to his roads, but constant vigilance was necessary to ensure they did not trick their way through by devious means. His rides with Leo gave him the opportunity, and when the driving lesson was over, provided the boy had kept to the prescribed speed and not broken out into an imitation of a Roman charioteer, which he invariably threatened to do, they would exchange the dogcart for a pair of horses and ride the boundary between Silvercairns and Willowbrae.

In retaliation for the closing of the Silvercairns road, Tom Diack had ordered a fence to be put up along the boundary line, and it had become the tradition for Fergus and Leo to patrol this fence at the end of their afternoon ride. At the back of his mind Fergus had formed an idea that he might need to relocate that fence one day, probably after dark, and he meant to memorize every yard of it, in case. Also, it gave him the opportunity to see what progress the enemy was making: a week ago, he had noted with satisfaction, they had made none at all. Nor had they now. His blocking of the road had obviously stopped them in their tracks.

'I can't see any sign of digging, Uncle Fergus, can you?'

'No, Leo, and I hope I never will.'

'So do I, the thieving bastards,' said Leo cheerfully and for once Fergus let it pass.

Today had been a good day. Leo had been tractable, had shown real promise as a charioteer, handling the vehicle with competence and developing skill, and had asked intelligent questions about the land and the quarry. Miss Drummond and her brother were expected for dinner and Leo, bribed by an extra half hour's riding, had agreed to disappear the moment they arrived and not to reappear till breakfast. Fergus, for once, was looking forward to the evening. He hoped that Philip Drummond would be able to report on the development of the Deeside railway and maybe put in a good word in the right quarters when it came to allocating the next set of contracts, and his sister Henrietta seemed to require no more entertaining than a magazine and a polite word of attention now and then. Drummond might be able to tell him whether it would be worth his while to put in for that quarry that was up for lease at Cairncry, too. Though it was on the wrong side of town as far as Silvercairns was concerned, it was close to the railway line north and there would be no problems when it came to shifting the granite. None such as Diack would have to contend with at Willowbrae, always supposing he found any granite worth quarrying.

Remembering, Fergus Adam smiled with satisfaction, though without mirth. He intended to make Diack fight for every chip of rock he extracted from that land, and to pay for it twice over. Nor would the fellow have the lifeline of the railway to help him, unless he bought up the land between and laid a road to meet it.

'Will we get another quarry, Uncle Fergus?' said Leo beside him. 'Now that that bastard Diack has stolen Willowbrae?'

Twice was too much. 'Where on earth did you learn that expression?' he demanded, and remembered too late.

'From you, Uncle Fergus. You said...'

[222]

'All right, all right. But it is one thing for a grown man to say it, and quite another for you to do so, especially on Sunday.'

'But will we get another quarry? I told Hamish we had two quarries and now he says I'm a liar because his uncle stole one of them.'

'We might,' said Fergus, not really listening. 'I am thinking about it.'

'Good,' said Leo. 'Anyway, he hasn't got a treasure cave like I have.' He dug his heels suddenly into his pony's flanks and with a shout of 'Race you to the stables,' took off in a swirl of dust and pounding hooves.

Fergus followed, in the usual ritual, and caught up with his nephew just before they rode into the stable yard to find a strange carriage blocking their way. The Drummonds must have come early.

'Tidy yourself up, Leo, then come to the drawing-room, just to say hello. Politely,' warned Fergus. 'Then you can disappear, as we arranged.' He ruffled the boy's hair with an affectionate gesture. 'You did well this afternoon. We'll make a charioteer of you yet.'

Leo disappeared towards the kitchen regions while Fergus made his way via the terrace to the front door and inside.

A servant intercepted him in the hall. 'The person is waiting in the drawing-room,' he said, indicating a polished chest on which was a silver tray, bearing a single pasteboard card. 'I am sorry, sir, but she insisted . . .'

Fergus picked up the card, glanced at it briefly then tossed it away. Some charitable lady, no doubt, collecting for the Nightingale Hospital or some other worthy cause.

He had better get rid of the woman, whoever she was, before the Drummonds arrived.

Lizzie Lennox was not quite as brave as she made out. It was one thing to call on Mhairi and Tom Diack, who had once lived down the stair from her in the same city tenement and whom she had known since childhood, and quite another to call at the big house where she had worked briefly as a scullerymaid until the young master got her pregnant. She had fled to Australia, to escape her own father's retribution as much as anyone else's, and, she remembered uneasily, she had taken a helping of Lettice Adam's jewellery with her. Wages, that's all, she told herself. Compensation for her troubles, and no

[223]

more than was her due. Nevertheless, the first time she had set out to call at Silvercairns House, she had lost her nerve and turned back at the gate.

The second time, she had braved it as far as the front door, only to learn with relief that the master was out. She had left her card, with a message that she was staying a while at the Douglas Hotel, and had expected a dinner invitation to arrive the next day. When the next day brought nothing, and the next, indignation began to stir and by the end of the week was raging. Who did that Fergus Adam think he was, ignoring her like that? Keeping her Leo from meeting his own ma. She'd soon sort him out, she would, gent or no gent. She looked out her most sumptuous and expensive garments, donned the lot, ordered herself a carriage and drove the two miles to Silvercairns, her temper nicely simmering.

It went off the boil slightly as she rounded the curve in the drive and saw the imposing frontage of Silvercairns, with its pillared entrance and elegant, terraced garden, but it was too late to turn back, and the expression on that insolent fellow's face when he opened the door to her was enough to fan it into raging fury.

'Oh. It's you again.' Anyone would think she was a piece of rotten fish the way his nose wrinkled.

'I've come to see Mr Adam, I have, so you can take that sneer off your face and show me in.'

'Mr Adam is not at home.'

'I've not paid a carriage to bring me all this way for nothing, so this time I'll come in and wait till he is.' She took a step forward and he moved swiftly to bar her way.

'I think you have mistaken the entrance. The tradesmen's door is at the back.'

'I ken that fine and if you think I'm coming in the scullery door with my best gownie on you can think again. You need your eyes sorted, you do, if you canna see your betters when they're standing in front of you. I'm staying in the Douglas Hotel I am, and I'm standing no cheek from the likes of you, you cross-eyed, stinking little runt, so get out of my way.' She pushed him hard in the chest so that he loosed his hold on the door and it swung wide.

'About time too,' said Lizzie, sweeping past him and into the hall, before he could regain wits enough to stop her. 'I know fine where to go so I'll show myself up.'

But in the silent elegance of the Silvercairns drawing-room her bravado faded as the minutes passed. In spite of her riches and her expensive clothes, she could not help remembering the last time she had been in Silvercairns, as a scullerymaid, and though she stamped it down the feeling of inferiority kept creeping back. She shouldn't be in the drawing-room: what would Ma Gregor say if she caught her? But with nervousness came the memory of daring: she had sneaked into that Miss Lettice's bedroom once, and tried on her clothes. That was when Mr Hugo Adam caught her and look what that led to. She had had some rare times with Mr Hugo before he got her pregnant, then you couldn't see the bastard for dust. But she'd made the Adams pay. And pay again when young Leo was born. Remembering, she felt her confidence return. Old Man Adam had wanted his grandson, sent for him half across the world, paid good money to get him back. She was Leo's mother and she had as much right as any of them to be in the Silvercairns drawing-room.

Nevertheless, when half an hour had gone by and still no one had come near her, she began to wonder if she might not leave after all. She moved restlessly round the room, picking things up and replacing them, admiring herself in the gilt-framed looking-glass above the mantelshelf. It was a good job there was no fire or she might have set her new skirts alight. There was a wifie up Ellon way in one of they country houses, turned round with her back to the fire, talking and laughing, and the next minute, whoosh. She was lit up like a candle and burnt to a cinder afore anyone could lift a finger. All on account of her crinoline. But there was only a tasteful arrangement of dried grasses in the Silvercairns fireplace, it being summer, and Lizzie was able to lean as close as she liked to the glass to adjust her straw hat and feathers, while every now and then she went to the window to see if Fergus Adam was coming.

She had just decided that she would ring the bell and tell that insolent fool of a servant to bring her tea or something, when she heard the sound of hooves and crossed to the window just in time to see two horsemen, a man and a boy, come pounding across the parkland, neck and neck, then round the corner and out of sight.

Fergus Adam and her Leo. It must be. Fancy her Leo, riding like a real gent, and with Mr Adam himself. Just like father and son. She chose a seat on one of the sofas, spread her skirts to show them at their best, patted her ringlets and prepared a suitable smile of welcome.

[225]

'Good afternoon. I was told that . . . ' Fergus stopped abruptly in the doorway, his eyes dazzled by the brilliance of her garb: scarlet skirts, purple cloak, yellow ribbons everywhere and a straw hat with the biggest ostrich feather he had ever seen. The faded elegance of his drawing-room served only to exaggerate the vulgarity so that for a moment he wondered if his visitor might be wearing fancy dress. He swallowed, retrieved manners, and extended a hand.

'Mrs Faraday, I believe, though I do not think I have the pleasure of your acquaintance?'

'You can have the pleasure all right, Mr Adam, any time. A handsome fellow like you.' Her smile stopped him in his tracks. He withdrew his outstretched hand, and put both firmly behind his back.

'I am afraid I don't quite . . . have you perhaps come on behalf of some charity? If so, I am afraid it is my sister you want and she, unfortunately is out of the country at present, though we do expect her back very shortly.'

'She can stay away as long as she likes for all I care,' said Lizzie. It was on the tip of her tongue to add 'patronizing bitch,' but she remembered those purloined jewels and thought better of it. Instead, she smiled invitingly and said, 'It's you I've come to see, Mr Adam. As for charity, if you call my Leo charity, then you are right.'

'Leo?' Fergus's face grew white with shock.

'Yes. I've come to see my Leo. The lad old Mungo Adam sent for, all the way to Australia.'

'My' Leo. Good God. He remembered Lettice's facetious warning, her jeers and jibes. *Suppose that dreadful mother of his comes back to claim him.* But surely she would not want him back now, not after so long?

'Do I understand that you are . . . ' he swallowed. 'The boy's mother?'

'Aye. Lizzie Lennox, that's me. Though I calls myself Mrs Elizabeth Faraday now, seeing as how I've come up in the world. If you dinna believe me, ask Ma Gregor and I reckon she'll remember, the spying old bag. Always nagging at me about the black-leading, she was.' Lizzie stopped short and changed tack. She did not want to remind anyone of that particular past, only of the present, and the future. 'But I'm not here to talk over old times, Mr Adam. I'm here to see my son. Mungo Adam was going to bring up like his own grandson, he was, and I should have been told when the old devil died. So I could see my Leo had his rights.'

[226]

'If you had written even once during the six years Leo has been with us, perhaps we might have had an address at which to contact you,' said Fergus carefully. He did not doubt her claim to be the mother: the red hair alone would have been sufficient proof. It was her motives he questioned. Was she after money?

'Aye well, I had no reason to write, did I?' bridled Lizzie. 'I was busy earning my living, I was. It was you as should have written to me, to tell me my Leo was being looked after proper.'

'Leo has been well cared for, I assure you.'

'Aye, but it was his Grandpa wanted him. Who's to say you haven't done him out of his rights now the old devil's dead.'

'No one has done anyone out of anything,' said Fergus, with slow patience. Suddenly, inside his head, a devil jeered, *Tom Diack's done you out of Willowbrae and his sister Mhairi.* Patience snapped. 'Kindly state your business. My time is limited.'

'I'll tell you my business, Mr Fergus Adam. I'm here to see about my Leo's money. The money his grandpa left him. And don't tell me he left Leo nothing because I'll not believe you.'

'Believe me or not, it is the truth. I have certain funds in trust for the boy, when he comes of age, but until then, he . . . '

'How much?'

'That, madam, is no concern of yours.'

'Oh no? Then let me tell you something, Mr la-di-da Adam. What concerns my Leo concerns me, especially if you're doing him out of what his grandpa left him.'

'I repeat, no one is doing Leo out of anything,' said Fergus with cold fury, 'and if you continue to suggest such a thing, I would remind you of the law of slander.'

'Remind till you're blue in the face,' taunted Lizzie. 'See if I care. I'm rich, I am, and I can buy myself the best lawyer in town.'

There was a pause, during which Fergus counted slowly to ten while Lizzie settled back on the sofa, spreading her skirts wide. She crossed one leg over the other, thus exposing a length of frilled pantaloon and Fergus, who had been studying her in frowning silence, looked hastily away.

Lizzie laughed. 'I was forgetting you was not married, Mr Fergus. You're blushing like a schoolboy. Haven't you seen a lady's ankle afore? I reckon we'll have to do something about your education.' She winked and wiggled a foot at him.

Oh God, it was appalling. What on earth had she come here for?

[227]

Surely, after all this time, she could not possibly want the boy back? Remembering Leo as he had been when he arrived six years ago and Leo now, Fergus vowed silently and through clenched teeth that she would take the boy over his dead body.

At that moment there was a knock at the door and Leo himself burst in.

'You said I was to come and say hello politely, Uncle Fergus but ...' he slithered to an astonished stop, and stared openly at the plump woman in the circus clothes who was showing her drawers. 'That's not Miss Drummond.'

'No, Leo, it is a Mrs Faraday who ...'

'Leo!' cried Lizzie, throwing wide her arms. 'Come and give your ma a kiss.'

'Ma?' faltered Leo. 'My ma's in Australia.' He sidled nearer to Fergus and felt for his uncle's hand.

'Not now she's not. She's right here in the room with you. I was in Australia right enough, but I made money, didn't I? More money than your uncle Fergus will ever see. So I says to myself, Lizzie, I says. You're going to take a trip to Scotland to see your family and your friends and show them how well you've done for yourself, so I packed my trunks and I came. Not steerage neither. I had a real cabin all to myself, with a bed and table and chairs and that, just like it was a house instead of a ship. But then your ma's rich, now, Leo, with her own hotel and her own wee gold mine. Look, I'll show you.' She fished about in the folds of her clothes, produced a draw-string purse and opened it. She took out a nugget the size of a walnut and held it out to Leo on the palm of her hand. 'See this? This is real gold, from the diggings. You can have it if you like.'

Mesmerized by the object in the woman's hand, Leo drew closer until he was standing just out of Lizzie's reach.

'There's no need to be afraid of your own ma, Leo. I'll not bite you. My, but you're a fine-looking lad, just like me, with maybe a wee touch of your pa about the eyes. You look a proper gent, too, in those clothes. I reckon you've looked after him well enough, Mr Adam,' she conceded, turning her head in his direction. 'So far.'

Fergus said nothing, though his mind raced with speculation. Suppose she demanded the boy back? Bribed him and cajoled him as she was doing now? If even half her tale was true, she had the means to support him. At the thought of losing the boy, Fergus's heart thudded hard with dread. Leo was all he had left.

[228]

'Well Leo, do I get that kiss now? You'll not get this wee lump of gold else.'

Gingerly Leo lent forward and kissed her on the cheek. Then he wiped his mouth on the back of his hand, and his hand on the seat of his pants.

'That's not very flattering,' said Lizzie. 'I maybe won't give you that gold after all.'

'You promised,' began Leo indignantly. 'You said...'

'Aye well,' interrupted Lizzie quickly. 'I'll maybe give you it this time, but you'll need to learn to kiss a lady better than that if you're to get on in the world. Hold out your hand. There,' she said, placing the nugget on his palm. 'That's a piece of real Australian gold, that is. See you don't lose it.'

Leo shot across the room to where Fergus was standing, his back to the sofa and glaring out of the window.

'Look, Uncle Fergus. It's just like a piece of rock from Silvercairns only it's gold. Look.'

Fergus picked the nugget up between finger and thumb, inspected it and returned it to Leo. 'So it is.' He added, with an effort, 'Say thank you to the lady.'

'Thank you, Mrs Faraday.'

'You mean "Thank you, ma,"' said Lizzie indignantly. 'I've not come half across the world to have my own son call me Mrs, as if I was a stranger.'

'But you are,' pointed out Fergus. 'You could hardly expect otherwise when you have not seen the boy for years.'

'Well I'm seeing him now, aren't I? You come back over here, Leo and sit beside me, and I'll tell you what Australia's like.'

Leo looked to his uncle for guidance, but Fergus was frowning at a point somewhere above Leo's head. After a moment, the boy sidled towards the sofa and sat down gingerly on the edge of the seat. He held the gold nugget tight in his hand.

'That's right, Leo, you hang on to that wee bit gold. That's money, that is, and plenty more where that came from. Diggings, they're called, only it's gold they dig, not like your quarry where all you dig up is stone. I thought when I came over here I'd maybe stay, build myself a house and settle down, but now I'm not so sure. It's not like I remembered, somehow. No life about the place. Not like where I come from. In Australia I'm famous, I am. Everybody's heard of Mrs Faraday's place and the bank manager opens the door for me

[229]

himself, when I goes in to count my money. Aye, I'm an important person in Australia, but then its not full of po-faced, mean-minded, sneering folk with a grudge against anyone who's done well for herself. Not like here. It's a rare life for a lad in Australia, Leo. You'd like it fine. The sun shines and there's strange animals with pockets on their fronts, called kangaroos. They can jump fences.'

'So can Mica,' boasted Leo. 'That's my pony. Uncle Fergus gave him to me for my birthday and he can jump a five-bar gate.'

'Aye well, I bet your Mica can't jump houses. Kangaroos can, on account of their back legs being so strong. Then there's birds called kookaburras what laugh instead of singing and all sorts of other birds, red and blue and orange, what you only see on women's hats here, but in Australia they're sitting in trees and flying about wild. Then there's dingoes that howl in the night.'

Leo looked apprehensive and edged further away. Lizzie laughed. 'There's no call to be nervous, Leo. They'll not get you. They're in the outback, see, not in the town. There's Originals in the outback, too. Natives, black as coal and with no clothes on. They hunt with a bent stick called a boomerang. They throw it away, see, and it comes back again, like a dog to a whistle, and maybe hits something on the way. If I'd thought, I could have brought you one.'

'Aunt Lettice is going to bring me a Russian helmet and a sword.'

'Is she indeed.' Lizzie's lips tightened. 'Well they wouldna come back if you whistled, would they?' She laughed at her own joke. 'They Originals is clever, see? They dinna like the white men on account of them killing and stealing land and all. And the white men dinna like the Originals on account of them being black and different and not doing what they're told and moving out of the way. But they dinna bother me. I've my own hotel, with a verandah and trees and that. Real pretty. I've a horse and trap, too. How do you fancy coming back to Australia with me, Leo, then you could drive it for me? I'll buy you a horse of your own as well, so that when you're not driving me about in my trap you can maybe go racing, or jumping hedges and fences and that. I reckon you'd like it fine in Australia. There's plenty more gold where that came from and good openings for fine-looking lads like you. The White Star Line ship's in harbour now and sailing for Melbourne any day. What do you say?'

Leo eyed her warily before saying, 'Can Uncle Fergus come too?'

Lizzie tossed back her head and laughed. 'You'd have to ask him that, laddie, but I reckon it's not a bad idea, eh Mr Adam? Here's me a widow and you needing educating ... We could have some rare lessons together.'

Fergus's face darkened with embarrassment and outrage. How dare the woman even so much as suggest that he and she ... He took a deep and steadying breath.

'You must excuse me. I am expecting guests for dinner.'

'Are you now? Isn't that convenient. I've always fancied eating in yon dining-room so you can send and tell Ma Gregor to set another place.'

'Mrs Gregor,' corrected Leo, an apprehensive eye on Fergus's face.

'My dining arrangements are already made and cannot be altered. Leo, tell them downstairs to send round the lady's carriage.'

Leo shot out of the room and down the stairs two at a time. Fergus could not have found a better way to remove the child: he knew Leo would take the message to the stable yard himself, and probably persuade the driver to let him ride on the box as far as the front door.

Lizzie's face was red with fury. 'You can send that carriage straight back, Mr Fergus Adam, because I'm not shifting from here till I've had my dinner, with my son. I've a right to ... '

'You have no rights,' cut in Fergus. Now the boy was out of earshot, he was free to speak his mind. 'You gave them up when you sold your son. I have the receipt in my desk, together with the agreement you signed and which you have obviously forgotten. You agreed to make no further claim upon the boy, whatever the circumstances.'

'Aye, well, I didna have the money then, did I, to bring him up proper. Now I have and I'm wanting him back.'

'How much are you offering, Mrs Faraday?'

Lizzie's mouth dropped open in shock and the belligerence drained out of her.

'Well?'

'I'm not offering anything,' she blustered. 'He's my son, isn't he? Folks don't pay money for their own sons.'

'Perhaps not, in the ordinary way of things.' Fergus felt his confidence return as he saw the result of his inspired question. He had not meant to descend to her level, had intended only to get her out of the house before she could do any more harm, but the words had come to him unbidden. Now he carried home his advantage.

'But then, as I recall, you sold your son for a hundred pounds. He

[231]

is now six years older, well nourished, tolerably well educated and in good health. If you take into account the cost of his upkeep over those six years, plus of course the original hundred pounds, and the undoubted improvement in manners as well as in the boy himself, I think we would be talking of at least a thousand pounds, don't you?'

'You're mad, you are, Fergus Adam,' gasped Lizzie, clutching her cloak around her and scrambling out of her seat. 'Mad as that evil old devil Mungo. I'll see my lawyer, I will. I'm nay paying you a thousand pounds for my own son.'

'What figure had you in mind?'

Fortunately at that moment the servant arrived to say madam's carriage was waiting.

'You've not heard the last of this, Fergus Adam,' she spat as she pushed past him into the hall. 'I reckon Leo would rather come with me any day than live in this miserable dump. And your ceiling's cracked!'

Outside, Leo himself was holding the horse's head and chatting to the driver. Fergus saw the woman speak to him, laugh, then climb up into the carriage. He watched it carry her out of sight with a mixture of relief and foreboding. He did not believe she loved the boy: if she wanted him, it could only be to spite him, Fergus, or as some sort of acquisition to take back with her and boast about. Nor did he fear the law. But Leo was susceptible to easy bribery. Like a jackdaw with a bauble. Suppose he actually chose to go?

And the wretched woman was right about the ceiling.

Suddenly it seemed to Fergus as if his whole life was cracking apart.

'Do I have to say hello again, when the Drummonds come?' asked Leo beside him.

'Not unless you really want to.'

'I don't.' After a moment he added, uncertainly, 'Is that Miss Drummond really setting her cap at you, Uncle Fergus, like Mrs Gregor says?'

Fergus was at the quarry even earlier than usual that morning, as he had been on every morning since that dreadful woman's visit but even so someone was there before him. Two shapes, a man's and a boy's, dark against the pale green sky. To the east, above the sea, the red and gold was strengthening into summer warmth, but in the shadows of the quarry yard the air was still cool, dew-laden. From the path behind them, Fergus saw the figures reach the yard, but instead of going to the quarry office as he expected them to do, they walked on towards the quarry itself.

Fergus opened his mouth to bellow 'Hey! You!' then closed it again as he realized who the intruders were: Donal Grant, the designer from the Wyness yard and his interpreter, Mhairi's son. Donal would not hear him, however loudly he called. As for the boy, Fergus spent every waking hour struggling to forget Mhairi Grant and had no wish to have his work undone in a moment by confronting her son. So he watched them in silence as they moved out from the shadowed yard and onto the rim of the quarry. Briefly, they were silhouetted dark against the aquamarine of the western sky, before shrinking gradually downwards until first one head, then the other merged with the bushy confusion of the horizon and disappeared. They would be on the spiral path now, descending to the quarry floor.

He could have stopped them, turned them back. The road to Silvercairns was closed to the Wyness camp: except that that agreement still stood, legally valid till the end of the year, by which Donal Grant was allowed to choose his granite slab in person. As for the boy ... technically he should not be there, but Fergus knew he came as Donal's ears and tongue. It must be the order for the Wyness monument. He would warn Bruce the foreman to keep an eye on the pair; see they did not outstay their welcome. As soon as Bruce arrived, Fergus wanted to settle the next stage of the blasting programme once and for all so that they could set to work on it without delay. That fresh crack in the ceiling was ominous: he must keep a closer eye on the house from now on, so that when the time came to move, they were not caught unawares. As for the woman who had pointed out that crack, she would have to be watched, too. And Leo. Frowning, Fergus unlocked his office and went inside.

Donal stood in the centre of the empty quarry floor, feet slightly apart and hands hanging loose, while he surveyed the granite walls around him. At that time of early morning, the quarry was in shadow except for a narrow strip on the northern wall where the first sunlight filtered through the intervening trees to touch the dull grey stone with gold. That was the abandoned wall, the roped off, disused wall, not cleanly sliced and hewn as the others were to a uniform smoothness, but jagged with the half-quarried debris of the old explosion which had wrecked the west wing of Silvercairns house and killed Old Man Adam. There were darker wedges of shadow cast by fallen rock, other shadows of scattered bush and fern, tenacious undergrowth clinging where no green thing ought to be. Donal stared for a long time at those shadows, especially at a dense patch some two thirds of the way down the cliff. Then he turned and looked a question at the boy beside him.

Hamish nodded. Yes, that was Leo's cave. Telling secrets to Uncle Donal was no betrayal of trust.

His uncle resumed his inspection of the rock face, moving closer now, till he came up against the rope which barred all progress beyond that line. Donal stepped over it. Hamish followed.

He moved in among the rocks at the foot of the cliff, laid his hand against the rock face, looked upwards and to either side. 'Water?'

Hamish understood not only the signs but the question behind the question.

'In the cave. Only a little at first, but more now. Enough to drink.' He cupped his hands in illustration. 'No one knows except Leo, and you mustn't tell anyone because he's not supposed to go there. It is forbidden ground.'

It is forbidden because of the water signed Donal. Water in the wrong place could flood a quarry. A little, and you could pump it out: too much, and the rock became impossible to blast, the quarry worthless. *It is forbidden because the water must not be disturbed.* But Hamish shook his head.

'No. At first there was no water. None at all. Then a little trickle. Now a stream. When there is a blasting, more comes. Enough to make a pool.'

Donald nodded, his face thoughtful, but before Hamish could ask him why, he heard distant voices and saw men at the top of the spiral path. The quarry workers were arriving. He tugged his uncle's arm and pointed upwards. In a moment, Donal and Hamish had moved out of forbidden ground and by the time the first men reached the bottom, Donal was tapping and inspecting well away from the northern face.

Nevertheless when he made his choice it was at a spot on the very edge of the boundary where a massive 'post' of weathered stone which had once been roped off was now, by the mere moving of that

[234]

rope, available for exploitation. Hamish fetched the foreman, Bruce, and Donal pointed out the particular block he wanted.

'It is for George Wyness's monument,' explained the boy. 'A double tomb with room for his wife and family to join him one day.'

Donal produced his sketches, showed the foreman his calculations of size and weight.

'Aye well,' said Bruce, looking from sketch to quarry wall. 'I reckon you've chosen the best rock in the place. I'll need to check with Mr Adam, of course, but you've made a lucky choice. Anywhere else and you'd be looking at five, six weeks waiting, maybe more. This section is next for blasting anyway. Take these figures to the office, lad, and tell them I sent you. Now, back up that path with you, at the double. We've work to do.'

At the gates of Silvercairns House, Leo crouched in the concealment of a rhododendron bush. 'Psst! Hamish! Come and see what I've got.'

Hamish touched his uncle's arm, made some hurried explanation, told him to go on ahead and he would catch him up, then with a quick look over his shoulder to make sure no one saw him, he joined Leo in the leafy thicket of rhododendrons. Huge pink flower heads dripped pollen and thick sap. Dark leaves were stiff as knife blades, glossy as polished green leather. There was a dank smell of leaf mould and hidden moisture.

'Where have you been all week?' demanded Leo. 'I've been waiting.'

'I've been busy,' whispered Hamish. 'Working. But what did you stop me for? What do you want? Hurry up and tell me because Aunt Fanny's ill and Uncle Tom's not working and Ma said I was to go straight back. I'm helping to run the quarry,' he added, with ill-concealed pride.

'So what. All you get is lumps of stone. Anyone can do that. Not like my gold mine.' He paused to savour the effect of his words.

Hamish jeered. 'Gold mine? You're soft in the head, you are. I'm going.'

He made to push his way past Leo but the boy stopped him. 'Look.' He held out his closed fist, then slowly opened it. 'That's gold, that is. From my gold mine in Australia.' When Hamish said nothing, but stared at the gold nugget in a mixture of disbelief and

[235]

awe, Leo went on, 'My ma gave it to me, from the diggings. She says she'll take me to Australia with her, to see my gold mine for myself. Then I can have as much gold as I want, to buy things with. Horses and racing chariots and that. Anything I like.'

But Hamish had recovered. 'I wouldn't go if I was you.' He was going to say something rude about Leo's ma, but stopped himself in time. Instead he said, 'What about your uncle, and Silvercairns?'

'They'll be all right. I'll maybe stay a year or two in Australia, spending my gold and that, then I'll come back again. I'll bring you a kangaroo if you like. And a boomerang. You throw them and they come back again, like a dog to a whistle. My ma told me so.'

But this was too much for Hamish, good manners or not. 'I don't like your ma. She said rude things about Uncle Donal and only ignorant, stupid people do that. I wouldn't believe a word she said if I was you. She'll treat you like a boomerang, making you do what she wants all the time. Or sell you. Like she did before.'

With that final taunt, Hamish neatly evaded Leo's lunge, slipped out of the bushes and ran till he caught up with Uncle Donal by the smithy at Hirpletillam, where, by great good fortune, they found Kit O'Brien, waiting for his horse to be shod, and begged a lift with him back into town.

'And how is poor Mrs Wyness this morning?' asked Kit when they were on the open road. He had been employed earlier in the week in laying straw on the road outside the house, to deaden the noise of horses and carriage wheels. Though with the poor woman demented anyway, he doubted it would make much difference.

'No better,' said Hamish, biting his lip. He was fond of Aunty Fanny and, though his mother and uncles were careful what they said in front of himself and Catriona, he had caught something of the general fear. 'She is very ill,' he added, almost in a whisper.

'So I heard, and her the mildest, kindest of women. But cheer up, Hamish,' he added, by way of reassurance. 'She is in good hands and nothing we poor menfolk can do except leave it to the ladies and the doctor and get on with our work. Tell you what. Would you like to try your hand at driving my cart for me? Just for five minutes, mind?'

Gratefully, Hamish accepted. The responsibility and the excitement took his mind off other things, until, as they approached the outskirts of town, he handed back the reins.

'Thank you, Kit. Did I do all right?'

'Like a charioteer,' said Kit solemnly, and winked.

[236]

After a short silence, Hamish glanced behind him to make sure Donal could not lip-read and confided, 'Leo says he might go to Australia.' He sounded hesitant and worried.

'Does he indeed? Well, I've thought of it myself more than once, but changed my mind. There's things here in Aberdeen I would not want to leave behind, not for all the tea in China – nor for all the gold in Ballarat or Bendigo or wherever the blessed diggings are supposed to be. I had enough of foreign parts when I was in Russia. Besides, I said to myself, if it was that easy to get rich, Kit my boy, why isn't everyone in Australia riding about in carriages, dressed to the ears in ermine and dripping with gold? Ask yourself that.'

'Leo says his ma owns a gold mine.'

'Maybe she does, in a manner of speaking,' muttered Kit, 'though it's maybe not the sort of gold mine young Leo has in mind.'

'I don't understand, Kit. Are there two kinds of gold mine?'

But Kit had reached his destination and pulled his horse up sharp, at the door of Abercrombie's Emporium.

'I'm sorry lad, I can't talk now. I've a load of wines to collect, among other things, and what with Merry casting a shoe I'm behindhand as it is. Just you tell young Leo,' he added as Donal and Hamish alighted from the cart, 'to take everything that woman says with a large pinch of salt. Go to Australia with her? I wouldn't even cross the street with her if it was me.'

He hitched his horse to a convenient post and disappeared into the shop, whistling.

They found Mhairi in the office at the Wyness yard and one look at her face told them that the news was no better. The yard was as busy as usual, possibly even busier, but a subdued air hung over everywhere and when the men spoke to each other they did so in murmurs. There was none of the usual rowdy bonhomie, the shouted insults, the laughter. It was barely six weeks since George Wyness himself had died and now his only daughter's life hung on a thread. Moreover Tom Diack, the new manager, had not been seen for days and the running of the yard left in the hands of his brother Lorn and Donal Grant. Lorn was out and about for much of the time, on company business, or helping his brother Will at the quarry, and though Donal was a good enough fellow, no question of that, and knew the job as well as anyone, it made a man uncomfortable to have to read and write instructions, especially if he wasna just that good at book learning. Or to ask a nine-year-old lad to interpret for him. Though Mrs Grant had explained to them, entreated their loyalty and tolerance, assured them that as long as the work was done they would be paid as before, there was a feeling of unease in the yard. The passing of the old order had been inevitable – just as death was inevitable – but the crumbling of the new order before it was even established was something else. Mhairi had realized that Tom had not had the same benign control over the business that Wyness himself had had: how could he, when Wyness had spent a lifetime building the business up from scratch whereas Tom had had barely six years of it and that mostly on the building side of things. But she had not realized just how far things had slipped.

Now she was beginning to find out.

The order book was up to date. She had been pleased to see they had no major orders overdue and that on the whole deadlines were being more than met. Until she realized the cause was not increased efficiency, resulting from the increased work force, but something far simpler: diminishing orders. She would go through the ledgers again, of course, for both quarry and polishing yard, in case she had misunderstood, but it seemed that Tom had not old Wyness's touch where attracting business was concerned. Houses, yes. But then they had always been Tom's province. But the rest of the business? Mhairi was beginning to suspect that those in the town who had known George Wyness all his business life, and had liked and trusted him, were chary of putting the same trust in his young son-in-law. Especially after that rumour that it was a boardroom row between father and son-in-law that had precipitated old Wyness's final illness and 'driven him to his grave'. She would study the ledgers again, but she was afraid that however many times she pored over them the result would be the same: since the old man's death the number of orders had shrunk to half, and was still shrinking. Something would have to be done, and soon.

Mhairi listened to Hamish's report of their visit to Silvercairns, asked one or two questions of Donal, checked the design of the monument with him yet again and nodded her approval. It was the best thing Donal had done and no wonder Mrs Wyness had approved – and agreed with him that only the white polished purity of Silvercairns granite would do justice to the design. You had only to look at that Drummond fountain to see what wonders Donal and the polishers could accomplish between them.

The fountain itself stood shrouded in protective sacking and locked away in a shed until the final frieze, of twined vine leaves and bunches of grapes, was finished. Every stalk and individual grape had to be not only carved but polished by hand, a tedious and time-consuming task, but one which Mhairi hoped would be finished before another week was out, when Philip Drummond was to come and make his final inspection. He had already seen it at various stages of completion and invariably praised its beauty and workmanship, so Mhairi had no fears on that score. But their work did not end there: there would be the difficult task of shipping it, unharmed, to London, for delivery to the Drummond estate. She made a mental note to ask at the Christie office, find a suitable ship. Then she turned to Donal.

'I must go now. I have to call in to see how Fanny is and to ask Tom's advice on various matters. Goodbye, Hamish.' She bent to kiss him briefly on the forehead. 'Look after Uncle Donal. And take care of things for me.'

'Yes, Ma.' Hamish's breast swelled with pride and responsibility. Kit O'Brien was right: there were things in Aberdeen Hamish would not turn his back on for a hundred gold mincs, not for the whole world.

The house at Elmbank was silent as the grave and for a moment Mhairi's heart stopped with dread. Then beat again, too fast. But when Jessie shook her head sadly and said, 'No change, ma'am,' Mhairi felt hope flicker into life again. 'But old Mrs Wyness sent to say the children are well, including the newest wee scrap of a quinie, though the lassie has been given no name yet, poor wee mite. I tried to speak to the master about it, but he wouldna listen, being that upset. As we all are.'

'I will talk to my brother about it,' promised Mhairi, 'when I have seen how the mistress is.'

She found Annys seated quietly at Fanny's bedside, an open book on her lap, and Fanny sleeping. But it was a restless, fevered sleep and Mhairi did not need to lay a hand on the dry skin of Fanny's forehead to know that it would be burning hot. The doctor had been and gone again, Annys whispered. He would come again in the

[239]

afternoon, but there was little more he or anyone could do, except hope, and pray. Yes, she herself was fine and needed nothing. She had books enough to occupy her when Fanny did not need her ministrations and Jessie relieved her now and then, for meals and rest. At night, Tom took over and kept vigil, Annys feared, all night. He was supposedly resting now, though she thought she had heard him pacing up and down in the parlour not five minutes ago. The parlour was underneath.

Mhairi stayed a few more minutes, said a prayer, kissed Annys on the brow and tiptoed out again. If she remembered Farmer Dickie's shameful allegations, she dismissed them as malicious gossip. Kit had been sent to fetch Annys to Fanny's bedside, that was all. If he had had his arm around her, as Farmer Dickie alleged, it was in friendly reassurance, nothing more. As for that other business, long ago, Farmer Dickie had imagined it. In his cups, no doubt. His appetite for ale on market day was renowned. Anyone who saw Annys caring so devotedly for her sister-in-law would know her to be incapable of such deceit.

At the foot of the stairs Mhairi paused, listened, crossed the hall to the door of the parlour and opened it. Tom was standing in the middle of the room, his head turned towards her. His eyes were tormented, his hair unbrushed, his clothes unkempt. When she stepped inside and closed the door he turned away and resumed his restless pacing, three steps this way, three steps that.

'Tom, I must speak to you.'

No answer. Merely the pacing, on and on.

'Tom, Jessie tells me that you have not named your little daughter. It must be done, and soon. You know that she is weak and ailing.'

'You mean she will die?' he cried, wheeling round to confront her. 'And why not, when her mother is dying?'

'The child may not die. And whether she dies or not, she is entitled to a name.'

'Then give her one, for pity's sake. Call her anything you like. Only leave me alone.'

'I never thought to say it to my own brother, but I am ashamed of you,' said Mhairi quietly, 'and furthermore, Fanny would be ashamed of you, too. How will you explain to her, when she recovers, that you could not find sufficient love in your heart to name the little child you and she made together? How will you justify yourself to her? Tell me that.'

'She will not recover.' His voice was flat and dead.

'Who are you to decide that? Where is your hope and trust? You should be up there praying for her, encouraging her, telling her her children love and need her, as you do. Not wearing out the carpet in self-indulgent misery and letting the business her father worked a lifetime for disintegrate and fall around your feet because you have not the backbone to brush your own hair, let alone do a day's honest work. And what about Willowbrae?' Mhairi spoke with deliberate cruelty now, in her last desperate bid to reclaim him, before he slipped beyond all rescue. 'You crowed enough when you bought it, like a rooster on a dung heap with your "cock-a-doodle-doo, what a clever fellow I am". Squandered the funds, ruined my happiness, and told us all what a brilliant investment you had made. And what have you done with it? Nothing. Fergus Adam closed his road, so you backed into a corner and sulked, like the great baby you are. Fergus Adam is worth two of you.'

'*Enough*.' If his roar of fury did not wake Fanny from her fevered slumber, it should have done, for it made Annys drop her book in fright and start to her feet, as well as rattling every plate on the kitchen dresser and sending the cat scooting for safety. 'Get out of my house.'

Mhairi stood her ground. 'Not until you have chosen a name for your daughter.'

Suddenly Tom collapsed into a chair, closed his eyes, let his hands hang loose on either side and groaned. 'I am sorry, Mhairi. I scarcely know what I am doing any more. I cannot think or speak or . . . I don't know what has happened to me. I am a burning knot of fear and guilt and helplessness and anguish. Please help me . . .'

'Of course, Tom, if I can . . .' she began, but he went on as if he had not heard her.

'If only I could make Fanny understand about Lizzie Lennox, that the wretched woman meant nothing to me, less than nothing, that I don't care about her father's will any more, that all I want is for her to be well again . . .'

'You must tell her,' said Mhairi gently. 'Sit beside her, take her hand in yours and tell her, over and over. But you must do other things, too. Sleep and eat, to keep your health and strength. Work, visit your children. And name your baby.'

'Frances. Frances Willow. For her mother, and for my folly.' For the first time a ghost of a smile flitted across his face, but it was quickly gone.

Mhairi was searching for the right comment when she saw with relief that none was necessary. Her brother, astonishingly, was asleep.

She tiptoed from the room and gently closed the door.

Leo Lennox crept down the front staircase of Silvercairns House on stockinged feet, his boots in his hand. Early morning, the note had said, but his uncle Fergus got up early to go to the quarry and he did not want to meet him. Already he was feeling guilty about Uncle Fergus. Last night, when he went into his uncle's study to say goodnight, Leo had said, 'I might go fishing tomorrow, with Leckie Bruce. We'll be going early. Is that all right?'

'Leckie Bruce? So that's why he was hanging around the stables earlier on. I wondered what he was up to. Yes, you can go, but mind and don't fall in. Get Mrs Gregor to pack you up some lunch and if you are really setting off early, then don't wake the household in the process.'

Remembering his uncle's words and his affectionate, 'Good night. Sleep well,' Leo's conscience, such as there was of it, stirred. He squashed it, flat. He was going to come back, wasn't he? And he had had to tell those lies. His uncle would have stopped him, else.

The packet of cold ham and chicken on the hall table jabbed his conscience into feeble life again, but he had to eat, didn't he? Even if he'd told them what he was really going to do, he'd still have needed food. There were bread rolls, too, he noted as he stowed the packets away in his pockets. And cheese and a couple of apples. Good old Ma Gregor.

He eased open the front door with infinite care, stepped outside and eased it closed again behind him. Then he sat on the steps to put on his boots. The morning was fresh and clean, little spider's webs festooned the grasses and sparkled with tiny drops of dew. Across the parkland he could see cows, misty in the dawn light, and on the terrace a pair of doves strutted and gurgled, pecking now and then at some invisible titbit in the gravel. It was going to be a warm summer day, the kind Leo liked. The sort of day when he could ride Mica to the very edges of the estate, or roll up his trousers and wade about in the stream at the back of the house, poking in the stones with a stick to see what he could flush out. Or help in the stables. Or climb down the cliff to his secret cave and watch the workmen in the quarry below. Instead, he was going into town to meet the woman who said she was his ma. He felt a moment's doubt: but she had promised him a goldmine and horses and a voyage in a real boat, with a cabin of his own, and he could always come back again, couldn't he? If he didn't like it? He tied the last lace and stood up.

It was a pity about Mica. He would have liked to take the pony with him, but he remembered what Uncle Fergus had said would happen if ever he rode her outside the grounds without permission, and she would still be here when he came back again. Dodging in among the rhododendrons which bordered the long sweep of the drive, Leo set off on his two-mile journey into the town.

Fergus did not know what made him ride over to the boundary with Willowbrae that morning, but when he did, he saw where only yesterday the dreary scrubland had stretched undisturbed a paler patch of newly cleared earth and a solitary figure, with a spade. Nearby and tethered to a tree, stood a horse, its nose to the ground and gently foraging among the unpromising plant life. The figure straightened, saw him, raised a mocking hand in greeting, then rammed the spade into the earth. Fergus heard the jarring ring of metal on stone and smiled with bitter humour. If the fellow was going to dig his quarry unaided Fergus need not worry too much about the competition. Nevertheless, he sat immobile on his horse, watching for a good five minutes, as Tom Diack tossed aside the spade, took a pick-axe instead, and laid into the ground with a succession of bruising hammer blows. Then he resumed the spade, cleared away the rubble until the stone defeated him, took up the pick-axe and repeated the process. There was no question that the man was strong, and he laid into the ground as if it was his bitterest enemy. Or as if he was driving an iron shaft into solid rock, to make a bore hole for blasting powder.

Was he? Would he? Unaided and with no apparent back-up? The thought was vaguely disturbing, especially as the spot the fellow had chosen was so close to the dividing fence. Not a good spot. Not the one Fergus would have chosen, but whether it threw up granite or not, it was too close to Silvercairns for comfort.

The thought reminded Fergus of his own quarry floor, where

[243]

boring was already in progress for the next blasting. Frowning, he turned his horse around and trotted back towards the yard.

On the long road into Aberdeen Leo walked with a swagger as befitted someone setting out to see the world and had a cheery greeting, man to man, for the few people he met at that early hour. Once, a farmer passed him and offered him a lift in his cart. On any other day, Leo would have jumped at the chance, but today he refused. The farmer would make conversation, ask questions, and no doubt mention it in the market place or one of the city bars and Leo felt safest from discovery alone, and on his own two feet. For, in spite of his excitement, Leo was uneasily aware at the back of his mind that he should not be where he was, when he was. That he ought to be fishing with Leckie Bruce, as his uncle believed him to be, and that if his uncle heard otherwise, he would be in trouble. The fact that twenty-four hours from now he would be on the high seas and beyond his uncle's reach did little to diminish the nervousness.

It was a fine morning, clear and bright, and as he was walking eastward the rising sun shone full in his face. But it was a cool sun as yet, with a pure gold light. Gold. That was why he was going to Australia with the woman who said she was his ma, instead of going fishing. He was going to have a gold mine of his own, and a pony and a trap to drive whenever he wanted to. His ma had said so. He felt in his pocket for the gold nugget she had given him and looked at it. It did not sparkle as much as it had done before. He rubbed it on the seat of his pants to brighten it, held it aloft to catch the sunlight, then put it back in his pocket. It was gold. The woman had said so. And there was a whole mine of it waiting for him in Australia.

The road was dusty under his feet, the hedgerows lush with grass and wild flowers. Birds strutted and foraged and sang. A cat streaked across the path ahead of him and disappeared, in pursuit of some unseen prey. Leo whistled jauntily to keep that niggling nervousness at bay and, as he approached the cottages at Stonyton, took out the bread and cheese Ma Gregor had provided and began to eat. He was only prevented from eating the lot by the thought that he ought to leave room for the feast his ma would undoubtedly provide for him when he reached the Douglas Hotel.

But when he stood in the pillared entrance of that august establishment in Market Street, his nose to the brass-buttoned chest of the uniformed doorman, Leo's confidence wavered. On his left was the incline leading up to Union Street, from where he had come; on his right the descent to the harbour where he could just see the tops of wooden masts and the rigging of a dozen moored vessels in the inner dock. One of them might be his ship, the one that would take him to Australia and his gold mine. Confidence returned.

'I've come to see my ma who stays here,' Leo announced. 'Let me in.'

'Tradesmen's entrance is at the back.' The buttons moved threateningly but Leo's innate instinct for self-preservation prompted him to jump out of reach before the gloved hand could clamp onto his collar.

'My ma is Mrs Faraday,' he shouted from a safe distance, 'and she's important, she is. She owns a gold mine in Australia and if you don't let me in this minute, she'll have you sacked.'

The doorman stared at him through narrowed eyes then, without moving those eyes, turned his head enough to call over his shoulder, 'There's another one, George. Shall I send him after the others?'

'I'm meeting my ma, I am. She's going to give me breakfast, with bacon and kidneys and that, in silver dishes,' declared Leo. 'Inside the hotel.' Beyond the doorman he could see the inviting red and gold interior, the white plaster ceiling, the glint of a chandelier. He edged his way sideways in order to dodge under the doorman's arms, but that gentleman moved too.

'Is she indeed? Then you'd best go down to the docks with the others. Mrs Faraday left no instructions here.'

'But...'

This time Leo was not quick enough on his feet and the large hand had him by the collar before he could duck under the outstretched arm. The next moment his feet left the pavement, his collar jammed up against his windpipe and he was jerking and squirming and fighting for breath.

'Out!' barked the doorman, letting go of the collar without warning. Leo fell, rolled over, and scrambled to his feet again, swearing. He launched himself at the doorman, fists flying, only to be caught as before and ejected.

He was scrambling to his feet for a renewed attack when he heard a crow of laughter behind him and turned to see what at first seemed to be one of the ships from the harbour, tacking up the street in full sail. Then his eyes cleared and he recognized Mrs Faraday, in a yellow crinoline and a green trailing coat thing with bits of white fur on it. Her hat was covered in feathers and ribbons and goodness knows what else, but it was her face Leo stared at. The woman was laughing. At him. Leo blushed with mortification, and glared.

Mrs Faraday laughed again. 'So you got here, did you? I was beginning to think you was not coming, till I saw you laying into that stuffed booby of a doorman. I knew you was a strong lad, the moment I set eyes on you. A lad with a bit of spirit about you. Though I did wonder, living with that Adam lot, if they'd have turned you into a spineless wee runt. Well, don't just stand there gawping. We're going inside, you and me. Remember this, Leo. Never let the likes of him shove you about, or you'll get nowhere in life. Out of my way, you,' and she pushed the doorman hard in his buttoned chest. 'That's for knocking my son about, and if you lay a finger on him again, you'll have me to deal with, so don't you forget it. I've a good mind to report you to the manager, I have. Attacking innocent folk on their own doorstep. You come with me, Leo, and I'll see you right.'

She gripped Leo's shoulder with a force that made him wince, propelled him in front of her across the sumptuous entrance hall and upstairs. Then along a short corridor to a door at the end.

'In here,' she said, pushing open the door and thrusting Leo inside. 'Dinna mind the mess. Yon housemaid is a lazy devil.'

It was a large room, potentially pleasant, but at the moment it presented a scene of devastation. Cupboard doors stood open, drawers likewise, and the unmade bed was strewn with a dazzling rainbow of assorted garments. Five cabin trunks stood about the room, lids open and variously filled. Two others, lids shut, stood under the window, with an assortment of hatboxes. Shoes littered the floor and there was hardly space to move. The windows were closed and the room stifling with stale air and cheap scent.

'Find somewhere to sit,' said Lizzie, lifting her skirts to step over a hatbox. Leo watched her in amazement: she was showing her drawers again. Long green and white striped ones with frills. No woman he knew ever showed her drawers, not his aunt Lettice nor the minister's wife, nor Ma Gregor nor anyone. Hamish's ma certainly didn't.

Mrs Faraday laughed. 'Haven't you seen pantaloons afore?' She lifted her skirts higher and kicked a leg. 'I can see you've led a sheltered life with yon po-faced Adam, but we'll soon change that.' She swept a hand across the cluttered top of the dresser, sending an

[246]

assortment of articles clattering to the floor, and lent forward to peer into the looking-glass. Leo watched in fascination as she plucked a hair from her eyebrow, dabbed red stuff on her cheeks and rubbed it into her skin, painted more red stuff on her lips, then picked up what looked like a bunch of dirty feathers and dusted flour all over her face with it. It made him sneeze. Then she rolled her hair round her fingers to make long orange sausages. That reminded him.

'When am I having my breakfast?' He added awkwardly, 'Ma.'

'Breakfast? What are you wanting breakfast for?' She looked briefly over her shoulder at him, one cheek white, the other red. 'You should have had it afore you came.' She peered into the mirror again, and put flour on the red bit, swishing it about with the feathers. Watching her, Leo felt anger rise.

'You said I'd get breakfast. Bacon and kidneys, you said, in silver dishes. You promised.'

'Well you should have got here sooner, shouldn't you? I can't hang about waiting for folk, not when I've things to arrange. The others was here an hour ago.'

'What others?'

Again she turned her head and this time both cheeks were white and her mouth bright red. 'Do you always go on like this? Asking questions? Annoying folk?'

'But I want to know. What others?'

'You'll find out soon enough. Now shut up, or you'll make me smudge.'

There was a short silence, before Leo said with curiosity, 'Are you going to be in a circus, Ma?'

He was unprepared for the reaction. She whirled round and before he realized what was happening had clipped him hard on the car.

'That's for your impudence. And that,' she added, clipping the other ear so that Leo's head buzzed with pain and indignation, 'is for asking so many bleeding questions. Now shut up till I'm finished.'

Leo sat in silence, heels drumming the side of the cabin trunk, ears scarlet and face creased with resentment. After a moment, he took out the last of his bread and cheese and began to eat it, scattering crumbs deliberately onto the floor.

Mrs Faraday laughed. 'You sly wee devil. You're not needing breakfast at all, not with a pocket full of food already.' She brushed the feathers over her face again, peered at herself, moved her lips

[247]

about in a chewing sort of way, then said, 'There. That's me ready. So when I can find that bleeding chambermaid to finish my packing, we'll go aboard. How would you like that?'

Leo stared at her, not speaking. Deliberately he bit into the bread and cheese.

'Well? You've a tongue in your head, haven't you?'

'Which ship?' he mumbled, his resentment obvious, even through the crumbs.

'We're going White Star line of course. The *Golden Era* it's called. Carries the Royal mail and all, to Melbourne. The cabins are real elegant, with mahogany furniture and that. I'll maybe let you share mine now and then. Not all the time, 'cos I'll have company and with you being young you'll be wanting to go to bed early, but there's hammocks and things below decks. You'll like it fine.'

'With the others?' said Leo and she fell into the trap.

'Aye. They're aboard already and ...' She stopped, looked at him, then laughed. 'You're a crafty wee devil, Leo. Just like your ma, eh?' She put a plump arm round his shoulders and hugged him.

The smell of sweat and mingled scent was overpowering and his nose stung and twitched, but he managed to grin and say, 'Aye. So tell me, Ma. Who are the others?'

'Well, let me see ... There's my sister Evie and a couple of my young brothers, then there's Doddie Henderson and two of the Bruce boys, oh and Squinty. That's their sister Jessie, but I tell't her she'd do fine in Australia and never mind the squint. It's not her face the lads will be interested in.' She laughed in the sort of way he didn't understand.

'Why? What will they be ...' but before he could finish she had him by the ear and was pulling it, hard.

'What did I tell you about asking questions?'

'Let go. You're hurting me.' Leo squirmed and tried to kick out at her, but all his boot found was the taut bell of her skirts.

'What did I tell you about asking questions?' repeated the voice, and the fingers twisted this time.

'OW! You said not to.'

Abruptly Lizzie let go. 'Yes I did,' she beamed. 'And there was me thinking you'd forgotten. But you'd best not forget again, see? I like my son to do as he's told. I mind years back, in Australia, afore I sent you to Scotland for your education, you was a disobedient wee tike even then. No matter how often I skelped your backside, you'd come whining back again, pestering me for attention. Real annoying. But now you've growed a bit, we'll get on fine, you and me. Just so long as you remember. Well now. Let me see. The ship sails on the evening tide, so we can go aboard any time. I reckon once my packing's done, we'll go, and there's plenty places on the quay for a meal and a bit of company. I've had enough of this place, one way and another. You'd think my money's not good enough the way some of they folk turn their noses up and sneer. Aye, we'll go to my cabin, soon as I've finished here. Now you sit there and dinna move till I tell you.'

Obediently, Leo sat. His ears burned, his pride was sorely bruised and his small body simmered from top to toe with resentment as he watched the battle between his ma and the chambermaid, and the second battle between the cabin trunks and the clothes. But at last every lid was closed, roped and firmly battened down. The chambermaid slouched off, grumbling under her breath, though her indignation had been considerably mollified by the generous tip Mrs Faraday had given her. That lady stood in the centre of the empty room, looking round her with satisfaction.

'Good. You stay here, Leo, and see no one steals anything, while I go and order us a cab.'

But Leo had realized what had been puzzling him throughout the turbulent packing. 'What about my clothes, Ma? You said not to bring anything. You said you'd buy me clothes, but there's none in those trunks. I saw.'

'Aye well, I haven't had time to go around buying clothes for folk that aren't there, have I?'

'I could send home for – ' began Leo, but his mother cut him short.

'Send to Fergus Adam? And have him storming down here to drag you back again? Not likely. We'll get you some in London maybe, or wherever the ship stops. But I might just ... ' Her eyes gleamed suddenly with mischief. 'How good are you at writing letters, Leo?'

'I can if I want to,' he said defensively. 'But my eyes are tired today.'

'No matter. I'd best write it myself after all.' She crossed to the door and rang the bell. She kept on ringing till someone came and when they did, ordered a sheet of hotel notepaper, with an ink stand and a pen. When they came, she sat down at the now empty dresser, dipped pen into inkwell and began carefully to write, speaking the words aloud as she did so, though in a voice meant only for herself. Leo listened.

'*Dear Mr Adam*, not that he is dear, the arrogant bastard. *In case you are wondering where my son Leo is, he is with me. He is coming to Australia with me, where he belongs, and before you go on about the hundred pounds what the bank paid me all those years ago, I am returning it herewith.* That's good, that is. Returning it herewith. *Leo is mine now and don't think to fetch him back because when you get this letter it will be too late. We will be at sea. So if you want the other nine hundred pounds you can come to Australia and get it. I might even make it worth your while, with a bit of that education you was needing.* Signed. *Elizabeth Lennox Faraday.*

'There. That should fix the bastard good and proper,' grinned Lizzie. 'And worth every penny.' She lifted her skirts, flashing her drawers yet again, fished out a draw-string bag from somewhere among the layers and took out a banknote. She folded it inside the letter and sealed it. 'Right. You guard our luggage like I said while I arrange about this and find us a cab.' Before he could answer she had gone.

The moment the door closed he shot to his feet and ran to it. It was locked. He ran to the window and tried to heave it open, but the sash was too heavy for him and it stuck fast. For a moment he felt panic, then he realized. His ma had told him to look after her luggage and had locked him in, to make sure he did. That was all. And to keep out thieves.

Nevertheless, he peered through the window glass in the hope of seeing someone he knew in the streets below, but the window was too high. All he saw was a corner of Union Street one way, with a glimpse of a top-hatted gentleman and a hansom cab, and a small strip of quay the other. But the quay was exciting. Shore porters trundled barrows loaded with cabin trunks like his ma's, or with barrels or sacks of grain. He could see the end of a ship. Was it called a prow or bow? Uncle Fergus would know.

Then he remembered. He remembered that letter, too, and wondered what his uncle would say when it arrived. Poor Uncle Fergus. And why had his ma put money in the letter? A hundred pounds of money. He hadn't been able to hear quite every word, but it had sounded as if she was sending it back. Uneasily he remembered Hamish's taunt. 'Maybe she'll sell you. Like she did before.' But his ma was rich now. She wouldn't need to sell him, would she?

And she was going to let him share her cabin, now and then. Again the twinge of unease. Before, she had told him he would have a cabin all the time. Now it seemed he was to be down in the hold somewhere, with the others. She hadn't told him there would be 'others' either. And she'd promised him breakfast. Uncle Fergus said it was wicked to break a promise. He felt in his pocket for the gold nugget and held it tight, for reassurance.

Mhairi Grant saw them from the window of the Christie Shipping Office, where she had gone to arrange about the Drummond fountain. She was standing at the window, idly studying the scene below while one of the Christie men went off to make inquiries about freight loads on their various ships, when she saw a handsom cab draw up at the gangplank of the White Star Line packet ship. The hatches were open, the deck hands busy, as all sorts of last-minute freight was lowered into the hold. Cabin trunks and personal luggage stood about the quay awaiting attention and from the general activity Mhairi deduced that the ship was preparing to put to sea. So when the hansom cab drew up at the gangplank she watched, from pure curiosity, to see who would alight. Then her heart turned over with dread. It was Lizzie Lennox, in full and vulgar finery, with the boy Leo beside her.

Perhaps he was coming to see her off? Look over the ship, then go home again? But in that case why was not Fergus there, with Leo? She watched Lizzie pay the cabbie, wave him on, but instead of going up the gangplank as she had expected her to do, Lizzie stood there waiting.

Then Mhairi saw a familiar sight: Kit O'Brien's bright green cart coming round the corner from the direction of Market Street. It was loaded high with cabin trunks and an assortment of hat boxes and came to a halt beside the White Star ship. Kit leapt down onto the quay and began to unload the trunks, while Lizzie watched, Leo at her side. Once it looked as if Leo stepped forward to help Kit and Lizzie slapped his ear, but surely she couldn't have? Then Kit carried the trunks on board, one by one, and this time Leo did help. He carried the hat boxes. Finally Lizzie paid the carter and he drove away. Leo waved. Then Lizzie and Leo went up the gangplank and on deck.

'Mrs Grant?' The voice behind her brought Mhairi's attention back to the business in hand, and she was forced to leave the matter of Lizzie Lennox till later. But when the business of the fountain was settled to their mutual satisfaction and Mhairi, making conversation, had inquired when the White Star Line ship was to sail, she took her leave and found herself at last outside on the quay. She did not immediately turn right and up the Shiprow, as she ought to have done, but instead turned left along the quay. The sight of Leo with Lizzie Lennox troubled her, as she knew it would trouble Fergus Adam if he knew. Did he know? And if he did, why had he done nothing to prevent it? Ought she to warn him? But she had not spoken to him since that dreadful New Year's eve, nor he to her. Ought she to go aboard, ask for Lizzie and demand an explanation? But after all, as no doubt Lizzie would tell her, it was none of her business.

She had strolled up and down in indecision for perhaps ten minutes, the clamour of seagulls overhead and the clamour of deckhands and porters all around her, and was wondering what further excuse she could find to linger without attracting undue attention when her eye was caught by a flash of yellow. She turned her head just in time to see Lizzie Lennox leave the ship, walk along the quay to the doorway of the Crown and Anchor, and disappear inside. Alone.

Leo must be on board. Suddenly Mhairi made up her mind.

She walked to the gangplank and mounted to the ship's deck. When someone in uniform asked her what her business was, she said, 'I am inquiring on behalf of Mr Fergus Adam whether his ward, Leo Lennox, has arrived on board. He is travelling, I believe, in the company of a Mrs Faraday.'

'Just a moment, madam, and I will check the passenger list.' The man disappeared to reappear again with a sheaf of papers in his hand. 'Faraday. Ah ... here we are. Mrs Elizabeth Faraday, cabin 4. No mention of anyone with her, though. Unless ... Yes. I seem to remember she brought a group of emigrants, travelling steerage.' He flicked the pages rapidly, then stopped. 'Here we are. Let me see. *Jessie Bruce, William Bruce, Douglas Bruce, George Henderson*. Ah. *Evelyn Lennox*. Was that the name?'

'Leo Lennox,' said Mhairi through her shock. The register of names had sounded like some evil roll-call of the schoolfellows of her youth. Lizzie's nursery school, she remembered. Lizzie Lennox had helped her child-minder mother by taking some of the older

[252]

children off her hands and into the streets, teaching them to steal apples and pick pockets, among other things. Once, for a brief time when their mother was dying, she had had Annys in her group. Mhairi shuddered at the memory. But the man was speaking.

'There is a Leo here but it is Leo Faraday. Would that be the one? Came aboard about half an hour ago?'

'Yes. I expect that is right. Thank you for your help.' She stood a moment in indecision, while the deck rocked gently under her feet with the stir of the harbour waters, and she looked about her at the masts and sails and ropes and enough rigging to make a hundred cat's cradles, hoping for guidance. None came. There was an air of cheerful expectation to the general bustle and activity, a salt tang to the wind and the familiar smell of fish. One or two passengers were strolling arm in arm about the deck, pointing out this or that to each other. Leo was not among them. Nor was he anywhere that she could see in the crowded melée around her. But after all, if he had been there what could she do? It was none of her business and she had no rights over the child. With a feeling of sadness she made her way carefully down the swaying gangplank and ashore.

Leo saw her from the cabin porthole and ducked quickly out of sight. But he looked out again almost immediately, to watch her walk slowly along the quay towards the town. She looked back several times, but she did not see him. When she reached the corner of Market Street he almost hoped she would, but instead she turned the corner and vanished.

He liked Hamish's ma. She looked really smart today, too, with a pretty blue dress on and a hat. Not huge like a haystack with feathers and things, but small and neat, with one blue ribbon and a bow, and her hair was smooth and black. She had been kind to him that time when Uncle Fergus had made him say sorry, and had given him the best stone ginger he'd ever tasted. She didn't shout or swear either, or show her drawers, and he was sure she never hit anyone. She had told him about promises, too, and about people doing what they said they'd do.

The woman who said she was his ma had promised him breakfast in a silver dish and what had he got? Two sore ears and an empty stomach. She'd promised him a cabin, too. This was her cabin, and it was nice enough, with little wooden cupboards and shelves and a porthole with a brass rim. It had a table, too, with edges round it so that things didn't fly off onto the floor when the ship rolled, and a lantern swinging on a hook, but it only had one bed in it and he wasn't going to share a bed with Mrs Faraday. She smelt. Then he remembered what she'd said about the 'others' and him sleeping with them. Suddenly he wanted his own bedroom at Silvercairns with his own bed and Uncle Fergus downstairs in case he had a nightmare. Suppose he had a nightmare here? Mrs Faraday would likely hit his ear again and tell him to shut up. As for the 'others' he didn't know who they were and didn't want to.

His ma had promised him dinner, too, and now she'd gone ashore without him 'to see a few friends'. But he'd seen her go into the Crown and Anchor and even from here you could hear the raucous laughter and the singing. She said she'd bring him a pie, but she was always saying things and not doing them. He felt hopefully in his pockets in case any of Ma Gregor's food was left, but all he found was the gold nugget the woman had given him. He took it out and looked at it. Bits of it were gold right enough, but other bits were dirty coloured and drab. He threw it away in disgust and it fell on the floor. He didn't bother to pick it up. She had said he could buy things with gold, but it didn't look like money. Not like that beautiful £100 note that she had wrapped up in the letter to Uncle Fergus, *the hundred pounds what the bank paid me all those years ago.*

Suddenly Leo went rigid with terror. *She'll sell you* Hamish had said. *Like she did before.* What if Hamish was right? She'd promised him a gold mine and a pony and trap but suppose that was a lie too and she was taking him to Australia to sell him for hundreds of pounds? *The other nine hundred.*

He shot across to the door and tried the handle, half expecting it to be locked, but the wooden bolt was on the inside. Gasping with relief, he eased open the door, slipped quickly through and closed it behind him. One minute later he was on deck, two minutes and he was dodging down the gangplank, a wary eye on the doorway of the Crown and Anchor lest she come out and see him. Three and he was on the quayside. Then he ran.

Fergus Adam dined late that night. He had had a long and arduous day at the quarry and the sight of Tom Diack and his one-man excavations just across the fence in Willowbrae had not improved his

[254]

temper. So it was not until he had disposed of Mrs Gregor's excellent roast lamb, with a cheese and a bottle of good claret, rounded it off with strawberries and cream and a bumper of desert wine and ordered coffee in the library that he thought to ask after Leo.

'The boy is back from his fishing excursion, I trust?'

'No sir,' said the parlourmaid, depositing the coffee tray on a low table and bobbing a knee. It was a habit he found particularly annoying.

'Then send him to me the moment he comes in,' said Fergus and forgot all about it. It was, after all, mid-June and still daylight outside, as it would be till ten o'clock or later. In fact, now he thought about it, it must be practically the longest day of the year. No wonder Leo was making the most of it. Fergus poured himself a large after-dinner brandy, took up the novel he was reading, Dickens's *Hard Times*, and settled down to enjoy the evening.

Some two hours later when the light was at last fading and the short summer night imminent, Fergus was recalled from the world of Thomas Gradgrind and the citizens of Coketown by a flurry of activity below. Startled, he remembered Leo and the fishing expedition. He would have to have a sharp word with the boy about returning so late.

But the expected knock on the door ushered in not Leo, grubby and belligerently apologetic, but the parlourmaid, bearing a silver tray on which lay a letter of some kind.

'Excuse me, sir, but the carter brought this. He said I was to give it to you at once, sir.' She bobbed a knee.

Fergus took the letter and while he was unsealing and opening it, said, 'I told you to send Master Leo straight to me when he came in. Why didn't you?'

'Because he's not home yet, sir.'

'Wasn't that him coming in just now?'

'No, sir. It was the letter, sir. Will there be any reply, sir?'

But Fergus's face had gone grey as death and the hand holding the open letter was trembling. Something white fluttered to the floor and the parlourmaid hastened to pick it up. It was a banknote for a hundred pounds. Trembling almost as much as Mr Adam himself, she placed it nervously on the tray and shrank back.

'Will there be any reply, sir?' she repeated, and bobbed twice in agitation. 'The carter is waiting.'

'Damn the woman to everlasting hell,' roared Fergus, leaping

[255]

from his seat and striding the room in white-hot fury. 'But she'll not get away with it. I'll fight her to the death. Get the law after her. The police. Tear her limb from limb if need be.' The terrified maid scurried out of the room, closing the door behind her. Fergus flung it open and bellowed after her down the stairwell, 'Send that carter fellow to me. At the double.'

When the idiot woman had disappeared, gibbering, into the servants' quarters below, Fergus leant his back against the door, closed his eyes and groaned aloud while the hurt and humiliation and helpless anger wrung his heart till he could have wept with the pain of it. Or cried his anguish to the heavens.

She had taken him, lured him, bribed and cajoled him. What did it matter how she had done it. Leo was gone. And knowing Leo, it could only have been voluntarily. The stupid little idiot. She had tempted him with baubles, promised him the earth, and he had believed her. That Fergus could understand. What he could not understand and what cut him to the heart was why Leo had lied to him, had slunk off as he did, without even a goodbye. He had thought Leo liked him, even possibly loved him, as Fergus loved Leo.

'Oh God,' he groaned aloud. 'How shall I bear it?' Then through the pain burst a new anger, ice-cold and relentless. How dare she steal Leo back again, for no reason but spite? And what would she do with him when she reached Australia? Undo all Fergus's patient teaching and drag the boy down into depravity and vice.

'*Over my dead body.*'

He would get the boy back even if it meant going to Australia to do it, even if it meant bankruptcy and ruin. What Leo's feelings would be he dare not contemplate, even in his innermost thoughts, for the pain of his rejection burnt on with undiminished force. First Mhairi's betrayal, now Leo's. Was he incapable of inspiring love in anyone?

If that was truly the case, then so be it. He would not lay himself open to hurt again. From henceforth he would be as cold and calculating and ruthless as his own father had been. If he could not compel love, at least he could compel obedience.

Kit O'Brien had been expecting the summons. Even so it startled him so that he almost dropped the slice of fruit cake Ma Gregor had given him. He pushed back his chair from the kitchen table.

'I'd better go straight up.'

'Mind and come back again Mr O'Brien,' said Ma Gregor. 'I'll be keeping a place for you, by the fire.'

'To be sure there's nowhere I'd rather be, Mrs Gregor, than in your gracious company, with the warmth of your hospitality wafting around me like the very breath of heaven.'

'Away with you for a smooth-tongued rogue, before the master dies of apoplexy.' But there was a worried edge to her voice, in spite of her smile. That boy Leo should have been home hours ago.

'Yes, Mrs Faraday gave the letter to me in person,' said Kit in answer to Fergus's question. 'About eleven in the morning it would be, maybe later. Didn't the doorman from the Douglas come looking for a cab, and the lady in question having so much luggage that the cabbie refused to take it? The road to the harbour is steep as a cliffside and him afraid that, with all that weight aboard, his precious carriage would run away with him and his horse, and tip all three into the water. But by great good fortune who should be passing but myself, and my cart with the best brakes in Christendom. Take my luggage to the quay, she says, the White Star Line. And when you've done, you can deliver this letter for me. But not till sundown, she says, on account of Mr Adam being out all day and her wanting the letter to be delivered into his own fair hand.'

'Who was with the lady?' asked Fergus, fixing O'Brien with a compelling eye.

'Master Leo, sir. The lady said her son was travelling with her in accordance with your wishes.'

'Did she indeed.' Fergus's expression grew even blacker. 'And Master Leo, did he say anything?'

'No, sir. Only thank you, and goodbye.'

'Do you know exactly when the ship is to sail?'

'On the evening tide, sir. That would be an hour ago.'

Fergus swore, for quite some time. When he recovered breath, he asked, 'Do you know the ports of call?'

Kit O'Brien did.

'Very well. This is what you will do. You will drive into Aberdeen. You will call at this address.' He wrote quickly on a card and handed it to O'Brien. 'You will bang on the door until someone opens and you will order my lawyer to come here to me. In his nightshirt if need

[257]

be, and if he won't come of his own volition, then you will fetch him. If necessary by force. I want him here, in my house, within the hour. Is that understood?'

'Yes, sir.' He added, with a tentative grin, 'I only hope he understands it.'

'He'd better,' growled Fergus. 'Or I'll see him ruined. Tell him so. Now get out.'

When the fellow had gone, Fergus went to his desk, drew out a sheet of paper, sat in thought for a few minutes, then picked up his pen and began to draw up a list of instructions. Send messages, by electric telegraph wherever possible and where not, by the fastest reliable means, to the ship's next port of call, and for safety, the next. Inform the harbour master, the city magistrates, and anyone else appropriate that the packet ship the *Golden Era* had a kidnapped child aboard. Said child to be removed forthwith and escorted back to his home in Aberdeen. His eye on that infamous £100 note, Fergus added that a generous reward would await those who delivered the boy safely into his uncle's hands.

That done, he strode the carpet, fuming, until his lawyer, bearing every sign of having been dragged summarily from his bed, arrived at the door, in a temper matching Fergus Adam's own. There followed a heated exchange of views on the desirability or otherwise of midnight for a business discussion. The cause of the summons explained, however, the lawyer simmered down. Mr Adam was quite right. It was a situation that required swift action. Together they mapped out what that action was to be and the lawyer left again in the small hours, to execute Mr Adam's orders with the least possible delay.

When Fergus had sent the fellow on his way in the half light before dawn, Fergus at last prepared for bed. With the ship already on the high seas there was nothing more he could do for the moment. But by God he'd get the boy back whatever it cost to do so.

But later, as he lay sleepless in the pale summer night, anger drained out of him leaving only grey despair. Leo had run away. Had chosen the company of that dreadful woman rather than stay here with him. There was no one to follow on. He had no wife, no son, no nephew. Even his sister Lettice preferred to live anywhere else but at home. What was the use of working the quarry with such meticulous care, day after day after day? What was the use of anything?

In spite of wearyness, anger, grief and sheer mental exhaustion, sleep evaded him and after two hours of wakeful torment he abandoned the attempt and decided to get up. It was daylight already and where better to take out his frustration and anger than on the bedrock of his quarry? He might even take a leaf out of his father's book one day and blow the place to smithereens. Why not?

He dressed, let himself out of the house, saddled his horse himself, for the idle stable lad was nowhere in sight, rode fast down the drive of Silvercairns and onto the quarry path. It was four o'clock in the morning.

From his hiding place in the rhododendrons, Leo saw him and cringed back in fear. His uncle looked angry. He would have got that letter by now. At the thought of the letter, Leo's fear increased, and he knew that he must not go back to Silvercairns. Not yet. Even if his uncle forgave him, and his face did not look as if he would, when Mrs Faraday found that Leo was missing, she might come looking for him and where else would she look but here? At the thought his mouth went dry. He had no doubt she would lay into him with all the strength of her brawny arm, tie him up and throw him back on board to be put in the dungeon till they got to Australia. He wondered fleetingly if they had dungeons on ships, but if they didn't there would be somewhere equally dreadful. Then when they reached dry land he would be sold, like a horse or a cow or a slave.

He must hide where she could never find him. He had thought of going to Hamish's ma and asking her to help him, but Mrs Faraday had been to Rainbow Cottage, Hamish had said so, and she might go looking there, too. As he had crept his furtive way homewards, keeping in the shadow of the hedgerow and hiding if anyone approached, he had seen Kit O'Brien's cart on the road at Hirpletillam and almost asked him for help, but Kit had taken that letter for Leo's ma and she might come after him and make him tell. No, there was only one place where he would be safe. He would get a message somehow to Hamish to bring him food, and lie low till Mrs Faraday had gone away again, on her way to Australia.

'Where are you going with that bread?'

His mother's voice stopped him in his tracks and Hamish turned, shamefaced, in the scullery doorway. 'Nowhere.'

[259]

'No one tiptoes out of the back door of his own house before anyone else is up with a whole loaf of bread under one arm and, let me see, a slab of cheese under the other, if he is going "nowhere".'

She looked steadily at her son who in turn looked at his own feet. They were clad in stout work boots and the boy was fully dressed, though it was a good hour before he normally rose from his bed. Behind him the door stood open to the yard and the morning half-light. The sky above the hill was pale green, the shadows soft and through the silence came the first stirrings of bird song.

'Well? I am waiting.' When Hamish still said nothing, she added quietly, 'Come inside. Shut the door. And tell me the truth.'

'I can't, Ma.' He looked up at her in anguish and his eyes were startlingly blue. And honest.

'Then let me ask a different question,' she said carefully, feeling her way. 'Is the bread for you?' He shook his head. 'For a friend?' He nodded. 'Can you say who that friend is?'

Hamish did not immediately shake his head, but his eyes were troubled.

'I think, if this friend needs you to creep about in the dawn in order to bring him bread, he must be in hiding. Is he a criminal?'

'Oh no!' cried Hamish. 'He has done nothing wrong. At least . . .'

'Tell me,' prompted Mhairi. 'I might be able to help.'

There was a long pause, before Hamish said uncertainly, 'I promised not to say where he was hiding.'

'Then you must keep your promise. But I think you could tell me who is hiding, and why. Especially as you seem to be stealing my food to feed to this hungry friend.'

'I am sorry, Ma, but Leo is starving and . . . oh.' He bit his lip and blushed scarlet.

'*Leo*? But Leo is on his way to Australia. Everybody knows it.'

She herself had seen him go aboard with Lizzie and it was common knowledge by now that the Lennox woman had snatched away her son from under Fergus Adam's nose and whisked him off to Australia, leaving poor Mr Adam out of his mind with grief and fury. Mhairi's own heart was not untouched, both on Leo's account and on Fergus Adam's. He must be so grievously unhappy.

'Leo jumped ship and ran away,' said Hamish, his face clearing now that he had no more choice in the matter. 'He says she was horrid and hit him and didn't buy him any dinner. He says the lump of gold she gave him was a cheat and that he was sure she was going

[260]

to sell him. So while she was in the Crown and Anchor, getting drunk, he ran away.'

Mhairi let the accusation pass. After all, it was probably true. 'Then what did he do?'

A wary look came over Hamish's face. 'He ran away, like I said. He couldn't go home, in case she came looking for him, so he gave Leckie Bruce a message for me and I'm to take him food.'

'Do you know where he is hiding?' asked his mother.

'Of course. I'm the only one who does, but I promised not to tell.'

'Very well.' Mhairi paused a moment to sort out her turbulent thoughts and keep them in some sort of check. Leo had not run off to Australia after all. Fergus was grieving for no reason and she had it in her power to lift that grief and bring him happiness instead. She felt excitement surge up inside her. This was the excuse she had been waiting for. At last she could go to him. Not to appeal. Not to threaten – though, after his proposal, she had every right to bring a breach of promise charge. But to tell him news to gladden his heart. In his resulting joy he would forget all differences between them and … But she was letting imagination run away with her. The first consideration was Leo.

'Is this hiding place warm and dry?'

'Oh yes. It's like a little house. With water to drink, too, and,' he grinned, 'a lovely view.'

'Is it safe?'

Hamish deliberately misunderstood. 'Oh yes. No one would ever find him there.'

'Then this is what I suggest we do. You take him the food, with a bottle of my stone ginger which I know he likes, and later on, at a more civilized hour, I will persuade Uncle Donal to drive me over to Silvercairns and tell his uncle that he is safe.'

'But you mustn't, Ma! I promised …'

' … not to tell where he is hiding. Yes. And you have kept your promise. I will explain that to Mr Adam and make sure he understands. But I think Mr Adam has a right to know that his nephew is safe and well, don't you? After all, he has been grieving for him. I am sure he will keep the secret, too. Then, when it is safe to do so, he will fetch Leo home. Meantime, shall I see if I can find some cake to take to Leo, and I think I might have a spare slice of ham. Then you must hurry, or you will be late for work at the yard.'

When the boy had gone, armed with his own lunch packet and

another, twice the size, for Leo, Mhairi busied herself with breakfast for the others while her mind went over and over what she would say to Fergus, what she would wear. Something plain, but elegant. Something that gave her confidence. Her best blue dress and jacket? Her new straw hat? And Fergus Adam's sapphire ring.

It was mid-afternoon before Donal collected Mhairi from the house at Elmbank to drive her over to Silvercairns. He had been giving the last touches to the Drummond fountain, a job which he preferred to do himself, and the delicate operation had taken longer than he anticipated. However, it was finished now, and once the Drummonds had inspected and approved it, which he hoped they would do on the morrow, it could be packed into the box which the joiner had made ready, padded all round with woodshavings, and sent on its way. At least that would clear the shed for his next major project: George Wyness's memorial. Donal had heard from one of the Silvercairns workers that his chosen stone was due for blasting at any moment. He had sent young Hamish off to check this very afternoon, and if the rumour proved true, the timing could not have been better. All in all, Donal was well pleased.

He was pleased about the news of Leo, too. No boy, however unruly, should be kidnapped from his home and shipped half across the world, willy-nilly. He was not quite so pleased at Mhairi's decision to tell Mr Adam the news in person, but that was Mhairi's affair, and he agreed that Mr Adam should be told. So it was with a cheerful air that he drove Mhairi's new chaise from its temporary housing in the Wyness yard and out onto the Elmbank road. But as he approached the house, the layer of peat and straw on the road reminded him of Fanny's continuing illness and the smile disappeared. Poor Fanny. It was nearly three weeks now and little sign of improvement in spite of constant care. Annys hardly left her, except when Tom took over.

At the thought of Tom, Donal frowned. First thing every morning, Tom spent an hour at Fanny's bedside, then rode out, alone, to Willowbrae. He knew that much at least. But why and what Tom did there, no one knew, except that he came back at midday, sweat-drenched and exhausted, to wash and eat and spend an hour with Fanny before riding off again to repeat the process. Rumour said he was touched in the head; that he was prospecting for gold, planting potatoes, digging a tunnel underground to Silvercairns. Whatever it was, it, and Fanny, occupied all Tom's attention, and left none for the Wyness yard or Rainbow Hill. But Donal and Hamish managed well enough without him. The yard did not suffer. If anything, business had improved and what mattered most was that Fanny should recover. Old Dr Marshall, though he confessed he had done all he could, continued to call twice a day, so it was no surprise when Donal turned the last corner to see the doctor's horse waiting at the door.

'I need that nephew of mine for a second opinion,' grumbled Dr Marshall. 'He wrote two months ago that he would be home "shortly" but his ideas of shortly do not coincide with mine. Consultations in London indeed. He should come home and consult here, where he belongs.'

'Perhaps they are waiting till their house is free?' ventured Mhairi, handing the doctor a cup of tea. In Tom's absence she had taken it upon herself to act as hostess and, his visit to the patient over, to offer the doctor refreshment in the parlour. 'I believe the Drummonds have taken it till the end of August.'

'Then they can un-take it. They must have homes of their own to go to.' Dr Marshall peered morosely into his tea-cup and Mhairi wondered if she ought to have offered him whisky instead.

'Would you like a dram, Dr Marshall? To help ward off infection?'

'I won't say no. When you spend your life peering down throats putrid with diphtheria, or diagnosing typhoid, or sorting out one villainous rash from another you need all the help you can get. Did you know that almost thirty percent of deaths in children under five are from scarlet fever, Mrs Grant? And it has been reported again in the city only last week. If we could stop it spreading, think how many lives we could save.'

'Do you think that Fanny's illness could be a kind of scarlet fever?' hazarded Mhairi and Dr Marshall grunted in dismissal.

'No rash. No swellings. Only the lingering fever and the wandering mind.'

'Then ... not childbed fever?' That was what they had feared above all else.

'If it was, she would have been dead by now. I'm damned if I know what it is, Mrs Grant. It might be a form of encephalitis, of course. A

[263]

brain fever. I'd like David's opinion on that. But if he chooses to kick his heels in foreign parts, instead of coming home, there's little I can do about it.'

Mhairi was tempted to point out that London was hardly foreign, but thought better of it. 'How is Fanny's baby?' she asked, steering him into calmer channels.

'Astonishingly well in spite of all expectations to the contrary. Old Mrs Wyness has done wonders with the child, and it's been the salvation of her, as she would tell you herself.' He emptied his glass and heaved himself out of the chair in almost the same movement. 'If I may so, Mrs Grant, you are looking very well yourself. Quite charming, in fact.'

Mhairi blushed and thanked him for his compliment.

'No compliment at all. The plain truth. But I must be on my way. As that brother of yours seems to be avoiding me, tell him from me to keep on as he has been doing. Talk to her, hold her hand, that sort of thing. See if he can get a reaction. If he does, tell him to send for me at once. I'll be in again tomorrow. No, don't get up. I'll see myself out.'

But Mhairi followed him into the hall nonetheless. She wanted to check once more whether Donal was in sight.

Donal drove the chaise at a brisk pace up the long drive of Silver-cairns. The trees on either side were stately with age, their branches spreading canopies of pale green across the drive. Near the gate, a tangle of rhododendrons offered opulent pink blossoms on a gleaming bed of darker green. Ahead, the house stood silver-tinted in the sunlight, its many widows glinting, its terraces flower-decked, and even the gap where the west wing used to be had been tidied into picturesque patterns of fallen rock. Stonecrop gilded the flagstones with splashes of brilliant yellow.

They drew up at the carriage entrance and, her heart beating painfully fast, Mhairi alighted and mounted the steps. She motioned Donal to follow. But when the servant answered the door, she learned, with disappointment, that Mr Adam was out and not expected back till late.

'If madam would care to leave a message?'

'No. That is ... Perhaps you would tell Mr Adam that Mrs Grant called, of Wyness, Diack & Grant, about a matter of mutual concern?' Then, in case Fergus should interpret that as referring to herself and him, added, 'Concerning Australia.'

'Certainly Mrs Grant.' He looked from Mhairi to Donal and made up his mind. 'Though if the matter is urgent, and concerning business, may I suggest you drive on to the yard? Turn right at the gate and follow the track to its end. You will find Mr Adam in the quarry office.'

Mhairi smiled. 'Thank you. But perhaps it would be better if I called again tomorrow.' She did not want to offer him her precious olive branch in public, in full view of the quarry work force. That would be to waste a heaven-sent opportunity. 'When can I expect Mr Adam to be at home?'

'Early evening would be the best time, madam. Though Mr Adam often looks in around mid-day. They are busy at the moment, blasting,' he added by way of apology. 'But I will tell him to expect you.'

'Thank you,' she said, taking Donal's arm. 'We are most grateful.'

Donal handed her up into the chaise and they drove sedately down the tree-lined drive towards the gate.

They had gone perhaps half way when, with a gasp, Donal suddenly pulled the horse up short. Mhairi turned her head in surprise and saw that he was white as death, and trembling

'What is it, Donal?'

Donal snatched up the pad which he carried with him everywhere and wrote, with furious haste, *Did the man say blasting?*

'Yes. But there is nothing strange in that, surely?'

They are blasting my rock.

Mhairi looked puzzled. 'But Donal. You said you were pleased. Tomorrow the Drummond fountain will go and the shed will be ready. You want your rock.'

He clutched her arm with a force that hurt before signing in agitation, *Where is Leo? Did Hamish say?*

'No, Donal. He promised not to tell. But he said Leo is in a safe place. Like a little house.' She signed with her hands. 'With water to drink.' She signed again. 'And a view. A secret place that only Hamish and Leo know.'

'Oh God!' Donal needed no pencil to convey his horror. Then, he snatched it up and scribbled, '*Cave. In the quarry. Blasting. DANGER.*'

Mhairi looked at him aghast and the blood drained from her face.

She reached for the reins, but Donal snatched them from her and, feet braced against the foot board, lashed the horse into furious speed, down the curved sweep of the drive, out of the gate and round the corner, axles straining and creaking and one wheel lifting dangerously high. Then the long, pounding straight of the track to the quarry yard and Fergus.

Fergus Adam felt curiously cold and washed clean of all emotion. He had felt like that since the morning after Leo's betrayal, when he had ridden to the brim of his quarry in the eerie light before the dawn and for a moment seen in the shadows of the pit the crouching beast which was the spirit of Silvercairns. The primeval beast which had lurked there in his imagination ever since childhood and which would one day rise up to devour him and his. He felt no fear. Only relief and satisfaction. The time had come as he had always known it would. What was it Shakespeare had said? *If it be now, 'tis not to come; if it be not now, yet it will come: the readiness is all.* And he was ready, as he had always been.

Whether Leo was returned to him or not, it made no difference. The contest was between him and that crouching beast, alone.

Since that morning, three days ago, he had driven himself and his men without mercy, every daylight hour, driving bore holes twenty feet deep into the rock of his father's folly. One man held the iron rod in place, two men smote it, turn and turn about, with eight-pound hammers, for twenty minutes at a time, then they changed places and repeated the process. On and on. Each blow bouncing off the quarry walls, echoing, echoing into the distance, as a new blow took its place. On and on, with remorseless rhythm. Five teams of men, working round the clock for every daylight hour, driving the bore shafts deep into the bedrock, gouging out the holes which, packed full of powder, tamped down with wooden ramrods and fuses inserted, would split open the wall of the quarry into monolithic pillars of pure granite, some weighing as much as thirty tons. He could picture them in his mind's eye, like refugees from Stonehenge, huge and menacing, each block vibrant with unearthly power. Could see them like a relentless occupying army, moving slowly across the landscape, while in the cavern which had spawned them, the black liquid bubbled and rose.

But he felt no fear. It was inevitable, as death was inevitable.

He and Bruce the foreman had worked out the programme together, pooling all their experience and skill to plot the exact lie of the granite 'posts', the position of the joints, the points of least resistance, and finally to choose where the bore holes should be driven. They planned to blast an arc of the quarry wall from one rope's end to the other, in carefully measured sections, beginning with that block the Wyness yard required for Headstane's monument and sweeping northward across the 'forbidden' side. The holes bored, the fuses laid, they would blast in quick succession, with only the shortest of pauses for clearing debris and sorting out the rock. The road metal and building rubble would lie where it fell, to be cleared at a later date. The larger blocks would be removed to a safe distance, to guard against damage from flying debris, but the teams of men were ready, the horses harnessed. As little time as possible would be lost.

Time. That was what drove him. The knowledge that there was so little time.

Once, Bruce dared to mention subsidence and possible danger to the house, but only once. Fergus, like his father before him, was driven by a power which would brook no opposition. He had forgotten family, house everything. He wanted only to blast his quarry to the heavens, to defy that sleeping beast to do its worst. And if he perished in the process, it would be no more than fitting. His quarry was his life: he had nothing else to live for. The thought filled him with a perverse excitement. The quarry was a worthy adversary and this time it would be a battle to the death.

He was poring over his diagram of the north face, checking for the last time what the order of firing would be, when the first group of workmen appeared over the rim of the quarry and spilled into the yard. Good. Bruce had cleared the quarry floor. The fuses were primed and ready. It was time.

Fergus rolled up the chart, tucked it into his jacket pocket, pushed through the milling men outside and made for the spiral path which led downwards to the quarry floor. He checked no one was left in the quarry, but that solitary figure. Raised his hand. Gave the signal. Then began to descend the path to the vantage point.

He had gone no more than ten paces when something made him turn his head and he stopped in his tracks. A horse and trap was driving at speed along the path to the yard. At first he thought it was the Drummonds, for there was a woman beside the driver, but it was not the Drummonds' usual style, nor their usual cabriolet. Then the vehicle careered into the yard, the driver reined in the horse with savage strength, the animal reared up to paw the air in whinnying terror and workmen scattered in all directions. While Fergus watched amazed, down from the vehicle tumbled a woman in a blue dress who seized hold of the nearest man, asked a question, looked wildly around her, then came running straight towards him, hair streaming, skirts flying and on her face a look of such fear that his heart turned over and he gasped aloud. For a moment he thought he had gone mad. She had run like that all those years ago, when her mother was dying and she had fallen at his feet. This time she did not fall, but came headlong towards him, shouting something unintelligible. He was powerless to move.

Then she cannoned into him, her feet skidding, and his arms came around her instinctively, to steady and support. But she did not pull away, embarrassed, as she had that time in Union Street, in the shipping office doorway. Instead she clutched his arm, crying 'Stop them, Fergus. You must stop them.'

He took her by the shoulders and gently shook her. 'Calm down, Mrs Grant. Calm down.'

The cold title, 'Mrs Grant', brought her to her senses. She stared at him a moment, startled, her eyes wide with fear. He had forgotten how achingly blue they were, their power to melt his heart. Then she shook her head, as if to rid herself of some annoyance, pushed the hair from her eyes and said, 'Don't you understand? You must stop the blasting. Now, before it is too late. Leo is hiding in the cave.'

The woman was mad. It was the only explanation. He said slowly, as to an idiot, 'Leo is on the high seas and there is no cave.'

'No he isn't and yes there is! Dear God, will you listen to me!' From the corner of his eye he saw someone push past them and run. Donal Grant. The fellow who had driven her.

'Hey! Come back!' Too late, he remembered it was no use. The man was deaf. He tried to shake off her arm, to follow after him, but she clung on, stumbling beside him.

'Leo jumped ship,' she cried in desperation. 'He ran away. He hid so his mother would not find him. He told Hamish. That is how I know. Fergus, you must believe me.'

He stopped. Looked down at her. She stared back, clear-eyed, imploring, without a trace of madness. His mouth was suddenly dry. 'Where did you say he is hiding?'

'Donal knows. He says it is a crack, a sort of cave, in the disused wall of the quarry. Behind the rope.'

Fergus looked at her for a wild moment, then at the rock face, seeing for the first time those patches of concealing bracken and other tenacious plant life. Then to the quarry floor, empty now but for a single figure, and that other, bounding and skidding down the spiral path towards the bottom.

'Dear God!' With an agonized cry of 'Stop!' Fergus leapt down the path after Donal, slipping and righting himself, jumping over potholes and boulders, waving his arm and crying 'Stop! Do not light the fuse!'

Mhairi followed, feet flying nimbly over the uneven ground, fear lending speed to her flight while above them, in the quarry yard, voices were raised in bewilderment and growing alarm.

But the man on the quarry floor seemed impervious to all around him. His back to Donal and the spiral path, he crouched over something on the ground, concentrating, not listening. Suddenly he rose to his feet, watched for a moment, then, apparently satisfied, turned and ran for cover.

The fuse was lit.

Leo watched the proceedings with interest, cross-legged on the floor of his cave, Mrs Grant's stone ginger bottle beside him and in his hands a slab of cake.

'Tell your ma she makes the best cake ever,' he mumbled, his mouth crammed full. 'And the best stone ginger.'

Hamish did not answer. He was beginning to think it had not been a good idea to join Leo after all. His uncle Donal had told him to find out about the blasting and he had thought the best way would be to spy it out from above, in secret, when he delivered Leo's food. After his mother had caught him that morning, he had been too late to visit Leo before work, so Donal's mission had seemed the perfect answer. Now, after watching the activity below, he was not so sure. Uneasily he remembered the last occasion when he had watched an explosion from the same spot. The ground had shaken, bits of grit had blown in his eyes, and the smell of the explosion had stung his nose for ages afterwards. Besides, this time the bore-hole was closer. Too close. He edged further back into the fissure which Leo called his cave and felt damp cold at his back. The water was dripping again. He wanted more than anything to go home. But with the quarry yard full of men waiting to go back down the quarry the moment the blasting was over, someone might see him. He shivered nervously and clasped his hands tight round his knees.

'See that wee flame, dancing along the floor,' said Leo. 'That's the fuse burning. When it gets to the bore-hole, we'll hear an almighty bang.'

It was at that moment that Hamish saw the man running. And higher up the path, another man, and a woman, running after him. He thought he heard someone shouting 'Stop'. The first man took no notice. Then, with a thud of fear, Hamish realized why. It was his Uncle Donal. Even as he watched, Uncle Donal reached the foot of the path and without a pause ran on, towards that sputtering flame. He can't have seen the fuse, thought Hamish with horror. And he couldn't hear them shouting. Hamish pushed Leo aside, scrambled to his feet and head and shoulders above the concealing bushes waved his arms in frantic warning to attract Donal's attention. 'Look out, Uncle Donal! The fuse is lit.'

Donal ran as he had never run before. A strong man, kept fit by the nature of his job, he nevertheless felt the breath rasp in his throat, and the pain in his chest was like knives. Once, he skidded on the loose sand and fell headlong, but he was up again in a flash and running. The ground shook under him, whether from the pounding of his own feet or others too he had no way of telling, and no time to turn his head. His eyes were on that crouching figure, his soundless voice straining to shout a warning, while in his head he calculated with desperation the burning time of the fuse and his own comparative speed. Would he make it? Could he make it in time to stamp out the fuse? If not, what would happen to Leo, hiding in his eyrie? At that moment he lifted his eyes to the cliff face and saw not Leo, but his beloved nephew Hamish, waving his arms and shouting. His dead brother's son whom he had vowed to defend with his life. Calculations became irrelevant. Unhesitatingly he flung himself forward towards that dancing spark.

Mhairi, too, had seen that waving figure and with a shriek of anguish caught up with Fergus Adam, passed him, and ran on like a mountain hare across the quarry floor. Then someone bellowed 'Down!' and she was flung to the ground, an arm around her shoulders, and someone's body pressing hard on hers. Her face was in the sandy earth, her breasts flattened by the weight above her, then the world became a thundering, roaring terror of wind and violence and flying rock and finally, a lifetime later, silence.

She lay bemused, while gradually her senses returned. Her ears sang and throbbed, but after listening for a while she decided it was with the rhythm of her own pulse. Her nose scented dust and smoke and, underneath, a familiar, acrid smell which she knew she would remember eventually, but there was no hurry. She managed to turn her head a little, opened her eyes, saw only blackness and closed them again. There would be time for seeing later. It was not all blackness, though. There had been something pale, like linen, and the blackness had been like woollen cloth. Very close. She thought about it for a while, lazily and without effort. Then she became aware that her knee was hurting, and her hand. She tried to move and could not. Something was pinning her down.

In mounting alarm she spread her hands against the ground and pushed. She squirmed and fought and struggled to heave off that smothering weight and to her astonishment heard a groan.

'Mhairi?'

The weight lifted a little, she managed to raise and turn her head and saw that it was Fergus Adam. He lay on top of her, his body spread over hers. His hair was white with dust, his bemused eyes two dark hollows in a mask of white streaked here and there with red. They stared at each other, at first in shock, then in burning embarrassment.

He rolled away, carefully easing and testing first one limb then another, sat up, held his head in his hands. There was blood on his fingers. After a moment, he said, without looking at her, 'Are you all right?'

Carefully, she rose to her feet, dusted down her clothes with trembling hands, opened her mouth to say yes, but before she could speak, memory hit her with shattering pain. *Hamish.* She must find Hamish. And where was Donal? Donal would find her son for her. Donal loved him.

'Donal?' Then as her voice bounced mockingly back at her from the surrounding rocks, she cried out in mounting terror. 'Donal? Where are you?'

All around her the air was full of dust which shrouded everything in a choking silver fog. She could see nothing ... Then, as the dust

[271]

began to settle, unfamiliar shapes rose from the debris, merged into rock formations, towers, castles, little terraces of houses, a miniature city in an unreal world.

'Donal?' she cried in desperation. 'Where are you?'

Hands outstretched in front of her, feeling each step with care, she moved forward into the chaos.

Behind her Fergus stood up, swayed unsteadily, said, 'No use. He was too late.' Then with more urgency, 'Mhairi! Come back.'

Mhairi ignored him.

'Donal?' She strained her ears into the silence for an answer, forgetting he could not hear her. Could not answer. Now there were voices behind her in the distance, a whistle, men shouting. They would be looking for Hamish, too. Someone would find him for her. They must. He was not injured. He couldn't be. It was his father who had been killed in a quarry explosion, not Hamish. Donal would find him. Donal would know where to look. Because she could not bear it if ... if. Then her foot touched something soft. She stood rigid, trembling, forcing herself to look down, down ...

'Donal?'

He could not have heard her in life. As it was, he lay outstretched, face upwards, eyes unseeing, beside the rock which was to have been his monument to old George Wyness. Miraculously, there was not a mark on him, though he was undoubtedly dead. She stood looking down at him, powerless to move or speak or weep as grief and terror gripped her. First Alex. Now Donal. Then ... dear God, not Hamish. Not her precious only son. Her whole body shook as she felt panic rise like a scream in her throat.

There was a step behind her and someone touched her arm.

'He was a brave man, poor fellow. Tried to put the fuse out, but was just too late.' There was weariness in his voice, and gentleness, and a world of pain. 'Come away, Mhairi. Leave it to the men.'

Angrily she shook free. 'No. I must find my son. I saw him, in the cave. He will be safe there, waiting for me.'

'But the cave is gone, Mhairi. There will be ... ' He had meant to say 'no one' but the words would not come. No one could survive a blast like that, not a grown man like Donal, and certainly not a child. Not her child, nor Leo. Leo. Tears stung his eyes and he brushed them angrily away. What was the use of tears?

'Come away,' he repeated, taking her arm. 'There is nothing you ... ' He stopped, suddenly alert. 'Listen.'

[272]

Expecting to hear her son calling, Mhairi froze, her eyes alight with hope. But instead of voices, she heard a different sound, a trickle which strengthened as she listened to a steady, bubbling stream, then a torrent.

'Water,' gasped Fergus. 'Water!' It sounded like a cry of triumph. Then he laughed. 'For years I have dreamt that some dreadful primeval beast would rise up and swallow my quarry and all the time the threat was only ... water.' Abruptly his voice cracked, his eyes blurred with tears. 'Wild beast or water, what does it matter? There is no one now. No one ...'

'Look!' Mhairi clutched his arm, her voice a horrified gasp. He felt her fingers dig into his flesh as wave after wave of terror washed through her. For at that moment the last of the dust cleared and for the first time they saw the devastation. Where there had been a weathered rock face, dotted with clumps of bracken and grass, even a rowan sapling here and there finding nourishment in unexpected places, was an open wound, white-gashed and raw. At its foot a heap of smaller, broken stones on which lay, tipped at an angle, just as it had fallen when sliced from the bedrock, the block which Donal had marked out and chosen. It was massive, unbroken, and without blemish. A perfect piece of quarrying. Beyond it, on the vertical dividing line between the quarried and the unquarried section, a fissure had opened up in the rock and through it gushed a white spout of frothing water, which tumbled down the cliff-side onto the quarry floor. Already it was spreading so that the foot of the cliff on that side was under water.

Then, from somewhere high overhead, came a thin cry, 'Help!'

Tom Diack heard the explosion from his solitary digging on Willow-brae. Even if he had not heard it, the ground would have given him the message for it shook and trembled under his feet with surprising violence. He straightened, pushed back the hair from his sweat-drenched forehead, and peered through the swirling clouds of dust and smoke towards Silvercairns. Surely the force of the explosion had been greater than normal? And beyond the patter of falling rock the sounds he heard were not the usual busy ones of men resuming their normal work. There was shouting, running feet, and some-where a warning whistle blew.

Something was wrong.

[273]

For a shameful moment he felt satisfaction. Mhairi's cruel words still rankled. *Fergus Adam is worth two of you* she had said, and though he knew she had said it deliberately, to taunt him into sanity again, who was to say she did not mean it? Mhairi had always spoken the truth. Uneasily, he remembered his business meeting with Adam, when the man had been undeniably courteous and straightforward. Remembered his own fuming resentment. Remembered Fanny's reproaches. Dear Fanny. She, like Mhairi, always spoke the truth. He remembered Fanny's face when he had left her this morning. She had been sleeping, still fevered, but quietly. He had taken her hand, spoken lovingly to her, kissed her burning forehead as he always did, told her he was going to work and would be back again very soon. As always there had been no response.

'She is a little better,' Annys had said, with determined hope. 'When you come home again, she may well be better still. I shall pray for her, as I always do, and you must do the same.'

He looked down at the broken ground around him. Rubble. Worthless dross. But whether or not he found granite on Willowbrae no longer mattered. This was his punishment and his prayer. He was powerless to help Fanny in her illness, but to hew and break the stone with the sweating strength of his own arm, and to do it till his muscles screamed with pain and he thought his chest would burst was the only way he knew to ease the guilt and the endless, dragging fear. Suppose Fanny were to die?

The familiar shudder shook him and he reached for his pick-axe, only to pause again, listening. There was definitely something wrong at Silvercairns. He himself had served his apprenticeship there, with Alex Grant, and the normal working sounds of a quarry were as familiar to him as breathing. He knew the pattern of blasting as well as anyone: the drilling of the blast-hole, the laying of the fuse, the explosion, the silence, then the buzz of activity as the results were inspected, and work resumed. Something had broken that pattern.

Suddenly he remembered Alex, killed in a quarry blast. His own father, killed by a fall of rock.

He tossed away the pick-axe, snatched up his jacket from a nearby bush, and unhitched his horse's bridle from the fencepost. He wasted precious moments soothing the nervous animal till it was calm again, then swung up into the saddle and dug in his heels. Fergus Adam might be his enemy, but if there had been some sort of accident, he would need all the help he could get.

[274]

'Help!' came the frightened cry again and together Mhairi and Fergus looked upwards to where, almost half way up the rock face, a bush still clung to what remained of a ledge – a ledge which had been split in half by the explosion, one half being swept away by the torrent of gushing water which roared through the fissure in the newly blasted rock. On the remaining half, spread-eagled in terror against the rock face and clinging precariously to a rowan sapling, was a small boy.

They were still staring in a mixture of relief and dawning horror, when the rubble at the foot of the cliff stirred, what at first sight appeared to be a mud-caked rock rose up, shook itself, fell back into the water which was steadily spreading, rose up again, and became a drenched, disreputable and terrified boy who, after one look, flung himself across the space between them and clung to his uncle, sobbing, 'I'm sorry, Uncle Fergus, I didn't mean to run away. I'm sorry, I'm sorry.'

Fergus swept Leo up in his arms and hugged him with over-whelming love and relief, before setting him down again to hold him by the shoulders and say, in an unsteady voice, 'First, are you hurt?'

Leo shook his head.

'Then quickly. Tell me what happened.'

'There was a bang and the cave shook and I was frightened. I looked for my rope and couldn't find it and . . .'

'What rope?' interrupted Fergus. If there was a rope, Hamish might yet be saved.

'My rope that I tied to a tree so I could climb down, of course.'

But George Bruce the foreman had joined them. After lighting his fuse he had retreated to his bolthole and crouched, hands over ears and eyes shut, till the explosion came. When the dust settled, he had emerged from his soundless, sightless burrow to find, as well as newly harvested granite, death, devastation and dismay. Now, rapidly taking in the situation, he touched Fergus Adam on the arm and nodded towards a length of frayed rope, thin as a clothes line, which lay among the rubble, one tattered and still attached to what looked like a gorse bush.

Fergus swallowed. 'You mean you climbed down the cliff on *that*?'

'It was a good rope,' said Leo in defiance. 'I used it lots of times.'

'You won't any more,' muttered Bruce, his eyes already searching for a means of rescue.

'Tell me what happened next, Leo,' said Fergus, while all the time

[275]

his eyes darted over the cliff-face, probing, assessing, searching for a way to reach that mewing scrap of terror before its fingers slipped, or the sapling gave way. 'After the cave shook.'

'It shook and shook,' said Leo, his face buried now in his uncle's chest, 'and then the floor split open and the bit I was standing on whooshed away when the water spurted out and . . . and it carried me with it down the waterfall. Like a raft in the rapids. Only it wasn't a raft because it sank and I landed in the water. Hamish's piece of floor was left behind.' He looked up at his uncle and added, in a subdued voice, 'Will he die?'

'I sincerely hope not,' said Fergus, with false cheerfulness. 'We'll get him down from there in no time.'

Already the men had been busy. At that moment there was a shout from the cliff-top and someone waved. Behind him was some sort of scaffolding and more men.

'They've got a hoist,' said Bruce, his voice suddenly light with hope. 'We could . . .'

'For God's sake tell them to keep quiet!' warned Fergus, but even as the foreman waved his arms in an urgent signal they heard the sudden patter of falling shingle. Then silence. They held their breath, waiting, then, from somewhere near where Hamish still clung to his pathetic sapling, a single stone detached itself, bounced with slow deliberation down the rock-face and smacked into the water at the bottom.

'Perhaps if he fell and the water is deep enough . . . ?' whispered Mhairi in vain hope, but Bruce shook his head.

'A foot deep at the most,' he murmured. 'It would be fatal.'

Other workers had joined them, silent men, looking up at the stranded boy with anxious compassion. 'We could maybe climb the cliff and help him down,' whispered one.

'And start an avalanche in the process? Look at that broken rock, man. It'd break off and bring the lad with it afore we was off the ground.'

'Lower a rope then. The men up there have brought the hoist.'

'A rope's heavy. Suppose it coiled and swung. Knocked him off before he could catch hold?'

Mhairi gasped and swayed, but her eyes did not waver from that point on the cliff-face where her son still clung. It was as if she thought she could stop him falling by the sheer force of her gaze. Fergus took her elbow in a firm grip.

[276]

'Come away, Mhairi. It is not safe to try to reach him from below. A man must be lowered down the cliff.'

'I'll do it and gladly,' offered Bruce, but Fergus waved him back. 'You will stay here. Get the men to fetch canvas, sheets, tarpaulin. Anything to stretch out and catch him in if . . . ' He looked swiftly at Mhairi's ashen face, then away again. 'If it should be necessary. I will go down the cliff myself.'

'But Mr Adam, it's not your place, sir, and . . . '

'That's an order, Bruce. Obey it.' Then he turned again to Mhairi. 'Come with me, Mhairi. You can do nothing here. We'll have the boy safely out of there in no time. Please God,' he added under his breath. 'So come to the top with me, then when we pull Hamish to safety, you will be there, waiting.'

'No.' She shook her head, her eyes still on her child. 'I will stay here, so he can see me.'

Fergus looked at her for a moment, then turned away, unable to bear such naked anguish. 'So be it.' He added, *sotto voce*, 'Look after her, Bruce.' Then he took Leo by the hand and together they ran for the quarry path and the long, zig-zag hawl to the surface.

'Can I help, Uncle Fergus?' panted Leo as they reached the top and the quarry yard where men were already waiting with coiled rope and harness. 'Can I come down with you on the rope, Uncle Fergus? Please?'

'No you cannot. It's a hot bath for you, my lad, and some of Ma Gregor's toddy.'

'Please, Uncle Fergus,' wailed Leo, bedraggled and tearful. 'Don't send me away. I want to see if Hamish is all right.'

For a moment Fergus hesitated, but it was a laudable sentiment on Leo's part. 'Very well. But you will stay with this man – it's Fraser, isn't it? – with Mr Fraser here and do exactly as he says. Do I have your solemn promise?'

'Yes, Uncle Fergus.'

'Good lad.' He turned to Fraser. 'Take him into my office. Strip those wet clothes off him. Towel him down, dose him with whisky and dress him in anything you can find. When he's warm and dry, he can come out again. But don't let him out of your sight. Understood?' Then he turned on his heel and walked towards the cliff.

The men had fetched from the yard a simple block and tackle, of the kind normally used for shifting heavy loads, and had rigged it up on the grass. Four of the strongest quarry workers stood ready to pay out the slack. They had laid sacking on the cliff edge, to prevent the rope fraying, but even so, when Fergus Adam eased his way over the edge and down, the sudden tautening of the rope stretched the fibres alarmingly. Gently, inch by inch they lowered him, his feet against the sloping quarry side, his hands gripping the rope, towards that terrified scrap of humanity that clung desperately to the rowan sapling, one foot on a ledge no more than six inches wide, the other hanging perilously in space, and beside him, a mere foot away, that gushing torrent.

'Don't look down,' called Fergus. 'Look up. To me. Guide me if you can. Tell me where to place my feet.'

In spite of the harness the men had fashioned, the rope dug into his chest and armpits, burnt his hands, and when his feet slipped, as they inevitably did, his knuckles banged against the rock and bled. Do not look down, he had told the boy, but he stole a look himself, to gauge how far he had come, how far still to go. The sight made his head swim and his stomach turn. A hundred feet below him water shimmered among fallen rocks. A part of his mind noted the water with interest – a weapon of retribution so simple it had not occurred to him. A weapon which would preserve the rock from depredation for ever after. Already it had spread over the smallest of the newly quarried stones. *Each one of which could kill or maim him if he fell.* As to the boy ... Fergus shuddered at the thought.

But Leo had fallen and survived. As he eased his way down that treacherous slope, walking his feet against the rock, inch by careful inch as the men, out of sight now on the cliff top, payed out the rope, Fergus clung to the thought with determined hope. Until he remembered that Leo was hardly human. When the west wing of Silvercairns house had fallen and killed Mungo Adam, Leo, who had been standing beside the old man, had been dug out unscathed. He was like a cat with nine lives: two gone, seven to go. But Hamish had only one life, and that hung by a sapling root which the smallest shift in the rock face might dislodge.

Or the smallest mistake on his part. Fergus glanced downward. Very close now. Below him, a little to his right, he could see the black sheen of the boy's hair, the child's white-knuckled hand clutching the sapling stalk. Mhairi's child. With infinite care, he moved one foot downward, then another, bracing his weight against the rope, his feet against the stone. If he were to lose his footing now, swing loose or bump against the rock...

In the quarry far below, Mhairi Grant stood motionless, her face lifted towards that tiny figure, as if by pinning him to the cliff with her eyes she could keep him safe till rescue arrived. Beside her stood Bruce the foreman, his eyes on Fergus Adam. Other men, who should have been roping up the newly-quarried rocks to load onto the wagons before the water spread, stood equally motionless, dotted like battered lead soldiers over the quarry floor. Others, knee-deep in water at the cliff-foot, held taut a pathetic canvas. Someone had covered Donal Grant's body with a cloth. Everywhere was silence except for the sound of water.

A similar silence hung over the quarry yard above and when Tom rode up from the direction of Hirpletillam, having had to make a detour round that pernicious boundary fence, his horse's hooves sounded loud in the unnatural quiet. He dismounted, hitched the bridle to a post and strode for the nearest group of men.

'What is happening? I thought I heard . . . '

'Sh!' said a dozen warning voices. Then, in a whisper, the nearest man told him.

Tom's face drained of all colour. Oh God. Oh dear God in heaven.

'Slowly. Only another yard. Hold on just a little longer.' Fergus talked now as much to encourage himself as to reassure the boy. 'Do not reach out to me until I tell you. Listen carefully. Do just as I say.'

This was the difficult bit. One slip and they could both be at the bottom. He could have clasped the boy in his arms, hung on while the men on the cliff top hauled them to safety. Except that if they bumped against the cliff, as they would inevitably do, or the men jerked the rope, he might lose his hold on the child. No. He must somehow slip the second harness over the boy's head, under his arms, adjust it into place. Then the men above would do the rest.

But he was almost level with the boy. Beyond the child, he could see the fissure through which the water gushed. It was closer than before and flowing faster, barely an inch away from the rowan's roots. 'Don't move, Hamish. Stay just as you are. I am going to try and find a foothold then I will tell you exactly what I want you to do. Do you understand?'

Blue eyes round with terror, black hair glossy as a raven's wing in spite of the dust. His mother's face, in miniature. He nodded. The

[279]

rowan sapling bent, quivered, strained, and in a patter of falling earth, gave way.

On the quarry floor, Mhairi screamed.

Simultaneously, Fergus struck both feet hard against the rock face to spring outwards, sideways and down towards that falling child while the rope spun burning through his hands. A split second later and he had caught the child in one arm, clasped him tight against his chest, the boy's arms locked round Fergus's neck while together they bumped and crashed against the granite wall of rock.

The scream abruptly stopped, cut off by Mhairi's own swift hand. Above that hand her eyes were huge with suspended terror and the first tremulous glimmerings of hope. She saw the rope swing slower, stop gyrating, hang steady, its double burden still intact. She saw Fergus slip the harness safely over the boy's shoulders, under first one arm, then the other, brace his feet once more against the quarry wall and, Hamish clamped to his chest like some primeval monkey-child, jerk the rope for the men above to start the long haul home. Mesmerized, she watched them go up, swaying now this way, now that. Once, Fergus's foot slipped and as the swaying bundle hit the rock the thud of bone against stone reverberated round the quarry. Once the men on the surface loosed their grip and the human bundle rattled down a terrifying ten feet before they found it again and the tortuously slow ascent resumed. And Mhairi watched, unmoving, scarcely breathing, her teeth digging hard into the back of her hand. Ten feet to go; five feet; three. Then they reached the rim, were hauled over it, and out of sight.

A great cheer of triumph split the heavens, beside her the foreman Bruce breathed a heartfelt 'Thank God!' and Mhairi slipped senseless to the ground.

'Ma? Are you all right, Ma?'

Mhairi opened her eyes to sunlight, white sky, and blotting out that sky a blurred face which took shape and became the anxious, loving face of her son. She blinked again and it was not sky, but white-washed ceiling, above plain wooden walls. She was lying on some sort of couch, in someone's office. Memory flooded back.

'Hamish! I thought you were dead.' She clasped him in her arms, hugging and kissing him till he drew away, embarrassed.

'So did I, Ma. The tree's roots came out and I nearly fell, but Mr

[280]

Adam caught me.' He turned his head and she realized that they were not alone. 'He saved my life. Everyone says so.'

'Then I hope you said thank you. As I must do.'

'He did, I assure you.' The familiar voice brought her, blushing, to her feet, where, in spite of herself, she swayed.

'Sit down, Ma,' said Hamish anxiously. 'You might fall.'

'Fall?' She laughed uncertainly and her eyes filled suddenly with tears.

'Hamish, now that your mother is recovering, why don't you run and find Leo? Tell him to make tea for your mother and bring it here. With two cups.'

Hamish hesitated, looked from one to the other, then when Mhairi nodded, he slipped from the room, closing the door behind him.

'And now,' said Fergus softly, 'What was it you said about thanking me?'

When Tom burst into the room some minutes later he skidded to an embarrassed stop. 'I did not realize. I . . . '

Mhairi stopped kissing Fergus and turned her head, though she kept her arms tight around his neck. Then she saw who it was that had interrupted them and whirled round, spreading her arms wide as if to protect Fergus from attack. Her hair was dust-streaked and dishevelled, her face streaked with tears, her clothes torn and bedraggled, and her eyes blazing.

'Don't you dare say it, Tom Diack. It will do you no good. Fergus Adam is a brave and honest man and I love him. You can rant and rave as much as you please but I am not afraid of you or your puny threats. I love Fergus and I am going to marry him, whatever you say.' She glared like an avenging tigress into Tom's astonished face. Deliberately she turned, pulled Fergus's face down to hers and kissed him, then, her arm around his waist, demanded, 'What have you to say about that?'

'Only . . . ' He spread his arms helplessly, shrugged, then took a step forward and offered Fergus his hand. 'Congratulations. I am proud to have you as a brother-in-law. And thank you for doing what you did. We owe Hamish's life to you and we'll not forget it.'

Then he turned and, like his nephew before him, slipped discreetly from the room.

[281]

There was a moment's absolute silence before Fergus said quietly, 'What was that you said about marrying me?'

She looked at him gravely, noting the bruising, the scratches, the bandaged hand and blood-matted, dusty hair. His usually immaculate trousers were ripped at the knee, his jacket torn, his eyes dark with sorrow and love.

'You asked me, remember?' She held out her hand on which still gleamed his sapphire ring. 'And if you change your mind again, for whatever silly, misguided reason, I do believe I shall sue you for breach of promise.' Then suddenly the tears came. 'Poor Donal. Poor, brave Donal. He loved Hamish so very much.'

'Yes, my love,' soothed Fergus. He drew her head onto his shoulder, his hand gently stroking her hair. 'And he deserves our grief. Mine as well as yours, for at first he did not know Hamish was there. It was for Leo that he ran. I will not forget that, ever. He was, I think, the bravest man I ever knew.'

They carried his body up the spiral path on a litter and laid it reverently on the grass.

'I saw him, Ma,' sobbed Hamish. 'I waved. I tried to stop him, but he could not hear me. Then there was a bang and he was gone. I looked and looked, all the time I was waiting to be rescued, but I couldn't see him . . . Then Mr Adam came down the rope and I knew Uncle Donal was dead. If he'd been alive, he would not have let anyone else rescue me. He would have . . . ' He threw himself on his dead uncle's chest and sobbed.

Mhairi's own eyes were brimming, as were Tom's beside her. At last Mhairi touched her son's shoulder, very gently. 'Come, Hamish. We will take Uncle Donal home.'

In his library the following morning, Fergus went over the notes which he and Tom Diack had made about the structure of the building. With careful shoring up and some rebuilding in the area of the fallen west wing, and providing there were no more explosions in the immediate vicinity, Diack had declared the house both retrievable and safe. The structure taken care of, the interior would need extensive attention, of course, but this would give the opportunity to introduce more modern kitchen arrangements and plumbing and, cost aside, could be looked on as a positive advantage. Diack had

[282]

offered to oversee the work himself. In fact, the man had really been most helpful, riding out at first light to inspect the damage with him.

Fergus had looked over the house himself, of course, the previous day, as soon as Leo had been enfolded in the loving bosom of Ma Gregor. He caught himself up short: 'Ma' Gregor indeed. Even he was catching the habit now. Remembering the previous disaster when his father had inadvertently demolished the west wing, and in so doing killed himself, Fergus could not let the household go to bed, nor go himself with a clear conscience, until he had inspected every ceiling, every wall for signs of damage. Miraculously there was none. None, that is, that had not been there already, and even the crack that ghastly woman had pointed out seemed no larger than before. But then Fergus's explosion, unlike his father's, had been meticulously planned.

This morning Tom's inspection had been more thorough, his notes copious. Afterwards they had ridden out to the quarry together, to see how far the water had risen in the night. Tom estimated eight feet, Fergus seven, and the level was still rising. 'Providing there were no more explosions' Diack had said and, looking down into that dark and glinting pool Fergus knew there was little danger of that. The quarry had won. In the early morning shadow, the water was black and thick as the liquid he had seen bubbling up through the quarry floor in his most lurid dreams, its devastation as complete as any more spectacular eruption. No pump could combat such a flow. No man take even one more rock from the quarry bed. His quarry was closed for ever, the contest over. Strangely, he felt no resentment, no sense of defeat. It was inevitable, an honourable amnesty.

As to the future, he had his house, his land, and a paltry holding of railway shares. That was all. But he still had Leo and, at last and beyond losing, he was to have Mhairi for his wife. The thought cancelled out all doubt, all fear. With her, he knew he could face anything the future held. If he had to start again from nothing, as his father had done before him, then he would do so, and, with Mhairi at his side, he would succeed, for her and for their children.

For a moment, out of habit, he turned his gaze towards Willow-brae, but without the usual rancour. Since the events of yesterday, how or why Tom Diack had snatched it from his grasp no longer mattered, though he had a suspicion that his own nephew's blabbing tongue might have had something to do with it. Since yesterday, the

[283]

only thing that mattered was Mhairi's love, staunch, undying, true. He had written to her already this morning, and would write again as soon as he was alone. *Darling Mhairi* he would say. *Ever since yesterday, when I held you at last, your heart beating hard against mine, I* ... Abruptly he broke off, pulled himself together, remembered his companion.

'How is it going?' he asked Tom, jerking his head towards the boundary fence. 'I noticed you had done some preliminary exploration.'

'So-so,' shrugged Tom, then looked away, avoiding Fergus's eye. 'But I am late already. I must be going.'

'Come back to the house and have breakfast with me,' offered Fergus. 'You have had an uncommonly early start to the day on my account. It is the least I can do in return.'

But Tom refused. 'I must go home, to see my wife.'

'Of course. Please forgive me. I should have inquired sooner. How is Mrs Diack this morning?'

'Still sleeping when I left. I thought it too early to wake her.' His face saddened. 'Last night she was no better.'

'Then I hope today brings some improvement.'

'So do I,' thought Tom as he tiptoed into the shadowed room. Sunlight filtered through the curtains to cast a soft light over the bedclothes and the white-clad woman who lay there, hair spread loose on the pillow, white hand lying half-curled beside her cheek. She looked so frail and vulnerable and helpless.

Annys rose from her chair, as she always did when Tom arrived. 'I think she is a little better,' she whispered. 'She does not seem quite so hot as she was last night. But I will leave you together,' and she went softly out of the room.

Tom sat on the side of the bed, took that lifeless hand in his and held it against his cheek.

'Are you awake, Fanny my love? Please try to wake up and listen, just for me. Such news I have to tell you this morning. Fergus and Mhairi are to be married.' For the first time since her illness he thought he felt her hand stir in his. 'Fanny, my love, did you hear me? Fergus and Mhairi are to be married. Isn't that wonderful news? So you are to hurry up and get well, for they want us to come to their wedding and I shall certainly not go without you.'

[284]

This time there was no doubt at all. She opened her eyes, looked at him, and said, puzzled, 'Mhairi and Fergus?'

'Yes, my love. Mhairi and Fergus are to be married. I have just come from Silvercairns this morning, where Fergus and I have been doing a little work together. He invited me to breakfast, but I told him I had to come home to my darling wife. Fergus loves Mhairi almost as much as I love you, Fanny. I said "almost" because no one could equal my love for you. I have missed you so dreadfully, darling ...' He said other, private things while she lay back on her pillows, eyes closed, but smiling, her hand in his. He hardly knew whether she was awake or sleeping, but it no longer mattered. Fanny had come back from whatever private world had claimed her and however long it took, he knew with joyful certainty that she would recover.

When Annys came back after the usual interval, Tom waved her away. 'Leave us alone a little longer, Annys. I have things to say to Fanny, in private.'

Annys looked from Tom to his wife in dawning excitement. 'Is Fanny recovered?'

It was Fanny herself who answered. 'I think so, Annys. A little. But very soon I will be quite well again.'

'Not if you talk too much, my darling,' said Tom, smoothing the hair from her forehead with a look of such tenderness that Annys bit her lip and turned her head away. At that moment she heard a carriage in the street and said, with relief. 'That will be the doctor. I will bring him straight up.'

'On the contrary. You will take him into the parlour and ply him with whisky, or brandy, and use whatever subterfuge you can devise to keep him there for at least twenty minutes. I told you, Fanny and I have things to discuss.'

Smiling to herself, Annys slipped quietly out of the room and closed the door behind her.

But it was not Dr Marshall who she found waiting in the parlour. It was Philip Drummond and his sister Henrietta.

'Please excuse us calling in this unorthodox manner,' began Philip Drummond, 'but we had an appointment to meet your brother at the granite yard and ...'

'We waited half an hour,' murmured Henrietta reproachfully.

'... and when he did not arrive, and as no arrangements had been made about the key, we thought ...'

'The shed was locked, so we could not even peep,' put in Henrietta with what Annys believed was called a *moue*. 'So tiresome.'

'We thought,' continued her brother with a frown in her direction, 'that perhaps there had been another accident, or Mrs Diack had taken a turn for the worse.'

'Oh no,' said Annys happily. 'On the contrary, she has taken a turn for the better. It is a miracle.' She smiled radiantly at first Philip, then Henrietta.

The girl was looking remarkably attractive this morning, thought Drummond with surprise. Why had he not noticed her before? But with her eyes shining and that aura of bubbling happiness about her he certainly noticed her now.

'And may I ask what wonder of the medical world brought about this miracle, Miss Diack?' He gave her his most winning smile.

'Oh it was nothing medical at all, Mr Drummond. It was my brother's news that did it.'

'News?' he repeated, puzzled. 'I knew there had been some sort of accident yesterday, at Silvercairns quarry. A man was killed, I believe. But I would not have thought . . . '

'Oh no,' cried Annys. 'Not that news. Poor Donal . . . ' For a moment her eyes blurred with tears, but she brushed them away. 'Tom would not tell her anything as terrible as that.'

'Then may we, perhaps, be permitted to know what news it was that achieved this miracle cure, Miss Diack?' This time his smile was teasing. She really was a most delightful girl.

'Of course. He told her that Fergus Adam and my sister are to be married.'

There was the smallest of pauses before Henrietta said, in strangely strangled tones, 'And is this news true?'

'Oh yes. They have been half-engaged since the beginning of the year.'

Henrietta Drummond rose to her feet. 'Miss Diack. I thought you to be a gentle, sweet-natured and honest girl. Otherwise I would not have invited you into my home and certainly not favoured you with the confidence I did.'

Annys's mouth dropped open with astonishment, not at the accusation which she had half-expected, but because for the first time in their acquaintance, Miss Drummond spoke in a perfectly normal voice.

'I find, Miss Diack, that I was sadly mistaken. You are underhand

[286]

and sly. You are deceitful. I do not wish you to enter my house again, as long as I live.' Head high with outrage, she swept past Annys to the door. 'Philip! Be so good as to take me home.'

Behind his sister's back, Philip shrugged and spread his hands in bafflement. He lingered long enough to say, 'Please convey our felicitations to your sister, and our good wishes to Mrs Diack for a full recovery. Oh, and please tell your brother that I will be in touch later about the fountain.' Then he followed Henrietta out of the house.

They had hardly turned the corner of the road when Dr Marshall arrived, accompanied by a bronzed young man too thin for his clothes.

'Good morning, Miss Diack. As my errant nephew has at last managed to tear himself away from the enticements of the Bosphorus and favour the north-east with his presence, at least for a day or two, I took the liberty of bringing him along, for a second opinion.'

'As you see, Miss Diack, I am to earn my keep,' said his companion with a smile. 'My wife has lingered in London, shopping, but she will join me later.'

'Meanwhile, I, and my patients, will have the benefit of my nephew's superior education and experience,' said the doctor, with only a hint of mockery. 'A most interesting case, David. A species of brain fever, though with no apparent cause. At one time I suspected encephalitis, but the symptoms...'

'Perhaps I had better examine the patient myself before hazarding an opinion, Uncle.' He turned to Annys. 'May we go up?'

'I am afraid you are too late.' Before they could draw the wrong conclusion, she added happily, 'Fanny is much better this morning. In fact, I believe she is cured.'

'Splendid news. Absolutely splendid,' cried Dr Marshall. 'Then we must certainly go up at once and congratulate her.'

'I am sure you can find your own way, Dr Marshall,' said Annys demurely. 'I was about to go out, for a breath of air.'

The moment she heard the bedroom door open and close again, she snatched her wrap from the peg, put her head round the kitchen door to say, 'I am going out for a while, Jessie,' and slipped quickly out of the house.

Once out of sight, she quickened her steps till she was almost running. There was a certain stance near the Castlegate where a certain Irish carter was in the habit of lingering, in the hope of trade. What better way to spread the happy news?

They buried Donal Grant in St Nicholas kirkyard, beside his brother. Every polishing yard and quarry in the area was closed for the day and quarrymen came from as far away as Kemnay to honour one of the best workers in polished granite the city had known, and one of the bravest. Though in life he had not been able to communicate freely, his death showed how many friends he had made in spite of that, and in what honour, affection and respect he had been held. The church was filled to overflowing as Donal Grant was laid to rest, and through her tears, Mhairi rejoiced that he had found such love and honour, not only within his family, but wherever he went.

In the sombre days that followed, the family mourned, each in his different way. Hamish and Catriona for whom he had been a devoted uncle, whispered quietly together in the evenings, the time their uncle had usually spent with them, and once Mhairi saw her daughter offer Hamish her handkerchief. Mhairi's own eyes were wet as she turned away. She had not realized what a gap in the family circle Donal's going would leave.

As for the others, Lorn had already taken upon himself the task of sorting through the innumerable sketches which Donal had left for the Wyness monument, for the Drummond fountain, and for the many other projects which the yard had handled in the past, or planned to handle in the future. All yearnings towards Australia long forgotten, he sank his grief in determination to take up the task where Donal had left it. He may not be as talented as Donal had been, but his interest had always favoured the polishing yard, he would do his best, and he could learn. Hamish helped him, as he had helped his uncle Donal, and found comfort in the familiar tasks.

With Lorn's new responsibilities, Will found himself in sole charge of Rainbow Hill and thrived under the challenge. As for Tom, he still spent much of his time with his wife, who was making a slow but steady recovery. When not at home, he could usually be found at Silvercairns, working on the renovations and repairs which were already under way. He had not been back to Willowbrae since the day of the explosion and it was never mentioned.

Annys stayed on at Tom's house, to help nurse Fanny back to health, and Catriona helped her mother in Rainbow Cottage and